About the Author

Janet MacLeod Trotter was brought up in the North East of England with her four brothers, by Scottish parents. She is a best-selling author of 16 novels, including the hugely popular Jarrow Trilogy, and a childhood memoir, BEATLES & CHIEFS, which was featured on BBC Radio Four. Her novel, THE HUNGRY HILLS, gained her a place on the shortlist of The Sunday Times' Young Writers' Award, and THE TEA PLANTER'S DAUGHTER was longlisted for the RNA Romantic Novel Award. A graduate of Edinburgh University, she has been editor of the Clan MacLeod Magazine, a columnist on the Newcastle Journal and has had numerous short stories published in women's magazines. She lives in the North of England with her husband, daughter and son. Find out more about Janet and her other popular novels at: www.janetmacleodtrotter.com

By Janet MacLeod Trotter

Historical:
The Jarrow Trilogy
The Jarrow Lass
Child of Jarrow
Return to Jarrow

The Durham Trilogy
Hungry Hills
The Darkening Skies
Never Stand Alone

The Tyneside Sagas
The Tea Planter's Daughter
The Suffragette
A Crimson Dawn
A Handful of Stars
Chasing the Dream
For Love & Glory

Scottish Historical Romance
The Beltane Fires

Mystery:
The Vanishing of Ruth
The Haunting of Kulah

Teenage:
Love Games

Non Fiction:
Beatles & Chiefs

Short Stories:
Ice Cream Summer

For two special women – my sister-in-law Barbara and my friend Mel – for their amazing courage, humour and love in the face of great difficulties.

***

Thanks to my brother Angus for his mad-cap suggestion of wild camping on the Outer Hebrides; to Uncle Donald and Auntie Astrid for leading us around ancient Gorrie sites and to copy editor Janey Floyd for her wise words and superior knowledge on hyphenating.

***

CHAPTER ONE

The Isle of Kulah, 1945

I heard the cuckoo this morning, but kept the news to myself. It's a bad omen. We women don't need any more sad news. Poor Margaret is in a terrible state since the mail boat came in last week. No letters from her boy Neilac and the newspapers full of his ship being torpedoed on a convoy to Russia.

'No news is good news,' said Simple Sam.

I thought Margaret's sisters were going to throw him off the cliff. Kate had him by the hair and Christina threw a punch like a prize-fighter before I pulled her off.

'He doesn't know what he's saying,' I tried to reason. 'He's only mimicking his mammy's old words.'

'Should have drowned him at birth!' Christina screamed. 'Why does Our Lady let a fool like him survive and take away our Neilac?'

It was no good pointing out that daft Sam was right; until word came through that Neilac MacRailt was either drowned or saved, why think the worst?

But we do. We're worn out by war; sick of our own company and the lack of our men-folk.

There's a visitor come to Kulah. He's beyond call-up age, so they say. I've been too busy over at Ostaig nursing old Seamus to see him. He's lodging down at the pier, though the house is half derelict since Donald-the-Pier went off to war. My girls tell me he has a camera.

It's a fine day. The sea is almost calm. I wonder if Tormod is out there and if so, is he leaning on the railings with his bulky arms, smoking? Or below in his hammock reading *The Sunday Post*? Or at action stations perched up high behind the gun, screaming at the pain in his ears from the din?

Cuckoos don't live on Kulah, but today I, Flora Gillies, heard one. Soon there will be bad news.

1

CHAPTER TWO

Isle of Battersay, present day

As the ferry stole into the bay, Ally Niven had the uneasy feeling that someone was watching her. She was on deck, scanning the rocky shoreline of Battersay for any signs of life. A scattering of squat grey houses clung on limpet-like, dwarfed by an ancient ruined fortress that glowered in the evening light. Not a soul was about.

But someone was staring; she could feel the prickle of discomfort down her back. Ally forced herself to glance round. Two women, laden with shopping, were chatting away in Gaelic. She had a sudden panic that she wouldn't be able to understand a word people said. Why on earth had she chosen such a remote place to escape her unravelling life? The metal gang-planks began to judder into action. The harbour closed about the ferry like scaly arms. Engines revved on the car deck.

'She lives over there.' A deep voice came from the shadows behind.

'Excuse me?' Ally turned sharply, pushing strands of auburn hair out of her green eyes.

A tall man stepped forward and flicked a cigarette overboard, next to the no-smoking sign. He was scruffy and unshaven, with unruly dark hair.

'On the far point over there. Not that you'll see her; she's as hard to spot as a sea otter.'

Ally stared up at him. Was he one of the ferrymen? She hadn't a clue what he was on about.

'I'm sorry – who does?'

'They all try to see her – all the tourists.' His rugged face was disparaging.

'I was just enjoying the view.'

'The view?' His mouth twisted. His disbelieving tone irked her. 'Well, make the most of it. You might not see it again for days.'

As the man disappeared down the metal stairs, Ally felt wrong-footed. 'I'm not a tourist,' she shouted after him, 'I'm here to work.'

If he heard her above the thrum of the engine, he chose not to answer.

One of the shoppers shuffled past her on the narrow deck, laughing with her friend. Ally's heart squeezed. Was it only three nights ago she had been in London sharing a bottle of wine with her friend Rachel, toasting her post-Lucas life? *He cheated on you, forget him, he's low-life'.* They had drunk to her new job as cook on Battersay and Ally had faked excitement. Rachel had joked, *'Good job they don't know you only make lasagne!'* She wished Rachel was there now with her cheap plonk and teasing optimism.

The younger of the women, with a tight ponytail and frameless glasses, turned and said in English. 'Don't forget your jacket; it's on the bench.'

'Oh, thanks!'

'And don't worry about Mr Moody;' she said with a jerk of her thumb, 'he's like that with most folk.'

Ally shouldered her one large bag, glad that she'd resisted Rachel's huge case on wheels, and offered to help carry the women's shopping. They declined but she stuck to them as they filed off the small ferry behind half a dozen vehicles: two cars, a builder's van and three camper vans. In one she recognised the family from Carlisle that she'd chatted to on the big Calmac ferry from Oban to Barra. The parents were breezy outdoor types and the three small children wore matching yellow cagoules even though it wasn't raining. The pang of envy for the excited family had caught her by surprise.

The flurry of activity brought a handful of people to the quayside to tie up ropes or greet travellers. Ally peered ahead, wondering if someone might have turned up to meet her with a sign bearing her name. *'Babe, this isn't Heathrow,'* she could hear Rachel giggle. Her instructions from Dr Rushmore of the Sollas Community were vague, merely to report to their village hall café the following day and ask for Calum. She looked around for a taxi. An ancient minibus belched blue exhaust fumes.

'Alec-the-Bus will take you down from Bay to Sollas,' the friendly woman with the ponytail told her. She laughed at Ally's look of surprise. 'You'll be the lassie from London who's cooking for the tourists at the village hall?'

'Yes,' she smiled, 'I'm Ally Niven.'

'Ishbel,' she replied, 'and this is Morag.'

Middle-aged Morag, plump and puffing from the walk up the steep jetty, merely nodded.

Alec, a gaunt, grey-haired man with startlingly blue eyes in a weather-beaten face, took her bag and welcomed her aboard. Morag sat up front – perhaps she was his wife? – while Ally sat behind two youths in overalls who kept glancing round. As the bus lurched away from the harbour, she scanned the place for shops or a café or pub, but in two minutes they were passing the signpost that marked the limits of Bay and out into empty landscape. A single track road bucked and dipped over moorland that was cratered with rocks like a moonscape.

This was madness. She appeared to have ended up on Scotland's most far-flung island on which to lick her emotional wounds. What did she know about this place? Virtually nothing, except what the job advert had said: Battersay was Catholic and Gaelic speaking. Usually Ally would buy a pile of travel guides before setting off travelling – Lucas said she was way too organised – but this time she had deliberately not researched the island. She wanted to feel her way in and not come with any preconceptions; she wasn't a tourist. This was a bolt-hole.

Five years ago – before her mother died and left her with a huge gaping void – she would have retreated to the Yorkshire Dales to get over her heartbreak. Her mum would have fed her home cooking, taken her on brisk breezy walks and knitted her something garish with cows on to make her laugh. Her mother had never met Lucas but Ally could hear her saying, *'that lad doesn't deserve you. Plenty more fish in the sea.'*

The Dales were solitary but accessible: not like here. From London it had taken two days of trains, buses and ferries. She could have got to Australia quicker. This wasn't a place for a thirty year old; she wasn't a loner and she'd go insane in a week.

As they reached a summit, Ally glanced back. The small ferry was already retreating out to sea. She swallowed down panic that she was now well and truly marooned on this tiny fragment of the Outer Isles. But this is what she'd wanted, wasn't it? to get as far away from Lucas as possible.

The three camper vans were tailing the bus and with the windows open she could hear high-pitched singing wafting through the still air. She calmed herself with practical thoughts; she was here to cook. It was just for high summer – Battersay's brief holiday season of two to three months – but it would give her a breathing space to get her head around what had happened with Lucas and to decide what to do next. That's what Freya, her understanding boss at *Lara*'s magazine, had said. *'For God's sake take the rest of the summer off and sort yourself out. Honestly, we'll manage'*. She worried that they might replace her, but she'd hardly been able to face going into work – sweats, palpitations – in case she ran into her ex. Her doctor had urged her to speak to a counsellor but she'd off-loaded on Rachel and Zoe instead. One had suggested a change of scene, the other castration for Lucas. The first seemed more practicable.

Ally wondered where Mr Moody had gone. She hadn't seen him disembark. Was he really called Moody or was it a local nickname? He hadn't sounded local; more posh Lowland Scots. Edinburgh University had been full of them when she'd studied there ten years ago: before London and journalism and Lucas. Why had he started going on about some woman as if she should know? An oddball, that was for sure, but handsome with it. Dangerous to think such thoughts though; another man in her life was the last thing she needed.

Ally felt queasy at the roller coaster bus ride. They passed a woman in a blue headscarf walking in the middle of nowhere, but Alec the driver did not stop. He dropped Ally outside an ugly square cottage; a former coastguard's lookout with a tin roof.

'Home sweet home,' he announced.

In the dying light, she couldn't see another house in sight. Her stomach knotted.

'Where will I get the key?'

'It won't be locked. But if you want to bolt the door against the tartan bogeyman, there's probably a key under the mat.' Alec chuckled at his own joke, called a farewell and with a toot of his horn he was gone over the next ridge.

In dismay, she surveyed the front door which was bleached silver where the red paint had peeled away. It was stiff to open. Musty damp greeted

4

her: a tiny porch and gloomy sitting-room at the front; a kitchen and narrow bathroom at the back. Ally smothered thoughts of her tiny bright second-floor flat looking onto a bustling high street. She tried a light switch. Bare strip lighting flooded the kitchen with harsh white light. At least there was electricity.

A note on the Formica-topped table read, '*Food in fridge. Come along to shop tomorrow and Calum will take you to the hall and show you the ropes. Sleep well – extra blankets in trunk in bedroom if you need them. Cheerio, Shona Gillies.*'

What shop? And bedroom? Ally wondered where that could be in this glorified hut that had no staircase. But she warmed to Shona Gillies immediately and her spirits lifted. The woman had put a carton of milk, a loaf of bread, butter, cheese, bacon and a jar of homemade jam in the fridge. Ally's eyes stung at the unexpected kindness.

After a thick cheese sandwich, she found the bedroom via a pull-down ladder that led through a hatch into the loft space. An orange nylon bedspread glowed in the final rays spilling in from the skylight. Ally forced the window open. Sea air, warmer than that inside, wafted in. She would unpack later.

Outside, a smudge of sunset sunk into the sea. She walked up to the rise where Alec's bus had disappeared. Mist veiled the rising moon, but it gave up enough light to show that the land beyond levelled out into two sandy bays, back to back. Then the land reared up again into a craggy promontory – where the man on the ferry had pointed – with a stunted lighthouse atop. In the shadowy dunes, a handful of tents were pitched and two camper vans had parked up for the night. Soft lights glowed through canvas. The Cagoule Family: Ally was comforted at the thought of them close by. The narrow road petered out at three or four croft houses; Sollas presumably. It was still and calm and she could hear the splash of some sea creature far off. Midges began to swarm in the stillness so Ally kept moving, tempted to walk along the beach in the dark.

Halfway down to the shore she heard someone right behind her: a long drawn-out sigh. She whipped round expecting to see one of the campers. Nobody there. Ally's heart punched. She stood stock still and listened but the only sound was the faint murmur of the sea. It was just her nerves after the endless journey and weeks of sleeping badly. She breathed deeply, allowing her heart rate to slow. It had sounded so human, so unhappy; like the way she had moaned and moped around the empty flat through recent long solitary nights. *Oh my God, perhaps it was me?*

Ally hurried back indoors. Silence hung about the cottage like a presence. She would ring Rachel and tell her she had safely arrived. Suddenly she was desperate to hear another voice. But there was no signal on her mobile. In mounting alarm, she walked through the house searching for contact but it made no difference. The silence was smothering.

Ally doubled back and looked under the mat for the key. She attempted to lock the door, but it was too stiff, or it was the wrong key. *Don't be ridiculous! Who's going to bother you here?* She tried to talk herself out of her panic. Hauling a large frayed armchair out of the sitting-room, she shoved it against the unlocked front door. *As if that's going to keep anyone out.* Feeling foolish, Ally retreated into the loft and pulled the ladder after her.

CHAPTER THREE

The noise brought her bolt upright in the pitch dark. What was it? Ally gulped for breath. It sounded as if someone was attacking the corrugated roof with hammers. She groped for the light switch. Rain was spattering in at the open window, wetting her clothes strewn over a wooden chair. Ally leapt out of bed, jamming shut the skylight. The temperature had plummeted. Outside was utter blackness. She pulled out two blankets from the old tin trunk and wrapped herself in both. They smelt musty, like old people's wardrobes. There was no way she could sleep with the din of rain overhead, and now she was chilled through.

With Lucas she had never been cold; he had given off heat like fire. She smothered bitter thoughts of who her ex might be lying beside tonight. She hadn't seen him for a month, had deleted him from Facebook along with his mobile messages – first pleading then angry – and (at her friends' insistence) changed the locks at the flat. '*You can never be too careful,*' Rachel had warned. '*Don't trust a man with a temper,*' Zoe had said.

Before she left London, she had bought a new mobile. Apart from her brother Guy who lived in Madrid, only friends Rachel and Zoe – and Freya at work – had her new number. Still fuming and hurt, she had vowed to be out of contact for the rest of the summer. Yet, huddled in this bleak strange place, Ally felt a treacherous yearning for her former lover. Annoyed with herself, she flicked on her mobile but there was still no signal.

***

Silence awoke her. The room was awash with a blue-grey light. Relieved it was dawn; Ally pulled on clothes, clambered down the ladder and made a pot of tea from her supply of Redbush. There was no view from the kitchen window; the house was wrapped in mist. Taking a mug of tea outside, she felt disorientated. Cloud had descended over the island like a fire curtain, thick and impenetrable. It was impossible to tell where the land finished and the sea began. Only the sighing of the waves below told her she was close to the cliff edge. There was another sound like deep breathing that made her call out, 'Hello! Is someone there?'

Suddenly a huge black crow flapped out of the mist. Ally ducked and it landed on the cottage roof squawking aggressively. Almost invisible, it kept up a loud and ugly cawing. Unnerved, she hurried inside.

It was still barely eight by the time Ally had taken a shallow tepid bath and dressed in jeans, warm sweatshirt and trainers, but she set off for Sollas to see if she could pick up a phone signal.

Sticking to the road, she found the village hall and a small shop just beyond the camping area. Both were locked and deserted. She noticed an outside tap for the campers but none were yet stirring. She decided to explore a little further, taking out her digital camera and snapping wild flowers in the mist: giant bluebells and purple thistles glistening from the previous night's rain. Ally always felt purposeful taking photos and it helped shake off her jittery mood.

As she crouched by the roadside, a van came hurtling out of the fog. She jumped clear as the vehicle braked and skidded to a stop just beyond. It reversed back.

'Sorry,' Ally said, leaning in the open window, 'didn't hear you coming.'

A fair-haired man in a bright yellow T-shirt grinned. 'I'll get you next time. You Ally Niven by any chance?'

'Yeah.'

'I'm Calum. Jump in.'

She liked him at once. He chatted easily about the weather and asked her about life in London. She told him she worked in catering. That's what she'd put on her application to the Hall Committee. No point admitting to being a journalist – even though her subject was mainly food – if she wanted to impress them as a cook.

'Long way to come to make soup and ham sandwiches,' he joked.

'Yeah, but I fancied a change.'

'From a stressful job?'

Ally hesitated. 'More than that – from city life – the commute – all that sort of thing.'

He flicked a look. He had amazingly long eyelashes. 'It's not paradise here, you know.'

'I'm not looking for that.'

'Good 'cos some folk think if you go far enough away you leave your troubles behind. You don't, they're just the same troubles with a different view.'

Ally quipped, 'just a view would be nice.'

Calum laughed and pulled up outside the white-washed village hall.

Inside it was wood-panelled with stag's antlers over the door. A long hatch, which had been cut into the wall, was hung with blue gingham curtains that screened a well-equipped and newly decorated kitchen. While they brewed up a pot of tea, Ally helped Calum carry in a crate of sliced bread, boxes of fruit and a sack of potatoes from his van. He chatted as he worked: his wife Shona would be down shortly to open up shop next door, they had twin seven year old boys who were away staying with Shona's parents on nearby Barra; Alec-the-Bus was his uncle, and there was a Co-op in Bay where she could buy alcohol and Redbush tea.

'Is there a public phone?' Ally asked. 'My mobile doesn't work here.'

'Missing city life already?' he teased. 'Aye, there's one in Bay, but you can come down to ours and use the phone any time. We're the house with the screaming dog and the barking kids.'

Ally smiled then surveyed the contents of the cupboards and decided to make lentil and carrot soup, potato salad, ham risotto and sandwiches.

'They'll want cheese and ham toasties, burgers and chips,' Calum warned her. 'And tray bakes. Shona usually makes brownies and flapjack to sell. The last girl to work here was a vegan. We made a loss. She lasted two weeks.'

'Okay, point taken,' Ally smiled. 'How many do you expect in today?'

'Saturday's always busy. There are about twenty campers at the moment – and another ferry in at midday from Barra – we'll get the tourists staying in Bay. And some of the locals will probably come in for a coffee to have a look at the incomer,' Calum grinned.

'Is there a bloke called Moody on the island?' Ally asked as she scrubbed vegetables. Calum shook his head. 'Must have been Ishbel's joke then,' she said. 'He was on the ferry yesterday – tall, dark, tatty waxed jacket – bit strange.'

Calum snorted. 'Och, that'll be John Balmain the painter. He's got a gallery of sorts north of Bay. He's harmless enough when you get to know him – but not many do – he doesn't encourage it. Shona'll give you the gossip on that one.'

The dank weather brought in the tourists all day and once the café was opened at ten, Ally never stopped till she closed at six. The Cagoule Family greeted her like an old friend which made Ally feel part of the place already. In the early afternoon, a small woman with short black hair and lively brown eyes in a round face, dashed in.

'Hi, I'm Shona. It's time you had a break. Get yourself home for half an hour. Cathy's minding the shop for me.'

'No I'm fine. I'd rather stay here,' Ally assured, thinking of the creepy cottage. 'I love being busy.'

Shona stayed to help and when she left, she sent teenager Cathy to lend a hand. Cathy had badly dyed blonde hair and heavy eye make-up accentuating pretty hazel eyes. She showed no interest in the piles of washing-up, preferring to linger over clearing tables and chat to the customers. Shortly before closing, a curly-haired young man in gum boots and working clothes came trudging into the hall. He stood awkwardly by the hatch trying to catch Cathy's attention as she joked with a couple of cyclists. He smelled of engine oil and fish. Ally had the impression the girl was deliberately ignoring him.

'Hi, can I get you something?' Ally smiled.

He shot her a hostile look and shook his head. Cathy laughed at something one of the men said. At this the young fisherman marched over and tugged her arm, muttering something. Cathy shrugged him off.

'Can't you see I'm working? I'll see you later.'

He turned on his heels and stomped loudly out of the hall. Cathy glanced after him. She smiled an apology to the cyclists. 'Local boys have no idea how to treat a lassie, eh?'

Later, as they cleared up, Ally asked, 'who was that who came in before?'

Offhandedly she answered, 'Oh, just Donny.'

'Boyfriend?'

Cathy pulled a face. 'Kinda.' She stared out of the window at the departing cyclists and waved. 'I can't wait to get out of this place and see

9

a bit of the world. I mean those guys there – I could fancy one of them – couldn't you?'

Ally said, 'Too skinny for my liking.'

Cathy gave her an interested look. 'You got a man then?'

'No.'

'Why not? You're dead pretty.'

Ally laughed. 'I've just got rid of one, thank you very much. I'm in no hurry to find another.'

'Just as well,' Cathy giggled, 'cos Donny MacRailt's about as hot as they get on Battersay.'

'Looked like he was carrying the worries of the world.'

Cathy grimaced. 'He's always moaning on about something – fish or money or worrying about –' Abruptly she broke off. Ally waited for her to continue but she didn't.

They washed up in silence for a minute or two. Ally recalled how, as an eighteen year-old, she couldn't get away quick enough from rural Yorkshire and her mother's fussing love. She'd taken off to Spain to work in a bar against her mum's wishes. Their relationship – always intense after her father's early death – had been turbulent for a couple of years and then calmed into adult friendship. She felt the familiar ache of her mum's loss and quickly focused on Cathy.

'Maybe you should try going somewhere else together?' Ally suggested. 'Do a bit of travelling.'

For a moment, she saw the yearning flit impatiently across the girl's face. 'No chance,' Cathy said. 'He'll never leave his precious boat and his smelly fish and all this.' She waved her tea-towel dismissively. 'MacRailts have always lived on Battersay and always will; his old man drummed that into him years ago.'

Ally saw how the subject rankled so changed it. 'I was expecting to meet Dr Rushmore of the Hall Committee but he hasn't been in.'

'Dr Ned? I think he's away.'

'Is he a medical doctor?'

'Suppose so. Think he's retired. Into all that herbal stuff.'

'What's he like?'

'Not bad looking for an old man. But don't get your hopes up; he's got a wife, Mary.'

'And you've got a one-track mind,' Ally said with a playful nudge. 'Rushmore's not a local name?'

'No, they're incomers. Did up Sollas House. They're a bit hippy, but nice enough.'

Calum returned to lock up. When they emerged outside, Donny was waiting in a pick-up truck, engine running. From Cathy's earlier chatter, Ally knew that the girl lived in Bay with a squabbling bunch of younger siblings and a mother who worked at the Co-op. Donny's home was a static caravan at the head of the beach that ran below Ally's cottage. 'Doesn't get on with his folks,' Cathy had said, 'and it suits him to have his own place.'

They roared off. Calum offered her a lift home but Ally preferred to walk. The mist was finally lifting and revealing fingers of land and knuckles of rock beside a glinting sea. By the time she reached the cliff house, the sky was a deep azure and the sun warm on her face. *See, this place isn't so bad, is it?* The view was hazy but beautiful; a crescent of white sand cut like a scimitar at the incoming tide and blue-green sea rolled out over the horizon.

A swim! That's what she needed. Twenty minutes later, Ally was running into cold waves, shrieking her head off and falling about in the shallows. A dark head popped above the water a few yards down and then disappeared. It resurfaced nearer and she realised with delight that it was a seal. It bobbed playfully around her for a couple of minutes then vanished.

Ally dried off and went for a run along the beach. Later, after heating up some of the leftover soup she'd brought from the café, she went out again with her camera, amazed at how light it still was even after ten o'clock. Skirting the village of Sollas, she was drawn towards the isolated promontory where the artist Balmain had said some woman was living. Climbing up to what she thought was a small lighthouse, she was surprised to discover a giant pale stone statue of a woman in a long skirt and shawl. Ally stood arrested; there was something fascinating yet disturbing about the monument. The face, corroded by the elements, was featureless and her robe pockmarked. Clutching her leg was the weathered remains of a stone child. They were a strange, forlorn pair. Perhaps they were religious – Madonna and Child? – this being a Catholic island. But why put them here so far from the main township, gazing out to sea?

Ally had an urge to touch it. She closed her eyes and ran a hand over the smooth cold stone. Abruptly her palm scraped against the jagged folds of the disintegrating child and a jolt went through her like an electric shock. She jerked away, feeling dizzy. A wave of nausea rushed through her as noise thundered in her head. For a moment she thought she would fall, and then the faintness and the roaring in her ears subsided.

Ally gulped a lungful of sea air; it was the precipitous view giving her vertigo, nothing more. *It's just stone, for goodness sake.* She turned her back on the sinister statue. Part of her wanted to rush back to safety and part of her – the nosy braver Ally – wanted to hurry on and discover who it was who lived out here. *'They all try to see her – all the tourists,'* the Moody man had said. Why should a reclusive woman be a tourist attraction? Something nagged at the edge of her memory, but she couldn't think what.

A night breeze was rising as she came over the final crag. A mournful sight greeted her: tumbledown stone cottages, long abandoned, huddled in the lea of a sheer cliff that reared up out of the sea. Peering through the gloom, Ally could see that one still hung onto its turf roof like a shaggy haircut. Could this be someone's home? It didn't look habitable.

11

On walking closer, she saw that there was glass in the tiny, deep-set windows and a narrow pathway had been beaten down through the thistles and bracken to the door. Ally stopped. What would she do if a stranger suddenly appeared? What if they were deranged or dangerous?

Ally took quick photos and withdrew to a rock above the grassy enclosure to watch. But neither sound nor movement came from the crude cottage, or wisp of smoke from its chimney. She stood up. Then she heard it; the soft moan of a woman, just like the night before. Ally stiffened and listened. It came again, closer this time, like an anguished sob. She looked about but could see no one. Night was closing in and shadows were growing out of rocks and hummocks. Heart hammering, she scrambled up the slope into the dying light. The next time she turned around, the small glen was in darkness and the stone cottage impossible to make out. The wind lifted her long auburn ponytail and whipped it into her eyes.

Ally hurried home along the opposite ridge that would take her back to Sollas; to people and life. Down to her left she caught sight of a large stone house nestled in trees beside a small strand of white beach. Warm light poured from an upstairs window and she caught the whiff of a scented peat fire. Sollas House perhaps? It looked cheery and welcoming and she had to resist the urge to run down and bang on their door.

By the time she got back to her cottage, Ally was shaking off the anxiety that had gripped her since touching the statue. She was being idiotic. Even if a woman had been there, she wouldn't have come to any harm. And the strange moaning was just the way the wind blew through the bracken and rushes. She was over-tired. Tonight she would sleep like the dead.

Drinking a final glass of water at the kitchen sink, she glanced out of the window. A hooded face was staring in. Ally screamed and dropped the glass.

CHAPTER FOUR

The tumbler caught the sink's edge and smashed on the concrete floor. Ally stepped back, crunching on splinters. When she looked up the face was gone.

Heart pounding, her first thought was to barricade the door. But adrenalin made her rash; she ran out at the front and round to the cliff side. The grassy ledge, illuminated by the kitchen light, was deserted.

'Hey! Who are you? What you playing at?'

The only sound was the restless tide.

'Come on, I saw you, stop messing about.'

Ally's alarm switched to anger: probably some local kid thinking it funny to scare the newcomer. She searched beyond the light along the cliff path. Was that a figure moving in the heather or just a shadow? She ran towards it, ploughing into bracken. A pain throbbed in her right heel, slowing her up. It was too dark to see her way. *What are you doing out here?* Ally was suddenly afraid; she was running around on her own in the dark on a strange island and somewhere out there was a hooded person who had given her the fright of her life. She turned and fled back indoors, slamming the door shut.

For several minutes she stood with her back jammed against it, trying to calm down. *Stop being so jumpy!* Tomorrow she would rig up a curtain at the kitchen window. Gradually the pain in her heel grew too sharp to ignore. She pulled off her trainer. A red rosette of blood stained her white sock. A glinting shard of glass had gone straight through the rubber sole and lodged in her heel.

Hopping into the bathroom, she pulled out the glass with tweezers and stuck her foot in the bath under running water. The cold was both numbing and made her queasy. *Come on, you're okay, no real harm done.* All that had happened was that someone – she couldn't now be sure if it was male or female – had looked through her window. It was probably someone curious to see lights on in a house that obviously hadn't been occupied for ages: a passing camper on their way along the cliff path, or that grumpy guy Donny curious about his new neighbour. Whoever it was hadn't tried to come any closer and had been easily scared off by her rushing out of the house screaming like a lunatic. She'd probably given them as much of a fright as she'd had.

Ally was worn out by it all; she'd clear up the mess on the kitchen floor tomorrow. She'd soon get used to island living, just as she'd have to come to terms with being on her own.

As she hauled herself up the ladder and sank exhausted into bed, she was aware of something else. A strange smell she had noticed outside – it was still hanging in the air – a fishy smell. Fish or seabirds.

CHAPTER FIVE

Kulah, 1945

The skin of the visitor is amber-coloured, like peaty water. He wears a deer-stalker hat and a huge greatcoat like the one my father came back wearing from the Great War. Rain drips off his beaky nose as he stands in my doorway, blocking the light.

'Good day, Madam, I'm Rollo.' He holds out a hand but mine are covered in flour so I do nothing. 'They tell me you're Tormod Gillies's wife? He's the village leader, isn't he?'

It's so long since I heard English spoken – my mother's tongue – that his words burst around me like soap suds as I try to make sense of them.

I know from my daughters that the man doesn't speak Gaelic. Two days ago he came into the schoolroom where my Seanaid was attempting to teach arithmetic to Christina's twin boys. But they're wild as goats this past fortnight since the news – the non-news – of their cousin Neilac's whereabouts. Seanaid has no patience with them, with their shouting and sticking out of tongues, and beats them over the knuckles with a ruler. My Bethag understands better; understands that their naughtiness is only the ricochet from the worry that is sending the MacRailt women half mad.

'My husband isn't here, Mr Rollo,' I say, trying out the words like old toys rediscovered in a trunk. 'I'm sorry.'

'No, dear lady, it is I who am sorry. I realise it must be a difficult time for you. I don't mean to impose, but I had heard that you are a mainstay of this community and I wished to introduce myself.'

His baffling words flap about me. All I can think of is to give him tea.

'Please come in, sit yourself down. Will you take a *strupach* – a cup of tea?'

He perches on a stool by the fire, leaving his coat on but removing his hat, while I swing the kettle over the flames. At his feet is a canvas bag. The smell of wet wool mingles with peat smoke.

'I met your daughters at the school; fine young ladies. Seanaid tells me that she wishes to train as a teacher and become a headmistress. What wonderful ambition from one so young!'

I busy myself with spooning tea leaves into the pot, the way my mother used to make it, not the Kulah way of boiling tea, milk and sugar (oh what I would do for sugar!) in one pan till it stews. This man will expect a proper afternoon cup. His black hair is greying at the fringes yet his face looks smooth and youthful.

'Seventeen is not so young, Mr Rollo, but Seanaid needs more patience to be a teacher.' I hand him tea in one of my mother's china cups that normally sit gathering dust on hooks on the dresser. 'Bethag would be better.'

He is too busy looking around to take in my comment. He stares into the dark corners as if he can't believe his eyes: my parents' dining table and chairs that stand on bricks to stop the damp crippling them like arthritis, the kitchen bench, the horsehair sofa, the treadle sewing machine and the box-bed curtained off in the corner which I've shared with Bethag since Tormod joined up.

'What brings you to Kulah, Mr Rollo?'

He drinks tea and thinks about his answer. 'I'm an ethnographer at Edinburgh University; I study remote tribes. But with the war on it's been impossible to travel. So for the past couple of years I've been touring around our far-flung islands collecting songs and stories – and taking photographs – bearing witness to a way of life before it disappears.'

I'm so astonished by his reply that I throw back my head and laugh. 'So we're a remote tribe are we?'

'I didn't mean – '

'Well, Mr Rollo, I can tell you that we're not about to disappear in a hurry. There have been Gillies and MacRailts on Kulah since the dawn of time – and we'll still be here long after you ethnographers have gone to your maker.'

Suddenly he's grinning at me, not at all crushed by my words.

'I'm delighted to hear it, Mrs Gillies. So perhaps you will allow me to take your photograph?'

CHAPTER SIX

Battersay

By morning, Ally decided not to mention the face at the window. She didn't want to stir up trouble or be labelled a nervous townie. It was another busy day at the hall café: a minibus full of hikers polished off her soup by midday and Ishbel, the friendly woman from the ferry, brought in four elderly residents of Bay House, the care home in Bay, for a cup of tea. They chatted in Gaelic and played dominoes. The old man flirted with Ally.

'I prefer my men more mature,' she teased back. Two of the women giggled. The third stared hard at her with faded blue eyes and said in agitation, 'Where have you *been*, Seanaid?'

'Bethag,' Ishbel said loudly, 'this is Ally. She's from London.'

The old woman frowned in confusion. 'London? You never come to see me.'

Ally glanced at Ishbel then answered, 'Would you like me to come and visit you?'

Bethag clutched at her hand with bony fingers. 'Oh please; it's been so long.'

'Will you come and visit me first?' Nichol, the old man, winked.

'If you promise not to tell your girlfriend,' said Ally.

She had to extract herself from Bethag's claw-like grasp. Ally promised to make them scones for their next visit. Cathy came in to help wash up. When there was a lull, Ally asked her about the crude cottage on the promontory.

'A guy on the ferry said some woman lives up there – a sort of tourist attraction.'

Cathy looked round in alarm. 'Keep your voice down.'

'Why? Who is she?'

The girl stopped drying, her look astonished. 'Don't tell me you've never heard of her? It's what Battersay's famous for.'

Ally shook her head. 'Didn't know it was famous for anything. That's why I came here.'

Cathy huffed in disbelief. 'The freak,' she hissed, 'the papers nicknamed her Birdwoman. You must have heard of her? Found her on Kulah over three years ago.'

A memory half surfaced. Ally vaguely recalled a story of some girl being found on an uninhabited stack of rock way out in the Atlantic. But at the time she had been lost in the fog of her mother's death and there were whole gaps in her memory of current events. Then miraculously this cheerful Aussie photographer called Lucas had knocked her off her feet and they had spent the summer – those first all-consuming, intense months of passion – travelling Eastern Europe with cameras on assignments for *Lara* Magazine, completely absorbed in each other. The story had largely passed her by.

16

'Was that the girl who couldn't speak properly?' Ally asked.

'Aye, her, Juniper; squawks like a seagull.'

'But I thought she went into care?'

'She was carted all over – hospitals, mental places – they didn't know what to do with her. Did all these tests – trying to find out her age and stuff. They think she was seventeen or eighteen but still a virgin, you know, so that shut them up about her being part of some sex ring thing.'

'Shut who up?'

'Journalists,' Cathy said with a curl of her lip. 'They were crawling all over Battersay for months trying to get stories; nobody likes them here now.'

Ally felt herself redden. 'But why Battersay? I thought you said she was found on Kulah – isn't that much further away?'

'Aye, about as far as you can go without bumping into America. Now that's a place I'd like to see. Pull a fit movie star, eh?'

'On Kulah?'

'No, don't be daft; in America.' Cathy abandoned her tea towel, keen on a chance to gossip. 'Kulah's just a bunch of old rocks – no one had a clue how she got there – still don't. But it was my Donny found her, you know.'

'Wow, really?' With an interested nod Ally carried on washing.

'Yeah, he was quite a celeb for a few months. Got himself smartened up for the cameras; bit of eye candy when he's washed and shaved and not stinking of fish. That's when we started going out. Three years ago last month on my sixteenth birthday. Donny was twenty-two.' She gazed dreamily at the bowl she'd stopped drying. 'We had the best time. This newspaper put us up in a hotel in Glasgow – all expenses paid! Sauna, pool, Jacuzzi and as much steak as we could eat. Fridge in the bedroom was full of wee bottles of wine and cans of lager.' Cathy giggled. 'My mum went mental when she found out I hadn't been staying with Auntie Jean in Dumbarton. But it was worth all the earache I got afterwards. Glasgow was so cool and Donny was – I dunno – different, you know, a good laugh.'

'So how come Birdwoman is living on Battersay?'

Cathy's expression tensed. 'Oh boy, don't let them hear you call her that round here. You have to say Juniper; it's the name the Rushmores gave her.'

'Juniper then. How did she end up in that hut that's half fallen down?'

Cathy pulled a face and grabbed some cutlery. 'Suppose people felt sorry for her. Folk from Battersay had found her so some said she should stay here. She won't live in a proper house so the men fixed up the old shepherd's bothy. Mad as a March hare – gives me the creeps. Rushmores keep an eye on her though.'

Ally itched to ask more about the mysterious woman, but Cathy abruptly lost interest and went off to chat to a group of walkers. If only her mobile worked she could check the story on the Net. She finished clearing up in the kitchen, struggling to remember anything about

17

Birdwoman. She had a vague idea that *Lara* had run a feature in their beauty section; something to do with treatment for chapped skin and a how a good haircut and treatment to chipped and rotten teeth could make the wild woman pretty. Perhaps she could do an article on Birdwoman's diet and find out more about what she ate on Kulah? It would keep her hand in while she was so far from the workplace; keep Freya happy. How long could anyone exist on a stack of uninhabited rock? She must be amazingly resilient; it made Ally's fear of being stuck in the coastguard's house look pathetic.

Just as they were about to close, Ally heard a commotion at the door: angry male voices.

'Just wanna speak t'her!'

'No Donny, not in that state.'

Calum was blocking the young fisherman's way.

'Need to tell her – '

'Go home and sleep it off.'

'Can't stop me – get out m' way!'

Ally crossed the hall. Calum was grappling the younger man and trying to steer him around, but Donny was resisting and shouting abuse. Cathy stepped out of the kitchen and barged past Ally.

'I'll see to him.' The girl confronted her boyfriend. 'What you doing turning up drunk as a skunk? And you better not have been driving. Give me the keys!'

Donny swore at her.

Calum said, 'Okay, that's enough. Out you go.'

Between them, they bundled him out of the hall, Cathy berating him for being useless and embarrassing and thanking God all the visitors had left. Donny snarled back and called her a tart. From the window, Ally saw Calum take the keys from the pick-up's ignition and Donny kick its wheels in frustration. Then he staggered off down the road.

Cathy was shaken, though tried to hide it. 'I'm finished with him. Don't want a stupid drunk for a boyfriend anyhow. He's a joke.'

'I'll give you a lift into Bay,' Calum offered. To Ally he said, 'Shona says come round for your tea tonight – then you can phone home too – just whenever you're ready.'

Ally accepted happily; she was keen to make friends here.

***

After a swim and a change of clothes, she was brushing her teeth in the bathroom when she heard a knock at the kitchen window. For a moment she stood letting the water run, thinking of the hooded figure. *Please don't let anyone be there.* Then she turned off the tap and steeled herself to enter the kitchen.

As she did so, something was hurled at the window. Ally gasped and ducked. A huge egg smashed against the glass. She felt foolish crouching but her heart banged in fright. The runny core dribbled down.

Rushing to the window, she peered out to see who had thrown it but there was no sign. Ally stared at the yellow mucus smearing the pane. At its heart clung a blob of blood; her stomach squirmed in disgust.

A seabird's egg. It was too big for a hen's, surely? So it could have dropped from a nest in the guttering, Ally reasoned. The knocking sound might have been that crow banging about. It didn't mean someone had deliberately thrown it; she would have seen them. It was nothing to get so worked up about. She would clean it off later.

All the same, she took a thin rug that covered a rip in the armchair and jammed it over the empty curtain rail above the sink. That way, she didn't have to look at the mess on the window and no one would be staring in at her after dark. Because deep down she knew – from the noise and force of the thud – that the egg had been chucked and that somebody out there was trying to scare her.

CHAPTER SEVEN

Ally found the Gillies' home at the end of the road: a modern kit house with a fenced-in garden strewn with plastic toys, a swing and a small trampoline. Calum's green van was parked outside and a sheepdog raced out to yap a welcome. Inside was untidy and fuggy from too much central heating. Shona shouted her into the kitchen, threw a pile of ironing off a chair into a plastic basket and poured her a tumbler of red wine.

'Hope you can eat fish pie. Calum's brother works on a salmon farm. We've got a freezer full.'

'Love it,' Ally said, taking a long glug from her glass that had Santa Claus painted on the side. 'When do your boys get back?'

'Another week, unless my mum and dad surrender early.' She talked rudely but adoringly about her sons Craig and Tor, and re-filled Ally's glass. 'Calum says you want to phone home.'

'It's just to let my friends know I got here safely.' Ally found herself telling Shona that her parents were both dead, her brother wouldn't expect contact beyond the occasional postcard, but Rachel and Zoe would. As would Freya her boss, who was more friend than colleague and had been brilliant about giving her time off to get away.

'Go ahead.' Shona nodded at the next room. 'And have a good blether.'

In the sitting-room, Ally was surprised to find a youth sprawled in front of the TV watching a Soap. They exchanged 'hi's' and she thought she recognised him from the bus over from Bay. Aware that the boy kept flicking her glances, she rang Rachel who was on her way home from work and had to shout over the traffic and voices. Ally could visualise the bustle and Rachel with her mobile jammed up against her corkscrew hair, swaying with the bendy bus. She had a pang of longing for London and crowds. All the things Ally wanted to tell her about the quirky place and her creepy house – things to make Rachel laugh – she couldn't say in front of the watchful teenager.

Instead she said, 'I'm having a meal at friends' – job's great – been really busy. I'll try and ring from the town; mobile's useless up here. You can ring this number if you need to leave a message. Tell Zoe will you?'

Ally wasn't ready to speak to Zoe yet. Her other close friend had been critical of her leaving London. *Why should you have to run away? Lucas is the one in the wrong. Don't let him win twice.* Somehow, in Zoe's eyes, she was letting down the sisterhood. She rang Freya's work number and left a message to say that all was going well and thanks again for her support – oh, and by the way, she had an idea for an article.

The youth turned out to be Calum's younger brother Rory who worked on the fish farm beyond Bay.

'Ally's already calling Bay a town,' he said with a sly grin, as they finished off the meal. 'You'll be as mad as the other incomers soon.'

'Don't be cheeky,' Shona scolded, 'and you shouldn't have been listening in to her phone call.'

'Bet you were too,' Rory snorted.

Ally offered to wash up but Shona said she'd done enough for one day and ordered Rory to do it. Picking up the remains of the red wine she led Ally into the sitting-room while Calum went to check on his dozen sheep. When Ally brought up the subject of Juniper, Shona pulled a face.

'Cathy had her tongue wagging, eh?'

'No, it was me who asked her,' Ally defended.

'I feel sorry for Juniper right enough,' Shona said, her tone grudging, 'but if she won't learn to talk we're never going to find out the real story, are we?'

'I just can't get my head round the fact that no one knows who she is or where she came from.'

'Well we don't, so we let the lassie live in peace. She doesn't bother us and we don't bother her.'

They chatted about Donny and Cathy's doomed romance.

'He's never been the same since Juniper came – all the fuss – he couldn't handle it. And he fell out with his dad over it all – the old boy said celebrity status had turned his head and he was no use at the fishing. Kicked him out.'

'Cathy said Donny wanted his own place.'

Shona shook her head. 'Have you seen the shack he lives in? No, poor old Donny's a lost soul. Drinks way too much. He's not stable in my opinion.'

'Someone was spying on me last night,' Ally confided, 'caught them staring in. Gave me a bit of a fright. And tonight someone threw an egg at the kitchen window. Do you think it could've been him?'

Shona looked concerned. 'More than likely. I'll get Calum to have a word.'

'No don't,' Ally said quickly, 'I don't want to cause him any more trouble.'

'Well if it happens again, you tell us, okay?'

Ally agreed and changed the subject. 'Calum said you'd give me the gossip on the painter.'

'John Balmain?' Shona broke into a grin. 'Now there's a mystery man.'

'In what way?'

'Came to the island about three years ago – there was so much fuss going on about Juniper that no one really paid him any attention at first. He said he was a painter, but you just had to see the stuff he called art – my Craig and Tor could do better – it was obvious he was covering up.'

'And was he?'

'Oh, yes. It turns out he used to be a priest!'

'A priest?' Ally's eyes widened in disbelief. 'He didn't look like one.'

'Well he isn't now, that's the point. Got the sack.'

'What on earth for?'

'Something to do with a woman – an affair, so they say.'

'And that's not allowed?'

Shona rolled her eyes. 'Not for a Catholic priest – celibacy and all that. Anyway, he keeps to himself and never talks about it.'

'So how do you know it's true?'

'Father Damien, the priest who comes over from Barra to take Mass twice a week, is a terrible gossip. He told Ishbel all about it.'

Ally drained the last of her wine as Calum came in.

'Mind you, he hasn't looked twice at any of the lassies since he got here,' Shona said. 'The only one he's got the time of day for is old Bethag and she's pushing eighty.'

'Don't sound so disappointed,' Calum teased.

Shona laughed. 'There's something a bit sexy about him, right enough. Don't you think so, Ally?' She gave an exaggerated wink.

Ally felt herself redden; she wasn't going to admit to finding him attractive. 'Not my type.'

'And what's that?' Shona asked.

Ally gave a rueful smile. 'I'm not sure anymore.'

'Ah, pass the bandages Calum!' Shona cried. 'She's had her heart broken. I bet that's really why you're here.'

Ally fanned her face. 'Wow it's hot in here.'

'I knew it,' Shona said. 'They all come here to mend their hearts.'

'Oh, yeah?' Ally snorted. 'Me, the priest and who else?'

'Well, there's the Rushmores.'

'Haven't met them yet.'

'You will,' Calum grunted. 'Dr Ned likes to organise us locals.'

'Don't listen to him,' said Shona, 'we're lucky to have someone who wants to take on village business. And Mary's lovely – a very private person but with a heart of gold – babysits for our boys sometimes over at Sollas House. Nothing's too much trouble for her.'

'So why do their hearts need mending?'

Shona's expression grew sad. 'Years ago they lost their little boy. Fell off a yacht and drowned.'

'God, how terrible!'

'They never had any more, but they've spent their lives since caring for other people's.' Ally heard the catch in Shona's voice as sudden tears welled in her eyes. 'They're so kind –'

Calum said, 'Don't go getting upset.' He gave Ally a look of embarrassment. 'She's a terrible softie; cries at the nappy commercials.'

Shona gave a swipe at her husband.

'Well,' said Ally, 'they sound like just the right sort of people to be looking after Juniper.'

Calum frowned.

Ally went on, 'I mean, it can't be easy with her not able to communicate properly, or are they trying to get her to speak?'

Shona gave Calum a nervous glance. 'No, the lassie's simple,' Shona said. 'Anyway, she doesn't need to speak; she lives like a wild animal.'

Abruptly Calum said, 'Come on, I'll run you home, you must be tired out.'

'Thanks, I am.' Ally knew he was uncomfortable at her mentioning the Birdwoman; it had broken the intimacy of her earlier conversation. Why was he so touchy?

Outside, the moon was up yet the sunset had not completely vanished. A breeze snapped at some washing that was still on the line. Shona waved goodbye and went to take it in. Calum drove in silence. Ally broke it.

'You don't like me talking about Juniper, do you?'

Calum shrugged. 'She's had a rough time. She deserves to be left alone.'

'And kept in a stone ruin like a wild dog?'

He gave her a sharp look. 'Have you been snooping round her place?'

'I went for a walk –'

'You shouldn't have,' he interrupted.

'You're kidding, right?'

He braked sharply at the end of her track. 'Promise me you won't try and approach her?'

'Why?' Ally was nonplussed. 'She's just a young woman.'

'She's not. It's like Shona said – she's simple in the head but she's strong – she'll have a go at you. The last thing we need is the press getting hold of a story that she's attacked a tourist.'

'You're all frightened of her, aren't you?' Ally said in astonishment, irked at being called a tourist again.

'Don't be daft.' His face set in annoyance.

'Well don't worry; I didn't even get a glimpse.' Ally opened her door. Without thinking she added, 'Though I'm pretty sure I heard her crying.'

'Crying?' Calum looked at her strangely. 'But she can't cry – not like normal folk.'

Ally shivered in the night air, remembering the sound of sobbing.

'Must've been something else then.'

Ally thanked him and he waved goodbye as he revved away up the hill. The sharp salty air made her feel dizzy; she shouldn't have drunk so much wine, it had made her say stupid things.

Buffeted by the wind, she hurried head down to the house. A pungent rank smell hit her. In the shadows, she stepped on something slippery and lost her footing. She landed with a thump on her right knee. Wincing in pain, Ally put out a hand to steady herself and recoiled at once: something cold and slimy.

CHAPTER EIGHT

'Oh God!' Ally cried out.

Pushing the door open and grappling for the light switch, she saw what it was. Spread out on the doorstep was a large rotting fish, its dead eye staring at her, a pus-filled milky yellow. Its scales were a dull dead grey, yet seemed to twitch and move in the light. Hand over mouth, Ally leaned closer. The flesh was alive with flies. Gagging, Ally picked it up by its tale and flung it into the heather at the side of the track. Slimy scales like a ghostly imprint remained on the stone step and clung to the soles of her shoes. She kicked them off in disgust and threw them outside the front door.

It took ten minutes of scrubbing under scalding water to get rid of the fish scales that clung to her hands. In bed, the smell still lingered. The thought of ever eating fish pie again made her nauseous and she cursed whoever it was who was playing tricks. Someone was watching her – knew when she came and went from the house – and wanted her to know. But why? Was it just high-jinx or something more malicious? Whichever it was, it was freaking her out.

Ally tossed and turned through the night, flinching at every small creak and sound, afraid to fall asleep. The red wine had left her dry-mouthed and craving water, but she was too spooked to lower the ladder and venture below. She had dragged the chest over the hatch to stop anyone lifting it.

Right now, Ally would have given anything, *anything*, to have had Lucas there lying beside her, warm and solid and unfazed. *Struth, Ally, it's just some kiddo got the hots for you trying to get your attention.* Lucas would've found it funny, rolled over and gone to sleep. But Lucas wasn't there because he'd let her down, and the only reason she was there was because she hated him and never wanted to see his lying, cheating face again, ever.

This was her problem, no one else's. It was harassment and she wouldn't put up with it. She'd complain to Shona and Calum, or maybe to Dr Rushmore if he ever showed his face. And if that didn't stop it, she'd tell them to stick their job.

Ally woke early, her head aching and her pillow smelling faintly of fish. Why should she have to go just because of some joker? She couldn't keep running away. She wouldn't give them the satisfaction. She'd deal with this on her own.

CHAPTER NINE

Kulah

Rollo helps me with the peat cutting. He learnt how to use a *cass-crom* on Skye when he lived there last year and we talk about the island – my mother's island – and I tell him about the holidays I had there as a girl, staying in my grandfather's cottage.

'He was gardener to a wealthy Glasgow banker,' I tell Rollo, 'my grandfather came with him from the city.'

'It's fascinating, isn't it, how much people have moved around? We think places have been the same for generations but there has always been to-ing and fro-ing. Probably some of your Kulah ancestors were passing Roman traders.'

He stands leaning on the long-bladed spade with his shirt sleeves rolled up and his thick hair lifting in the breeze and enthuses about people. And somewhere inside I feel a small fluttering like a wounded bird and wonder what it means.

'Take my own family, for instance: father's half English, half Irish and my mother's from a long line of Armenian merchants.'

As he chatters, I carry on throwing out the cut peats to dry in the wind and wonder if he has a family to carry on the bloodline of English-Irish-Armenians.

Later, the girls appear with a flask of tea, oatcakes and cheese. Seanaid practises her English while Bethag perches on a creel and giggles. Rollo says they can help him write down the songs that the old folks sing.

'My Gaelic's pretty rough so you girls can help me translate, and I'll help you with your English writing. Do we have a bargain?' He holds out his hand.

Seanaid gives him a bold look and shakes on it. Bethag hides her blushing face behind her hands.

He squints at me in the sunlight. 'Do I have your permission to recruit your daughters as my assistants, Mrs Gillies?'

I laugh. 'If it improves their education then yes, I agree.'

It's then that I notice that his eyes are not exactly blue, but more of a green: the green of a stone glimpsed under water.

'Mother,' says Seanaid in Gaelic, 'it's rude to stare.'

CHAPTER TEN

Battersay

'Hail Helpers!' A tall fit man with a sweep of pale greying hair strode waving into the hall. Dressed in baggy shorts and faded African print shirt, Ally took him for a camper, until he thrust out an arm covered in tattoos and shook her hand.

'Ned Rushmore; how are you Alison? Settling in well I hear. Sorry not to be around when you arrived – been to the mainland for a few of days. Great to be back. Hate going away.'

He turned at once to Cathy. 'How's your mother? Over the worst of that cold I hope. Got some Echinacea for her.'

The day up till then had dragged. No ferry came into Battersay on Mondays or Thursdays and most of the campers had already cleared off; apart from the Cagoule Family. From the window, Ally had watched them dart along the shore like yellow sandpipers collecting small treasures and waving to their parents. Ally had been trying to pump Cathy for information on Donny, but she was less chatty than the previous day and kept giving her sidelong glances as if she couldn't make up her mind about something.

'Does he have a problem with me for some reason?'

Cathy had been dismissive. 'That scene yesterday wasn't about you – it's me he's angry with for not giving him what he wants.'

'It's just that someone left rotting fish at my door last night and I wondered if it could be him.'

'Ugh, sick!' Cathy had grimaced, and then shrugged. 'Anything's possible when he's had a few.'

'So you weren't with him last night?'

'No way.'

The girl had started cleaning her nails with a kitchen knife, and when Ally had asked her to stop, she had gone into a sulk. Ally had tried to coax her out of it by chatting about her evening with Shona and Calum.

'Found them a bit touchy about Juniper though. What does Donny think of her?'

Cathy's look had been sharp. 'What do you mean?'

'Well, he was the one found her so does he have any ideas about her?'

'God you're just like a journalist – questions, questions! Why's everyone so bothered about her? I wish I got half the attention.'

'Sorry,' Ally had said. 'I was just being nosy. I didn't mean to upset you.'

'I'm not upset.' Cathy had turned away. 'But don't go bothering Donny about her, okay? He doesn't like it.'

So Ned's appearance was a welcome relief.

Straddling a chair, the doctor refused a cup of tea, but downed a pint of water.

He told them about his trip to Oban to charter a boat for a trip around the islands in September. 'Friends come up from Wales every year to do a bit of sailing. Mary and I like to join them.'

'Can't think of anything worse,' Cathy pulled a face, 'boats make me seasick.'

'Ginger biscuits,' Ned answered, 'that's the remedy.'

Ally felt a pang for the man; how brave to continue sailing after his son had drowned. She could only imagine how devastated he must have been. He offered to cycle into Bay and fetch Ally provisions.

'That's kind, but I thought I might walk in after work and have a mooch around.'

'Walk?' Cathy cried. 'It's over five miles. Co-op'll be closed by then.'

'Okay, I'll run.'

Ally laughed at the look of horror on the girl's face.

'Good for you!' Ned cheered. 'If you're the active type, we'll have to see about fitting you up with a bicycle, then you can explore our beautiful island on your days off.'

Cathy rolled her eyes. 'Not that there's anything to see.'

They watched the doctor cycle away. 'Fit isn't he,' said Cathy, 'for an old man?'

'Hardly old – fifties maybe,' Ally mused.

'That's ancient.'

***

Straight after work, Ally changed into running clothes and trainers and set off for Bay with an empty backpack. The rotting fish was still noticeable by the track; she was happy not to linger at the house. Clouds were ballooning on the horizon yet the day was still warm and the breeze gentle and she saw no need for a waterproof. Sticking to the narrow road, she waved at Alec's bus as it rattled by, with Cathy its only passenger.

Ally welcomed the familiar rhythm in her feet, and the sound of her breathing as she settled into a good pace. It set her thoughts free.

Ned was good-looking in a fading alpha-male sort of way; body in good shape but tanned face scored with life's experiences. Lucas would probably look like that in twenty years; his fresh blond looks corrupting, his body thickening. He might no longer get away with a boyish smile or honeyed words of apology from sensuous lips. She used to love watching him as he slept, his face untroubled as a child's, his fair hair tousled like a Greek god's. She would kiss his brow and wonder how she had found such a beautiful man.

'How serious are you about Lucas?' It was Freya who had first flagged up a warning. They had gone to Freya's exclusive gym one night after work; her boss was middle-aged but with the lean muscled body of a fit thirty-something which Freya put down to not having had kids. 'Semi-serious', Ally had answered, though what she really meant was head-over-heels mad about the guy.

'*I saw him with someone last weekend when you were away at the food fair.*' Freya was always brutally upfront. '*Coming out of a Greek restaurant arm in arm.*' Ally had felt gut-wrenchingly sick but made excuses; it was probably someone from back home in Oz. He was always meeting up with nomadic friends from Sydney.

Freya had stopped towelling her short fair hair and long limbs, and given her a penetrating look. '*So he didn't tell you about it? Beware of men who keep secrets.*' Ally had protested that Lucas wasn't like that.

'*I'm going to keep an eye on him,*' Freya had warned. '*I'll not have him causing upset in my team.*' She was fiercely protective of her female staff and had power over Lucas; he was one of her freelance photographers and she gave him lucrative work. Equally she could offer the shoot to another ambitious freelancer. What a mistake it had been to relay this conversation to her boyfriend. Lucas had been hurt – '*what woman? There was a crowd of us* – and angry that Freya was interfering in their private life. '*She's a bloody stirrer. Don't listen. You know I'm crazy about you.*'

Ally picked up her pace, attacking the hill in front, trying to smother the memory of the rows that followed once the poison of doubt had been injected. They always began over something petty – like forgetting to pick up the dry-cleaning – and ended with her flinging accusations. '*So why were you so late last night? Who were you with? Who is it keeps hanging up when I answer the phone – number withheld*'? He grew tired of making denials. '*Struth! You're right. I'm shagging Princess Anne. That keep you happy*'? She would snatch her trainers and go off for a long run. By the time she got home he was usually gone. Only later, when she had consumed a lot of wine alone and he had returned waving a bunch of supermarket flowers, did they fall into bed and make furious love. '*You know how much I love you.*' Nobody was tenderer than Lucas after a fall-out.

But she'd been right not to trust him; he had been unfaithful all along. The other woman was a model from his autumn shoot and it turned out he had a key to her place too. He'd tried to blame the leggy model for coming onto him, for using him to get noticed by Freya. Ally's anger fizzed once more. Excuses, bloody excuses! She hated him for spoiling things so badly.

Bay stretched out before her as she pounded down the last slope, trying to clear her head of Lucas. Her right heel was beginning to throb from the recent cut. The sky had gone hazy and the landscape colourless. The stout fortress was hardly distinguishable from the rock beneath it, and the houses had retreated into the blue-grey background.

She found the Co-op in a large shed close to the ferry terminal. She bought pasta, pesto, olive oil, grapes, feta, shortbread and two bottles of Orvieto wine. The woman on the till looked like Cathy's older sister and wore a name badge: Sandra. Ally took a gamble. 'You must be Cathy's mum? I'm working with her down at Sollas.'

Sandra gave her a tired smile. 'Aye, she's told me. Would you like a bag for those?'

Ally declined. The woman watched her load up her backpack. 'You can tell me what that lassie gets up to down there. My spy in the camp, eh?' she gave a chesty smoker's laugh.

'Agent Ally at your service,' Ally agreed.

She explored the rest of the harbour: a post office-cum-newsagent that was closed, a pizza-kebab takeaway that wasn't yet open. Beyond were a gift shop, a café and an ironmonger's that sold camping gaz that were all closing up for the day. The public telephone was coin operated and she had little change. Ally decided she would ring her friends when she was more settled, worried that hearing their voices might make her hanker all the more after London and her flat. She felt too close to jacking it all in.

Steps lead up to the junction that branched one way to Sollas and the other to the east side of Battersay. A tourist sign promised a list of attractions along the latter: The Heather Hotel, a Standing Stone and an Art Gallery.

Ally dithered. The ache in her heel was getting worse, yet she didn't want to go back. It would be light for another three or four hours and the hotel was only two miles away. Perhaps she would treat herself to a bar meal? She was hardly dressed for going out but who around here would care? All at once, the thought of a cheery hotel rather than an evening alone in her dank cottage, spurred her to fork right.

Fifteen minutes later, Ally felt the first spots of rain. She broke into a jog, but was astonished at the speed at which the sudden storm caught her. Black clouds whipped in from the sea, trailing skirts of rain like giant jellyfish that stung her face and arms. Hailstones bounced off the tarmac. Within seconds she was soaked through and visibility had narrowed to a few paces ahead. Head down, she battled on, hoping for a car to flag down.

Abruptly the road deteriorated and she was splashing ankle deep in muddy puddles. Ally stopped, wondering whether it was safer to turn back to Bay. She peered through straggly hair, her heel raw and stinging from her waterlogged trainer. There was a building ahead – it couldn't be the hotel yet – but somewhere to seek shelter. She hobbled on.

No one answered her knocking. She huddled under the guttering for a moment then skirted the low cottage, squinting in at its deep-set windows and looking for a back entrance. Behind was a yard littered with ancient farm machinery and broken lobster pots; the beaten ground was a mud-bath.

'Hiya!' she called. 'Anyone at home?'

A seagull screeched overhead. She spun round in alarm. A door in the dilapidated barn opposite banged open. Ally's breath froze in her chest as a hulk of a man loomed out of the doorway, brandishing an axe.

CHAPTER 11

Advancing towards Ally was the man from the ferry: John Balmain.

'What do you want?' he shouted above the deluge.

She stared, speechless.

'The gallery's closed!'

'Hotel! I was looking for it.'

'You've taken the wrong turning.'

'Yes, sorry.' Her teeth chattered with cold, her gaze fixed on the axe. She stepped back quickly.

'You're soaking,' he said, following her. 'Come in the house till it eases off.'

'It's okay,' Ally said, slithering about the mud trying to get away.

He caught her wrist. 'Don't be foolish.'

Ally gasped and pulled herself free.

He dropped the axe. 'I was just sculpting. I'm not a psycho. Come on, we're both getting soaked now.'

Against her better judgement, Ally followed him into the house. John switched on a lamp whose base was a smooth boulder, and threw some more peat on a smouldering fire. She stood shivering beside it, curious despite her misgivings. Without another word, he disappeared through a far door. She stared about her. Two downstairs rooms had been knocked into one to create a large living space: part sitting-room, part dining area with a sturdy pine table that was covered in paints, brushes and pieces of driftwood.

From beyond came the sound of a tap being run and the hiss of a kettle being thumped on a stove, followed by heavy footsteps on the stairs and across the floor above her head. She thought about bolting. '*Don't be so trusting in future,*' Freya had warned. Her boss was a far better judge of character than she was; she was happily married to wealthy easy-going, Rich. '*Rich by name, rich by bank balance*', Lucas used to say with envy. John reappeared with a pile of clothes.

'The bathroom's upstairs. You can put these on.'

He held them out: a pair of thick cords, a check shirt, a coarse woollen jumper, socks. Their ordinariness was reassuring but still she hesitated. All her instincts were telling her that there was something risky about being here; that this man spelled trouble. His look challenged her as if he sensed her unease over him. 'Not the height of fashion for a London girl, but I don't think either of us cares.'

'Thanks,' Ally took them. What was she doing here? Curiosity about this reclusive man, this wayward ex-priest, made her take the stairs with a thumping heart.

A large open area under the eaves gave access to a bedroom on one side and bathroom to the other. Glancing in the open bedroom she was startled by the sight of a large iron-framed double bed covered in a blanket of animal skins with small pointy heads still attached. She hurried in to the bathroom.

Its walls were decorated in a mosaic of shells and pebbles embedded into swirls of plaster. The mirror was framed in tiny pieces of coral. She found a pink comb – a woman's? – and pulled it through her tangle of long hair. Large solemn green eyes peered back at her, her full lips purple with cold. Even rolled up, the trousers were ridiculously long. She tied them up with string that lay coiled on the windowsill and hoped it wasn't part of some sculpture. The shirt was brushed cotton and soft on her raw skin, the jumper heavy and instantly warming. Ally felt an uncomfortable intimacy in wearing his clothes that was strangely erotic. The socks were well darned, perhaps old kilt socks. They were too scratchy for her lacerated heel so she just wore the one. Leaving her running clothes dripping over the bath, she ventured back down.

Waiting on a table made from a tree stump, was a cup of tea. The fire had taken hold and was filling the room with an earthy, smoky aroma.

John returned carrying a plate of chocolate biscuits. He raised an eyebrow at sight of her. 'Not exactly Versace.'

Ally said, 'No – much more Battersay.'

His face cracked into a smile. For an instant he looked boyishly handsome. He offered her a biscuit and plonked himself down on a battered sofa. She perched on the armchair by the fire.

'So you're running away from Sollas already?'

'I like to run, but I misjudged the weather.'

'Newcomers always do. How's the job going? Cathy pulling her weight?'

Ally exclaimed, 'Does everyone know everything that goes on here?'

'Pretty much.'

She sipped tea and wondered whether she could confide in him. His expression was severe – apart from the deep brown eyes. Up close, he looked younger than she'd first thought, no more than forty.

'So who is it that doesn't want me here?' Ally asked quietly.

John frowned. 'Meaning?'

She told him about the snooper, the smashed egg and the stinking fish. He looked concerned.

'Sounds like boyish pranks, but you should tell the Gillies.'

'I told Shona,' said Ally, 'but maybe I should mention it to Dr Rushmore. He gave me the job and seems very approachable.'

'Ah, so you've met the charismatic doctor,' he grunted.

'You don't like him?'

John blew on his tea. The mug looked lost in his large hands. 'I steer clear of the organising types.'

Ally remarked, 'if there was no one to organise us, we'd live in anarchy.'

'Umm,' he murmured, 'wouldn't that be a fine thing.'

'An anarchist and an artist,' she said in amused surprise. He regarded her but did not respond, so she added, 'Calum tells me you run a gallery. Is it in the barn over there?'

He snorted. 'People will insist on calling it a gallery. I wouldn't pay for anything in it.'

'We all have to make a living,' she said.

He shrugged. She sipped more tea. 'I can't make out if you're just undervaluing your art or being a snob about tourists wanting to buy your stuff.'

His dark eyebrows arched. 'Well, you speak your mind, don't you?'

''Fraid so. It comes with being a j –' She bit her tongue.

He contemplated her with knowing dark eyes as if he guessed what she had meant to say; eyes that seemed to encourage the confessional. But he didn't question her unfinished words, just pushed the plate of biscuits across the floor. 'Help yourself.' She ate three. He offered to heat up some soup. When she declined, he didn't insist.

A seagull flapped onto the windowsill and squawked.

'That's Mungo,' John said, 'my greedy friend. He must've seen the biscuits.'

'I have a big black crow that wakes me up early every morning,' Ally said. 'He's a pain. Between him and the sea, it's noisier than the city.'

They talked about the hall and the Gillies and her need to get out of London for the summer. She didn't mention Lucas.

'What brought you to Battersay?' Ally asked.

'I'm sure you've heard the gossip.' Abruptly he got up and went to refresh the teapot.

When he returned, she asked, 'Were you really a priest?'

He eyed her. 'Is it the fact I was a priest or the reason I was sacked that interests you?'

Ally blushed. 'Sorry, it's none of my business.'

'No it isn't.'

He poured out more tea. The silence was awkward. The rain was beginning to ease, but the fire was now blazing and the room cosy. She should make a move but her limbs were heavy.

Abruptly John said, 'what's wrong with your foot?'

'Oh, I dropped a glass and nicked the heel.'

He leaned down and peered closer. 'Hey that's a nasty cut, looks infected.'

'I probably shouldn't have run so far.'

He left the room in three quick strides saying, 'I'll get something.'

Returning with a battered biscuit tin full of plasters, string, loose batteries and scissors, John emptied the contents on the rug and seized on a tube of antiseptic cream. He took hold of her ankle in a firm grip and squeezed the ointment onto the cut. Ally flinched. The sensation that shot up from her foot was electric.

'Sorry,' he said, relaxing his hold.

'No, it's me, I'm ticklish.'

She watched him as he gently rubbed in the cream, trying not to gasp with pleasure. She felt ridiculously and instantly aroused. He rested her foot on his knee as he reached for a fat roll of plaster and cut a generous

32

square. John frowned in concentration as he lined it up over the cut and smoothed it in position with dextrous paint-flecked fingers. She gazed at his tangled hair and dark lashes and wondered if he felt the same internal kicks and shocks that she did.

He placed her foot carefully back on the floor and looked up. 'Operation over.'

Ally swallowed. 'Thanks.'

'You okay?'

Ally thought: he has no idea how sexy he is. How had she not noticed before? She had been too overawed by his initial rudeness and unkempt appearance.

'I'm fine.' She reached for the other sock and pulled it on, glad of the distraction.

'You look like you want to say something,' John puzzled.

She shook her head. He scooped up the spilled contents and rammed them back in the tin.

'There is something actually,' Ally said. 'When we met on the ferry I didn't know anything about the Birdwoman. That's not why I came here. I just want you to know that.'

He put the lid on the tin, and glancing at her said, 'her name's Juniper.'

'I know that now.'

He sat back, abandoning the tin on the floor. 'So what else have you learned about her?'

Ally thought before answering with a question of her own. 'Are people here afraid of Juniper?'

She expected another denial like Calum's, but he leaned forward and said, 'intriguing question. What gives you that impression?'

'I saw her hut on a walk. I mentioned it to Calum and he got worked up about it – said she was dangerous and I shouldn't go near. And Cathy's funny about it too – tells me I'm not to say anything about her to Donny. It's just, the islanders cared enough about her to take her in and protect her from the outside world, so I'm surprised they seem to avoid her.'

He nodded. 'It's a strange relationship. People feel responsible for her, because it was the MacRailts who found her. But there's also this feeling that she's a bad omen – that nothing good comes out of Kulah.'

'A bad omen?'

He looked uncomfortable and shrugged as if he'd said too much.

'Go on tell me, please. I want to understand – I'm living here now.'

After a considering look he said, 'Some of the islanders – the older ones especially – think that Kulah is cursed.'

'Why's that?'

'Because of the shipwreck.'

Ally had a vague recollection from a social history lecture at Edinburgh years ago that Kulah had once been inhabited but that the islanders had been resettled elsewhere.

'Was that something to do with the island being evacuated a long time ago?'

'In a way, yes.' John stared into the fire. He took a deep breath. 'A boat full of servicemen returning to Kulah after the Second World War hit rocks in a storm and sank. Most of the male population was wiped out – drowned right in front of the eyes of the women waiting on the shore to welcome them home. They'd been away for years and then died within sight of their homes and families.'

Ally was stunned. 'That's appalling!'

John nodded, his face grim. 'It was said that the people of Battersay could hear the wailing of the women eight hours boat ride away.'

Ally felt a chill go down her spine. *A woman crying.*

'But communication was so infrequent and the storms that spring so bad that no one really knew what had happened till weeks later. When the first supply boat reached Kulah they found only a handful of traumatised islanders left.'

Ally sat in disbelief, trying to take in the enormity of the disaster. Something he said nagged.

'Why only a handful?'

John got up and went to the fire. He hunkered in front, needlessly prodding with the poker. His voice was reflective as he stared into it, his strong profile lit up by the flames.

'It's too tragic for words. It appears there was an outbreak of flu that winter that carried off many of the women and children – including their leader Flora Gillies who had kept them strong all through the war.'

'Flu?'

John nodded. 'That's what the survivors said. I suppose after years of half starvation they were weakened and susceptible to an epidemic. The remaining islanders were evacuated to Battersay and the mainland.'

'How terrible,' Ally whispered. 'No wonder they think the place is cursed.'

'Not just cursed, but haunted,' John said, shaking his head. 'Plenty locals think Juniper is the reincarnation of Flora Gillies. They won't say so to the media, but they think it.'

'But you don't?'

He looked at her in astonishment. 'Of course not – it's superstitious nonsense. The only explanation possible is that the girl was abandoned by passing trawlermen – or maybe people traffickers.' He scrutinised her. 'Don't tell me you believe in such things as ghosts and possession?'

'I'm open-minded about ghosts,' Ally replied. Despite the heat of the fire she felt shivery.

'There's nothing open-minded about it,' he mocked. 'It's pagan rubbish.'

'As opposed to worshipping saints?' Ally sparked back.

His face darkened. 'I'm no longer a practising priest.'

'But you still believe in something?'

'That's personal,' he said defensively.

'And so's the belief that Juniper might be Flora in some mystical way.'

He jumped up and paced to the window. 'God, you'll get on well with the woolly-headed thinkers around here.'

She got to her feet. 'Good. What's so wrong with that?'

He whipped round. 'Because it means they don't treat Juniper as a normal human being – like you said, they steer clear.'

'But if they think she's Flora come back again, isn't that a positive thing? You said Flora was a strong leader. Why should they think that's a bad omen?'

She saw the tension in his jaw, as if he struggled with whether to answer. Finally he spoke in a low voice, 'They think Flora will somehow take her revenge for all the bad things that happened, for neighbouring Battersay not coming to their rescue quick enough.'

Ally laughed. 'Now that is far-fetched!'

But his expression was deadly serious. 'Not for superstitious minds that believe in ancient prophecy. There was a seer on Battersay who predicted it all three hundred years ago.'

'Predicted what?'

'Calamity.'

Ally's heart began to thud. 'So what's the prophecy?'

John went to the alcove next to the fire and reached over a small desk with a computer to pull a book from the shelf. It was battered and grubby with age. He went to a marked page.

'"When the Woman of the Birds is joined with the Flame-haired One, there will be death on the island and so much weeping that the children of the long boats will drown in tears". They say that Flora was red-headed.'

John looked across at her. Suddenly his expression changed as if he were seeing her properly for the first time. Dread prickled the back of her neck. Nervously, she pulled back her drying auburn hair. Surely he couldn't think …? She got up.

'I must go. It's getting late.'

'Sorry, I didn't mean to spook you.'

'You didn't,' Ally lied. 'I'll just fetch my stuff. Thanks for the tea.'

He gave her a lift in his battered blue van but they hardly spoke. It was all too weird; she couldn't work out what to believe. Something about this place was unreal, as if the past was all about her but she just couldn't see it. *Don't talk rubbish!*

But as they arrived at her cottage, a sense of foreboding stole in like mist. The house stood dark against the setting sun with the crow perched on the cold chimney, cawing. She dreaded going in alone.

CHAPTER 12

John didn't drive straight home. He felt restless: energised but unsettled by Ally's sudden appearance out of the rain. She'd looked bedraggled but beautiful, hair writhing around her face and neck, her curvy figure revealed in the flimsy wet running gear. *A temptress*, he could hear his mother say. Old Bethag would be kinder, call her a *silkie* – a mermaid – lured ashore by curiosity.

He parked over the brow of the hill, out of sight of the coastguard's house and cut back to the beach. He pulled off his canvas shoes and plunged his feet into cold wet sand, walking briskly. What was he to make of this new arrival? She was attractive and friendly, but far too nosy for her own good. All those questions about Juniper and the Prophecy could lead to dangerous ground. He had stopped short of telling her more. Her blunt questions about his own personal situation had taken him by surprise, and she had known just how to rile him over matters of faith.

Yet it alarmed him how easily he found himself confiding in her. He wouldn't be surprised if she were a journalist, trying to winkle information out of him on Juniper. Reporters had come in various guises over the past three years; Ally might just be the latest. Worse still, she might be there to uncover the truth of his doomed affair with Caroline; he had come to Battersay to prevent lurid tabloid headlines and he relished his anonymity. He must be on his guard.

John strode to the end of the bay and looked back. A dim light shone through the skylight of the cottage; she must already have gone to bed. The thought was unsettling. Had she discarded his clothing with relief, or was she still wearing his shirt to sleep in?

Digging fingers into his tousled hair, he let go a sigh of frustration. He'd been fine up till now. Nobody had troubled him or caught his attention since coming to Battersay; it had been a blessed relief. There had been no one since Caroline – could never be again – he couldn't trust himself not to cause harm.

Sitting on a rock, John lit a cigarette and smoked steadily as the light left the sky. What had possessed him to talk to Ally on the ferry in the first place? At his sarcastic remark she had turned and fixed him with large green eyes, her plump lips opening in astonishment. The effect had been like a punch to the guts.

Just as Caroline would have done, she had challenged him back, flinging a riposte after him that he'd pretended to ignore. He'd picked up snippets about Ally from a trip to the Co-op and gossip at the care home. She was already attracting interest – not all of it healthy – if her tale about dead fish and a hooded snooper were true.

John glanced up the dune at the dark hulk of Donny's caravan, and wondered. Perhaps it was time to have another chat with the young fisherman; to play the father confessor role once more? There was something Donny still wasn't telling him.

He ground out his cigarette and leapt up the dune in three strides. The ancient caravan was in darkness and there was no sign of Donny's pick-up. John retreated up the path towards his car. Glancing back, he could just see the corrugated iron-roof of Ally's cottage jutting up like a loose tooth. What to do about her? He had a bad feeling that she was going to be disruptive and uncover things he would do anything to keep secret. He was torn between keeping well clear and keeping a watchful eye on her.

John drove home, still undecided.

CHAPTER 13

Kulah

It's midsummer before word reaches us from a passing yacht that the war on the Continent is over – has been for over a month. We let the children out of school and they run around the cliff paths, squawking like gulls, spreading the news to the most isolated homes. I declare we will have a celebration.

All week we gather driftwood for a bonfire and make scones on the griddle and pots of broth; Simple Sam and Seanaid clamber down the cliffs for eggs, for they are the only ones left on the island who will dare. I don't like Seanaid taking such risks but she's nimble and fearless of the fulmars and she's doing it for the village. We will put eggs in the hot ashes and they will remind us that soon our men will return and we will have as many eggs as we wish.

Rollo goes fishing with the yacht people and returns with a crate of flapping, shimmering mackerel. The old men gather on the shore to gut the fish and discuss the month-old news in the yachtsmen's newspaper, and Rollo captures their wrinkled faces and myopic gaze with his camera that he carries everywhere in the canvas bag like a giant's eye.

'Please let me take one of you at your sewing machine,' he begged me a week ago, 'you have such expressive hands.'

He makes me blush so easily with his funny comments and unexpected compliments, but I wouldn't let him. My hands are long and calloused and dirt-engrained no matter how hard I scrub them; they are ugly as garden tools.

'Photograph the girls not me,' I told him firmly. 'My husband wouldn't want me making a spectacle of myself.'

Rollo stopped badgering after that; whenever I mention Tormod it brings an end to our conversation. I haven't heard from my husband for months, but I know that nothing bad has happened to him. No matter how far away he is, I feel his presence; the moment he stops drawing breath I will know it.

We have a feast; spirits are high. Even the MacRailts have pushed to the back of their minds the dread thought that Neilac might be at the bottom of the Arctic Sea. News still hasn't come, but tonight they hope that he might be safe, just as the others must now be safe. Only widow Kate from Stavaig stays at home and mourns her dead husband and her dead son, for no amount of bonfires and fish will take away her pain, and I feel a guilty relief that I don't have to comfort her tonight. I want this to be a special night.

Susan Munro plays her father's fiddle and people get to their feet and dance on the grass above the shingle.

'Dance with me,' Rollo says, stepping out of the shadows beyond the fire and pulling me up.

I hear mutterings from some of the older women but I don't care what they think. I've worked every day for nearly six long years to keep roofs over our heads and food in our stomachs and by the saints, I'm going to dance!

I've never drunk whisky but this is how I imagine intoxication to be; I feel as light and free as a curlew as we spin around in the reel. A strong arm around my waist then the clasp of a warm hand on my upper arm, and then our hands entwined and holding on tight in case we fly away in the reel. These are what I feel while my ears ring with shrieks and laughter – my laughter.

Afterwards, I sit catching my breath while Rollo dances politely with my daughters. My body burns from the contact – I can still feel the impression of his hands in my flesh – and I can't keep up with the racing in my heart and throat. I want the excuse to touch him again, to be touched. I have been starved of this pleasure. And then I think of Tormod and something inside rises up like a frantic bird caught in the chimney, and suddenly I'm sobbing. I scramble into the darkness for I mustn't spoil the moment for anyone else, but I can't possibly stop. I can't remember the last time I cried; Flora Gillies never cries.

Bethag finds me. 'What's wrong Mammy? Are you crying for Father? Does the dancing make you think of him?'

I nod. My youngest is wiser than her fourteen years.

'Don't worry, he'll be back soon and he'll never have to go away again.'

CHAPTER 14

Battersay

Thursday was Ally's day off. Rain set in. She abandoned plans to explore the island and went back to bed. The last two days at the hall had been hectic again. Waking in the afternoon to sunshine, she felt disorientated, as if she had missed a day. She did a wash and hung John's borrowed clothes out to dry in the wind. *'I'm in no hurry for them back,'* he had said. Or to see her again, she felt he had meant. The whole red-haired thing seemed to have unnerved him, despite his protest that he didn't believe in the seer's prophecy. *'Myth and poetry, that's all it is. Don't think for one minute I was thinking of you.'*

But Ally couldn't stop thinking of it: the Woman of the Birds and the Flame-haired one. Juniper and Flora or Juniper and her? What if her coming here could accidentally trigger off some terrible disaster? It was nonsense, of course. Yet others on the island who believed in such predictions might view her with real suspicion, even fear. Enough to lay rotting fish on her doorstep. And would it stop there? Could she possibly be in danger by being here? Ally shook off the idea immediately. All the same, as she gazed through the flapping washing at the jagged cliffs of the promontory, she thought that perhaps she should steer clear of Birdwoman's cottage. It would only cause trouble.

She went for a swim. 'Hello Mr Seal,' she called to the sea creature that bobbed to the surface beyond the waves. The bracing water and her swimming companion lifted her spirits. In London, millions would be sweltering in stuffy offices or battling through dusty, fume-filled streets, while she floated like a cork on a turquoise sea, dazzled by sun on a bleached white beach. This was heaven. There was nothing here to trouble her. Men like John Balmain were merely eccentric; tales of Birdwoman being possessed and strange prophecies were simply quaint folklore. Donny MacRailt was just an unhappy guy with a drink problem who was probably venting his frustrations on the newest newcomer. The hooded figure at her kitchen window had been about his height.

The swim over, Ally dressed, wrapped her bikini in a towel and took a stroll up the beach away from Sollas and the far cliffs, in the direction she hadn't yet explored. After ten minutes, she rounded the headland to find a pale green caravan tucked into the dunes. Donny's place? She scrambled up to it, deciding to take the track back across the top to her cottage. There was no sign of his truck.

Ally circled the rusting caravan, peering in on tiptoes where the ground rose behind. It looked surprisingly tidy – spartan even – no dirty dishes or piles of clothes, no empty beer cans or unmade bed: nothing to betray a troubled mind or a man going off the rails.

Intrigued, she tried the door. It was unlocked. A smell of fish pervaded, and something else sweeter, more cloying. Spare overalls hung from a wire hanger and gum boots stood on newspaper by the entrance.

A mug, bowl and spoon were propped on the draining board, and a choice of children's sugary cereals stacked on a shelf above. There was an old TV and an acoustic guitar gathering dust but no sign of any other electrical gadgets. A sleeping bag was rolled up on the narrow couch; an almost empty packet of tobacco and Rizla papers the only items of clutter. Perhaps he smoked dope; that would explain the sickly under-smell. The place felt monkish; the home of a much older, world-weary man. Donny obviously lived in this one room.

All the same, Ally couldn't resist a peek at the adjoining bedroom. Perhaps that's where he kept all his belongings, his youthful junk. In there the curtains were closed, so it was hard to see after the glare of outdoors. There was a table and chair, and loose paper scattered across the surfaces of both.

Drawing back the curtains to take a better look, she saw that they were cartoons. She looked more closely and recoiled. They were grotesque drawings in black and red biro of semi-human creatures. She caught her breath at their savagery: monsters with men's torsos and dragon's tails copulating with women with giant breasts and scaly limbs; witch-like soldiers bayoneting frog-children; fish with bald baby heads being carried off by fierce eagles. They were the brutal imaginings of some nightmarish graphic novel, well-drawn but stomach-turning.

Not really wanting to, Ally picked up a sheaf of papers clipped together. The first was a naked woman standing on a black rock with arms outstretched to the sky and dark hair snaking around engorged breasts dripping with blood. She was screaming open-mouthed, and had huge wings spread as if in take-off. A Birdwoman?

In fascinated horror, Ally saw there was a series of pictures of the same woman: falling from the rock, being stabbed through the eyes by a fishing hook, lying in a boat bound by seaweed. The final figure was that of a curly-haired warrior drawn from behind, standing on a rock with a large bird tattooed across his back. Was Donny portraying himself? In one hand was a dripping dagger, in the other the severed head of the woman. Ally dropped it in disgust.

It was then that she saw the one of the red-headed mermaid swimming in the sea with huge powerful arms and fish tail. Behind her, the same warrior was chasing in a boat with harpoon raised.

Was it her? Ally felt bile rise in her throat. Someone should know about these. She took out her camera and hurriedly snapped shots, then turned and rushed from the room. Ally was halfway down the sandy track to the gate when she saw Donny's pick-up approaching.

CHAPTER 15

Ally stopped in fright. Donny mustn't see her; one look and he would know she had been snooping round his place. She was no better than he was and cursed her nosiness. Doubling back, she skirted the caravan and hurtled down the steep dune. The sound of the engine grew closer and then cut out. Ally was onto the beach when she heard a shout.

'Hoy, wait!'

Glancing back, she saw Donny, hair wild in the wind, waving at her or shaking his fist. Not waiting to see if he followed, she turned and fled. She sank in the soft sand; the harder she tried to run the more it seemed to pull her back. Running against the wind, her lungs heaved like bellows. Round the headland, she didn't let up till she was level with the path in the cliff that led back to her house. At the top she stopped, heart pounding, and scanned the beach. There was no sign of him.

***

Who should she tell? Ally was still shaking an hour later. The guy was seriously disturbed, and obviously fixated on Birdwoman. Was she, Ally, now also an object of his unhealthy obsession? Was he dangerous to women? Did Cathy know about his drawings? Or is that all they were – merely the bored pornographic sketches of a loner?

It was a bad time of day to go bothering the Gillies with her findings – they would be busy with sheep and the evening meal – and she would have to admit to trespassing. Ally opened a bottle of Orvieto wine and a bag of nuts bought on the ferry almost a week ago. It felt as if she had been on Battersay much longer. The wine made her light-headed.

Feeling braver, she went outside to gather in the washing and peg out her wet swimming things. It was then that she realised there was no bikini top; it must have dropped out of her towel somewhere between the house and Donny's caravan. Her stomach lurched to think it might have slipped out when she'd put down her towel to take a better look at the drawings.

She couldn't get the violent images out of her head. It wasn't Juniper who was a danger to the islanders; it was much more likely to be the young fisherman. Wasn't it always the solitary types, estranged from family and friends, males with chips on their shoulders, who turned into killers?

Ally hurried inside and dragged the chair across the front door. As she did so, there was a frantic banging on the kitchen window. She froze, stranded in the passageway, imagining Donny's hostile face leering in. Her heart drummed. What should she do? Make a run for it? Then anger stirred her; she would not be made a prisoner in her own home.

Ally forced herself back into the kitchen. She gasped in shock. A giant crow, wings outspread, had flown straight at the window. It was thumping and flapping and scattering feathers in a desperate attempt to get in. She watched in horror as its beak smashed against the pane. Then it gave up and veered away, leaving a smear of fresh blood across the glass.

Ally rushed to look outside, but there was no sign of the injured bird. Shaking, she sat at the table and poured out more wine. Another glass later, she was telling herself not to be such a wimp. The poor bird had been dazzled in the low sun and crashed; it wasn't a bad omen or a warning or anything crazy like that.

And Donny's bizarre drawings were just dope-fuelled fantasies – the equivalent of dirty magazines on an island where you probably couldn't buy such things – or if you did your girlfriend's mother would be the first to know. She should pity him, not be frightened by him.

But concern for Birdwoman nagged and made her restless. Perhaps Donny was stalking Juniper? Maybe Cathy knew of his compulsion and that's why she was giving him the cold shoulder. Ally felt she should be doing something, yet didn't have the nerve to go out again now it was growing dark.

She'd have a chat with Shona about it tomorrow. Ally fixed up the blanket over the blood-smeared window – another cleaning job – and grabbing a bowl of cold pasta out of the fridge, took it upstairs with the remnants of the wine.

CHAPTER 16

Somehow Ally never got the chance to talk to Shona about Donny; her new friend was busy in the shop and sounding off about some camper's dog that had got in among their sheep.

'Calum's doing his nut. I'm sorry I haven't got time to make flapjack today. That is what you came in for?'

'Not exactly.'

'What then?'

Ally could see she was stressed. 'It's okay; it'll keep.'

Cathy turned up late for work and in a bad mood. Ally guessed that if she started asking personal questions about Donny she'd have her head bitten off. Instead, she kept Cathy in the kitchen peeling potatoes, stirring cake mix and washing-up while she served customers, ignoring the teenager's stroppy looks and huffy sighs. Even a cheery Dr Ned calling by, didn't shift Cathy's surliness.

'Just to say, Alison, drop in anytime. Mary is desperate to feed you.'

'People call me Ally,' she smiled, 'and thanks, I'd love that.'

'Ally it is then.' He left with a breezy wave.

She went back to the cottage, cleaned the crow's blood off the window and ran a bath. As she swirled her hand around getting the temperature right, Ally decided she would get Calum to fit a new lock on the front door and ask Shona if she had a spare curtain for the kitchen. She thought of John Balmain's cosy sitting-room with its haphazard bits of colourful sculpture and its well-used fireplace.

This place must have been home to someone once and she could make it so again. She stripped off and sank into the deep bath. The cottage never seemed sinister in the daylight, just a bit neglected and unloved. What it needed was a bit of attention, just like Donny's caravan.

Ally wished she hadn't thought of that. The image of the fisherman's dim curtained den with its disturbing drawings made her heart lurch. She felt uneasy lolling in the water, trapped and naked in the confining tub with its stained enamel.

She washed, climbed out and dressed again quickly. Pulling on her fleece jacket and trainers, she grabbed her camera and went out.

***

Looking down on the old stone cottage, Ally thought she detected movement. Crouching down in the heather, she watched through the zoom lens of the camera. As shadows grew across the ruined settlement, she saw something dart out of the cottage door – too small for a cat – maybe a stoat. A moment later, a figure in a green poncho and long rusty coloured skirt came out barefoot in pursuit. As Ally took photos, Birdwoman made chirruping noises and clicked her fingers as if to entice the animal back. When it did not return, she laid a bowl at the door and disappeared around the far side of the hut.

44

Ally waited but Birdwoman did not re-emerge. Only when she stood up did she glimpse the almost camouflaged figure further off, moving swiftly through the bracken towards the cliffs. Ally followed. Passing the crumbling walls of the old homestead she saw that a stream ran parallel, cutting deeply into the hillside and providing a grassy pathway that was hidden from view by thick gorse bushes.

The stream ended in a dramatic waterfall that rushed over the cliff edge. Spray blew back at her in the stiff breeze. Birdwoman had vanished and Ally could see no way down to the shore. The view below of sheer black rocks was dizzying; she backed away quickly, having no head for heights.

Suddenly, there was a great flapping of seabirds above. A gull screeched right behind. Ally wheeled round, almost losing her balance. It was Birdwoman, broad-faced and with black hair writhing in the wind, screaming at her just feet away.

'It's okay,' Ally shouted, 'I'm your friend.'

But her eyes rolled in terror or fury. She was wielding a stout, crooked stick.

The cacophony grew deafening as the massive birds circled in agitation. They flew at Ally, pecking her hair. She grabbed at bracken to stop herself falling, trying to fend them off.

'Please,' she cried, 'stop them. I'll go. I'm sorry. Help me!'

Yet her words seemed to madden the woman further. She raised the stick above her head and let out a harsh bark like a bird of prey. Instinctively, Ally ducked and then lunged. She grabbed at the flailing arm and knocked the stick from her grasp. But Birdwoman tore at her with horny nails and kicked her with huge hard feet. One caught Ally in the stomach and sucked out her breath. She doubled over.

Birdwoman seized her stick. Ally waited for the blow, struggling to breathe as she tried to shield her head. Nothing happened. When she opened her eyes, Birdwoman was retreating through the bracken, a flock of noisy companions wheeling overhead like minders. Ally sat hunched, gulping for breath, wondering how she had escaped being beaten over the edge by the crazy woman. She was strong as a wild pony and the way she had called on the seabirds was terrifying. The tabloids had named Birdwoman well. It suddenly struck home. It was Donny who would need protection from the Birdwoman if he tried anything on. She was dangerous; the locals were right to be afraid.

CHAPTER 17

Kulah

A supply ship anchored off Black Rock two days ago and waited for the swell to die down. Today I lost all patience and with the help of Sam, Rollo and Christina, rowed out to meet it. I feel full of a feverish energy and have to be busy; it's as if I've woken from a long, sluggish sleep. We took turns at the oars.

'You're a Boadicea of the waves!' Rollo shouted above the scream of birds.

We came back like pirates with a boat full of booty – flour, margarine, tinned meat, candles and soap. The captain and crew followed with further supplies of vegetables and paraffin (last winter we were reduced to lighting our houses with dishes of burning fulmar oil like our ancestors).

At present, we are gathered in the school room (now that Morag the teacher has declared the summer holidays begun) and give the crew tea and oatcakes and bombard them with questions. Is it really true that the war is over? When will the men be de-mobbed? What's showing at the pictures in Glasgow? Are we still at war with Japan? Have you brought any thread and needles?

Our old men, Sandy and Iain, carry off the week-old newspapers like holy books to read and discuss over a fresh packet of Woodbines.

In all the excitement of the ship's arrival there is one thing I fear, that Rollo will take this opportunity to leave Kulah. He has been here over a month now and he must have photographed everyone five times over. Most evenings he ends up at our home, sitting outside watching the fiery ball of sun go down or by our fire sharing the stories he has collected that day. The girls look forward to these moments too, hovering beside him like moths around a bright lamp, laughing and adding to his tales.

So when the crew get up to leave, my heart stops in my chest. But Rollo makes no attempt to go with them. He catches my look and winks. I feel my face glow hot as a griddle and the bird in my heart sings for joy. We walk side by side up the stony path and wave to the departing sailors. As my hand drops to my side, it brushes his and I have to fight the desire to knit our fingers together.

I know my time with this man cannot last, but today I feel like a prisoner given a stay of execution.

CHAPTER 18

Battersay

To avoid going anywhere near Birdwoman's cottage, Ally did a wide sweep of the promontory and came down the western side to the back of Sollas House. This time, she did not resist the welcoming lights glinting through the bank of hazel and rowan trees. When Ned answered the door to her knocking, Ally burst into tears.

Sweeping her through a darkly panelled hallway, he steered her into a large kitchen warmed by a huge red stove where a woman was sewing at a scrubbed pine table. She looked up over large framed spectacles.

'Mary, this is Ally Niven. She's had some sort of shock.'

The woman dropped her mending and came to her, not waiting for further explanation.

'Dear girl!'

The quilted waistcoat, the baggy purple trousers, the grey hair tied back with a scarf, the smell of lavender and cooking as she enveloped her in a hug: it all made Ally cry harder. This stranger reminded her of her mother – before the weight had dropped from her – before the chemo.

They stood holding on until Ally pulled away in embarrassment. 'Sorry,' she sniffed. Mary produced a cotton hanky.

'Don't be.'

The couple fussed around her, pushing her into a wooden captain's chair lined with bright cushions, letting her explain about Birdwoman while they fixed her a hot lemon with honey and emptied homemade shortbread out of a well-worn tin from a yellow painted wall cupboard. Mary looked older than Ned, or perhaps had just aged faster.

'I blame myself,' Ned said. 'I should have warned you what she could be like. She doesn't know her own strength. It's not her fault really – it's just the way she's adapted to fending for herself. She probably thought you were trying to steal her cache of eggs – buries them in secret places along the cliffs.'

'How stupid of me.'

'You weren't to know,' Mary said.

'Calum warned me not to go near.'

'He's a sensible chap,' said Ned.

'But they misunderstand her,' his wife added.

Ned said more sharply, 'they are right to be cautious, Mary. She's never going to be civilised.'

'She has a child's heart.'

Ned smiled at Ally, 'my wife finds it impossible to think badly of anyone.'

Ally's eyes prickled; so like her mother.

'Have you had any supper?' Mary asked.

Ally had to think before shaking her head. At once, Mary was moving around the kitchen gathering food: a leafy salad, soda bread and butter that smelled cheesy. They must churn their own. She unsheathed a knife from her belt and cut a hunk of game pie, then plucked two ripe tomatoes from a row of plants on the deep windowsill and popped them onto the plate whole. They gave off a subtle pungent smell like nettles. The kitchen was festooned in drying herbs and ropes of onions and the dresser shelves were a multi-coloured array of pulses and preserves stored in re-used coffee and jam jars. A kitchen for real foodies: her kind of people. Mary slid the lid off a hive-shaped jar and sprinkled mixed seeds onto the salad.

Ally ate ravenously. Ned poured her water from an earthenware jug into a misshapen pottery mug. He chattered about the island; he was knowledgeable about geology and wildlife and sites of historical interest.

'The Standing Stone's an impressive example of Pictish art – carved with strange beasts – one has a trunk, possibly a mammoth – very rare. You won't have had time to see it yet. It's beyond Bay.'

'Yes, I saw the sign. Only got as far as the gallery.'

'Balmain's place?'

Ally nodded, scraping her plate. 'Got caught in that storm on Monday and had to find shelter.'

'Won't have got much of a welcome there, I imagine.'

Ally heard the contempt in his voice and looked up. 'Actually, he gave me tea.'

'You should be honoured then.'

Mary said, 'Ned,' like a gentle warning.

Ned gave a snort of laughter. 'Sorry, my wife doesn't like me beefing on about the de-frocked priest. It's fine for Balmain to snipe at us for being do-gooders or the locals for their Highland culture, but I mustn't be uncharitable about *him*. She's quite right of course; Balmain should be pitied. He's a failed man of God and a second-rate artist.'

'Enough,' Mary chided, removing Ally's empty plate and replacing it with a bowl of strawberries and small purple berries.

'Bilberries?' Ally cried. 'Gorgeous.'

'You can have it with Myrtle's cream if you like. It's an acquired taste,' Mary smiled, placing a small jug on the table.

Before Ally could ask, Ned was saying, 'Myrtle's our goat – one of the family. We have our own hens too. We trade eggs with the Gillies for the odd piece of salmon.'

'Sounds wonderful,' Ally said, spooning cream onto the fruit, 'so self-sufficient.'

'Not totally,' Ned grinned, 'but we do our best to live sustainably.'

That led to talk about the Slow Food movement and its promotion of local seasonal ingredients, and how the Rushmores gathered recipes from the old folks that had been passed down for generations. Ally made a mental note that it would make a great feature for the magazine.

'Oatmeal and herring were staples,' said Ned, 'but it's surprising how many vegetables and fruits can grow here if you shelter them from the wind – and keep out the sheep. It's a mild climate for so far north – we grow palm grass to make baskets – the Gulf Stream comes this way, did you know?'

'Doesn't feel like that when I'm swimming,' Ally grimaced.

'You've been in the sea? Brava!'

'We used to swim a lot,' Mary murmured, 'before ...'

'It's terribly good for you,' Ned interrupted, 'just wish more of the locals did likewise. Some of them can't even swim. Dangerous when you live on an island. The chances of drowning ...'

Mary tensed; Ally remembered about their young boy.

'I'm sorry about your son,' she said, filling the sudden quiet, 'Shona told me.'

The Rushmores exchanged looks, their sorrow passing between them like a live wire.

'It was a long time ago,' Ned said stiffly.

'Twenty-two years and nine months,' Mary added softly. 'Ossian would have been thirty in September. In some ways he's still with us.'

'What Mary means is that we feel closer to him here. We were sailing around the Outer Isles when he – was taken from us.'

Before her mother died, Ally would have squirmed at the turn the conversation had taken, but now she understood about grief: you grew a skin over the wound which dulled its pain but couldn't replace what was missing.

'Ossian's an unusual name,' Ally said gently.

'Little Deer,' Mary smiled, 'in Gaelic. There's a legend about his mother Sadbh being turned into a deer by a bad wizard –'

'Ossian's a famous warrior-poet,' Ned interrupted, 'from the Third century. He kept alive the great Celtic legends and laws. Have you heard of the Ossianic Cycle?'

'No.'

'One of the four great cycles of Celtic mythology. Ossian was a bard – like a troubadour – and his tales were as important as any Arthurian legend.'

'The great warrior Fionn saved Sadbh,' continued Mary, 'so she became human again and they stayed together and had their beloved son Ossian.'

'My wife loves a sentimental story,' Ned said, 'but the point is that early Celtic society was rich in culture – not just the stories they told but their elaborate metalwork and stone sculptures, their feasting and physical prowess – not to mention their incredible mental agility. They had to learn everything orally. Did you know it took seven years of training for their druids to learn all their laws and beliefs?' Ned said animatedly, 'that's as long as a student doctor!'

'They sound amazing people,' Ally said.

'I can lend you some books to read, if you like?'

'Sure.'

Ned jumped up and left the kitchen. As Mary cleared away Ally's empty bowl, the older woman touched her lightly on the shoulder and said, 'You're very sweet.'

49

Ally was sent home with a hessian bag full of earnest reading. Mary hugged her at the door and urged, 'come again.' Ned walked her as far as the campsite. The moon was up. Someone was playing a guitar in the dark.

'It's so beautiful,' Ally whispered.

'Will you be okay from here?'

'Yes. Thanks. You've been really kind.'

Ned leaned forward and brushed her cheek. 'Please call on Mary anytime; it'll do her good. She doesn't like to leave the house so I encourage company.'

Ally promised she would.

***

Unable to sleep, Ally curled up under a rug on an armchair – she had dragged it from the fusty sitting-room into the kitchen – and started to read one of Ned's books. She chose one with pictures: black and white photos of ruined stone circles and hairy archaeology students on digs, circa 1972. She yawned. This would do the trick. Cathy was right in her pithy opinion; the Rushmores were a bit hippy, but nice. Perhaps Dr Ned was a shade too full of himself but she found his enthusiasm endearing. And Mary was lovely; a tender echo of her mum.

Ally dozed off. She woke with pins and needles in her tucked-up legs. The book had slipped to the floor. Groggily she got to her feet and stretched, relieving the cramp. It was dark, except for a faint glow of reddish dawn glinting on the window. She trailed the blanket up the ladder and lay down.

Something tugged at her sleepy mind, and wouldn't let go.

Ally sat up. She fumbled for her mobile and checked the time: 2:17. Since when had sunrise been quite that early?

Back downstairs, she pulled on her trainers and went out. Lurid light flickered beyond the eastern headland. The air was still but she caught the whiff of burning. Racing towards the cliff path, she ploughed through dark heather. With every metre the smell grew more toxic.

Ally ran along the uneven sheep track, stumbling and skidding on loose stones. She heard a low roar like a train. She reached the bluff. The heat bounced off her. Flames leapt high. Donny's caravan was a ball of raging fire.

CHAPTER 19

Calum was the first to notice the truck was missing. He had rallied volunteer fire-fighters from around Battersay once Ally – hair scorched, hysterical, stinking of smoke – had raised the alarm. But by the time they reached the inferno and pumped up water from the sea, the caravan was a white-hot melting shell. Ally stood wrapped in a blanket looking on with Shona and Rory and a score of others – campers and locals – from the cliff-top.

Alec-the-Bus was trying to calm a distraught woman in overcoat and slippers. Ally knew before Shona told her that it must be Donny's mother.

'Where's his van?' Calum called out.

It was still dark, chaotic, and the field around the track was littered with cars abandoned in the rush to help. But through the acrid smoke it appeared Donny's pick-up was gone. Ned Rushmore was soon galvanising them into a search party. A new buzz of hope went round. Car lights swept the hillside as a posse headed off. There was aimless milling around.

'Let's open up the hall,' Shona said.

Ally, still numb with shock, was glad to be told what to do. Twenty minutes later, Shona and she were pouring out tea and coffee from catering-sized metal teapots to a clutch of worried neighbours. Mrs MacRailt hovered by the door waiting for news and fretting about her husband being away on his boat.

Later the local policeman from Bay arrived. From what they could tell, from the smouldering remains, there was no sign of Donny. Could he have gone out fishing with his father?

Effie MacRailt shook her head tearfully. 'They weren't speaking.'

PC Melville had only been on the island for three months but was aware of the strained relationship.

'Have you been and asked that Stewart lassie?' Effie demanded.

The constable nodded. 'He's not there, Mrs MacRailt, and Cathy's not seen him in a couple of days.' Effie gulped back tears. He put a hand on her arm. 'We'll find him. His boat's at Bay, so he can't have gone far.'

Melville took Ally aside and asked her to describe what she'd first seen.

'So the fire had already taken hold? And you didn't see Donny or anyone else?'

'No.' Ally's heart began to thud. 'Do you think it was deliberate?'

'I'm just trying to get a picture.'

Ally swallowed. Should she tell him now that she had been snooping inside the caravan just hours before? She thought of the graphic pictures and felt queasy. Suddenly, the telephone in the hall rang. Melville went to answer it. People turned and fell silent.

'Where?' He frowned. 'Any sign …? Okay, I'm on my way.'

As he hurried towards the door, he said, 'They've found his truck.'

'Donny?' Effie gasped.

51

'Not yet. I'm going over now to help look.'
'Where?'
'Balmain's gallery.'

CHAPTER 20

Ally never went back to bed that night. Dawn came up. They waited.

'Thank goodness my boys are away,' Shona had said, but slipped out at seven to ring her mother and check on them.

Effie MacRailt was persuaded to go home and rest. John Balmain claimed to have heard nothing and was unaware of the abandoned truck down his track until the searchers woke him up. He hadn't seen the fisherman for a couple of days. All this, Calum relayed when he returned exhausted from further fruitless searching.

'Probably drunk,' he suggested, 'collapsed in the heather somewhere and is sleeping it off.' His eyes were tired smudges in his fair face. Ally became aware of his younger brother Rory staring at her. She felt anxious. A faint alarm bell was going off in her head but she was too tired to think straight.

Ned Rushmore arrived looking as fresh as the day before and sent everyone home.

'I'll man the place for a couple of hours while you all get a shower and breakfast.'

All of a sudden, Ally couldn't bear the thought of going back to the cottage. Ned seemed to understand. 'Mary has a pot of porridge on the go. I'll ring ahead. It's absolutely no bother.'

The Gillies gave her a lift as far as the path up to Sollas House. While Ally ate porridge with cream and newly baked bread with heather honey, Mary ran a lavender-scented bath and looked out clean cotton trousers and T-shirt.

'Take your time,' she urged.

Ally stripped off her smoky clothes in the cavernous bathroom with its ancient claw-footed bath and wood panelled walls painted white, and relaxed into the steamy water. Even lying down, the view through the large sash window across to the crescent bay was stunning. The sky was cloudless and that intense blue that promised a warm day ahead. Donny would be found, hung-over and contrite for causing such a fuss. He would move back home and be reconciled with his parents, get his act together and win back Cathy's interest. Good would come out of the terrible fire.

Ally closed her eyes.

Birdwoman: dripping blood, skewered on a fishhook, screaming like a gull, pulled by the tide, deeper and deeper. Ally's eyes snapped open. She cried out, spluttering water in a panic.

'Are you alright?' a voice called beyond the door.

For a dazed moment, she wondered where she was.

'Sorry; I'm fine,' Ally shouted, 'just dozed off.'

Her mind jarred with anxious thoughts. She must've been one of the last people to see Donny the night before. Had she upset him by running off and not speaking? Did he know she'd been in his caravan? What was he doing out at Balmain's? Did he accidentally set fire to his own home or was it malicious? Should she fess up to that policeman? And if so, how much? The more she worried, the more agitated and tense she became.

Ally emerged, flushed and wet-haired, Mary's clothes too tight for her. She blurted out about seeing Donny. 'I was exploring – just peered in. I think he saw me. He looked angry.'

'Oh dear,' Mary said with a worried frown. Then she squeezed her hand, 'poor girl, don't worry yourself. I can't imagine that's got anything to do with it. Donny's been a very troubled young man for a long time. The shock of finding Juniper – all the media circus – it's left its mark. His parents were very hard on him – well his father in particular. Donny has addiction problems. Ned's tried to help. The mother blames Cathy as the bad influence, but no mother likes to think ill of their son.'

Ally's feeling of guilt eased. 'He's been behaving bizarrely, that's for sure.' She told Mary about the pranks at the cottage. 'I think Donny's got it in for me. John Balmain says there's this prophecy about Juniper and a red-headed woman – when they come together then bad things will happen. Perhaps when Donny's had a few, he thinks I'm some sort of threat.'

Mary looked reflective. 'Ah yes, the prophecy.'

'Balmain seems to think plenty of people still believe in stuff like that round here.'

Mary said, 'Mr Balmain has a bit of a chip on his shoulder about people's belief systems. Since the church rejected him, he seems very prickly about things religious. What we see as a healthy interest in culture, he confuses with dark superstition.'

'So you don't think I should bother that policeman with all this?'

'Why don't we wait till Donny turns up? PC Melville's got enough on his plate just now.' Mary smiled. 'Put your head down for an hour.'

'I should be helping at the hall …' Ally wanted nothing more than to lie and close her eyes.

'Ned will ring if there's any news.'

Ally capitulated. Mary showed her upstairs to a small back bedroom: yellow curtains, bright patchwork quilt, faded kilims on the wood floor, and old photos of seascapes above the single bed. Within minutes Ally was asleep.

The sound of a helicopter clattering overhead woke her. She found Ned and Mary outside on a makeshift bench drinking coffee in the shade of a rowan. The sun was overhead and the day hot. Ned jumped up.

'Ah, sleeping beauty! I'll get you a mug.'

'Any news?'

He shook his head. 'Not yet.'

'The helicopter?' She shaded her eyes as she squinted into the sky.

'Coastguards. The search goes on.' He dashed inside.

'How long have I slept?'

'You needed it,' Mary answered. 'Morag Gillies and a couple others are helping out. You don't have to rush.' She made room for her on the bench.

'I didn't know it could be this hot up here,' Ally said, leaning into the shade.

'High pressure over the Atlantic; we'll have a few days of calm, sunny weather.'

Ned returned with more coffee. He sat the other side of Ally. She caught him watching her; the blue of his eyes intensified by his craggy tanned face. She felt a nervous fluttering in her gut.

'Mary's told me about you seeing Donny yesterday,' he said, 'near his caravan.'

'Oh.' Ally found the way he looked at her unsettling, as if he knew all about her rifling through Donny's pictures.

'We found an empty petrol can in the pick-up; so it looks like he might have started the fire,' Ned said. 'We also found a red bikini top which obviously doesn't belong to Donny. And it's too big to be Cathy's.'

Ally flushed. 'It could be mine. I dropped it after my swim.'

He scrutinised her, then nodded. 'That explains it then. He must've picked it up on the beach and thrown it in his truck. But you need to tell the police. Don't look so worried; I'll come with you.'

He didn't press her for any more details and she felt a surge of gratitude for his support. Nevertheless, she was nervous going back to the hall and was glad that Ned was with her. He took Melville aside and together they explained about the bathing top.

Cathy came in looking defiant in extra mascara and glittering eye-shadow, but Ally could see the girl was worried. She chewed on her nails.

'They can't blame me for this,' she hissed at Ally in the kitchen, 'you saw the way he shouted at me the other day? Nobody should put up with that shit. I'll give him such a mouthful when they find him.'

To Ally's relief, she didn't seem to know about the bikini top.

***

Over the following two days, extra police arrived from two islands away. The area surrounding the caravan was taped off. An RAF helicopter scanned the sea around Battersay, and teams of islanders helped comb the land, but Donny appeared to have vanished into thin air. The Rushmores were asked to help supervise the search around Juniper's homestead. Ally went too. Birdwoman fled into her hut and only Mary could calm her. Ally hovered outside, wanting to go in but Alec-the-Bus pulled her back to stand at a distance with the other locals.

On a bright Sunday morning, an oar-less rowing boat was spotted bobbing far out beyond the point. There was no Donny, but his clothes were strewn around, damp from bilge water. There was a note in his jacket pocket, the wording smeared but just legible. He hated himself.

55

He hated his life. The Devil was after him but he couldn't stop the bad things happening. He asked for forgiveness. He didn't say from whom. Effie and Cathy each believed it referred to them. The police said the fisherman might never be found. Father Damien said special prayers at Mass to ask that he would.

Two days later, as Ally was taking her evening swim, Donny's body came in on the tide.

CHAPTER 21

Kulah

'Old Kate told Rollo about the Seer's prophecy,' Seanaid says drying her hair by the fire. They got caught in the rain coming back from Stavaig. 'I told him to take it with a pinch of salt.'

'Seanaid tells me you are sceptical of such predictions?' Rollo is smoking a pipe, relaxing back in Tormod's chair in collarless shirt and braces. He no longer looks like the eccentric visiting ethnographer amused by the local tribe; he looks like one of us.

'I think they are invented to frighten people,' I reply, pausing at the sewing machine, 'to make us suspicious of outsiders.'

'Go on,' Rollo encourages.

'Well the prophecy is so vague it could be applied to anyone at any time. It doesn't even say it's about Kulah.'

'But let us just suppose that it did,' Rollo prompts.

'Very well: "A Woman of the Birds meets the Flame-haired One". Every woman on Kulah could be the woman of the birds – the place is chockablock with the blessed creatures! And the Flame-haired One – we Gillies have always had red-heads among us. But when my mother came to the island as a young bride people took against her because of her bright red hair, frightened she might bring about the drowning of all their children. She had a terrible time of it until she became a mother and was accepted by the old wives – and all because of a silly prophecy.'

Seanaid laughed and shook out her long hair. 'See, I told you that's what she'd say.'

'But isn't there always a positive side to a prophecy?' Rollo asks, picking a flake of tobacco from his pink tongue. 'A promise that things will go right in the end; that's a common theme I've found elsewhere.'

'Yes,' Seanaid jumps in with an answer, 'Old Kate never told you the other half about the ancestors returning – she only likes to tell the gloomy stories.'

'Tell me, please,' Rollo smiles.

'After the time of blood,' Seanaid begins.

'There's a red boat and a red-haired woman,' Bethag joins in excitedly.

'I'm telling him,' Seanaid cries. 'A blood-red boat will be seen at sea and a red-haired woman will give birth, and then the ancestors will return and laughter will be heard –'

'In the place of tears!' Bethag shouts.

'Bethag!' her sister protests, flicking a towel dangerously over the flames. Bethag squeals and grabs it.

'Girls, stop it!'

Abruptly, Rollo starts to sing *Red Sails in the Sunset*, diffusing the argument. We all stop to listen; the words falling on us like caresses. No man has ever sung such a romantic song under this roof.

I stare without blinking, storing up the memory like a photograph, of this handsome man sitting in my husband's chair singing a love song to me.

CHAPTER 22

Battersay

Every time Ally closed her eyes she saw Donny's bloated grey body tangled in seaweed, half his face eaten away. She had thought it was a dead seal. Her screams had brought a camper tearing over the dunes. She vomited on the beach and every time she thought of it, couldn't stop retching. Shona and Calum were soon on the scene, but they were too distraught to notice Ally succumbing to the cold. It was Ned Rushmore who found a blanket and whisked her to Sollas House for a bath and warm food.

'You can't possibly stay in that cottage on your own tonight,' he was adamant.

She was tearful and grateful, but found it impossible to sleep. Mary discovered her wandering downstairs in the middle of the night, mixed her something herbal and offered to sit with her. After that, Ally curled up in a kitchen chair and slept fitfully.

It made national news: the suicide of the fisherman who had rescued Birdwoman from Kulah. That was the conclusion of the police investigations. When Ally was interviewed about her bikini top, she told them about the dead fish and smashed egg episodes. The police wrote it off as the bizarre behaviour of a man in crisis and let the matter drop. She never mentioned the drawings; what was the point now? It would only cause more distress to Donny's parents.

The MacRailts remained tight-lipped, but Cathy was persuaded to give a tearful TV interview about Donny's drinking and rift with his father. She had loved him; they were going to get married. But their lives had been wrecked by all the publicity. Battersay was a normal place before Juniper came. Now the world treated them all like freaks.

Cathy was packed off to Auntie Jean in Dumbarton till local anger at her speaking out subsided. As a mark of respect to the MacRailts, the hall and campsite were closed until after the funeral. The Cagoule Family left a note of goodbye and thanks jammed through the hall letterbox. The villagers were subdued, but the beautiful weather continued, cruelly indifferent to the suffering of Donny's family.

'It won't last,' said Shona. Yet it did, day after day.

Ally felt in limbo. Ned and Mary pressed her to stay on at Sollas House, but she knew if she didn't go back to the coastguard's cottage soon then she never would. So she hung around her cottage as little as possible; it seemed full of creaks and noises she couldn't explain. The huge black crow that had smashed into her window the evening of Donny's death had never returned, but sometimes she thought she heard it cawing. Worst of all, she couldn't shake off the feeling that someone was there in the cottage; though she knew that was only her mind under stress from finding Donny's corpse.

The Gillies' twins, Craig and Tor returned, and she found focus in helping entertain the lively pair while Shona opened the shop for half days. Craig was fair and bashful; while Tor had Shona's animated round face and dark hair, and gave out a constant stream of chatter. Ally took them on picnics and swam with them in the safe shallow bay by Sollas House. The boys were used to Mary keeping an eye on them in the holidays and ran in and out of her kitchen for drinks of homemade cordial as if it were their own. It touched Ally to see how Mary's lined face came alive whenever the boys were there; she looked ten years younger. Ned would appear out of his workshop with hastily made catapults and teach the boys how to hit targets with pebbles or skim flat stones across water.

In the afternoons, Ally would sunbathe and swim; it was too hot to go running. In the evenings, when it cooled, the midges were too ferocious to risk going out. She stayed on at the Rushmores' late into the evening writing postcards to her friends, wondering if she could call round to Shona's for a glass of wine and chat but fearing it might somehow be disrespectful when the islanders were in mourning.

She hadn't expected to enjoy hanging around the Rushmores' kitchen as much as she did: its smell of herbs and ripening tomatoes, the table strewn with Ned's sea charts, the click of Mary's knitting needles, all conjured up a feeling of home that made Ally feel safe. They had no TV and never seemed to have the radio on, but she found she wasn't missing news of the outside world or any of the programmes she and Lucas used to flop down in front of in the evenings out of sheer habit.

With the Rushmores she helped prepare the evening meal while they chatted about books and folklore and, after eating, sat around drinking Mary's heady homemade mead and listening to one of Ned's folk albums. Occasionally Mary could be persuaded to sing – ancient Gaelic songs – in an emotional quavering voice that made Ally's eyes smart. Even though Ally did not know what the words meant she could hear the longing and heartache. Afterwards, silence would descend and she would think of her dead parents and feel strangely, comfortingly, connected to them.

When finally Ned dropped her off, Ally would sit up half the night reading, trying to rationalise the creaks and sighs as the cooling of the corrugated roof after the hot day. She turned to Ned's dry books on the Celts, reluctantly at first, then with increasing interest.

It fascinated her to think how these remote islands, on the very fringe of the known ancient world were once populated by this vigorous race: fearless seafarers, traders and warriors whose women led them into battle too; a sensual people who adorned themselves in beautiful jewellery and body paint and marked the seasons with feasting and fertility rituals; a spiritual people with an intimate relationship to the heavenly bodies, to whom a stone or a tree could be a living spirit or the moon their mother.

Ally could imagine them living on a place like Battersay where seals were their brothers and the tribal ancestors could appear to them at the strange limbo times of dawn or dusk. A place where they could see their heaven – Tir nan Og the Celts had called it – in the setting sun and believe with such conviction in this final resting place, that they buried their dead with food and equipment for the journey.

Staring out at one blazing sunset after another, Ally could see how overwhelming such evidence would be to an ancient people so in tune with the natural world. The joyous, passionate, elemental, mystical Celts: Ally began to envy them.

The day before the funeral, restless at the enforced idleness, she borrowed Shona's bicycle and headed off for the Pictish Standing Stone, packing Balmain's borrowed clothes into a nylon pannier. She would drop them off afterwards.

The Stone was smaller than she had imagined, like a large tombstone embedded in the peat on the hill summit. One side was smothered in yellow lichen, the other covered in carvings so worn it was difficult to make them out. She traced the swirls and curling patterns with her hand, pressing the palm against the cool rock. There was none of the unwelcome nauseous reaction that she'd had at the white statue near to Juniper's cottage. Closing her eyes she willed her mind back over the centuries to when the carvings were new, when the artisan understood what the strange symbols meant. There was symmetry to them, an attraction of opposites: bird versus mystical beast; boat versus figure on a horse.

This was no tombstone; she was sure of it. There was nothing dead or mournful about the art, it was vibrant and sensual. This was more like a marriage certificate: two tribes brought together in alliance – the sailors and hunters maybe. Ally felt a shudder of excitement course down her arm and into the pit of her belly. Perhaps there had been dancing and feasting on this very spot, music and love-making.

She opened her eyes, surprised by her sudden arousal. Lucas pushed his way into her thoughts and she tried to smother the sudden, sharp physical yearning. They had once had sex on a beach in Cornwall under the stars with the sound of the sea drowning out Lucas's grunting. She could imagine how he would have taken enthusiastically to having it in the heather. There was something Celtic about Lucas.

Ally turned and leaned up against the stone, sighing out her frustration. To the south she could see the white statue, Our Lady of the Seas (it was Mary who had told her its name), standing stoically on her hilltop, a modern counterpoint to the Celtic monument. The new religion of the Christians depicted women as gentle virgins or mothers, no longer warrior leaders and heads of lineages. Yet she had found the other monument far more sinister and threatening than this.

Something caught her eye away to the left: a woman with a blue headscarf walking along a sheep track. Her lower body was hidden by the curve of the hill, but even from this distance she looked overdressed in heavy tweeds for such a hot day. Something about her was familiar. Ally watched her progress. She disappeared behind a large rock. Ally wondered if she was making for the stone or the road below. She waited to see which way the woman would go.

61

A skylark that had been singing brightly, stopped. The hillside went into shadow. Ally looked up to see a cloud, conjured out of nowhere, passing over the sun like a frown. A breeze stirred, causing goose-bumps on her arms. Shivering, she moved away from the cold stone. Picking up the bicycle she pushed it over the stony ground, glancing leftwards, but the woman never reappeared.

CHAPTER 23

Ally gained the road again, puzzling on where the solitary walker had gone. There must be a track across the hill that linked down to the Sollas road, perhaps a shortcut that only the locals knew. She would explore it another time.

John Balmain was up a ladder, stripped to the waist, whitewashing one of the gable ends. His shoulders were ruddy brown, his unshaven face glistening in the heat. Someone was talking animatedly in Gaelic from a radio on the window sill.

'I've brought your clothes back,' Ally called, shading her eyes and squinting up. 'Not that you'll need them today.'

John hesitated, then balancing his brush on the paint pot, began to descend. He wore old black jeans cut off at the knees; his feet were bare. He stood for a moment regarding her with his distrustful look. Was he angry at the interruption? His unruly hair was flecked with paint; she could smell his sweat. His chest and stomach were hard-muscled with not a trace of flab. The desire she had felt at the stone flared again.

'I have iced tea,' he said, pulling on his discarded T-shirt. 'Want some?'

'Please.'

Ally left the bicycle propped against the wall and unhooked the pannier, following him inside. It was cooler and shadowed. She unpacked the clothes and put them on the stairs, while he brought out a jug and two tumblers from the kitchen. He led her across the cluttered yard and round the far side of the barn to a grassy area where a faded camping chair was placed under a stunted hazel tree. She could hear the sound of a stream gurgling over stones close by.

'You take it,' he gestured at the chair, poured them iced tea and wedged the jug into a dip behind the tree where the hidden stream ran. John perched on an upturned bucket and spread out his long bare legs, draining off a tumbler in one go.

Ally gulped at hers; it was cold and very sweet. Normally she hated sugary drinks but today her body craved it.

'Help yourself,' John said, as if he knew. He lit up a cigarette.

She refilled her glass, forcing herself to stop staring at him.

'It must have been hard for you,' John said quietly, 'finding Donny's body.'

Ally's stomach churned as the dreadful image came once again. She swallowed down bile and nodded.

'Nothing prepares you for something like that,' John murmured.

After a pause, she asked, 'Are you going to the funeral tomorrow?'

'Yes. Are you?'

'I don't know,' Ally sighed. 'Should I? I hardly knew him. The locals might think I'm intruding.'

'They don't treat death that way. If you want to feel a part of the community, then you should go.'

'Is that why you're going?'

'Yes. Is that such a surprise?'

Ally shrugged, 'Well I know how you like to keep to yourself. I didn't think you'd want …' her voice trailed off.

'You don't know me.'

'No, sorry.' Ally felt awkward in the silence that followed.

'I liked Donny,' John said, surprising her. 'He was one of the first to make me feel at home here – took me out fishing. My past didn't interest him. He was a sensitive soul. He wasn't always a drunkard.'

'He must have been so unhappy,' Ally said, 'to have done what he did.'

'Nobody knows another's breaking point.'

'But everyone has their own theory. The MacRailts are blaming Cathy and Cathy's blaming them. Ned and Mary say it was his alcohol addiction that made him depressed.'

'Dr Ned,' John snorted, 'with his quack remedies. He was always getting Donny to try some ridiculous herbal cure dredged up from somebody's great-great-grandmother. What he needed was counselling.'

'Well at least Ned tried to help. Anything's worth a go when you get that low, isn't it?' When John didn't answer, she said, 'I think he was smoking cannabis.'

John ground out his cigarette butt and eyed her. 'What makes you say that?'

Ally couldn't admit to being in the fisherman's caravan, so she just shrugged.

John said, 'you're probably right. He was in a mess and getting out of his head was his way of dealing with things.'

'We all do that at times,' Ally murmured, 'but suicide? That's pain on a different scale, surely?'

'Donny had his reasons to drink,' John replied. 'There were things which preyed on his mind – not just family trouble or hassle with the girlfriend.'

'You mean Juniper?'

John nodded.

'But what was so terrible? He'd saved the girl's life for heaven's sake!'

'There was more to it,' John said quietly.

'What?'

When he did not answer, Ally blurted out, 'was it to do with those drawings he did?'

'Drawings?'

'Horrendous cartoon type things of monsters and violence – of Birdwoman too – being caught on a fishhook.' She could tell from his startled look that he hadn't a clue what she was talking about.

Suddenly she was spilling out her guilt at having searched Donny's caravan and found the graphic pictures.

'There was one that I think was meant to be me too, so I took photos. He came back as I was leaving and chased me to the beach. I was dead

64

scared and he seemed really angry. But now I'm not so sure. The more I think about it, I wonder if he was trying to wave me back.'

'Did he say anything to you?' John asked sharply.

'No.' Ally closed her eyes. 'But it haunts me. The police say I was the last person to see him alive. If I'd just had the guts to stop and face him, he might still be here.'

It was only as the words were spoken that Ally realised how the burden had been sitting like a lead weight in her stomach all week. She flinched at a sudden touch on her arm and opened her eyes. John's warm, paint smeared hand was resting there. Her heart thumped.

'That's nonsense. You didn't cause his suicide.'

As quickly as he'd touched her, he withdrew his hold. Ally felt a kick of disappointment. He asked, 'Have you shown the photos to anyone?'

'No,' she admitted, 'though I keep wondering if I should. I still have them on my camera. What do you think?'

'I think it might do more harm than good.' He stood up. 'Come on, I'll show you something.'

John led the way down a rutted track, his hardened bare feet oblivious to the rough surface. It reminded Ally of Birdwoman. She wondered where on the track Donny's pick-up had been found. There was a low thrum in the heather of insects and bees. The sun bounced off the sea in the bay below.

John stopped and pointed to tyre marks across the verge. 'Donny's truck was parked here.' He walked on.

As they neared a narrow inlet laced by shingle rather than sand, Ally saw debris heaped along the shore: crates, buoys, planks, frayed ropes and a rotting upturned boat. John stood gazing out to sea; then he spoke.

'Donny took the rowing boat we used to go fishing in together. He pushed it out to sea and rowed. He was a strong rower. When he was far enough out, he drank a bottle of whisky which he'd taken from my house while I was asleep. Then he threw the oars overboard. That's what I think happened.'

Ally watched him; the muscle working furiously in his cheek to curb any emotion.

'We hadn't been out in it for over a year – I think one of the oars was half splintered off – I'd meant to replace it.'

He turned to look at her, his dark eyes glinting fiercely. 'I heard something outside that night – thought it was Magnus the seagull knocking at the window as he often does – and turned over to sleep. I should have got up and gone to look, but I didn't. I should have done more about getting Donny help.'

'You weren't to know –' Ally began.

'He confided in me,' John cut her off, 'confessed you might say, knowing I wouldn't tell anyone. I knew what was eating him up – what had caused the split with his father – and I did nothing.'

Ally saw how his body clenched. It struck her that John's anger was directed at himself more than at others.

65

'Do you want to tell me?' she asked.

He nodded. The tide sighed and raked over the shingle as he carried on, his voice low and thick with anguish.

'When Donny and his father found Juniper on Kulah, it wasn't the first time.'

'What do you mean?' Ally's heart thumped.

'When Donny was much younger – still at school – his father took him out to Kulah as a special treat. Nobody went there anymore, mostly because of the distance and all the tragedy, but also 'cos it was now owned by some bird trust that didn't want the nesting grounds disturbed. It was an adventure for the lad – a bonding experience for father and son.'

'So what happened?'

'They didn't land – the swell was too big – but they got close in. Donny swears he saw a girl on the cliff-top with long black hair and dark clothing. The birds were making such a racket that he couldn't hear if she was shouting or not.'

'Did his father see the girl too?' Ally asked.

John shook his head. 'MacRailt was below deck. By the time Donny had shouted for him to come and look, the girl had gone. He just wouldn't believe him.' John sighed. 'It spoilt the trip. MacRailt told him not to say a word – said it would upset a lot of folk. By the time they got home two days later, he'd convinced Donny he'd seen the ghost of one of the Kulah women and sworn him to secrecy.

Over time, Donny came to believe it himself – until they were fishing out that way several years later. A storm was forecast and forced them to make a landing on Kulah. That's when they found Juniper living in one of the old bothies.'

Ally shuddered. 'So Donny was right all along; she'd been there for years. What did his father say to that?'

John shook his head. 'Still wouldn't allow himself to believe Donny's original sighting – and threatened that he'd cut him out of the family business if he dared breathe a word – not even to his mother. But it tore them both apart. Donny was full of guilt that he could have saved Juniper sooner – that she might have been able to lead a more normal life – go to school – that sort of thing.'

'And they might have found out who left her there too, I suppose,' Ally said.

John looked at her with deep sorrow and nodded. 'That's what was eating him up more and more. The drawings you found were proof he was tipping over the edge. I meant to go and see him just recently – Cathy's mum said he was turning aggressive and she was scared for Cathy. But I did nothing about it.'

Ally stepped towards him. 'You didn't do nothing – you listened and that's what he wanted. It was up to him to tell people what he had seen – if you had, it would have been a betrayal.'

John almost growled, 'He came to me on his final night, and I turned over and ignored his knocking.'

'Don't blame yourself.'

In a wave of pity, Ally held out her arms but John held back. They stood gazing across the inlet as the sea murmured.

***

Ally had no idea how long they sat on the rocks and talked, only that by the time they stopped the tide was lapping around their feet and the sun had swung away to the west. A strong breeze was blowing and high Cirrus clouds were drawing across the sky like a net. She told him about working for a magazine and about Lucas and her real reason for escaping to Battersay and spoke of her mother's illness and her brother Guy's wanderlust and her London friends.

'I used to know what everyone was doing every hour of the day,' Ally laughed ruefully, 'now I can't even text them.'

'That's one of the joys of this place,' John snorted.

'The strange thing is I don't really miss all that being in touch – not after the first week. I don't have to let everyone know my every move or worry about theirs. It's a relief.' She glanced away. 'It makes me think what a pain I must've been to live with – always hassling Lucas to tell me where he was or who he was with. No wonder he went off with that model he was photographing – probably anything for a quiet life.'

John stubbed out another cigarette and said, 'Don't let him off the hook that easily.'

What he told her about himself was sketchy: only child of loving parents who grew up in a comfortable Glasgow suburb; his mother was devoutly Catholic and encouraged him to become a priest.

'I find that strange,' Ally had said, 'I thought most mothers wanted their sons to give them grandkids to fuss over.'

'Not mine,' John had answered, lighting up another cigarette to hide his discomfort. His voice had hardened. 'It's the last thing she seemed to want when I told her I was leaving the church to get married. She's never got over the disgrace – hasn't spoken to me in six years.'

'But you didn't get married?'

'No.'

Ally had waited for him to elaborate but he hadn't. 'So you could have stayed on as a priest – maybe somewhere else?'

Blowing out smoke John had said, 'I was a square peg in a round hole. I resigned before I was sacked – contrary to what people like Rushmore will tell you.'

Ally had longed to know more about the affair, but he had deflected the questions back onto her.

Now he stood up and led the way off the shore; from behind he looked boyishly scruffy in his faded T-shirt and cut-offs, leaping among the boulders and grassy tufts. He invited her to stay for a meal and Ally was amazed to see, by the clock in his sitting-room, that it was already seven in the evening.

'Let me help,' she offered, 'I love to cook.'

To the sound of a jaunty ceilidh band on the radio in the small galley kitchen, they cooked up a Spanish omelette with leftover potatoes and herbs that John grew in a huge tractor tyre at the back door. She made a salad from carrots and nuts and he pulled out two batons of bread from the freezer and stuck them in the oven. They said little, but the silence was companionable not awkward.

As John opened a bottle of Chilean red, Ally asked if she could check her emails on his computer. He booted it up.

'Help yourself,' he said and disappeared upstairs.

Ally could hear water running in the pipes. She took her wine and logged on. There were loads of messages: short, breezy, hope-you're-fine-come-back-soon-we-miss-you-love-you!-type. But she could see from the chat flying around between her friends that they were getting on with life as usual without her.

Instead of feeling put-out, Ally felt relief. Despite the traumatic event of Donny's death, she didn't want to be anywhere else right now. It struck her with sudden clarity; the strange island and its people were getting under her skin – and so possibly was the man upstairs.

Ally flushed at the thought as John emerged from his shower in clean jeans and shirt, his hair wet and dripping onto his collar. She noticed how he'd pulled a comb through it, but had given up on a frizzy knot at the back. He put on music: mellow jazz with pianos.

'Swedish,' he told her.

The ceilidh music played on in the kitchen. They ate in the dwindling light with Magnus the seagull peering in at the window. They talked about the Standing Stone; John liked her idea of it being a marriage stone.

'I saw a woman in a blue headscarf and a thick coat up on the hill,' Ally said, 'she must have been boiling. I remember now where I've seen her before – walking along the road to Sollas when I first arrived. The minibus was half empty but Alec didn't stop for her.'

'Some people prefer to walk,' John said with a wry smile.

'Funny I've never seen her around Sollas, yet she must live there.'

'Why?'

'Well, she's always walking towards it.'

'Nobody springs to mind.' John got up and cleared their plates. 'There's ice-cream – or I think I might have tinned pears.'

'Just coffee for me,' Ally said, sharing out the last of the wine between them.

They took their drinks to the fireside, though the grate was full of ashes and hadn't been lit in days. There was a creeping chill to the air. Outside, the wind was getting up, whistling into the blackened chimney.

'Looks like that's the end of the good weather,' Ally said, her skin still glowing from the heat of the day.

'I'll give you a lift home,' John offered, 'it's too dark to cycle without lights.'

'You don't have to.' Ally felt a twinge of disappointment that he wanted to wind up the evening.

'I can stick the bike in the back of the van no problem.'

It was darker than she had expected; the first time in days without a moon. The van rattled over the hardened track and onto the road.

When she got out at her cottage, she leaned across and kissed his cheek. 'Thanks, I've really enjoyed today.'

He nodded, and then was unloading her bicycle. The wind moaned across the dune grass as she watched him drive away.

Ally couldn't work him out; he was much more difficult to read then Lucas. She wasn't sure if he felt the same attraction that she did. There was something guarded about the man. Despite his unburdening about Donny, she felt sure he was holding something back, protecting some secret – or someone – perhaps?

CHAPTER 24

Kulah

August has come, and the long light nights which I love are beginning to shorten at the fringes. Walking up to the shieling to count the goats, Rollo and I see a warship edging along the horizon. The sight should no longer frighten me, yet I feel fear rear up in my belly.

'What is it?' Rollo asks. He touches my chin with his finger, tilting my face round so I must look into his green eyes between their dark lashes.

I whisper, 'I'm not sure I can bear life to go back to how it was before.'

He doesn't have to ask what I mean; we both know I'm thinking of when the men come back, when Tormod will stride up the shore to reclaim his possessions.

Rollo takes my hands in his and squeezes his warmth into me.

'Don't think about that now. Live for the day; that's my motto.'

We bend into the wind and carry on walking the steep path to the high pasture. Anyone watching us from below would think that Rollo was helping to pull me up the slippery scree, not that we are holding hands for the sheer joy of it.

The shieling is half fallen in – there has been no one to re-thatch the roof in five years – but we find a sheltered corner and Rollo lays out his coat like a blanket. We sit down facing each other and he strokes my cheek with his hand.

'I think I might take the girls and go to Skye,' I say, 'get a job where my grandfather used to stay.'

It's a fantasy I've been having during the short sleepless nights of late, and I surprise myself when I speak it aloud. From where am I getting such courage?

'I think you should,' Rollo says, 'this island is far too small and limiting for a woman of your intelligence – and too stifling for your daughters. Why stop at Skye? Why not head for the big city where there are opportunities galore, and you can more easily start afresh; reinvent yourself.'

My heart nearly bursts with excitement. Does he want me to go away with him to Edinburgh? I'm about to ask, when he leans close and kisses me softly on the lips. Tears well up inside and blur my sight. He kisses the hot trickle of tears that run down my face and into my mouth.

'What did he do to you?'

I can't answer him for the sobbing. Sitting up, I undo my coat, take off my cardigan and unbutton my blouse. I point to the red scars on my stomach – the round swirls of cigarette burns that I carry on my body and which itch from time to time, so that I never go for long without being reminded of the shame.

'My poor darling!' Rollo exclaims.

He bends over me and begins to kiss my scars with warm lips. I lie back, shaking at the power of his gentleness. I watch his bowed head licking and kissing me; I don't want to close my eyes in case he vanishes like a dream.

We make love in the draughty damp corner of the shieling with the sound of the goats snuffling and grazing on the other side of the stone wall. My mind is cocooned; cut off from all future consequences. I am in the here and now – the ecstasy of loving – and no harm can come to me while I'm in this man's arms.

CHAPTER 25

Battersay

The modern concrete, hexagonal church, built beside the ruins of a much older one, was packed for Donny's funeral. Shona and Calum gave Ally a lift, but by the time they'd dropped off the twins at the Rushmores and driven up the winding single track road to the north of Battersay, there wasn't even standing room inside.

A gale was ripping in from the Atlantic. They huddled in the lee of the church while others crouched by the tumbledown ruin, gripping onto their hats, their coats snapping in the wind.

Ally could hear little of the service, except for intermittent bursts of hymn singing that rose out of the church like a wave and was taken up by those outside. She saw the sorrow etched into their faces as they sang – almost wailed – their response: faces that she recognised from coming into the hall or shopping in the Co-op or unloading freight from the ferry. They seemed to be joined together at some deeper level, through generations of common endurance and ties of kinship, which made Ally feel excluded yet in awe of them.

The funeral procession eventually emerged, the MacRailts hanging onto each other, anchored by the supporting arms of others. Cathy, weeping loudly among a clutch of Stewarts, was followed by dozens of others: some kinsfolk and former school friends who had travelled from other islands and distant cities to attend. Ishbel came out with old Nichol from the care home and, to Ally's surprise, John followed pushing Bethag in a wheelchair. He was dressed in a crumpled black suit that was too short in the arms, his hair wild in the wind. She smiled but he was too lost in thought to see her.

As they fell in behind, Shona slipped her arm through Ally's and gave it an encouraging squeeze. On the walk up to the cemetery, a photographer followed at a distance.

Donny's coffin was laid into the open grave on the steep-sided hill that was peppered with much older tombstones. The priest said final prayers for his soul, then one of the MacRailts – a thick-necked man who looked constrained by collar and tie – spoke something to those around the grave. Word rippled back that all were invited to the wake down the road at the hotel.

It was a relief to get out of the wind. Tea and sandwiches were laid out in the hotel dining-room; a group of young men of Donny's age thronged around the bar. There was an awkward atmosphere: the family wrapped in grief while others tried hard to lift their spirits, joking about the old Donny. Ally heard Juniper's name in muttered conversations.

She picked two shots of whisky off a tray and pushed her way over to John who was sitting eating sandwiches with Bethag. When he turned and smiled, her stomach flipped.

'You okay?' he asked.

'My ears are still ringing from the wind, but yeah, okay thanks.'

Ally gave him one of the drams. She sat the other side of Bethag, putting her hand on the old woman's knee. 'I haven't forgotten about coming to see you. I'm Ally from Sollas hall café, remember? I baked you scones the last time you came in.'

'Scones, aye,' Bethag repeated with a smile of recognition. 'The English lassie. I liked the scones, right enough.'

'Good, I'll make some more when the hall opens again.'

'Why is it closed?' Bethag asked.

Ally and John exchanged looks. He said gently, 'because of Donny dying.'

Bethag's face creased in sadness. 'Och aye, poor Donny. They say he fell off his boat?'

'Yes, he did.'

'Terrible thing. He was a happy wee boy, just like his father Neil.' She sucked in breath and sighed. 'One of my favourites.'

'Bethag was a children's nurse,' John explained.

'Aye,' Bethag nodded, 'I've always loved the wee ones. Trained in Glasgow, so I did.'

'Must have been a big change from Battersay,' Ally said, 'going to the big city.'

'Not as big a change as going from Kulah to Battersay,' Bethag sighed.

Ally stared at her in astonishment. 'You lived on Kulah?'

'Aye, till I was fifteen. I'd never seen a stove let alone the electric!'

Ally glanced at John, but he didn't seem surprised.

'You knew?'

He nodded, but his eyes seemed to hold a warning. He changed the subject, encouraging the old woman to talk about the care home outing to Barra earlier in the month. Ishbel came over.

'Time to get you back home Bethag. Have you been having a grand chat with your new friend Ally?'

'Ally?' she queried.

'Me,' Ally reminded, squeezing her gnarled hand.

The old woman studied her with puzzled blue eyes and then scanned about the room. She asked Ishbel, 'Is it somebody's funeral?'

Ishbel gave a sigh. 'Yes, its Donny MacRailt's remember?'

'Donny's dead?'

The carer raised her voice, 'Yes, come on now. Don't upset yourself.'

John stood up. 'I'll help.'

Ally stood up too; Bethag was growing distressed. As John manoeuvred the wheelchair, Bethag suddenly grasped Ally's hand, her eyes wide and voice urgent. 'I didn't know what to do! Why did you leave me? I did all I could to save her.' Then she lapsed into a babble of Gaelic.

Ishbel fussed and tried to break the woman's hold, but Ally said, 'It's okay,' and walked beside her.

John wheeled her into the car-park where the care home minibus awaited. Bethag let go, shrinking into her coat in the wind. They stood around as Nichol and three other of the elderly were helped on board, Nichol blowing Ally beery kisses. The bus drove off. John pulled out a packet of cigarettes, and then changed his mind.

'Impossible to light up in this,' he said. They regarded each other.

'What was all that about?' Ally asked. 'Bethag keeps mistaking me for someone. The first time we met she called me Seanaid.'

John gave her a sharp look.

'You've heard of her?'

He glanced away. 'It's a common name up here.'

She knew he was holding back. 'I suppose I should go inside,' Ally said, 'Shona will want to head home for the twins soon.'

As she turned, he said, 'come back for a drink if you like.' He looked tense, as if bracing himself for her saying no.

She smiled and said, 'yes, I would like.'

Ally found Shona in the Ladies and told her she'd make her own way home. Shona gave an exaggerated rise of the eyebrows and grinned. 'See you tomorrow at the hall then. Don't stay out too long.'

***

As they reached John's cottage, the first spatters of rain began. He lit the fire while Ally put on the kettle and made tea. When she returned with the tray, he had discarded his jacket and tie, shoes and socks, and was hunkered by the fire feeding it sticks. It crackled and spat.

She wanted to ask more about Seanaid, but sensed it was too soon. Instead she said, 'Can I put on some music?'

'Help yourself.' He nodded at an untidy pile of CDs on the floor by the small desk. There was lots of jazz and classical, as well as northern soul, salsa and Latin-beat. She chose Rachmaninov; it was one of the few things she knew about her long dead father: a love of the Russian's music.

Over mugs of tea, Ally talked about this. John spoke of his own father – a quiet, patient, gentle soul – with affection. The senior Balmain kept in touch, encouraging his art.

'Show me what you're making,' Ally said abruptly, 'in your workshop.'

'What now?' John was incredulous. 'It's chucking it down.'

'Just quickly,' Ally grinned.

They ran across the yard, John in bare feet, Ally in thin flat pumps and burst into the barn laughing and shaking off the wet. When he switched on the light, she saw among the jumble of driftwood and bits of machinery, a huge sculpture of a bird made out of scrap. Its wings were thin planks of wood painted white, its eyes metal cogs and beak bashed out of copper. Despite its size, it was quirky and humorous rather than frightening.

'It's Magnus,' John said.

Ally circled around, stepping over junk. 'I love it.'

74

John was disbelieving. 'Bet you think it's hideous.'

'No, it's cool. I really, really like it. It's like a giant cartoon.'

She watched him struggle with the praise. 'You mean it?'

'Believe me, if I'd thought it was rubbish I'd say so.'

'Umm, I bet you would.'

She crossed the workshop to stand beside him. 'I've covered enough Arts events for *Lara* to know what's good and what's not. And this is good. You're an artist – start believing it.'

To her amazement, his eyes glistened with emotion and he swallowed before he could speak. 'Thanks.'

Ally slipped her hand in his. 'That's okay.'

The next moment they were facing each other, and then she was stretching up and brushing his lips with a kiss. It felt dangerous – there was so much about this man that she didn't know – yet exciting. She pressed closer and he cupped the back of her head and kissed her again with more certainty. Parting her mouth, she felt the hunger in him match her own. They broke apart, her heart drumming in her chest.

'Will you stay?' he murmured.

Her instinct screamed, *this is mad, you'll get hurt again – you're just doing this to get back at Lucas.* Desire drowned out her doubts.

Yes,' she answered.

He took her hand and they hurried back to the house. Upstairs, the shedding of their damp clothes was distracted by kisses and caresses. In stages they reached the high iron-framed bed. Ally flung off the macabre-headed animal skins that covered the duvet – it reminded her of Ned's Celts – and pulled John to her.

She'd expected him to go at it quickly – had felt the pent-up energy in his taut muscles – but John made love slowly, covering her body with exquisite touches and languorous kisses, savouring every moment. She was almost feverish with wanting him by the time they climaxed. He was a revelation; beneath the taciturn mask of the solitary artist was a sensual passionate man.

Outside, daylight had dissolved into grey twilight before they finished, lying entwined with fingers laced together. Ally hadn't felt such contentment in months, possibly years. For the first time on Battersay she felt completely safe. It was then that she asked about Seanaid.

After a long pause, John said, 'She was Bethag's older sister.'

'Where is she now?'

'Bethag says she died on Kulah – one of the flu victims.'

Ally let out a breath. 'How awful.'

'With her dementia Bethag's retreating more and more into the past – thinks she's back in a time when her sister's still alive. You obviously remind her of Seanaid. It hadn't struck me before but I suppose there's a similarity.'

'How on earth do you know that?'

'Bethag has an old photo album from Kulah; pictures are good quality. Maybe one of the islanders was an amateur photographer – or they did get the odd summer visitor with the supply and mail boats. She doesn't remember who took them.'

Ally scrutinised his face. 'How do you know so much about Bethag?'

He hesitated. 'Years ago, in Glasgow, I went into hospital with a broken arm – fell out of a tree. Bethag nursed me. Somehow she kept in touch – my parents befriended her – had her over for Sunday tea, 'cos she didn't seem to have family. When my life went into freefall, it was Bethag I turned to. She told me about this place. It was half derelict, so I bought it with help from my father.'

For a long time they lay in silence, listening to wind in the eaves and Magnus hopping across the tiles. Ally's mind wandered outside to the Standing Stone and the woman with the blue headscarf whom she had failed to spot among the mourners. Who was she? And the thought of how Bethag kept mistaking her for the tragic Seanaid, pecked at Ally's peace of mind, destroying the warm feeling of being with John.

CHAPTER 26

The hall reopened the following week, but Sollas remained shrouded in sorrow by Donny's suicide. The locals stayed away. The weather turned wet and blustery and the number of campers never revived. Time dragged. Ally made more food than was needed – broths, fish pies, baked scones – that ended up in the freezer. Cathy didn't return; after the funeral she headed off to Inverness with the promise of a bar job from one of Donny's old school friends.

'If it picks up again,' Calum said, 'we'll find someone else from Bay or the campsite. Some campers are happy to help out for a few free meals.'

Craig and Tor ran around the hall, bored and fractious with pent-up energy, demanding to be taken to the beach.

'It's raining,' their father grew tired of pointing out, 'no beach today.'

The small boys howled with disappointment; Ally tried to distract them with the box of toys in the corner but this usually ended up with them hurling plastic cars at each other.

One day, Calum finally lost his temper and dragged them both out, squealing and kicking, for Shona to deal with in the shop next door.

That night, Ally went round to their house with a bottle of wine she had picked up from the Co-op on her way home from John's on her day off. It had been a fantastic day despite the weather. Ally had helped John scavenge along the rain-lashed shore for driftwood and got so wet they'd stripped off and plunged into the choppy waves. *'It's warmer in the sea than out,'* John joked. Afterwards they made a picnic which they took up to his bedroom and alternated between food and love-making. But on Friday nights John went to the care home to read to Bethag and Ally didn't want to muscle in on their routine. Instead she called over to see Shona.

'You're a star,' Shona greeted Ally, taking the bottle and leading her through an assault course of toys, coats and drying boots to the fuggy chaos of the kitchen.

Calum's teenage brother Rory was hunched over a bowl of cereal, plugged into his iPod. He looked up startled at Ally's sudden appearance.

'Hi Rory.'

Blushing, he got up and took his bowl with him, nodding as he went.

'I didn't mean to chase him out,' Ally said.

'Don't worry; he's always under my feet. It's like having another kid in the house. Sit yourself down.' Shona tipped a colouring book off one of the seats and rummaged in a drawer for the corkscrew.

Upstairs, Ally could hear the muted thud of small feet and tired bickering.

'Calum's bathing them tonight.' Shona glanced ceiling-wards. 'They've been a nightmare since they came back from Mum's. She's spoilt them rotten for three weeks.' She poured wine into cups. The sink and counters were piled high with unwashed glasses and crockery.

'Cheers!' Shona said, clinking cups and taking a long slug. Her face was grey with fatigue, her brown eyes dulled and dark-ringed. Ally saw her tense with irritation as the noise from upstairs grew to a crescendo of Calum shouting and one of the boys – probably Tor – screaming in defiance.

'They're just picking up on all the unhappiness around them just now,' Ally suggested.

Shona downed her wine and refilled. 'Child psychologist, are you?'

'No.' Ally hesitated. 'Just saying, don't be too hard on them – or yourselves. It's a bad time – everybody's feeling it.'

Shona looked about to protest, and then sank back with a sigh. 'Aye, sorry, you're right. It's all pretty hellish. I just keep thinking of the poor MacRailts and what they must be going through – but I can't stop snapping at the boys – and Calum's on a short fuse too – it's not like him – and I hate myself for feeling angry at them all. I feel so bad 'cos I really love my boys to death –' She broke off, her eyes welling up, and stuffed a fist in her mouth.

Ally reached over and put an arm about her, squeezing her shoulders.

'Go on, let it out, have a good cry.'

Shona shook her head and gulped down tears. 'If I do, I'll never stop. Do you know what really makes me angry? It's that freak over the hill in her witch's bothy.'

'Juniper?'

'Aye, *Birdwoman*,' Shona spat out the word. 'I wish they'd never found her.'

'You don't mean that.'

'I do! If it hadn't been for her, Donny would still be alive and he would never have fallen out with his father – and we islanders wouldn't have been splashed all over the tabloids – none of it would have happened. And it's all because of that girl – that *thing* that lives up there. Don't look at me like that; we've all done our best to make her feel at home, but she doesn't want any of it. She doesn't want a normal home or to learn to talk – she attacks anyone who goes near her. If you ask me they should lock her away where she can't do any more harm.'

Ally was shocked by the sudden outburst. 'Does Calum think the same way?'

'We all do,' Shona declared. 'Donny's final note said he was being chased by the Devil; plenty people think he meant that creature. If it wasn't for Dr Ned and Mary, someone would have pushed her off a cliff long ago.'

'But it's not her fault she was abandoned on Kulah,' Ally said, 'just think what she must have been through. No one could be normal after that. Donny and his father did the right thing rescuing her – of course they did.'

It was on the tip of her tongue to tell Shona how Donny had been plagued with guilt for not having rescued her sooner, but the woman was in such a fraught state that it would only compound her anger at Juniper.

'She's nothing but bad luck,' Shona snapped, 'we've put up with her for long enough, if you ask me.'

'But she's not doing any harm living where she is.'

Shona fixed her with a look. 'Don't know why you're defending her; I bet she was the one put stinking fish on your doorstep. I think she's dangerous and I don't want her anywhere near my kids!'

Ally got up, pricked by the memory of Birdwoman wielding a stick at her. 'When's the last time you ate?'

Shona shrugged.

'Okay, sit tight, I'm going to make you something.'

'No, don't be daft.'

'I want to,' Ally smiled, 'I can't take away grief, but I can make a meal for you, so please let me.'

Shona retreated with the wine bottle to the bean bag in the corner amid a sea of books and crayons and, sinking down, closed her eyes while Ally searched cupboards for food and clean utensils. She made vegetable risotto then tackled the mountain of unwashed dishes. They said little; the brooding presence of Birdwoman seemed to hang between them. John was right; the islanders were spooked by Juniper. What if they turned on her as a scapegoat for their grief over Donny's death?

Half an hour later, Craig and Tor clattered into the kitchen, pink-faced and in pyjamas with an exhausted Calum – fair hair on end like corn stubble – pursuing.

'Look at you relaxing,' Calum cried, 'like the Queen of bloody Sheba!'

Craig threw himself into his mother's lap, spilling wine. Instead of scolding him, Shona grabbed him and gave him a fierce kiss.

'Ally!' Tor spotted their visitor and came crashing round the table, kicking obstacles out of the way. 'Will you read me a story?'

'Sorry Ally, I didn't see you there,' Calum said embarrassed. 'Leave her be, Tor. Say goodnight then upstairs.'

'No!'

'Yes! Now!'

'Don't shout at him,' Shona complained. Craig was burrowed under her arm.

Ally saw the annoyance on Calum's face and said quickly, 'Come on Tor, you choose the book and we'll read it in bed.'

'No, down here with Mummy,' he shouted.

'But if we stay here then we can't play hide and seek, can we?' Ally said, pulling a disappointed face.

'Hide and seek?'

She nodded. 'You have to hide in your bedroom and I have to find you, yeah?'

'Okay.' Tor's face lit up as he turned and scampered out of the room.

'Can I play?' Craig piped up.

'If you're quick,' Ally promised.

The fair-haired twin scrambled out of his mother's lap and headed after his darker brother. Ally went to the fridge, took out a can of lager and handed it to Calum on her way to the door.

'Fairy godmother,' he murmured with a weak smile, taking it.

It was late by the time the boys finally settled and the adults managed to eat the dried-out risotto, but the atmosphere mellowed and Shona began to quiz Ally about John Balmain.

'So what happened after the funeral?'

When Ally hesitated, Shona pounced, 'You stayed over didn't you? Oh my God! Does that mean you're seeing him?'

'Shona, give the lassie a break,' Calum protested.

'Go on, tell!'

'It's too early to say,' Ally smiled.

'But you'd like to?'

'Maybe – yes.'

'Oh, look at her, Calum,' Shona teased, 'she's like the cat that got the cream.'

'Shona!'

'Ally's in love! I think that's great. It's what that grumpy painter needs too.'

'He's not really grumpy,' Ally defended, 'I think he's just been through a hard time – people have let him down so he keeps them at arm's length.'

'But not you,' Shona grinned, 'arms are wide open for our Ally.'

Calum groaned. 'That's enough.'

Shona ignored her husband. 'Have you been back there since?'

Ally nodded. She wasn't going to admit that as well as her day off she had been there three evenings this past week, or how impatiently she waited for John's rusty blue van to turn up in the rain to collect her.

'Well good for you,' Shona said. 'Best remedy for a broken heart, eh? You can forget about that guy in London who gave you the run-around.'

Ally wished she hadn't told Shona quite so much about Lucas; she didn't want to think about him now.

Calum stood up. 'Come on Ally, I'll run you home.'

In the car Ally said, 'Shona got pretty upset earlier about Donny. She's angry at Juniper – says you all are – is that true?'

Calum's face set grimly. 'Donny was my fourth cousin; we're all close round here. He shouldn't have died. He was a fine boy – just a normal happy guy until she came – and now he's dead. Everyone's life has changed for ever.' He gripped the steering wheel harder. 'And what for? That witch with her stoats doesn't give two hoots about Donny – probably doesn't even understand or care someone's died because of her. That's why we're angry. Wouldn't you be, if it was your family?'

'Yes,' Ally admitted, 'I suppose I would.'

CHAPTER 27

'Hold still just a moment more,' John said, making quick lines and smudges across the sketchbook. He felt like pinching himself to see if this was really happening: such a sexy, attractive woman posing on his beach just for him.

'Hurry up, I'm getting cold,' Ally protested. 'Can't we do this in the comfort of your sitting-room?'

'I just need to catch the light on you.'

Ally sat perched on a rock by the shore in the dying sunlight. They had just swum in heavy surf and as she dried off, John had grabbed his pad to capture the moment. She was at her most beautiful; her strong-limbed body glistening golden in the soft light and hair twisting around her shoulders. He could gaze at her for hours. He never expected to feel this way again, after Caroline. *It's wrong; it won't last.* He stifled malign thoughts.

'You're my next project,' he said, 'a ship's figurehead.'

Ally wrapped a towel around her and came towards him. 'You mean I'm getting goose pimples just so you can turn me into some bits of metal and polystyrene?'

He smiled. 'I can't take the risk of you disappearing like a *silkie* back into the sea when the sun sets.'

She plucked the sketchpad from his hands and licked his chin. 'Umm salty.'

He tugged at her towel, but she pulled away.

'Later,' Ally grinned, 'in your nice warm bed.'

As they walked up the track, an evening breeze whipping around them, he held her hand tight as if that could keep dark thoughts at bay. John ran Ally a deep bath and made a supper of bacon and mushroom pasta while she thawed out in the hot suds. He found her dozing in the steamed up bathroom, stripped off and climbed in too. Water sloshed over the side onto the bare floorboards.

'This is too cramped,' Ally laughed, 'pity we don't have one of those huge retro baths like the Rushmores'.'

John felt his stomach twist. 'When have you been bathing at Ned Rushmore's?'

'Don't pull that face,' Ally said, throwing a sponge at him. 'I've bathed there a few times, if you must know. They had me to stay after Donny –'

John saw her expression change, that haunted look that came with remembering Donny's dead body in the seaweed.

'Sorry,' he said quickly, 'I didn't mean to remind you.' He leaned forward and kissed her raised knees.

She climbed out. 'I think I can smell the pasta burning. It's making me hungry.'

'Spoken like a true foodie,' he grunted.

***

81

'Why is it I feel constantly hungry when I'm with you?' Ally asked later as they sat eating, the table only half cleared of paints and driftwood.

'It's all the exercise we do,' John answered with a smile, shovelling down pasta and sliced white bread.

She chattered on about the day at the hall and some campers who had complained that the vegetable soup had been made with chicken stock.

'As if I'd do a thing like that,' Ally protested. 'They just didn't want to pay, cheapskates!'

John sat back in contentment. Then the invidious thought stole in: was this how it might have been with Caroline? Would she have been satisfied with a simple meal in a rough and ready cottage like this? He doubted it. She was used to a comfortable life and ready money. *I'll be the breadwinner for a while,* she had said, *just till you find your feet as a painter*. They had talked of going to America where she had contacts. He imagined them sitting out on a wide deck, cooking up steaks and drinking Chablis to the sound of cicadas. That is the future that had been snatched from him by his spiteful, needy mother.

'What's wrong?' Ally said.

John shook off bitter thoughts. 'Nothing.' He stood and cleared the plates.

She followed him into the kitchen. He rummaged around for biscuits and cheese.

'You're doing it again,' she said.

'What's that?'

'Shutting me out.' She stepped in front of him and put a hand on his chest. 'You haven't listened to a word I've been saying. You go off somewhere in your head, and it really bugs me.' Ally scrutinised him with vivid green eyes. 'Are you thinking of her?'

'Who?

'You know who. Do you look at me and compare me with Caroline?'

John's gut tightened.

'How do you know her name?'

'Half your CD collection seems to be from her. Why don't you tell me about it and we can get her out of the way, like I did with Lucas?'

'Don't spoil it Ally.'

Her hand dropped to her side. 'I don't care that you have a past – we all do – but I've never known anyone who's so secretive and hung up about it. Why won't you tell me anything about her? I've been really open with you about my relationships. It's weird not knowing anything about you.'

John felt his jaw tighten.

'Believe me, the more you know about me the less you'll like me,' he said, keeping his voice flippant. 'I'm not a very nice person.'

'Rubbish! Who told you that – your holier than thou mother?'

'Don't judge people you don't know.'

'Well that's all I can do unless you tell me more about them,' Ally said in exasperation.

He stepped towards her, struggling to keep hold of his temper. 'Okay, Miss Prying Journalist: this is the scoop. I'm the product of a dysfunctional marriage, of a weak father and a mother who so dislikes herself that she thinks her son is equally dislikeable. It's a religious guilt-trip thing which I'm not going to begin to try and explain. I don't do intimate relationships – I *fail* at relationships – so if you want more than a summer fling then you better look elsewhere.'

'Summer fling?' Ally sounded offended. 'Is that all I am to you?'

John ran agitated fingers through his hair. 'Let's not kid ourselves. We both know you will be going back to your busy London life in a matter of weeks and I will just be part of your traveller's tales. I don't mind, I'm happy to take what you can give me in the meantime.' He took her by the shoulders. 'I want you every minute of the day; I can't get enough of you Ally. But don't ask me for more than this. You can come here as often as you like – eat with me, sleep with me – but don't try and change me.'

Her look was a mix of alarm and defiance.

'So that's what Caroline did to you; forced you out of the church and the life you'd chosen, into something else you couldn't be. Was that it?'

John's grip tightened. 'No! She wasn't to blame.'

'Then why isn't she here with you now? She encouraged you to take this massive life change and then what happened? She changed her mind and left you high and dry.'

John let go and turned away, shaking with anger. He mustn't do something he would regret – not again. He stared out at the dark hillside and its flickering shadows.

'I knew it would be something like that,' Ally said. 'But just because Caroline let you down, doesn't mean that every relationship has to go the same way.'

John spoke through clenched teeth. 'She didn't let me down.'

'So where is she then?'

He could hear the disbelief in her voice. Why not just go along with her version of things and put an end to the painful subject? His words came out like a growl.

'Caroline is dead.'

He didn't have to look round to know that her face was wide with shock. The silence was like a dead weight. It was the first time he had ever said those words out loud to anyone. He felt as if he had uncaged some part of him; some raw hurting wild thing inside. He should stop being such a coward and tell her the whole truth: *and God help me, I was the cause of it.* But he couldn't say it. And he no longer believed in God so it didn't matter what he'd done. There was no Hell and Damnation to come in the Afterlife; just the Hell he had created in this one.

Ally came close. He felt her warm breath on his neck.

'What happened?' she said softly.

'Car crash.' He amazed himself that he could speak the words.

'I'm so sorry.' She put a hand on his shoulder.

John flinched away. 'Don't be. The last thing I want is your pity. The affair was already over by then. If she'd lived, she wouldn't have chosen to spend her life with me.'

He finally looked at Ally, expecting that he'd done enough to put her off him for good. He hoped for her sake that he had. She was pressing slender fingers to her lips as if to prevent a stream of words. He couldn't read her expression.

'So, do you want me to run you home now?'

She looked up at him with a strange fierce look.

'No John, I bloody well don't. I want you to take me upstairs and give me some more summer fling.'

CHAPTER 28

Kulah

Margaret's shrieking can be heard from the top of the village. I'm pegging out washing when it happens. My stomach flips over like gasping fish. Dropping the peg bag, I tear down the path with Bethag running at my heels shouting for me to wait.

A group of women in pinafores flock around her door. Acrid peat smoke belches out.

Margaret is keening her son's name, over and over. 'Neilac, Neilac, Neilac!'

I look into her face and see raw terror. She is clutching a telegram. Christina snatches it and thrusts it at me.

'Read it!' she demands.

I stare at it with shaking hands; I wasn't even aware the mail boat had come in. These days I don't see what I don't want to see.

The MacRailt women watch me as if I can decide their fate. I take it out of the brown envelope.

'"On hospital ship appendix out back home soon love Neil".' They stare at me. I know they understand but I translate it into Gaelic anyway, to make it real. 'He's *alive,* Margaret; your boy's alive!'

She buries her face in her pinafore and screams. Her sisters throw their arms around her and praise the saints and the Virgin Mary. I hug Bethag and Christina's children dodge around shrieking and whooping like cowboys. My heart bursts with happiness and relief for my childhood friend as I go to hug her too.

Margaret tenses and turns away, grabbing at one of the twins and ruffling his hair. Her look slides away from mine. Christina takes the telegram from my hand with no word of thanks. It is as if a sea fret has descended between us.

Then Bethag is tugging at my sleeve. 'Look Mammy.'

My gaze follows her pointing finger to the distant ledge below where the pier is carved out of the rock. A familiar figure stands outside the pier house in coat and deerstalker hat, a canvas bag slung over his shoulder and suitcase at his feet. Opposite him, the bobbing boat that has come from the mail ship, tugs impatiently at its moorings.

I gape with incomprehension. Rollo is leaving. Without another thought, I'm tearing down the rocky steps cut into the cliff-side, howling at him to wait.

CHAPTER 29

Battersay

After that night at John's, with its half revelations and angry words, Ally found it easier to come and go as she pleased. She had been in danger of becoming too involved with this secretive man. Now she knew where she stood with John; their friendship was casual, physically intense, sometimes playful, even tender, but without promises or commitment. Well that suited her too; a Summer Bloody Fling, as they came to jokingly call it. Without it, Ally wondered if she might have given up the job and left this strange, sad island. The atmosphere remained tense over Donny's death and resentment towards Birdwoman festered.

One evening, as they lay naked in the stuffy attic, the windows closed against devouring midges, Ally spoke of Juniper. 'If she had been left there by passing trawlermen, then they must have thought they were leaving her there to die. Who would do a thing like that? And why?'

'I don't like to think why,' John murmured, one of his muscled legs hooked over hers.

'But she hadn't been sexually abused – she was still a virgin.'

'But still abused,' John said, 'physically deprived and emotionally. It must have been terrifying.'

Ally had wrestled with that too. 'I just don't get it. If they wanted rid of her for whatever reason, then why go to all the trouble of sailing out to Kulah? Why not just dump her overboard?'

She could feel the strong regular thump of John's heart beneath her head. His deep voice vibrated in her ear.

'I've no idea. The whole story is so sad and bizarre.'

Ally didn't know either, but she felt better being able to ask her questions aloud. All day, she bottled up her thoughts about Birdwoman. In the light of Donny's suicide, to talk about her to the locals was even more taboo than before. Yet the whole place seemed infected by her presence.

John traced a finger across her chest setting off small tremors of yearning. 'We'll probably never know,' he said. 'But what's more important is how she spends the rest of her life, isn't it?'

'Umm,' she agreed, 'especially with the locals turning against her.'

'It'll pass. They're not bad people – just hurting.'

'Aren't you worried someone might have a go at Juniper?' Ally asked. 'Push her off a cliff like Shona said.'

'I can't believe –' John broke off and sighed. 'It's all Rushmore's fault.'

'How come?'

'For his pseudo folklore – going around stirring up superstitions that have been dead for decades.'

'I don't think it's superstitious to worry that a crazy Birdwoman might harm your kids. Ned's got nothing to do with it. If anything, he's the one person standing between Juniper and a lynching, if a tipsy Shona's to be believed.'

John was scathing. 'Or look at it another way, he's the one person keeping her like a semi-domesticated animal.'

'That's what I thought at first, but it seems to me she's content enough where she is,' Ally said.

'Happy as a wildcat? John snorted. 'You sound like Rushmore.'

Ally was irked. 'Okay then, what would you do? Pack her off to boarding school like your parents did to you?'

'That was cheap.' John shifted her off his chest.

'Sorry,' she said at once, but he was already swinging out of bed and reaching for his cigarettes. In frustration she asked, 'What is it with you and Ned Rushmore anyway? Are you jealous of the way he shows me attention, is that it? Macho pride hurt that I might fancy him?'

'Do you?' John said sharply.

Ally snorted, 'I can't believe you're even asking. Do you think I'm capable of two flings at once?'

He pulled on shorts and without answering, went below.

'Mr Moody,' she muttered after him.

They dropped the subject but Ally didn't stay that night; she said she had an early start at work. Two could play at the moody game, and it rankled that he didn't trust her with Dr Ned. But after he'd dropped her off, she instantly regretted not spending the night snuggled up next to him. She tracked the argument back to her mentioning Juniper. Perhaps she should stop bringing up the subject if it was beginning to cause friction with John?

Yet Birdwoman flapped around in her head, giving her no peace. Finally, Ally determined that on her next day off she would go back to the isolated cottage and face her strange tormentor.

CHAPTER 30

Ally crouched in the wet heather, eyeing the stone cottage through the zoom in her camera. Smoke was seeping from a hole in the thatch. The pearly grey of the sky bled into the sea; the white statue shimmered on the skyline like a ghost. A shadow passed by the tiny window. Birdwoman was in there.

Plucking up courage, Ally waded downhill through the bracken, ignoring her sodden jeans and wondering why she felt so drawn to this strange young woman. It was madness; she'd probably get attacked again. People would say, I told you so. But she had to find out for herself what Birdwoman was really like.

Ally had no time to rehearse her greeting; before she was out of the rough and into the clearing, the cottage door banged open. Birdwoman flew out in hippy skirt and bare feet, brandishing a gnarled stick and screeching. A flock of seagulls took off from the roof and began a noisy circling overhead.

'Okay, okay,' Ally shouted, stopping in her tracks, 'I won't come any nearer.'

Birdwoman bared her teeth, her dark eyes wild beneath tangled black hair. The gulls screamed and dived about. Ally waved them off with frantic arms.

'Please, tell them to stop. I want to be your friend. Look, I've brought you something to eat.'

Ally scrabbled in her coat pocket and pulled out a small parcel of homemade shortbread. Unwrapping the silver foil she held out the biscuits in open palms. A huge herring gull swooped down and snatched at them. Ally dropped the package in fright. At once, a frenzy of gulls attacked the shortbread, ripping and breaking it with sharp beaks. They took off again in a shower of falling crumbs and manic screaming.

'They were for you,' Ally cried in frustration, 'not those bullying birds.'

Birdwoman spun on her heels and swooped back under the low doorway. Ally felt rebuffed; ridiculously disappointed.

She stood for a few moments wondering what to do, and then retreated up the hill. What on earth had she expected – tea and a cosy fireside chat? This whole thing was way beyond what she could handle; she was a foodie journalist and knew nothing about the psychology of the traumatised.

Then she heard it: that eerie moaning she had dismissed as the wind the first time she had come to the shieling. Now she was sure it was a cry of distress. Ally swung round and ploughed downhill again. Without knocking, she pushed open the weathered door and bowled in.

At first she couldn't see anything in the dank gloom, the peaty smoke stinging her eyes. The hut reeked of rotting vegetation and a scorched acrid smell. Birdwoman was hunched on a bed of heather on the far side of the smoky fire, rocking back and forth, her mouth wide open and yet making no sound.

Ally went to her. Birdwoman shrank back, her eyes rolling in terror. Her left hand was clasped tight. She waved it at Ally as if to ward off attack.

'I'm not going to hurt you. I know you don't understand me but I want to help you – I want to be your friend and I want to stop others harming you. You have to trust me. Do you understand anything I say at all?'

Birdwoman stared at her, shaking violently.

'Someone's been in here before haven't they?' Ally guessed. 'Someone who frightened you. It's okay, I won't let anything happen Juniper.'

At the mention of her name, the girl un-tensed her hand a fraction. She was clasping something.

'What is it?' Ally asked. Cautiously she reached out and touched her hand which was chapped and thick knuckled like an old woman's. John's words came back to her about the locals believing Birdwoman was a reincarnation of Kulah's heroine Flora Gillies.

Ally cupped the hand in hers and slowly unfurled the fingers. She gasped and recoiled. The palm was bloodied and the skin ripped. At its centre lay a small metal brooch of purple flowers whose pin she had been using to stab her flesh. Birdwoman seemed not to notice. Her eyes were fixed on the scarf around Ally's neck. Juniper reached out with her right hand to finger it.

Swiftly, Ally unravelled the scarf. 'You like it? Go on take it.' She held it out. 'It's yours if you want it.' Juniper hesitated. Ally folded the brightly patterned Indian scarf into a triangle and reaching around the girl, tied it loosely in the front. Juniper put it to her nose and sniffed, all the time keeping wary eyes on Ally.

'It's my favourite scarf, but you need it more than me. Don't suppose you go on many shopping trips do you? Looks like you're dressed from a charity shop – or maybe Mary's hippy cast-offs?'

At the mention of Mary's name, something shifted in Birdwoman's look – a flicker of comprehension perhaps?

'Mary is your friend, right? She's my friend too.'

Birdwoman gazed at her, squatting on her haunches and rubbing the scarf against her nose.

Ally cast around looking for some common interest, the smoke stinging her eyes. It looked like the home of a squatter. A few blankets, a low wooden stool, a couple of ancient packing crates and a basket for an animal. An old blackened kettle and a large pan were balanced on stones next to the fire. Strands of drying seaweed hung down from the thatch like brittle hair. How on earth did she survive in such a place? But then she had probably lived in worse conditions on Kulah, Ally thought.

Abruptly, Birdwoman stood and darted forward. Ally flinched, but the girl lunged beyond, grabbed a handful of limp nettles, threw them in the kettle and hooked it over the fire. Her movements were swift and noiseless for someone so solidly built.

Ally peered through the smoky dimness as Juniper rummaged in a chest and scooped grain into a pan. Adding a splash of water from a jug she mixed it in with a grubby hand. Producing a flat iron disc, she smeared it in fishy-smelling fat and placed it on the fire. Ally watched in fascination as the fat melted and spat and Juniper dropped the mixture onto the skillet, pressing it into a large flat cake. After a few minutes, she flipped it over, staring intently while it cooked. From her throat came a low gurgling noise that was almost a hum.

Breaking off a hunk of the cooked cake, she handed it to Ally.

'Ah, that's red-hot,' Ally winced, blowing on it hard. Birdwoman rammed a large piece into her mouth and munched.

Ally gave a tentative bite: hot, smoky oatmeal with a faint taste of fish.

'Oatcake,' she smiled. 'Umm not bad – tastes better than it looks.' She ate some more. 'Did Mary teach you how to do this?'

Birdwoman showed no sign of understanding as she poured out nettle tea straight from the kettle into chipped bowls. It looked and smelt rancid.

'God, what's in it – goat's milk?'

The girl slurped hers and dipped in a chunk of oatcake. Ally sipped and tried not to gag.

'Possibly the worst cup of tea in my life,' she murmured. 'I'm going to introduce you to Redbush.' She forced it down. 'No, no more thanks.'

Birdwoman poured the remains of hers into a dish by the basket and crumbled some oatcake around. A moment later, something scuttled around the loose-fitting door. A stoat dashed across the earthen floor, stopped, listened then carried on to the dish.

'Hello little fella,' Ally began. The stoat flicked around and shot back out again. Birdwoman scowled at her. 'Sorry, Juniper.'

With a squawk, the girl snatched at Ally's bowl and threw the half drunk tea into the ground. Ally judged it time to go.

'Thank you for the oatcake and tea.' She made for the door. 'I'll bring you some more shortbread next time, if I can get it past your guards.' Ducking out of the door, she looked around nervously for aggressive gulls.

Birdwoman followed her to the edge of the grassy clearing.

'Do you know where I live?' Ally turned, knowing she would get no answer. 'Perhaps one day you'll trust me enough to come to my place. It's got a great beach. I haven't dared swim there since I found Donny. But maybe we could go together.' She mimed a swimming action; the girl's eyes widened in alarm.

'I bet you can't swim though; stupid suggestion.'

Suddenly, Birdwoman screeched and grabbed at Ally.

'Hey, get off!' Ally panicked. Her grip was vice-like. When she tried to pull away, Birdwoman screamed louder and gulls appeared in an empty sky, wheeling overhead. 'Let go, that hurts,' Ally cried.

Then she saw the look on the wild woman's face; she was staring at something beyond. The girl wasn't angry but frightened. Ally craned round. Not a person in sight. Was someone hiding in the bracken, watching them? She scanned the rocky hillside but could see nothing.

'It's okay, there's no one there.' Ally tried to prise off the grimy hand. Birdwoman was rigid, her eyes bulging and chest heaving. Again Ally searched the waving bracken. For a moment she thought she caught sight of something – a shadow, a flicker of movement that wasn't the wind – then it was gone.

'Really, there's no one –' Ally began, but Birdwoman was already relaxing her grip and backing away.

In a few short strides she had retreated to the cottage and slammed shut the door. Ally stood shaking, wondering what on earth had just happened. Birdwoman had seen something out on the hill – something to fear.

CHAPTER 31

'Bethag's not well,' Ishbel told Ally on an outing to the hall. Only three of the old people had come from the home on a blustery August day. 'She's getting very confused.'

The holiday trade had dwindled; stories of Donny's suicide and indifferent weather appeared to be putting off the tourists despite it now being peak school holidays. Ally often closed the hall early and took leftovers up to Juniper and her pet stoat, where they sat in the shelter of a tumbledown wall and communicated by food. The young woman grabbed at things as if suspicious that Ally would take them back, but was generous in sharing out her ration with her animal friend. Ally felt there was watchful intelligence behind the wary frown.

That evening, when John came to collect her, she suggested they visit Bethag at Bay House. They found her sitting in a small conservatory, gazing out to sea. She looked hunched and tired, yet smiled at them and raised a cheek for John to kiss. Ally noticed how she sparked into life whenever he came near.

'I've brought you some cake,' Ally said, 'seeing as you missed out on tea at the hall.'

She nodded but made no attempt to eat it. They sat either side of her while John told her of his latest sculpture: a figurehead for a ship made out of scrap.

'It's a *silkie*,' he said, 'inspired by Ally.'

'It's not very flattering,' Ally laughed, 'she's fat and muscly.'

'Not fat, powerful. She's a great swimmer.'

Bethag gave a puzzled look. 'Swimmer? When did you learn to swim?'

Ally said, 'when I was little I suppose – I can't remember – I've always swum.'

Bethag put a trembling hand on her arm. 'That's good; I'm glad. I wish I had learnt to swim. If only ...' her voice tailed off and her head drooped.

They sat in silence as she nodded off. Ishbel came bustling in with the tea trolley.

'Time for a last *strupach*. Would you like one?'

John stood up. 'No thanks, we'll just go. She's very sleepy.'

As Ally moved, Bethag jerked awake. She looked around in alarm.

'I saw it! Don't let her come in here! Mary Mother, don't let her!'

'It's okay,' Ally said, 'you've had a bad dream.'

'No,' the old woman quailed and pointed outside, 'she was there, and I saw it. She wants to hurt me.'

'Now, now,' Ishbel soothed, 'there's nothing to get excited about. She's not there – and even if she was, we wouldn't let her in.' She turned to Ally as if Bethag couldn't hear. 'We try and get her to sit in the lounge but every time I turn my back she's off in here and looking out the window. We think she's seen Birdwoman on the cliffs.'

'Juniper wouldn't harm her,' Ally protested. 'She's too frightened of others to go anywhere near them.'

Ishbel shot her a look. 'How would you know?'

'I visit her.'

'You silly lassie!'

John intervened, 'Come on Bethag, take my arm. Let's get you to your room. We'll manage her Ishbel.'

Back in her neat pink bland bedroom, the old nurse calmed down and sank onto the bed.

'I told you they were ganging up against Juniper,' Ally murmured. 'There's a bad atmosphere.'

'You're exaggerating,' John said, 'and I don't think it helps telling them you go and see her.'

'You're joking? You're the one encouraged me.'

'Not exactly.'

'What then? It's okay to talk about treating her as human but actually, let's stay away 'cos it might upset the locals?'

'No –'

'I can't find them,' Bethag broke in. 'I had them here.' She was patting the bed covers and scrabbling on the top of her side table.

'What are you looking for?' John asked.

'My rosary.'

'You had it in your lap in the conservatory,' Ally said. 'You must have dropped it. I'll go and look.'

'No, I'll go,' John said and quickly left.

Ally sat down beside Bethag and sighed. 'I think he's annoyed I go and see Juniper because he's never dared. Dr Ned's the same – wants her for his own pet charity. All I do is take her food. She likes chocolate brownies best. You're not frightened of her are you, Bethag?'

'Who?'

'Juniper.'

The old woman looked blank.

'Doesn't matter.' Ally patted her shoulder.

Bethag reached into a drawer and pulled out a small black photo album. 'Show me the lassie.'

The old leather creaked as Ally opened it. Inside, black and white photos were stuck down with old-fashioned corners that were losing their stick.

'Wow, these are really old. Who are they?' Her heart jumped. 'Bethag, is this on Kulah?'

The woman nodded. Ally peered at the photos: rows of stern-faced women outside stone hovels, barefoot children with blurred faces and sheer cliffs with tiny figures standing above. Two larger photos were tucked into the back of the album. Ally held them up to the light. One was of a handsome woman with high cheekbones in a voluminous blouse, an elaborate cross around her neck. The other showed the same woman sitting on a chair with two teenage girls – one round-faced, one pretty and elfin – standing either side. Something about the coy expression of the plumper younger girl was familiar.

'It's you, isn't it?' Ally pointed. 'And this one: is she your mother?'

'Aye,' Bethag sucked in her breath.

'She's beautiful. You all are. You should have these on display.'

The old woman traced the figures with a trembling finger and let go a deep sigh. 'I'm sorry.'

'Don't be. I'll find you a frame at the gift shop.' Ally turned over the photo and saw there was something written in ink so faded it was almost illegible. *For Flora, with sincere regard, R.*

Ally gawped at Bethag. 'Your mother was *the* Flora Gillies – the one who kept everyone going through the war?'

'The war,' Bethag echoed. 'Oh it was a terrible time.'

'I bet it was. And then for it all to end so badly.'

The old woman suddenly shrank away from her, 'it wasn't my doing; I couldn't have stopped them – nothing I could do!'

'Of course not, I didn't mean –'

John marched into the room holding out the string of beads. 'Found them down the side of the chair.'

Bethag began to wail, 'tell her it wasn't my fault! Tell her!'

Ally gave a helpless look. 'Sorry. The photos upset her.'

John pressed the rosary into Bethag's hand and whisked the album off her knee, his look thunderous. He kneeled down and cupped her shaking hands.

'She didn't mean anything,' he said quietly.

'Why has she come back? After all these years.'

'It isn't Seanaid. It's Ally, the English girl. She doesn't understand.'

Ally was irritated; it felt like a put-down. John stroked the old woman's hands and she began to finger the beads, muttering under her breath. They left her praying.

***

Later, eating poached salmon and new potatoes, Ally broached the subject they had been avoiding since leaving the care home.

'Did you know that Flora was Bethag's mother?'

He pushed away his plate. 'All the Gillies are related in some way.'

'But not so directly.'

'Does it matter?'

'Well yeah! You said lots of the old people believe Juniper is possessed by Flora's ghost. What if Bethag believes that?'

'She doesn't.'

'How do you know? It must be really upsetting to think your mum's not at peace – that she might have taken over someone else's life – someone that everyone's scared of. No wonder she's losing it.'

'Drop it Ally.' John got up and cleared the plates, even though he hadn't finished.

94

She followed him into the kitchen. 'Why are you so touchy all of a sudden? Talk to me John. You're the one who told me about Flora coming back to curse everyone for not saving them. God, I can't believe I'm taking this seriously!'

'Then don't. I should never have mentioned it.'

'But if that's the real reason why people are turning on Juniper then we should get it all out in the open and deal with it.'

'No!'

'Why not?'

'You can't just confront people like that – they'll only deny it. It's more complicated. People are angry about Donny's death.' He turned away and started washing-up.

Ally felt her frustration boil. 'I think there's more to this Kulah story than we know. I mean, why is Bethag blaming herself all these years later? People drowned in a shipwreck or died of the flu – how can that be her fault?'

Ally saw the tension in John's shoulders.

'It's not. Listen, digging up Bethag's past isn't going to help anyone – least of all her.'

'You know more than you're telling me, don't you? Why can't you trust me?'

He glanced round, frowning. 'All I know is that you remind her of her dead sister and that upsets her. Promise me you'll leave her alone?'

'That's ridiculous; you can't stop me going to see Bethag,' Ally exclaimed.

'I'm asking you,' he snapped.

'God, you complain about Ned being possessive over Juniper, but you're just as bad with Bethag. She's not your personal property.'

Suddenly, John was thrusting his face at hers. 'I'll protect her from your interference if I have to. It's just a game to you, isn't it, a summer's diversion? Well the rest of us have to get along here as best we can and that means respecting each other's privacy, and not raking up the painful past. Can't you understand that, Ally?'

She pushed him off. 'Oh, yes, I understand alright. It's not Bethag whose frightened of me finding out the past; I think it's you, John.'

CHAPTER 32

Kulah

I, Flora Gillies, live in semi-silence. No one, apart from my girls and daft Sam, speaks to me. I know the women gossip around their peat fires; how the reckoning will come when Tormod and the men return.

Six years of back-breaking work – growing potatoes, milking goats, mending thatches, nursing the sick, burying the dead – count for nothing. Flora Gillies has shamed them by taking a stranger into her home and letting him sit where her man should sit. I have shamed them by pleading on the quay for the outsider to stay, hanging onto his arm and shouting profanities at him for daring to leave without a word of goodbye. And when he smiled with regret and said that his work here was done, I called down curses on his head like a heathen. This brings shame; this frightens. I smell the fear on them.

As the autumn gales rattle the door and set the peat smoke billowing about our house, I think back to that high summer day when Rollo kissed my shame away. It happened just the once; just enough to remind me that I am a woman to be loved. Sometimes I wonder if I just imagined our coupling – wanted it so much – that I conjured it up from my feverish thoughts.

CHAPTER 33

Battersay

The sea was a choppy purple-grey as the dawn light spilled onto the beach. Ally, tucking Juniper's long skirt into its waistband, led her by the hand down to the surf.

'Just put your toes in; the sea won't bite.'

Ally said the words as much to give herself courage as Juniper; the beach felt haunted with Donny's unhappy presence. The tide rushed around their feet. Juniper shrieked and sprang back, pushing Ally over. The water was an icy slap. Ally sprawled in the shallows, her shorts and sweatshirt soaked.

'Juniper!'

But Birdwoman was fleeing up the beach into the dunes. Ally stripped off her wet clothes and flung them on a rock. There was no one around; that's why she'd chosen this early hour to coax Juniper onto her beach. People who lived on islands ought to know how to swim. Ally ploughed into the sea, instantly exhilarated by the salty cold on her naked body. It reminded her of skinny-dipping in the surf in Cornwall with Lucas. The pang of regret that washed through her took her off guard. She thought she had driven her ex firmly out of her thoughts since John had become her unexpected passion.

John, John! She struck further out to sea. Ally craved everything about him: his strong body, his deep posh voice, his company, his quirky house, his deep bed. But would she ever really get to know him? At the end of the summer she would leave Battersay still ignorant of his past, his tragic affair and deepest thoughts. The islanders seemed as wary of him as she had once been; all except Bethag who appeared to love him like her own.

They had argued over Bethag, yet it was Juniper who was proving the real problem between them. Ally thought how ridiculous it was that John should be taking this attitude to Birdwoman when it was he who had first championed her cause. The more Ally's strange friendship – one-sided John called it – with Juniper grew, the more John cooled towards her. Yet she blamed herself for their latest standoff, after too much wine. They'd been talking about families – or at least about hers – and how hard it must have been in the old days to bring up kids on Kulah.

'Wouldn't it be amazing to go and visit the place?' Ally had said.

'Maybe, but it's not possible. They don't do cruises to uninhabitable bits of rock.'

'The Rushmores are sailing out that way with some friends in September before the summer's over. Ned's gone to Oban to sail the yacht out here.'

'God that sounds like a trip from hell, stuck on a boat for days with Know-all Ned and Mystic Mary. Horses couldn't drag me.'

'It would be an adventure; see where Juniper survived for so long.'

'Typical journalist; always after the sensational. I've no interest in the place.'

Ally had lost patience. 'You're no bloody fun! No one is. Everyone's uptight or in a mood. Even Shona and Calum do nothing but argue.'

'They're grieving – and you're drunk.'

'Boring sod. And yes they are upset about Donny – but it's more than that. This place is beginning to get me down – it's like there's a black cloud over it all the time, a big black curse of a cloud.'

'Don't say that, Ally.'

'What? Cloud or curse?'

He had got up from the sofa. 'I'll run you home.'

'Gone off sex have we?'

He had picked up the van keys.

'Well I think this place is cursed,' she had pursued him loudly. 'Everyone's scared of something and Juniper sees things too. And what about that woman I saw up by the standing stone? Who the hell is she? Maybe that's who Bethag sees when she's staring out the window. And all that wailing –'

'Ally shut up,' John had snapped.

She hadn't seen him now for the past five days.

Ally turned in the sea, treading water, and looked at the early sunlight creep across the land. Juniper was standing in the shadowy dunes. Ally strained to see well. Was that someone with her? Her heart thumped. Immediately, she struck back for the shore. Wading out of the waves, she grabbed her clothes, but by the time she'd struggled into them, she'd lost sight of Juniper.

Frantically, Ally searched the dunes, calling her name. She had disappeared. Perhaps she'd been mistaken about the other figure – a trick of the dawn light – and Juniper had got bored and walked home? There were indistinct prints in the dunes but they could have been there before. She cut back to the beach and continued the search along the shore as the sun rose higher. Ally went all the way up to Juniper's cottage but there was no sign of the girl anywhere. Panic gripped her. Someone had been watching them – watching her swim naked and then seized the moment when Juniper was alone to take her. What else could have happened? The girl never ventured beyond her own isolated peninsula and there was no trace of her here.

Ally ran down to Sollas House. A slender yacht was anchored in the bay, so Ned was back from Oban. She hammered on the Rushmores' front door. Mary answered.

'Dear One, you're soaking! Whatever's the matter?'

She spirited Ally inside to the kitchen as she gabbled her story of losing Juniper on the beach. Ned, in a faded kaftan, turned from stirring porridge.

'And I'm sure I saw someone there with her.'

'Oh dear,' Mary gasped.

'Man or a woman?' Ned frowned.

'Too far away to tell. I'm sorry, I didn't know who else to turn to – I know you're the only ones who really care about her.'

'You did the right thing,' Ned assured. 'She's probably just wandered off to one of her secret places.'

'But this other person?' Mary worried.

Ned said, 'I'll go out and have a look, my love.' He turned to Ally. 'Sit down and have some of this. Mary will get you something dry to put on.'

'But I want to help – it's all my fault – I shouldn't have made her come down to the beach. I just had this stupid idea of teaching her to swim.'

'Goodness me,' Mary exclaimed. 'You must have gained her confidence.'

'Yes, I think so. Now I've spoilt it.'

'How on earth did you communicate?'

'Just through miming. I've tried teaching her words for things but I don't think she gets it.'

Ned patted her shoulder. 'That doesn't surprise me – we've tried without success. But well done for having a go. Now eat and then we'll look for her.'

'Shouldn't we –'

'It's highly unlikely that Juniper would go with a stranger – and if anyone had tried to grab her, she would have raised the roof and you would have heard, wouldn't you?'

'Yes. Thanks,' Ally smiled, feeling the first flush of relief.

***

They searched all morning without success. Ned grew so worried that he phoned PC Melville in Bay. Word soon spread. Every vehicle leaving on the afternoon ferry was searched. People were asked to look in their outhouses in case she was hiding; the MacRailts were questioned.

'Can I stay with you tonight?' Ally asked the Rushmores. She couldn't bear the thought of a night alone in the dismal cottage with a potential abductor on the loose.

The three of them stayed up late drinking nettle wine; Ally and Ned played backgammon while Mary sewed. Ally felt totally at home. She glanced at Mary, head bent over her tapestry work, and with a sweet pang was reminded again of her mother.

Despite the potent wine, Ally didn't sleep well. Thoughts of her mother came to her so vividly that she could almost smell the peachy powder she used to wear and hear the rhythmic sound of her brushing out her long hair. She was engulfed in a fresh wave of loss. Five years and suddenly, coming to Battersay, the pain was like a raw wound again. How had she managed to keep her feelings buried? She could talk about the facts of her mother's cancer and the chronology of her illness without upset; but she realised now that she had too often avoided talking about the woman, the mother.

Yet who could she have had that intimate conversation with? Her close friends, Rachel and Zoe still had their mothers living and delighted in complaining about them. Lucas was breezily casual about his faraway parents. She didn't know about Freya. Only her older brother Guy could share childhood memories – or maybe not even Guy – his memories were different and he obviously didn't feel the same.

Why had she never talked properly about the death with him? They had only ever discussed the practical things, nothing about feelings. Guy had been too hasty to move to Spain and the time had never been right. He hadn't wanted to take any of the furniture or even a few mementos. She had filled a trunk full of personal clothes and trinkets that she could neither bear to unpack nor throw out. It sat in the bedroom corner covered in a throw and was a dumping ground for clothes and magazines.

But perhaps she was expecting too much of her brother. Guy, as a twelve year-old, had been traumatised by witnessing their father's fatal heart attack; whereas Ally, aged three, barely remembered him. Some bereaved boys (so she'd read in *Lara*) took upon their young shoulders the role of father-figure-man-of-the-house to try and compensate. But she and Guy were never close and, before her tenth birthday, he went off to university and never came back.

As she turned restlessly in bed, Ally was gripped with regret that she hadn't known her mother for long enough as an adult. She yearned for those conversations they could have had about her mother's early life, meeting her dad, what music she'd liked, any boyfriend disasters, what having a baby felt like.

Dawn was breaking before she finally succumbed to sleep. As she drifted off, she thought about John and the rift with his mother and wondered how painful that was. Did that have anything to do with his keeping people at arm's length? What had really happened between him and his fiancée Caroline? It struck her that the only woman he felt truly comfortable with – had turned to when in trouble – was Bethag. Why was their bond so strong?

CHAPTER 34

Kulah

My girls miss Rollo too. They argue over petty things – a ribbon borrowed, a pencil broken. Our evenings stretch out endlessly. Seanaid refuses to help Morag with the schooling of the children. Her eighteenth birthday has come and gone. She sits at home writing stories.

'I am making my own folklore collection,' she says grandly. 'Rollo is going to help me get it published. As soon as I've finished, I'm leaving this place. You'll not catch me marrying a smelly islander.'

'Don't call them smelly,' Bethag protests.

'That's what they are – fishy smelly dullards!'

Dullards? A Rollo word.

'Father won't let you go,' Bethag says, looking at me for confirmation.

But I don't throw cold water on my eldest's dreams; I want my sharp-eyed, quick-tongued daughter to escape.

'Father's going to be back soon,' says Bethag tearily. 'We're going to be a family again and everyone will be happy like before the war.'

Seanaid snorts. 'That's silly baby talk.'

My stomach is twisted into knots at the thought of the men returning. When Bethag is out milking, I give Seanaid an advertisement I have cut from one of Rollo's newspapers and kept in the dresser drawer. It's for a domestic agency in Glasgow.

'I don't want to be someone's servant,' she is dismissive.

'It's just a start. It's your way off the island. If you write a letter now, you might get a reply before the mail boats stop for the winter – and before your father comes home.'

She looks at me with her restless blue-grey eyes and I see something of myself at her age; vitality, an impatient passion. I used to wear them carelessly like a plaid; it's why Tormod the Strong had to have me.

Seanaid takes the cutting and doesn't question why I should have kept it hidden in the dresser. Not in her wildest dreams does it occur to her that I might have done so for myself. And that's what my leaving Kulah feels like now: a wild dream. How is it possible, now that Rollo has gone and Tormod is growing ever closer?

CHAPTER 35

Battersay

Ally woke to the sound of animated voices below her window. Struggling out of bed, she saw that it was Calum's young brother Rory talking to Ned. Heaving up the sash window, she leaned out.

'We've found her,' Rory called up.

'Juniper? Where?'

'Your house.'

'*What?*'

Ned looked annoyed. 'Ally, I assumed you'd checked your own place.'

She felt such an idiot. The youth was excited. 'Saw smoke in the chimney last night, but we knew you were over here. She won't come out.'

Blushing furiously, she said, 'I'm coming.'

Rory drove Ally and Ned over in Calum's van. She got the feeling he was enjoying being at the centre of the fuss. He revved up the track and skidded to a noisy halt in front the coastguard's cottage. A score of locals were milling about, armed with spades and one with a rifle. Donny's father was there, gesticulating and shouting in Gaelic. Calum's twins were dashing about knocking on windows and running away. PC Melville was trying to restore order.

'She's here now, you can all go home.'

But the crowd jostled about her as she pushed towards the house, their faces angry. One or two tried to bar her way.

'We're not budging till we've seen that witch gone,' MacRailt cried in English. As Ally approached, he bawled, 'look at the trouble you've caused. I had the police at my door accusing me of abduction.'

'I'm so sorry –'

'No one was accusing you Neil,' the policeman said.

Ally's heart began to hammer as the crowd jostled about her.

'My Effie's in such a state. Have we not suffered enough?'

Ally's mouth went dry. 'Mr MacRailt it's all my fault and I'm sorry. It never occurred to me Juniper would come here. But let's just calm down; she's probably terrified in there.'

A chorus of protest erupted. '*She's* terrified? It's us you've put in danger!'

'You've no right to bring her down here.'

'Let us deal with the evil bitch!'

She tried to press forward but others pushed back and barred her way. Her knees went weak as panic rose in her throat. Her head buzzed as if she would faint. Calum muscled his way through.

'Come on, move away. Let Ally into her house.' He steered Neil to his van, barking at his sons to follow.

Ally stood shaking. Ned took her arm. 'It's okay, I'm with you.'

She clung on as he led her forward. Juniper had barricaded herself in. Ally gulped for breath, trying to calm her racing heart. She put her face to the door.

'Juniper, it's me Ally, let me in.'

There was no answering noise. Ally coaxed again without success. She turned and faced the sea of angry faces.

'Please everyone, she's not going to come out while you're all here.'

This galvanised PC Melville into herding them back down the track, with Ned chivvying too. Ally went round behind the house and peered in the kitchen window. She had a view of the corridor; Juniper was huddled in the hallway under a blanket. The window was ill-fitting and Ally managed to lever it up from outside and haul herself in. The room was icy; it made her skin crawl. She heard weeping.

'Juniper, don't panic, it's just me, the others have gone.' Ally scrabbled across the kitchen table, noticing how the rickety chair had been smashed up and fed on the fire.

All at once, there was a stench of rotting seaweed and Birdwoman sprang up and loomed out of the dark corridor, snarling and screeching. Ally went rigid with fright. She backed behind the table.

'I'm Ally your friend, remember?'

Birdwoman towered over her, huge in the small kitchen, her eyes hard with hate. She threw her meaty hands in the air to strike. Ally shoved the table at her. The room rang with the sound of screaming and crying.

Ally shouted, 'I'm not afraid of you. I don't know who you are, but get out and leave us alone!'

Birdwoman yelled back, face contorted. Then her body went stiff and started to shake, her arms still suspended. Suddenly she fell to the floor and went limp. Ally stared, frozen in horror. Ned was banging at the front door.

'Are you all right? What's happening?'

Ally rushed to unblock the doorway. 'Quick, she's collapsed.'

Ned barged in and took over, checking for a pulse and heartbeat.

'Is she –?'

'She's fainted; she'll be okay in a minute or two,' he reassured, putting Juniper into the recovery position and gently placing a cushion under her head. 'What about you?'

Ally nodded, too shaken to answer. The doctor steered her into the armchair and fetched a glass of water.

'You look like you've seen a ghost.'

She shivered. Ally was not sure what had just taken place.

'She really scared me. She was so angry and didn't seem to recognise me – like this sort of hatred had taken hold of her.'

'I heard you shouting,' Ned said, eyeing her curiously, 'I thought there was someone else in the room.'

Ally glanced away. It seemed ridiculous to say Juniper had seemed possessed.

'Ned,' she trembled, 'can I –?'

She was about to ask whether she could stay over at Sollas House again, when Birdwoman's eyes flickered open. The girl looked at them in confusion and struggled to sit up. She clutched her head.

'It's okay,' said Ned, 'easy does it.'

She batted away his attempt to help her up. She was looking directly at Ally, her dark eyes huge and bewildered. She stretched out her arms, her mouth opening and closing.

'Mm-mm.'

Ally caught her breath. 'Did you hear that Ned?'

'Is she trying to speak?' he whispered.

'I think so.'

'Mm-mmm,' Birdwoman made the noise louder. 'Mummu.'

'Oh Juniper,' Ally reached forward, arms wide. A sob rose out of the strange woman as she embraced her in a hug.

CHAPTER 36

Kulah

I have been away nursing Old Seamus at Ostaig, glad to put myself out of the gossips' way. He is bed-bound and thinks I am his mother. Walking back over the top I see a ship anchored off the Black Rock and my insides turn to bilge water.

I stop in my tracks and scan the shore for signs of men with duffle bags, of welcoming women. Surely Bethag would have sent word that the ship of the men was in? Helping Morag at the schoolroom, she is my eyes and ears in a village where I am no longer welcome. I nearly faint with relief when I see it is just cargo being unloaded.

Only as I reach the house do I see Seanaid panting up the hill, clutching a large envelope to her chest to stop the wind whipping it away. Her face shows excitement. I go ahead and put the kettle on to boil, eager for her news.

'Is it from the agency?'

She flops onto the sofa and catches her breath. 'No.'

'No?' I turn and peer at her in the gloom. 'Your father?'

'No!' She tears at the package and hunches over the letter.

'Who then?' I step closer.

'Rollo, of course.'

My heart thumps. There are pages and pages; photographs too.

'What does he say?' I want to ask if he mentions me but I can't. 'Is it about your book?'

Seanaid glances up. Her look is impatient. 'He wants me to go to Edinburgh.'

'Edinburgh? But we can't afford that. You'll just have to post it to him.'

'Not just the collection,' she says, waving the letter, 'he wants *me*!'

I stare at her.

'Rollo says I'm too bright and lively to be stuck away here. I should be studying in Edinburgh.'

I redden. 'It's not up to him; he's not your father and we don't have the money.'

'No he's not my father,' she repeats, 'he's the man I want to marry.'

'What in all the saints –!'

'I love him, Mother,' she says, as if explaining to a slow-witted child, 'and he loves me.'

I am about to dismiss this as nonsense, when she shifts position and slides a hand over her belly, that protective gesture that I remember myself from long ago. I sink onto the sofa beside her, my mind trying to fend off my dread thoughts. They stack up like creels: Seanaid's withdrawal from the village, her secretive writings, her weather-cock moods, and the lack of blood-stained rags in the washing pile. They amount to one thing.

The words seep out of my mouth like whispering smoke.
'Holy Mother of God! Are you carrying his baby?'

CHAPTER 37

Battersay

Shona came marching into the hall, oblivious to customers and banged a newspaper down on the counter.

'Look what you've done,' she blazed. 'We're a laughing stock again: "'The superstitious locals don't understand her', says Alison Niven, undercover reporter for *Lara* magazine." You're a bloody journalist! What the hell are you playing at Ally?'

Ally read in disbelief. Somehow, a tabloid had got hold of the story of her friendship with Juniper. *Mermaid and Birdwoman, a match made in the Hebrides.* A short salacious article and a picture of her skinny-dipping were splashed across an inside spread.

'I'm not undercover. This has nothing to do with me.'

'It's everything to do with you. Look at you – dancing in the waves. You look as mad as she is.'

'Shona, I'm as annoyed as you are.' Ally tried to keep her voice down; people were looking over. 'Who on earth took that photo?'

'Who cares? Probably that priest you're having it away with – maybe that's how he gets his kicks.'

Ally flushed scarlet; she was furious. 'Well whoever it was, it's me they've harmed not you or anyone round here. It's my privacy that's been invaded – and Juniper's.'

'Well you should have thought about that before you dragged her back into the limelight,' Shona snapped. 'If you'd left her alone in the first place none of this would've happened. Now we'll have reporters ringing us up again asking about poor old Donny.'

Ally glared at the article. Freya was quoted as saying that her employee was taking time out from a stressful situation and should have her privacy respected. She appreciated Freya's support, but it just added to the tone of the article that Ally was unstable.

'Look Shona, let's not fall out over this - '

But the indignant woman had already turned her back and was halfway to the door.

'And I don't ever want Birdwoman in the coastguard's house again,' Shona called out. 'It reeks of fish and you can pay for a new kitchen chair.'

Ally fumed. She might have known that, even though Calum had changed the lock on the front door, Shona wouldn't have any qualms about letting herself in.

The last visitors in the hall – a birdwatcher and a couple of kayakers – gave her odd looks as they paid and left.

As Ally cleared up she was tormented by who could be doing this to her? Was it the same person who had planted rank fish at her door and not Donny after all? Whoever it was wanted her gone – or wanted her to stop befriending Juniper. Right now that could be any of them.

Well she wasn't going to give up on the wild girl; these past few days she had felt a greater connection between them and knew that Juniper was beginning to trust her – even like her. Whenever she went up to the shieling now, she was waiting at her door as if she sensed Ally coming long before she appeared. Ally had helped her clear out rubbish and line the hut with fresh heather and spare blankets from the coastguard's house; Juniper had kept the place tidier since. And best of all, she greeted her with her new humming sound that almost sounded like 'mum'. It made Ally believe that Juniper might have a past that she could eventually help the girl recover.

But Shona's waspish words about John being the possible snooper plagued Ally as she made her way home. She didn't think for one minute that he was capable of it, but then again, what did she really know about the man?

Then it struck her: he was the only person she had told about working as a journalist for *Lara*. It had to be him. Ally felt nauseous. How could he do such a thing? She trusted him, loved him. Was it because he was afraid of her finding out something about him that he now wanted her gone? Something that she was close to discovering? Something – God forbid – about him and Juniper? It was time to confront him.

***

She was in the cottage just long enough to change into running gear and trainers and then she was pounding up the road towards Bay, working off her aggression.

Thoughts churned as she ran. How long could she stay on here if locals like Shona were turning against her? She shuddered to think of the hostility shown to her the day Juniper was found at her cottage. When had things on Battersay begun to go so sour? It can't only have been her befriending of Juniper that had caused the bad feeling; mostly it must be down to Donny's tragic suicide. It had poisoned the island. Rather than pull people closer, the young man's death had shown up the cracks. The place was full of unexplained tension. How much could Juniper tell her about the island, if only she had the power of speech? And how much could she tell her about John?

All her thoughts kept coming back to her strange lover, his original hostility and aloofness towards her, then his sudden unburdening about Donny and Juniper. She thought of their recent arguments and his defensiveness over Bethag; John was burdened with some guilt, she was sure of it. She had assumed it had to do with Caroline, but what if it was something closer to the recent tragedy? Donny had come to John on his last night alive; she only had John's word for it that he had not spoken to the young fisherman before he drowned.

Ally came over the crest to Bay. The afternoon ferry was pulling out to sea; the one that had brought the unwelcome newspapers. She pounded up the back road towards John's, passing the drive to Bay House Care

Home. On the spur of the moment, Ally swerved left towards Bethag's home. She was at the front entrance before she really knew why she had come.

'She's in her room today,' Ishbel smiled in greeting, 'I thought you'd stopped visiting.'

The manager can't have read the papers, Ally thought with relief.

'Sorry I haven't been lately. How is she?'

'Not too grand. And she's already had a visitor – your Mr Moody.' Ishbel's look was enquiring. Ally's stomach knotted.

'I won't stay long. I promised to frame a couple of photos for her.'

'Go ahead.'

Ally found the old woman dozing in an upright chair. When she put a gentle hand on her knee, Bethag looked up and her eyes widened.

'It's just me, John's friend Ally.'

'Ah, John,' she sighed, 'such a good wee boy.' She looked suddenly tearful. 'You must be very proud of him.'

'Me?' Ally smiled quizzically.

'Aye Seanaid, you.'

Ally's heart thumped. 'Why should I Bethag? Remind me.'

'That's the one thing you should thank me for.'

'Why should I thank you for John? Is he special to me?'

'I found him. I promised to take care –' her face grew troubled; her fingers scrabbled in her lap. 'Where did I find him?'

'You found him in a Glasgow hospital, didn't you? You were a nurse and John was your patient.' Ally held her hand. 'But what else was he to you – to us?'

The old woman's pale blue eyes cast around in bewilderment. 'Why did you go? I didn't want you to go. We should have been together.'

'We are now.'

Bethag looked close to tears. Ally stroked her hand and made comforting noises. Gradually the old woman grew calmer and her eyelids drooped. Her head lolled as she dozed. Ally moved Bethag's hand back into her lap and stood up quietly, but the movement jerked her awake.

'Ally?' she asked in surprise.

'Yes, I just popped in to see you.'

'You have to help me,' Bethag grew agitated, 'she's here – she wants to harm me – please –'

'Hey, don't get upset,' Ally reassured.

'Don't leave me alone with her.'

'With who?'

Bethag's face crumpled. Ally squeezed her hands in hers.

'It's okay, I won't leave you. Come on, I'll get us both a cup – a *strupach*.'

Before she left, Ally slipped the two family photos into her daypack. She wanted to have a closer look at the Gillies women.

CHAPTER 38

Kulah

All week, words rage between Seanaid and me like crashing waves. Bethag takes refuge in the box bed behind sooty curtains while I battle with my eldest.

'The shame of it! You've brought disgrace on us all!'

'I didn't mean for it to happen. He said it wouldn't happen.'

'You shouldn't have been with him – a man more than twice your age! You're just a girl.'

'I'm a woman! You were married at my age.'

'Yes, I was married – not carrying on with a stranger.'

'You can't talk. You made a fool of yourself over Rollo and you've got a husband.'

I slap her mutinous face. It makes no difference. She glares at me with desperate eyes and doesn't flinch; bites her lip to stop herself crying.

'He loves me, that's what you can't stand, isn't it, Mother?'

'Give me the letter,' I order.

She refuses. It is tucked into her bodice. I try to snatch it but she fights me off. I want to rip it to shreds and burn it in the flames. How dare Rollo do this to me? He pretended to love me and all the time he was fornicating with my daughter. I can't bear to think of it. Where did they do it? On the very same spot where he made love to me?

'Your father will kill you when he finds out – he'll kill us both!'

'I won't be here,' she shouts in defiance, 'I'm leaving on the last boat.'

'And how will you afford a ticket? Or get yourself to Edinburgh?'

'I have money saved from helping Morag – and Bethag will lend me some.'

'You will not take money from your sister.'

'I'll walk all the way if I have to,' Seanaid screams, 'I love him and I have to be with him. You can't stop me!'

I round on her. 'Does that man even know you're carrying his baby?'

When she doesn't answer, I say, 'No, he doesn't, does he? So what makes you think he'll want you turning up on his doorstep in your condition?'

'He loves me; he hates us being apart.'

'So why didn't he take you with him when he had the chance?'

'He had other islands to visit before returning to Edinburgh.'

'And no doubt other women.'

She flinches at my bitter words. I know the pain I am inflicting, but I can't stop.

'What do you know about this man? No doubt he's married with a family. He might not even work for the university. We only have his word for it.'

'I believe him!'

'So tell me about him. What's his full name?'

'Rollo …'

'Rollo what? Is that his surname or his Christian name?'

Her eyes glint with angry tears.

'You see, you don't even know that.'

'I hate you!' she cries and slams out of the house.

Outside it is dark and blowing a gale. My heart is so hot with fury that I don't care that she's gone. Let the wind shake some sense into her.

Bethag climbs out of the box bed and stands shaking in the firelight. I go to put my arms about her, but she brushes me off and heads for the door, snatching her coat from the hook and carrying Seanaid's over her arm.

'I'm going to look for her.'

I feel a tide of shame rise up and choke me. How can I be so cruel to my firstborn? I should be protecting her, not wishing her evil thoughts. I know in my heart that it is Rollo whom I want to punish, that I am only lashing out at Seanaid because she is here.

'Wait!' I call after Bethag and pull a plaid around my shoulders.

CHAPTER 39

Battersay

'Not gone off sailing on the hippy ship then?'

Perhaps John had meant it as a joke, but it infuriated Ally further.

'I'm not staying. I just have to ask you something.'

He led her inside, looking uneasy. She had interrupted his painting: bits of driftwood daubed in bright yellow and red. When she refused a glass of wine, he poured her water from a pottery jug. The fire wasn't lit, so Ally pulled on the sweatshirt from her daypack. The photos fluttered to the floor. Before she could reach, John had picked them up.

'Bethag's photos?' he frowned. 'What are you doing with these?'

'Getting them framed.'

'Has she asked you to?'

'Not exactly, but –'

'Take them back.'

'Why shouldn't she have them on display?' Ally demanded.

'Because they're upsetting. They remind her of a time when she had a family.' He waved them at her. 'She looks at these and all she sees is ghosts. If she'd wanted them framed, she'd have done it years ago.'

Ally sparked back. 'Or maybe it's because no one will ever talk about what went on all those years ago. She's still feeling guilty about something and it's eating her up; she's a frightened confused old woman.'

John threw the photos on the table and paced to the window. 'She's got dementia. Leave her alone, Ally.'

'This isn't just about Bethag is it?' Ally said. 'It's about you too. She talks to me about you John – when she thinks I'm Seanaid. What's that all about?'

He turned with a furious look. 'It's got nothing to do with you.'

'No, I'm just Ally the English girl who doesn't understand. It's okay to have me around now and again when you're feeling horny, but not important enough to bother explaining to, is that it?'

'For God's sake,' he said in exasperation, 'no.'

'Are you related to Bethag and Seanaid?'

He turned away again.

'Why won't you talk about it?'

'It's personal.'

Ally lost patience. 'Yeah, and so is this.' She yanked the newspaper article out of her bag and waved it at him. 'That's what I came about. Some jerk has put the tabloids onto me and Juniper. I'm being watched and it's not a nice feeling.'

John came forward and took it.

'Someone wants to break up my friendship with Juniper – or get me to quit.'

He read it then looked up, his face grim. 'You don't think I had anything to do with this, do you? Tell me that's not why you came.'

'You're the only one who knew I work for *Lara*,' Ally accused.

The look he gave her was hard to decipher. 'The journalist who put this together could easily have found out where you worked. And I don't need to sneak around taking photos of you Ally – I know what you look like with no clothes on.'

She felt her face burn. Ally picked up the photos and made for the door.

'Maybe I'm wrong about you tipping off the press, but I'm not wrong about you shutting me out. Well you can keep your secrets, whatever they are.'

'It's complicated,' John growled, 'don't judge me.'

'This isn't about judging,' Ally cried, 'it's about trust. You don't trust me and now I don't know if I can trust you. And you don't need me John; you're happy here on your own, I see that now. That's your choice. I'm different. I need to be with people – people who are honest with me – and loving.'

John followed her outside. 'Ally, don't – at least let me drive you back.'

'No John,' she said, fending him off, 'I won't bother you again. And I don't want you coming round – not unless you're prepared to be straight with me.'

She started to run, picking up speed along the track, John shouting something that was carried off in the wind. All the way home, she raged that she had allowed herself to fall in love again with a man she couldn't trust. Ally didn't stop till she reached the cottage.

In the gloom, she was startled by two crows rearing up suddenly round the corner of the house. With a loud cawing they landed on a dark shape lying at the top of the beach path. For a stunned moment she watched them peck at the deathly still body.

'Juniper!' Ally screamed.

Rushing over, she kicked and shooed the protesting birds away. Her insides heaved at the stench. She gasped for breath, her lungs aching. Not Juniper. She stared in disbelief. It was a dead seal; its head bashed to a pulp and its body putrefying.

Ally doubled over and retched into the grass.

CHAPTER 40

Kulah

Winter has come. It is dangerous to walk near the cliff's edge for fear of being whipped into the sea. To go outside to bring peats in from the stack or to feed the goats takes away all my strength; it is a tug of war.

The endless days are spent sitting in the gloom, unravelling old jumpers to knit into new and sewing together scraps of tweed and worsted wool to make a bed cover.

'Old Seamus won't need them anymore,' I tell Bethag when she protests at us cutting up his old suit. 'He'll never get out of bed again.'

'But Father's as well? It's not right.'

I cut and stitch and cut and stitch, straining my eyes in the bad light. I do not say that her father's wrath will be so great, that it will not have time to waste on the petty crime of cutting up his old Sunday suit to make a blanket. I see his fury sweep around us like the gales that batter the island, whipping and roaring and pushing us towards the edge. His anger will keep us prisoner until he decides what is to be our fate.

Bethag kneels in front of me, holding yarn between skinny trembling hands as I wind the oily wool, looking up at me with anxious eyes. And I realise that I am already a prisoner, cut off and condemned for tasting forbidden fruit. That is why I have retreated with my daughters to Ostaig and the house of Seamus who is dying in the box bed in the next room. It is winter and no one will come – the tracks are too sodden and the days too short. Bethag no longer goes to the schoolroom to help Morag; I know she misses the children but she doesn't complain. She sings to the old man who thinks she is his long dead wife.

Seanaid sits staring into the fire for hours at a time. She has run out of paper but I know she is making up stories in her head. There is a light in her eye and a stillness about her that tells me she is travelling to some far off place where I can't reach her.

'Keep to the house,' I order, hoping that the winter will be long and we can hide her until the baby comes. She has grown less mutinous as her belly has swollen, and is outwardly obedient. But I can't stop her mind rushing off to be with Rollo.

I knit and knit with a clack of angry needles: a shawl and swaddling clothes of scratchy wool. My knitting is bitter and brooding: one minute tight enough to strangle, the next careless and loose with dropped stitches.

My firstborn sent a letter with the final mail boat last autumn: an SOS to her lover.

'Don't be so foolish,' I told her, 'he'll never help you. I'm the only one who can.'

'We are going to be together,' she repeats like an incantation.

But until the spring comes, neither of us knows who is right.

I watch her from the shadows. She is still a wisp of a girl, dreaming by the fire, hugging her secret thoughts. Only when she stands to stretch and her pinafore pulls tight over her full belly do I see a woman before me. Then she is a stranger, the carrier of Rollo's bastard child – a cuckoo for Tormod's nest.

Fear swells my empty stomach. I remember that I alone heard the cuckoo last spring – that herald of disaster – just before Rollo came. Now I know that Rollo's child is our disaster. So I make up my mind. I know what I have to do when the baby comes. I pick up my knitting and stab out a new row of angry stitches.

CHAPTER 41

Battersay

Calum helped Ally bury the seal. Come daylight it was clear someone had dragged the carcass up from the beach. Judging by the decay, Calum thought it had been dead for a couple of days.

'Someone's got it in for me,' she said. 'Who would do something that disgusting?'

He eyed her. 'You know who. There's only one person not right in the head round here who would, in my opinion.'

'Not Juniper.'

'Yes Juniper. She's strong enough and mad enough. Listen, Ally, you need to take care of yourself. Stop putting yourself in danger. She's wild; you can't change someone's nature.'

She knew it was pointless to argue. She was just thankful that Calum was still speaking to her; Shona wasn't.

Over the next few days, word of the tabloid article spread and Ally felt the islanders retreating behind a frosty politeness. She began to long for her London friends and tried to speak to Rachel from the kiosk in Bay but got only her answerphone. She took copies of Bethag's photos with her digital camera and took back the originals. The old woman was sleeping and Ishbel too busy to chat. She tried Rachel again and got through. Her friend's bubbly voice sounded surprised and rushed.

'Great to hear you, babe. What's up? Keep talking; I'm on my way out. No nothing much happening here. What about you? Still shagging that painter?'

Ally began to explain about Juniper, but Rachel laughed, 'It's true then? Zoe saw something on the Net. You'll have a great scoop for *Lara* when you come back; keep the boss happy.'

The telephone started beeping; Ally rammed in her last pound coin.

'The phone, it takes coins, just a sec.'

'What's that?'

'Rach, I'm not doing this for *Lara*, I'm trying to help Juniper.'

'Listen babe, there's something I should tell you. I bumped into you-know-who the other day – he was with –'

Abruptly the line went dead. Ally hit the machine in frustration. What was her friend about to say? Was it Lucas? She pushed at the heavy glass door and went out into the wind. Rachel was probably going to tell her he was with another woman. She waited for the twist of jealousy, but it didn't come.

Running home, Ally had to admit how much of her enjoyment of Battersay had been bound up with John. She missed his company and the shabby charm of his croft. She had been too hasty in believing him capable of stirring up the bad publicity but the truth was that she had wanted more to come of the relationship than he had. And now that she

116

had wrecked their friendship with her accusations, it was dead in the water.

She took refuge with the Rushmores, thankful they accepted her for who she was. Increasingly, Ally spent time at Sollas House, some nights not bothering to go home at all, preferring to bed down in the cosy yellow room than face the cottage that seemed haunted by unhappiness. Mary and Ned didn't try and stop her seeing Juniper either – Mary would help make the chocolate brownies the girl so liked – and they couldn't have cared less that she'd been made notorious by a tabloid.

Ned snorted, 'we've had rough treatment too in the past. After we lost Ossian.'

'They didn't pick on you about your son, surely?'

'Oh they did,' Ned said bitterly. 'Said we'd been irresponsible to take him on such a remote sailing trip.'

'It was very cruel,' Mary said, her voice shaking, 'Ned is a very experienced sailor. Ossian knew all about safety too – we'd drummed it into him – but he was such a lively little boy.'

Suddenly Ned's chin trembled. 'I should've had better hold of him –' he stopped and swallowed hard.

Mary continued, her voice quiet but full of emotion. 'The gutter press saw us as easy meat – they rubbished Ned's alternative medicine and my way of dressing.'

'That's terrible,' Ally sympathised.

Ned cleared his throat. 'And they found some bonkers priest to say that it was God's judgement on us for sailing on the Sabbath.'

'Never?'

'Oh yes, it was all very unpleasant. We turned our back on it all for a while – joined a community in Galloway. They loved that too of course – fitted in with their judgement on us as weirdo hippies who couldn't take proper care of their beloved only son.'

'Ned stop,' Mary whispered.

Abruptly he got up and left the room.

'You poor people,' Ally said, moving from her cushion on the floor to squeeze Mary's arm. 'Your world just ended and still they put the boot in. I don't know how you've coped so well.'

'We have each other,' Mary replied. 'I'd be nothing without my Ned. And coming to Battersay of course. I can look out of our bedroom window to the west and know that Ossian is there.'

CHAPTER 42

Kulah, 1946

There is rumour flying over the island like a giant eagle: powerful, circling, thumping like a heartbeat. The men are on their way home. Bethag brings the news after a rare trip to the village to trade goat's milk for oatmeal. Conflicting emotions chase across her pale face like clouds: excited, nervous, wanting reassurance that this is good fortune. The winter has been hard and hungry.

'How can they possibly know?' I demand. 'We've been cut off for months.'

Her words trip over themselves in their hurry to be told.

'Sam said that Susan said that old Iain got a message in a float that was thrown overboard from a ship on its way to America and it says the men of the Isles are coming and it's going to be any day now!'

'Sam says!' I snort. 'Susan is telling him a tall story.'

'Any – day – now!' Bethag repeats.

Her words punch my heart. I don't believe it, but I have to go outside and look along the cliff path, scanning the wild sea for signs of the ship. There is nothing but mist and rocks and water churning far below. I return breathless; even the shortest walk now feels as if I have climbed the Black Rock.

'No skipper in his right mind would set out in that,' I declare to my daughters.

Seanaid looks at me and I see the fear claw at her thin face. 'It's too soon,' she whispers, clutching her distended womb. 'The baby must come first.'

'It will come first,' I snap, 'stop fretting.'

But it is I who cannot be still. I pace the earthen floor, in and out of old Seamus's room with its sickly stench, to check on his fluttering pulse. He doesn't eat and it no longer takes two of us to lift him onto the chamber pot, but somehow he clings onto life and won't let go.

Bethag says, 'he won't go to the ancestors until the men come back; he's keeping watch over Kulah.'

'You're just repeating what Morag says,' Seanaid scoffs with a flash of her old spirit. 'It's Mother's care that has kept him alive so long.'

My eyes smart at her words, grateful for the brusque love with which they are said. I want to put my arms about her and breathe in her sharp smell but if I do I might feel Rollo's baby kicking at my emptiness. I turn away and blink back tears.

'It's not what Morag says,' Bethag whines, 'it's what I say. Father made Old Seamus promise to keep an eye on us, didn't he Mammy? So that's just what he's doing.'

CHAPTER 43

Battersay

Mist had covered the island all day. Noises were magnified and distorted. Walking back from work Ally heard the sound of a ship groaning as it put out to sea, though the ferry was five miles away in Bay. She hated weather like this and didn't intend to stay at the cottage longer than it took to grab a change of clothes before heading over to Sollas House. Mary and she were going to make vegetable curry and chapattis.

Ally hurried up the ladder to the bedroom and dug out a change of underwear and a clean T-shirt; she would sleep in her old one. As she stuffed them into her backpack she heard something below: the squeak of the front door opening. She stood holding her breath. There was silence, and then the sound of footsteps. The tread was heavy like a man's. Calum or John perhaps? But whoever it was didn't call out a greeting. She heard them walk past the ladder, into the kitchen and then stop.

Ally clutched her bag, heart hammering as if she were the intruder. Should she call down and confront them or make a dash for it? She felt trapped. Light flooded along the corridor; the man had switched on the kitchen light. Then the footsteps returned. They stopped at the ladder and she heard it shake and creak as someone began to mount.

Seized with panic, she cast around for something heavy to throw. Ally snatched up one of Ned's heavy books. A hooded head appeared through the hatch. Ally raised up the book to strike. He pulled down his hood to look around and she saw his face.

It was Lucas.

'What the hell are you doing here?' she gasped.

'Ally?'

'Of course it's me,' she cried, fear subsiding into anger. 'You nearly gave me a heart attack.'

'Struth, this place is a dump. I can't believe you swapped London for this.'

'Don't come any further,' she brandished the book at him.

'Okay, okay,' he said, halting on the ladder.

'You've no right to be here. What do you think you're playing at? How did you find me? I bet it was Rachel and her big mouth –'

'Hey girl, put that down. I'm sorry I frightened you. Was a bit spooked myself. This place is fucking creepy.'

Ally lowered the book but said, 'get back down now.'

Lucas retreated and Ally followed. Cold mist swirled around the open door. He made as if to hug her, but she warded him off. 'Don't even think about it. You've two minutes to explain what you're doing then I'm out of here.'

He looked sheepish. 'I did bump into Rachel, but it wasn't her. I saw you in the paper – there's stuff all over the Net about you and Birdwoman – it wasn't hard to find you.'

Ally went hot at the thought. 'What sort of stuff?'

Lucas gave a wry look, 'you two being a couple of lezzies. Had one hack ringing me up asking for personal details on you; told him to go screw his grandmother.'

'Oh God,' Ally groaned, 'I've made things ten times worse for her.'

'What? Birdwoman? By the sounds of it she's having a ball. You're her first buddy.'

'She's called Juniper,' Ally snapped, 'and she's not having a ball – the locals have turned against her –' Ally bit off her remark; she wasn't going to trust him with confidences. He was probably here sniffing around for a scoop. 'So why are you here Lucas?'

'I was worried about you.'

'That's crap.'

'It's the God's honest truth. I miss you girl. It's been driving me nuts not knowing where you'd gone, not being able to speak to you, explain –'

'Apologise you mean?'

Lucas sighed, 'yeah, okay, apologise.' He stepped towards her. 'Ally I've been an arse and I'm really sorry.'

She steeled herself against his hang-dog look; he knew just how to get round her defences.

'You're wasting your time – and you've come a long way for nothing.'

He looked at her desperately, 'I just want to be with you, Ally, no one else. I realised that the moment –'

'What? The moment you jumped that model?' With satisfaction she saw his fair face flush. 'Can't you see I'll never be able to trust you again?'

His broad shoulders sagged. 'Yeah, I don't blame you.'

Her anger deflated. Now that he looked defeated, Ally wasn't sure what to do. They stared at each other. He looked away first and leaned to pick up his sports bag, dumped by the door.

'You can stay here the night if you want,' Ally relented. Hope lit his face, so she quashed it at once. 'I won't be here; I'm staying over at friends.'

He grunted, 'No thanks, this place is as friendly as a morgue. I'll book into the hotel.'

'How do you know about the hotel?'

'Struth you're suspicious. There's a thing called the internet – even Battersay's on it.'

She allowed herself to smile as she shooed him out of the house and slammed the door behind them. They walked down to the road in the mist.

'What the hell's that noise?' Lucas asked, stopping in his tracks.

Ally listened. All she could hear was the usual screech of birds on the cliffs.

'Seagulls,' she said, 'they never stop. I'm used to them now.'

'Sounds more like people crying,' he said, his face suddenly tense.

She seized his arm. 'What sort of crying?'

120

'Well, like those Afghan women on TV when their villages are bombed; high-pitched sort of wailing. Can't you hear it? You must be hearing it too.'

Ally's heart thumped. He looked at her strangely. 'You know what I mean though, don't you?' Lucas said. 'You've heard it before.'

She nodded.

Lucas took her hand; she had never seen him look scared. 'Ally, what the hell's going on around here?'

CHAPTER 44

Kulah

I wake in the night and know something has changed. I can hear Bethag mumbling in her sleep and Seanaid turning restlessly on the truckle bed, its springs squeaking. The thatch creaks. Beyond there is silence.

That is what has changed: the rhythm of the night. I climb down from the box bed and feel my way in the dark across the damp floor. Pushing open the door to Seamus's room I move with stealth, though I know in my heart that there is no need.

His hand is cold and his brow is clammy to the touch, yet I feel him still lingering in the dark, filling the space. The back of his neck is warm as a baby's. His spirit is half way gone, but not quite left. Perhaps it was his dying sigh that woke me, or his soul passing through the room and taking one last look around his home of eighty years.

I lean against the wooden bed and hold his hand between mine as if I could heat it up again with life.

'Oh Seamus, Seamus,' I whisper, raising his fingers to my lips and kissing them. 'Don't leave us.'

My tears drop onto the blanket. The girls will cry a pailful at his dying when they wake and I tell them in the morning.

Then it strikes me like a forge hammer: it is too quiet. The silence is not only the absence of the old man's breathing, but also in the stillness beyond.

I leap up and knock into things in my haste to get outside. There is no wind; not a breath. The sea whispers below as if all its energy has been spent after weeks of raging. It is early March and there should be storms for another month; the sea should be a tight plaid around our rocks keeping out invaders till the spring.

But Seamus is dead and the sea is calm. There is nothing to keep the men from coming across the water.

I must not cry out; I must stifle my fear.

It is only in the light of morning as I serve up thin porridge that I tell my daughters. 'The old *botach* died last night.'

CHAPTER 45

Battersay

Ned nearly ran them down in the mist. He'd been collecting supplies from the ferry for his and Mary's forthcoming boat trip. To Ally's embarrassment he started talking enthusiastically to Lucas about sailing, who acted as if he hadn't been scared out of his wits minutes before.

'Let me give you both a lift,' Ned said.

'Lucas is going to the hotel,' Ally said firmly.

'How about a bite to eat with us first?' Ned suggested. 'The food at the hotel is processed and microwaved to death.'

'If that's okay with you?' Lucas turned to her, his look pleading. He'd had a shock. The thought of the wailing women made her relent.

Ten minutes later, they were rattling down the drive to Sollas House, and then Lucas was helping Ned unload boxes and being introduced to Mary. It was no surprise to Ally that Mary liked the Australian at once and wanted to mother him. He was as boyishly charming and helpful as only Lucas on the scrounge could be.

Over candlelit curry and large amounts of homemade wine, conversation turned from the forthcoming sailing trip to the tragedy of Donny's suicide and the worsening attitude towards Juniper.

'There's a climate of fear about the place,' Ned said, 'that's never been there before.'

'People are naturally upset,' Mary said.

'It's more than that; there's a general suspicion. Look at the way Ally's being picked on for trying to help Juniper.'

'Picked on?' Lucas queried.

'Well, yes, someone's trying to frighten her or turn folk against her. Surely she's told you about the dead seal and all the carry-on at the house?'

Lucas shot Ally a concerned look. She shook her head, not wanting to explain.

'And then there's the question of who took the photo and leaked sensational material to the press,' Ned went on. 'I have my suspicions of course.'

'You do?' Lucas asked.

'Balmain; it has to be.'

'Balmain?'

'Ally's painter friend – the de-frocked priest.'

'Oh yeah?' Lucas gave Ally a surprised look.

'He's not my painter,' she said flustered.

'Well, he's taken rather a shine to you – and an unhealthy interest in Juniper if you ask me. Strange as a kettle of fish. '

'Ned,' Mary chided, 'don't embarrass Ally.'

'Have I?'

Lucas intervened, 'I heard the creepiest noises in the mist earlier, like people going hysterical, sobbing their hearts out.'

Mary put down her tumbler with a clatter. She and Ned exchanged looks but said nothing. The sudden silence was tense.

Ally's insides knotted. 'Have you heard it too?'

'I knew it,' Mary whispered. 'It's a sign things are getting worse.'

'What things?' Lucas asked, baffled.

'The prophecy,' Mary trembled.

'You're beginning to scare me,' Lucas joked.

Ned said, 'it's no laughing matter, I'm afraid. Such things are deeply embedded in the culture here. The roots go far back to our Celtic ancestors.'

Just as John had told Ally, Ned began to tell Lucas the prophecy and of the long ago shipwreck of servicemen off Kulah and how the Battersay locals thought their fate was somehow linked to those tragic events.

'You're not the first to hear the weeping women,' he said, 'it was claimed people on Battersay could hear them at the time of the shipwreck, though it's impossibly far away. But it's an indication of how out of sorts things have become.'

'Do you really believe that?' Lucas asked.

'Yes,' said Mary, 'we believe in the power of the dead to connect with the living. Why not? To the Celts such communication was as natural as you and I sitting round this table talking. We've lost the ability to trust in things that we can't see or explain, that's all.'

Her grey hair glinted in the flickering light, her expression faraway. Lucas looked at her wide-eyed.

'So what are you saying? That Donny's suicide has stirred up some sort of ghostly past?'

'It's possible,' said Ned.

Lucas gave a nervous laugh. 'You guys have been living here too long.'

Mary laid a hand on his. 'But you said yourself you heard the weeping of the women.'

'I dunno. I was creeped out by the mist and that dump of a cottage, that's all.'

'You know you heard it Lucas,' Ally said, 'I saw the look on your face.' She felt a sudden desire to unburden. 'It can't just be Donny's suicide that's triggered things, 'cos this stuff was happening before that. Don't laugh but I'm really frightened that my coming here has somehow had an effect. At the beginning I thought it was just that someone didn't like me – all the pranks at the house – but some of it simply can't be explained.'

'Come on Ally,' Lucas reasoned, 'someone was trying to scare you, that's all. Probably some jealous girl. There's no way you could be mixed up in this nutty prophecy.'

'Let her speak,' Ned said firmly. 'Go on Ally; tell us what's worrying you.'

Ally hesitated. The shadows in the dark beyond the candlelight shifted, like a listening presence. The others sat still, waiting. Even Lucas, who was trying to make light of it, held his breath. She could tell he was as unnerved as she was.

'I first felt it when I came across Our Lady of the Seas.'

Tentatively, Ally spoke of her violent reaction to the white statue with the corroded baby, of unexplained crying since the day she arrived and of the phantom woman with the blue headscarf.

'I know this sounds really far-fetched, but could the woman in tweed possibly be the ghost of Flora Gillies? I'm sure that Juniper sees her as well,' Ally said. 'Something frightened her up at the shieling that just wasn't visible. And Bethag seems haunted by someone too – a woman walking the cliffs.'

Her question hung in the dimly lit kitchen. Lucas was the first to stir, pushing back on his chair and taking a glug of wine.

'After what Juniper's been through,' he said, 'she should be frightened of her own shadow.'

'It's more than that,' Ally insisted. 'And sometimes she terrifies me – she can change mood so quickly – gets so angry and aggressive like she's …'

'What?' Ned asked.

'Possessed?' Mary suggested.

Ally shrugged and then nodded.

Lucas began to protest, but Mary hushed him and took hold of Ally's shaking hand. 'You mustn't be afraid, dear one; for some reason you've been chosen.'

'Chosen?' Ally's pulse began to thud.

'I believe,' Mary said gravely, 'that the spirits of Kulah are trying to communicate with you.'

CHAPTER 46

Kulah

We bury old Seamus behind the house; that is as far as Bethag and I can carry him, even though he is thin as dry reeds. It takes me all morning to dig the grave. Bethag is worried that he is not going to lie in the burial ground with the ancestors, but I tell her that he will be at peace here and if the men wish to move him after they return, then so be it.

My youngest asks, 'Can we wrap him in the patchwork blanket?'

'That would be wasteful and not what Seamus would want.'

'But it's mainly his suit, Mammy!'

'Blankets are for the living.'

We pack him in a bed of heather with his cap, pipe and sea-boots. Bethag insists on putting in his Bible, a tin mug, postcards from his son killed in the Great War, a cut-throat razor and the remains of his tobacco. When she tries to add a jug of water and some oatcakes, I stop her.

'Don't be wasteful.'

'But he'll need these for his journey,' Bethag says.

'He's dead,' Seanaid cries, 'he doesn't need any of this.'

They bicker over the grave like crows. They are both right, but one has her mind in the future and one takes comfort in the past.

'We will share the meal with him now,' I end the argument by breaking the oatcakes and handing them round. We drink from the jug and say prayers and bury some crumbs with Seamus. Bethag sings a psalm in her sweet voice while I replace the stony turf. I am so weary and slow that I see myself in my mind's eye as an old woman ready for her own grave.

Suddenly, Seanaid is weeping, sinking to her knees and calling out for the old man. The strength of her grief takes me by surprise. Bethag stops her singing to go and comfort her sister. They cling to each other and I drop the spade. Stepping round the grave, I put a hand on each head and wish I had the power to protect them forever.

We are exhausted by this day of burial. Soon we will have to send word of the passing of Seamus and then the questions will flock to our door: How did he die? Why didn't you come and fetch us? Why is he buried in unhallowed ground? And all my efforts to hide our shameful secret will be undone, for they will see for themselves the fruit of Rollo's sinning.

CHAPTER 47

Battersay

'How's Cathy getting on in Inverness?' John asked Sandra in the Co-op.

The woman snorted as she checked through his purchases. 'How should I know? She never rings me. But that's a good sign; she'd be straight on the phone if she was short of cash.'

'Well at least she's making her own way in life,' John grunted, 'got to admire her for that.'

'Aye', Sandra sighed, 'that's true, right enough.'

She helped pack his hessian bag. 'You drinking that funny tea now too?'

Embarrassed, John muttered, 'Yes, I'm acquiring a taste.' It was a lie; he was buying Redbush for Ally in the hope she would reappear in his life for a cup of tea if nothing more. God, he missed her. She hadn't been over for a week. He wished he could lie as easily to her as to Sandra, make up some sob story about him and Caroline and his mother that would satisfy her and stop the awkward questions, and – more importantly – throw her off the scent about Bethag and Seanaid. But he couldn't bring himself to do so. Heaven help him, he must be in love.

Sandra eyed him. 'Ally give you the taste for it, eh?'

John felt himself go red. She laughed as she popped the box on top. Perhaps he'd go on over to Ally's cottage and give her the tea as a peace offering.

He asked as casually as possible, 'has she been in recently?'

Sandra glanced away, busying herself with tidying carrier bags. 'Aye, she was in yesterday with Dr Ned and another man.'

John's stomach knotted.

'They were buying tinned food by the box load. You'd think we were in for a month of storms.'

'Maybe I'll take her over some teabags if she's planning for a siege,' he joked.

Sandra flicked him a look. 'You'll not find her at home. Seemingly, she's moved into Sollas House. Can't blame her. Coastguard's house isn't fit for humans. Rory says it stinks round there since the Bird-witch was caught inside.'

'You shouldn't call Juniper that,' John frowned.

Sandra's look hardened. 'That's what she is, everyone thinks so.'

'Come on, nobody really believes she's a witch. People are just people; they don't have supernatural powers.'

'Well Ally and Dr Ned believe in the supernatural. Kept asking me if I'd seen a ghost with a blue head scarf. I said aye, she comes in every day for cigarettes and the papers.' Sandra snorted with amusement. 'And that foreign boy started larking about making ghost noises and grabbing Ally from behind.'

John tensed. 'Foreign boy?'

'Aye, he sounded South African or something. Friend of Ally's from London.' Sandra eyed him. 'Thought you'd have met him by now. Came on the boat the other day. Ally not brought him out to the gallery yet?'

John felt winded. Sandra's look was turning from interest to pity.

'Not yet,' he said, heaving the bag from the checkout. As he turned away, John couldn't help asking, 'could he have been Australian?'

'Aye, something like that. Had a fancy name.'

'Oh?'

Sandra wrinkled her nose trying to remember. 'Lucas. Aye, that was it.'

John walked out, trying not to show how much he minded. What a fool he'd been over Ally. She must have invited Lucas up from London days ago; probably the day she accused him of being behind the salacious article. Or maybe she had planned all along to get back with the photographer? Had she used their affair to make Lucas jealous and come running back to her?

John revved the van in angry frustration and tore out of the car park.

CHAPTER 48

Things were moving too fast for Ally. She worried over the latest development. That morning Ned had said to Lucas, 'why don't you come on the trip too? It's a chance for some stunning photography. You said your time is your own. You'll never get a better chance to see the Outer Isles.'

'I'm not much of a sailor,' Lucas had laughed.

'You'll soon pick it up.'

'Will you really get as far as Kulah?'

'If the weather holds. Can't guarantee it.'

'It would be amazing to have a look around.'

Ned had cautioned. 'The pier they once used is unsafe after years of storms. It would be risky to go ashore unless there's no swell.'

Lucas had shown his disappointment. 'Hardly worth all the effort then.'

'Not at all,' Ned had enthused, 'you'll still get a good feel of the place. And if we don't get that far, there are other uninhabited islands where we can land. The sea fishing is superb.'

'Well I love to fish. I'm just used to warmer seas.' He had looked at Ally. 'What do you think? Would you mind me tagging along?'

'It's not my trip,' Ally had shrugged.

'That sounds like a yes to me,' Ned grinned. 'Welcome aboard, Lucas.'

As Ally busied herself in the kitchen at work, she wondered crossly why she hadn't opposed the idea of Lucas joining the sailing trip. In four days time the Rushmores would be sailing. Ally had worked a seven day week so that she could join the expedition for four days – the stretch to Kulah and back – and then Ned and Mary would carry on north, meeting up with their friends en route.

Four days stuck in a cramped boat with Lucas sounded like a bad idea. A week ago she simply wouldn't have contemplated it. So what had changed? *Lucas has changed.* She allowed the treacherous thought to worm its way into her head. Her friends at home would have a fit if they knew she had not only allowed Lucas to stay under the same roof but begun – begrudgingly – to enjoy his company again.

She hated to admit it but Lucas was being kind and considerate to her, helpful and funny with the Rushmores. They loved him. Like a son. Ally sighed; who was she to deny them the comfort of a young guy around their home?

'Shona doesn't have time to make flapjack today,' Calum came in and told her. 'Tor's in bed with a sore throat and temperature.'

'Oh, poor kid. Don't worry, I'm making brownies. Can I do anything to help? Take Craig off her hands for a couple of hours?'

Calum hesitated, his look awkward. 'That's okay. I can take him with me today.'

Ally felt a pang of disappointment. Before the damaging newspaper article the Gillies would have jumped at her offer.

'Thanks anyway,' Calum said as he hurried away.

Anger at the unknown person who had betrayed her flared in Ally once more. She hoped it wasn't John; deep down she didn't believe it could be. What did he have to gain by it, except a fat fee? Unless in some warped way he wanted her alienated from the other islanders so that he could have her to himself? Or maybe it was a ploy to upset Ned and force a rift between her and the Rushmores by exposing Juniper to the press again. The article had made Juniper seem more human, just a young woman having fun in the sea. John was always going on about needing to show the world the real Juniper: eccentric maybe, but essentially ordinary.

The more Ally dwelled on it, the more she was nagged with doubt about John. And he had made no attempt to try and see her. The thought caused her pain. Well if his plan had been to cause annoyance to Ned and turn him against her, then it had failed badly. The Rushmores were the only real friends she had on the island now. Them and Lucas.

Ally stirred the soup with vigour. She didn't like to think that she was forgiving Lucas too easily just because John was no longer interested. She must smother the aching feeling of loss of being without John. Somehow she would find out if her doubts about him were true.

CHAPTER 49

Kulah

Seanaid lies restless in the box bed. She is hot to the touch yet shivery. We were out too long the day before yesterday in the cutting air burying the *botach* and she is frightened of what is to come. Her belly is hard as a sack of oatmeal and she cannot get comfortable. The thought of Rollo's child weighs on my heart like a grinding stone.

'I'll go over to old Kate's for a remedy,' I tell my daughters, 'it'll help you sleep tonight.'

It is an excuse to be out of the cottage; the reclusive widow Kate stopped making cures when her husband and son were taken by the war. I can put up with any amount of work and busyness, but I cannot stand the idle hours. I realise how much I have come to depend on caring for Seamus to fill my days; his absence nags like sleeplessness. No longer can I bear to knit or sew or churn milk into butter; these everyday duties mock me as I wait. There is only the disaster coming.

Anxious thoughts fly after me as I labour over the hill towards Stavaig: what if I cannot manage to bring the baby out? What if Bethag tells all? What if Seanaid dies?

I stop, out of breath. The sea washes the rocks below. Today it is playful and caressing. It is blue as Our Lady's mantle, like the colour of midsummer. The calmness sparks my anger. Fickle sea! You have cradled my husband through the war and will bring him safely home to torment me once more.

I pick up a stone and hurl it over the cliff. 'Is that what you want? That we women must be punished? That Rollo wanders free to scatter his bad seed? Why should Tormod return to a hero's welcome when he is the enemy that threatens my family? Answer me that!'

My yelling brings a circling of birds overhead. Fulmars and gulls beat their wings in agitation, screaming back at me. I pull my blue plaid over my head in protection and shake my fist as they wheel and dive. But something strange – like a vision – is happening. They do not touch me; they are like my armour and my battle cry. My twin emotions – fear and fury – have spun into the air and taken on the flesh of birds.

I am powerful! I will not be beaten. I will take on the bad men and the bad sea because I have the spirit of good ancestors and the protection of saints at my command. Suddenly, all is clarity. Seamus is travelling at this very moment to join the heavenly band of angels and plead my case. I am not a bad woman and I only looked for love because I was starved of it. Rollo is the treacherous one – he betrayed me and my precious daughter.

I fling my arms into the air and cry out, 'Let there be revenge! Punish Rollo for his wickedness. Come ancestors; keep Tormod from my door and save my daughters. Take away the shameful seed that grows in my firstborn's belly.'

I am ablaze with righteous passion and step so near the edge that I feel loose stones crumble beneath me and drop into the dizzying void. But I know that the birds will protect me and stop me from falling; they will lift me up on wings of fire. My anger makes me clear-headed; I have cowered away in fear all these months for no reason. Neither the gossips of the village can harm me, nor Tormod's fists and burning cigarettes.

'I am Flora Gillies,' I scream. 'I curse you Rollo and I curse your bastard child! I curse you Tormod. You no longer have power over me or mine.'

I feel the stirrings of the sea trembling up the rock-face and through my bare feet; Sea Mother is waking from the spell of the bad men.

Reaching out, I call, 'Come, Sea Mother and protect your own kind. You have the power to turn back the men. Keep them from Kulah until I have dealt with the cuckoo child. Come Sea Mother, I command you. Rise up and save us!'

The birds swoop around, frantic in their screeching and beating of wings. Together we make such a noise that I am deaf to all else, spewing out my hatred for Tormod and Rollo into the salty air.

I do not realise that anyone else is there, until a hand grabs at my plaid and pulls me.

'Mammy!' Bethag's face is contorted in horror – or fear – as she clutches my arm. '*Mother.*' She repeats my name over and over and babbles words that make no sense. I no longer understand the language of the ordinary; I speak only with tongues of fire.

Then she says my firstborn's name. *Seanaid.* The ringing in my ears ceases.

She is sobbing. 'It's Seanaid. Please, please! Come quickly.'

CHAPTER 50

Battersay

Ally knew John would be out on Friday evening visiting Bethag. It was three days before the sailing trip and she could no longer stand the not knowing.

'I'm going over to the cottage after work,' she told Mary, 'but I'll be back for supper.'

To her dismay, Lucas came by the hall as she and Calum were locking up.

'Okay mate?' Lucas punched Calum playfully on the arm.

Calum grunted a reply, gave Ally a questioning look and swiftly left.

'Not very friendly round here, are they?' Lucas said.

'They were fine till the Donny business – and that article about me and Juniper,' Ally said tensely. 'What are you doing here?'

'Going to keep you company – fend off any unfriendly ghosts at the haunted house,' Lucas grinned.

Ally began to walk. 'I really don't need you there. I'm not going over for long.'

'Thought we could go for a swim.' He slipped an arm around her waist. 'Happy to make it a skinny dip if you want.'

She shook him off. 'Just 'cos we're getting on okay doesn't mean we're back together.'

He kept pace as she quickened. 'Is it 'cos of this priest guy? Am I getting in the way?'

'That's my business.'

'So are you planning to go over to his? Mary thinks you are.'

'It's nothing to do with her,' Ally said in annoyance.

'Hey, don't get angry with her. She cares about you. Asked me to keep an eye on you 'cos she thinks this John guy's upset you.'

Ally slowed down. 'Yeah, sorry, I know she means well. But I'm okay; I can handle this myself.'

Lucas grabbed her hand. 'Tell me what's going on. If you think he's behind the article on you, then don't give him the time of day. Stay away. Ned thinks he's bad news – all bitter and twisted after leaving the church and being dumped by his fiancée.'

Ally flushed. 'Enjoyed a good gossip about me and John did you?'

'No, course not. I feel really bad. It's my stupid fault you came to this weird island in the first place. I just want to do what I can to make it up to you, girl.'

As the coastguard's cottage came into view, Ally felt a familiar twist of anxiety. Perhaps having Lucas around wasn't such a bad idea. She decided to be straight with him.

'I am going over to John's, but only because I know he won't be there. I want to check his computer to see if I can find the article.'

'Wow, you really don't trust him, do you?'

She shot him a look. 'No, I don't seem to attract men who can be trusted.'

'Okay, I deserved that one.' Lucas gave a sheepish grin as they carried on past the cottage. 'So how you so sure the priest won't be there?'

'Stop calling him a priest,' she said in irritation. 'On Fridays he visits old Bethag at the care home and reads to her.'

Lucas smirked. 'That guy knows how to have a good time.'

Ally tried not to laugh. 'It's very sweet of him. I think they're somehow related but he's very touchy about it.'

'Is she the old girl from Kulah? One of the survivors that Ned was talking about the other night?'

Ally nodded. 'She's got dementia – lives more and more in the past and it seems to frighten her – thinks I'm her long dead sister.'

'Struth, that's creepy.'

'She's got some fantastic family photos from the 1940s – really professional – look at these.' Ally fished her camera from a pocket as they strode along. 'These digitals don't do them justice.'

'Wow, these are beauties,' Lucas whistled. 'Can I see the originals?'

'No, Bethag keeps them hidden in a drawer.'

'We could do a great spread for *Lara*,' said Lucas, 'the old and the new. Get you posed next to Ned's Standing Stone.'

'I had thought of doing something on traditional recipes,' Ally admitted, 'but now the locals are too wary.'

They stopped and bought bottles of water and a packet of biscuits in Bay, then skirted round the shoreline towards John's gallery to avoid meeting him on the road. Ally felt a pang of longing as they picked their way across the pebbled beach with its flotsam of creels and rope, smothering the memory of recent swims with John.

There was no sign of his van at the house. Ally took the front door key from under a polished boulder and steeled herself to enter. She felt deeply guilty yet had to end her torment of not knowing.

'You can wait outside and shout if you see anyone coming,' she told Lucas. But a minute later he followed her in, too curious.

Ally's heart hammered as she waited for the computer to boot up. There was a smell of coffee and smoky peat; the fire had been damped down to keep it smouldering. She imagined John coming in later and poking it vigorously to bring it alive, uncorking a bottle of red wine and leaving it on the hearth to breathe.

'Strange sort of art,' Lucas said, picking up bits of junk sculpture from the table.

'Leave his stuff alone,' Ally was sharp. She typed in the password *bethag_gillies* and clicked on his documents. Lucas began leafing through sketch books. Ally found poems in various drafts and letters to John's father, notes for art projects. She skimmed them just long enough to make sure they weren't about her or Juniper. There was nothing remotely related to the article or contacts with the newspaper; nothing incriminating. She felt a wave of relief and shame at her doubting. She

134

checked his website history but there was no link to *Lara*, just a few about South West Scotland. Wasn't that where he'd practised as a priest: Dumfries or Galloway? He'd also been researching Kulah and bird sanctuaries. Why would he be doing that now?

'Ally Niven, you hot girl,' Lucas crowed, waving a sketch in the air. 'This is you practically naked on a rock, isn't it?'

Ally's face burned. 'Put that down now,' she cried. 'You've absolutely no right.'

'Okay, okay,' he quickly dropped it. 'Have you found anything?'

'No, nothing.'

'Does he use a camera?'

'Yeah, for his work.'

'Might as well check for photos while you're on.'

Ally searched for pictures. She could hear Lucas pulling out a drawer in the large table. She was about to tell him off again when she clicked open a file called Donny.

'Oh my God!' she gasped. 'These are my photos.'

Lucas came over. 'What the hell are they?'

'Drawings that Donny did. I found them in his caravan. They're of Juniper.' Ally felt nauseous as she pointed. 'I think that one's me – the mermaid.'

'One sick guy,' Lucas said, staring in fascination. 'How come the priest's got these on his computer?'

'He must have downloaded them from my camera,' Ally said in shock.

'Cartoon porn,' Lucas said. 'S'pose that's what you do up here when you're sex starved.'

Ally's insides squirmed with disgust to think that John had secretly copied the images for his own titillation. What other reason could there be? Was this what had given him the idea of making a mermaid figurehead? She hugged herself, embarrassed at the memory of posing for him.

'Sick bastard,' Lucas said. 'He's been using you to get his kicks Ally; you do see that don't you? He's obviously well capable of writing a raunchy piece on you too; probably just deleted it.'

Angrily, she deleted the file and closed down the computer. Lucas was already making for the door. Passing the table, something glinting in the overhead light caught Ally's eye. She stopped and picked it up: an elaborate cross in lapis lazuli and silver, on a thick chain. Why was it so familiar?

'Found it in the table drawer,' Lucas explained. 'Beauty, isn't it? Looks Eastern or Orthodox.'

It weighed heavily in her hand. Ally ran a thumb over its ornate curves. On the back were engraved initials, but so worn they were hard to decipher: maybe S.G?

'I've seen it before, but not here,' she puzzled. Then it came to her. Ally scrabbled for her camera and searched for Bethag's photos. 'Here,' she gasped, 'the cross that Flora Gillies is wearing. F.G. – Bethag's mother – does it look like the same cross to you?'

'Could be,' Lucas nodded.

'Bethag must have given it to him, unless ...'

'What?'

'Unless John's always had it.'

Lucas took the cross out of her hands and chucked it back in the drawer. 'Or maybe he just pinched it off the old lady,' he said in disdain. 'Come on Ally, let's get out of here.'

CHAPTER 51

Before he even entered the house, John knew that someone had been there. The way the key was half in view under the stone and the way Magnus screeched from the barn roof, disturbed from his usual perch on the windowsill. His heart quickened. Had Ally come over to see him? Was she waiting inside or even upstairs?

John pushed at the door, but it was locked. Whoever it was had left and locked up again.

Switching on lights to banish the gloom, he saw his sketchbooks scattered across the table and that the painted driftwood left to dry had been moved. Picking up a painted cork, he saw smudge marks from large fingers. The table drawer was pulled out.

'Who the hell's been mucking about?'

Angrily, he strode to the fire and poked it hard, unleashing a flame. He threw on a fresh peat. Three people knew where to look for the key: Bethag, Donny and Ally. He went to the window and gazed out. Perhaps he was imagining it – wishing too hard – but he could almost smell her perfume as if traces of her lingered in the room.

Turning back, he saw the light on the computer winking. It was on standby. He always turned it off completely. It was faintly warm to the touch. Ally had been here – he was sure of it – and she'd been trawling through his computer. Perhaps she'd brought someone with her: bloody Dr Ned or her lover Lucas? He went cold inside. How dare she? What had she been after? He switched on the computer. Did she distrust him so much that she had to snoop through his private files for evidence that he was something to do with the tabloid article? Maybe this Lucas had put her up to it, feeding her paranoia about him. Or more than likely, Ned would be behind it.

Impatiently, John fidgeted. The computer thrummed into life; he checked his files and recent documents. Something made him check his deleted files. There it was in the recycle bin: the file named Donny. Ally's photos of Donny's obscene pictures.

John slumped back in the chair. He closed his eyes, burning with shame. What would she think of him now? All her worst suspicions would be confirmed.

Magnus tapping on the window stirred him. John sprang up. He was not to blame for any of this. Ally must be made to see that. He paced across the room. He would go to her now and confront her; he did not care who else was there. No quack doctor or Australian photographer was going to stop him.

Then he caught sight of Flora's cross, its chain half spilling out of the drawer. He froze. What had they been doing with that? John grabbed it and squeezed so hard it left red marks in his palm. Had she guessed?

John let out a groan. He was gripped by a feeling of dread. No matter how hard he tried to protect Bethag – protect them all – things were spilling out of control. There were forces at work that he could no longer combat; forces taking possession of the island just as the seer had predicted. He had scoffed at it all; now he couldn't deny it any longer. There was evil stalking the island.

John packed up a small bag that night. He wrote a note and shoved it through Sollas village hall letterbox. At six the next morning he was on the drive-on ferry to Barra. By ten, he was crammed into the small plane taking off across the sand and heading for Glasgow.

CHAPTER 52

Kulah

Seanaid is screaming and writhing on the bed. At first I am thankful that she is not dead. Bethag was so distraught, I feared the worst. But she is entering the dangerous straits of childbirth. I fire out instructions to my youngest.

'Get me water from the pail. Mix it in the tin bowl with hot from the kettle. Fetch the pile of newspapers from Seamus's room. Hurry.'

The lumpy mattress is already soaked. Seanaid's waters have broken. She is burning with fear. I stroke the hair from her brow.

'Wheesht now, Mother is here.' I loosen her clothing, roll up my sleeves and wash in the bowl that Bethag brings spilling in her haste.

I have done this for most of the women on Kulah, but my fingers fumble and my voice dries when faced with my own daughter's labour. Seanaid is rigid with terror; she smells my fear.

'I'm going to die! I don't want to die!'

'No, no,' I croak. I try to lift her but the bed is too high and I am too weak. Tears blind me.

All at once, Bethag begins to sing. Her voice rises over our panic like a curlew, high and clear. Seanaid still weeps but my tired spirit rallies.

'Sit up,' I coax, 'it'll be easier. Soon you have to push the baby out.'

I press a damp towel to her brow. The women of Kulah used to bite on a twisted gag to stop their screams, but I tell Seanaid to yell all she wants. We breathe as one, in and out, in and out. I feel the crown of the cuckoo child pressing down on my trembling hand. Nothing can stop this now; not all the wishes or cursing in the world.

'Push, girl, push!' I urge.

Bethag sings louder to drown Seanaid's roaring and my shouting. Our noise fills the damp smoky room. Rollo's baby slithers onto the old newspapers that carry stories of the war. The room is filled with the stench of blood, strong as iron. It is done.

Seanaid pants, 'Let me see, let me see.'

I stare at the bloodied, slimy creature, ugly as a skinned stoat. It makes no sound. I hope it is dead and then I can just wrap it in the soiled newspaper and bury it along with the stories of war and all the pain of the world. Bethag stands at my side, wide-eyed with shock.

'Is it a boy?' Seanaid asks, trying to raise herself to look.

'Best not to know,' I murmur. I stand, counting in my head. How long before I can remove it?

'Mother!' Seanaid wails. 'What's wrong, tell me!'

We can bury it with old Seamus, so that if it has a soul it can travel with him to Limbo or as far as it can go.

Bethag nudges me out of the way and seizes the creature, lifting it up and gathering it in skinny arms. She does not seem to care about the mess on her pinafore or the cloying smell of the womb. She pulls mucus from its face and tugs it clear from its mouth. It gives a tiny cough and splutters into life. The bleating that follows is like the sound of a kid goat from far off.

My youngest lifts the baby into her sister's arms. 'I think it's a girl.'

Seanaid's tear-streaked exhausted face bends close to Bethag's as they gaze at the newborn, exploring its limbs with gentle hands.

'Look Mammy,' Bethag says, rubbing its head, 'she's got your red hair.'

My heart twists tight as a rope, even though it is probably blood that colours the tiny slick of hair. I dare to look closer. It is neither monster nor devil; this thing that has held such fear over me these wretched months. It does not even resemble Rollo. It is a small, wriggling scrap of a baby – my granddaughter.

CHAPTER 53

Battersay

Ally allowed Lucas to help her at the hall on Saturday, knowing they would be busier with two ferries in. She caught snatches of his jokey chat with the customers as he cleared tables and brought in trays of washing-up.

'I've never had so many conversations about the bloody weather,' he laughed, tipping dirty cutlery into the sink with a clatter.

'They'll make a local out of you yet,' Ally snorted.

She had to admit that it helped having him there; he was someone to talk and laugh with while Shona was still giving her the cold shoulder and Calum pretended he was too busy to chat.

Ishbel brought in two residents from the care home, but not Bethag.

'She's taken to her bed,' Ishbel said, 'can't even get her to sit in the conservatory.'

'I'll try and pop round before I go,' Ally promised.

'Go?' Ishbel looked surprised.

'On the trip to Kulah with Ned and Mary. We go Monday, but I'll be back at the hall Friday.'

'Why the heck do you want to go there for?'

Ally just shrugged and smiled. She could not explain that going there might reveal some clue about Juniper that would lead to discovering the girl's past. And it would be fascinating to know more about the strange tragedy of Bethag's family, though she doubted there would be anything to find after all this time.

'Well it would be nice if you visited the old girl,' said Ishbel, 'seeing as Mr Balmain won't be around.'

Ally's stomach fluttered. 'Oh? Why's that?'

'Didn't you know?' Ishbel gave her an odd look. 'Alec-the-Bus said he left on the early ferry.'

'Oh, right.' Ally knew she was blushing.

'Seemed in quite a state.'

'What does that mean?' Ally asked. Was it possible John had seen her and Lucas leaving his house?

Ishbel pulled a face. 'You know our Mr Moody, says the strangest of things. Something about an eagle and the devil. I tell you, we get all the weirdos on Battersay.'

Ally hurried away to the kitchen. She knew then that John had discovered his Donny pictures had been deleted; the spear-throwing man with the eagle stretched across his back, chasing after Juniper. He'd obviously been horrified at being caught out – she could imagine his shame – and so was running away rather than face her. She felt leaden inside. He might stay away till she left. She might never see him again. Her eyes stung with angry tears.

'What's the matter, girl?' Lucas asked.

'Nothing,' she said, swallowing down bitter disappointment. She realised how much she had still hoped she was wrong about John and that he would have come to seek her out and explain it had all been a mistake.

Lucas swung an arm around her shoulders. 'We're going to have a swim after work. Then I'm going to treat you to a meal at the hotel, cheer you up. Deal?'

Ally gave a watery smile. 'Deal.'

CHAPTER 54

At six that evening there were other people still on the beach: a family of campers playing a noisy game of rounders in the mellow light.

'This place is cool when the sun shines,' Lucas grinned.

'Best time of the day,' Ally agreed. He dived underwater and grabbed her by the ankles. She tried to shake him off but he held on and pulled her to him. They thrashed around, Lucas planting a salty kiss on her lips before she wriggled free.

'Unfair,' she said, trying to be cross.

He laughed. 'I've missed doing that.'

She noticed how he still wore the Maori charm she had given him; a symbol of virility. The piece of carved bone glinted on his tanned chest. Ally swum off but he followed alongside.

'Doesn't feel like the same place as that creepy first night,' Lucas said. 'I must've been wrong about those noises. Just the wind or something.'

'That's what I used to think,' Ally said. 'But it was happening too often. And I've definitely seen that woman with the blue shawl over her head. How do you explain that?'

'Ooh, the spooky Flora,' Lucas teased.

'Well no one else can come up with an explanation.'

'Okay, tell me the truth, have you seen or heard anything since I've been here?' Lucas asked.

Ally swam on without answering.

'No, you haven't, have you?' Lucas pressed.

It was true: Ally had had no more disturbing sightings or sounds these past few days. Even on their way back from John's yesterday, going via the Standing Stone to avoid the road, she had experienced none of the powerful feelings of before. She relaxed, treading water. It hadn't struck her, but Lucas was right.

'You know what I think?' Lucas said, floating on his back. 'It's all been the strain of Donny's suicide and living in that dump. It's got to you, girl.'

'You think I'm going bonkers? Thanks a bunch.'

'Not bonkers, just really upset. Hey, I don't blame you. I'd be the same if someone had been dumping rotten fish and seals on my doorstep. Gross.' He drifted closer. 'And seeing that pervy priest can't have helped.'

'Leave John out of this,' Ally snapped.

'Okay, sorry, but Ned tells me Balmain was the one who got you all up tight about this prophecy and Kulah stuff in the first place.'

'Maybe,' Ally admitted.

She didn't know what to think anymore. Gazing out over the tranquil sea and listening to the laughter and shrieks of the rounders players, she found it hard to imagine how fearful she had been. The pranks had stopped since she'd left to stay at Sollas House; whoever it was must have got bored and given up. *Or gone away.* No, she simply would not accept that John could have been behind any of it.

'And didn't he pester you right from the start, on the ferry?' Lucas said. 'Ishbel told me he was winding you up about Birdwoman even then.'

'Just drop it, okay?' Ally struck back for the shore, wondering how many other people Lucas had been chatting to about her. She didn't want to think that John could have had an unhealthy interest in her all this time. She knew him better than they did; and he wasn't like that. *You don't know me.* He'd said those words to her once. *The more you know about me the less you'll like me. I'm not a very nice person.* Ally plunged her head underwater to drown out her mounting doubts.

Towelling down and dressing on the shore, she said, 'I want to go over to Juniper's with some leftovers. You go on ahead and tell Mary we won't be in for supper.'

'Let me come with you,' Lucas said, 'I don't like to leave you on your own.'

'I'm fine. And I don't want you scaring her.'

'I won't go near, I promise. I can just stay outside and wait.'

Ally was unsure. Lucas, towel around his neck, raised his hands.

'Look, no camera; I won't be a threat to her in any way. Just want to be with you, girl.'

Ally relented, though she wasn't going to tell him that she quite liked the idea of him tagging along. She'd forgotten how happy-go-lucky and uncomplicated Lucas was; so much easier to cope with than her intense encounters with John.

Juniper's cottage was bathed in evening light. The only sounds were the soft chomping of nearby sheep and the sweet call of a skylark, invisible in the sky above.

'Stay back here,' Ally ordered, thrusting her wet swimming things at Lucas, and heading off down the slope.

Juniper came out to meet her, the pet stoat scurrying at her heels.

'Cheese scones today, Juniper,' Ally said.

The girl bounded forward and flung arms around her, almost crushing the breath from her lungs. She had no idea of her own strength, but Ally put up with the bruises in return for seeing Juniper's trust and social skills grow. Not even Mary had managed to get as physically close as she had. It was a positive sign that maybe one day Juniper would be able to build normal relationships.

They went into the hut and sat on stools. Ally tried to explain about the boat trip.

'We'll be gone a few days but I'll leave plenty of food on Sunday before I go.'

Juniper slopped nettle tea into bowls, frowning in concentration.

'I know you can look after yourself anyway, but you've got used to me coming, haven't you?'

Juniper began a low humming, like bees droning. It was a sign of happiness or contentment, Ally was sure.

144

'And you must be used to Ned and Mary going away sailing at this time of year, so I'm sure you'll be okay.'

The girl squatted beside Ally and slurped her brew.

'God, Juniper, your tea doesn't get any better,' Ally winced. 'Where's the proper stuff I brought you? Real tea.'

The girl watched her, and then pointed to the windowsill behind. Arranged on the deep ledge was a pyramid of teabags with a large clam shell on top. Small balls of tin foil left from Ally's food parcels were scattered around the pile and her Indian scarf hung from a nail like an attempt at a curtain. Ally's heart squeezed.

'Wow, Juniper, that's cool,' she smiled. 'It's a shrine to tea. Maybe on special occasions we can drink some.'

Birdwoman's humming grew louder. She darted over to the window, plucked a bag from the display and dropped it into Ally's bowl, stirring it with a grimy finger.

'Thanks,' Ally laughed. 'Served with style.'

Abruptly, Juniper went silent and cocked her head.

'What is it?'

The girl made a low growling noise. Ally got up and peered out of the window.

'I think I might know. You're not to worry but I've got a friend waiting for me outside on the hill. He won't harm you, or come any nearer, okay?'

The noise in Juniper's throat grew louder. Ally made for the door.

'I'll come again tomorrow.'

Juniper followed her out. Ally saw Lucas stand up at her reappearance and wave. Ally waved back.

'See, he's dead friendly; nothing to be frightened of. Do you want to meet him?'

Ally turned to see Juniper disappearing into the gorse, the stoat leaping after her leathery heels. Reaching Lucas, she said, 'Well I told you she was camera-shy. She wasn't in the mood to meet you.'

Lucas was staring into the distance. 'Where the hell did she go?'

'She's got a secret path down to the cliffs. See those seagulls gathering over there? She'll be underneath; it's the only way you can tell where she is.'

Lucas whistled. 'Wild. Like something out of a vampire movie.'

Ally felt irritated. 'Don't say that. She's showing real signs of understanding me.' She told him about the teabags.

'Still sounds wacky,' Lucas grinned. 'Come on, I'm starving. I've booked our meal for eight.'

With a last glance back, Ally thought she saw a distant figure on the cliff edge. But the harder she looked, the more she thought it a stunted tree and not a woman at all. She shivered. Was it possible that her sightings of the mysterious head-scarfed woman had simply been tricks of the light or of her own overwrought imagination just as Lucas believed?

Maybe she had wanted to believe in the ghost of Flora Gillies too much, drawn in by Bethag's mistaking her for Seanaid.

'What's wrong?' Lucas asked, taking her hand.

'Nothing,' Ally said, turning her back on the ancient cottage, 'nothing at all.' She felt a stirring of relief. With Lucas here, things didn't seem so sinister and difficult to explain. She let him hold onto her hand.

CHAPTER 55

Kulah

I call her The Baby. Seanaid calls her Rosamund after some girl in a book and Bethag added Marie because she said her niece needed a Kulah name and a Catholic name to carry through life. My daughters baptised her in the burn that runs in front of the house while I made oatcakes.

I did not expect to find room in my heart for her, but when I showed Seanaid how to suckle her at the breast, I felt a tug at my own as if I had milk coming in too. She is small but sturdy and asks little of us, and I fall asleep to the sound of her snuffling in the box bed with Seanaid and Bethag while I lie close to the fire in the truckle. The March air is raw and I cannot get warm even though I go to sleep in old Seamus's oily jumper and my tweed coat and bound in a plaid.

There is no use fretting about what to do next; fate will have a path for us and we will face it when it comes knocking. But what the world does not know is that we are knitted together – we Gillies women – and will not be torn apart by the hot tongues of gossip or the censure of men. They think we hide at Ostaig in shame and trembling, but we are as one. We do not need them. What we have here is enough. We are bound together by The Baby, swaddled in love for her.

No longer am I interested in walking the cliffs. I prefer to sit in the house, wearing Seamus's peaty jumper, and to stir the porridge. It is hard to think of a time when I did anything else. That woman who strode about the village as busy and commanding as a general is a stranger now; her energy has drained into the earth.

147

CHAPTER 56

Battersay

Ally was glad there were others in the hotel bar eating. Morag and Alec-the-Bus were having a birthday celebration with friends and there were a dozen tourists.

'How much longer are you going to stick it out here?' Lucas asked, pushing away his empty plate. He wasn't drinking as Ned had lent him the ancient Citroen.

Ally toyed with her wine glass. 'Late September I suppose – when the summer trade dies off.'

'Will you go back to *Lara*?'

'Yes, why shouldn't I?'

Lucas shrugged. 'Thought maybe part of the reason you left London was that you were sick of the job and not just me.' His look was sheepish. 'Least that's what I hoped.'

'I love the job.' She eyed him. 'It's you I couldn't handle.'

He leaned towards her and took her hand. 'You know how sorry I am about that. What can I do to make it up to you?'

Ally pulled back her hand. 'You can pay for this lovely meal,' she smiled.

It was late when they got back to Sollas House but Mary was still up knitting by candlelight.

'I'll make a night drink,' she said at once. 'Come and sit by the fire.' Ally thought her distracted; she didn't ask them about the meal.

Lucas asked. 'Okay if we open Ned's whisky? I've stayed off the booze all evening.'

Mary didn't seem to hear, so Lucas just helped himself, pouring two large glasses, topped up with water and gave one to Ally. She sat by the fire, the flickering light and peaty whisky making her feel drowsy. Lucas sat on the floor at her feet. Finally Mary handed them hot drinks smelling of honey.

'Hope this is better than the nettle tea Juniper gave Ally,' Lucas grunted.

Mary looked troubled. 'It's Celtic mead.'

'He's just teasing,' Ally assured.

'It's herbal and very calming, just the thing for a restful sleep,' Mary said.

'It's delicious, isn't it, Lucas?' Ally nudged him.

'Dynamite. These Celts knew how to party.'

Mary didn't take up her knitting, but moved about in the shadows straightening jars and opening and closing tins. Lucas tried to make her laugh with exaggerated tales of travelling round Eastern Europe, but Mary wouldn't settle.

'Is everything okay?' Ally asked.

Mary flinched as the back door banged open. Ned appeared.

148

'I was worried,' Mary said, going to him.

'No need. Missing a party I see.'

'We thought you'd gone to bed,' Ally said in surprise.

'Been for a walk to check on the boat.'

'He never sleeps well before a sailing trip,' Mary explained, her face tense.

'Ned, you should have one of these,' Lucas said, holding up his half-drunk mead. 'It's a knockout.'

'Prefer a dram,' Ned answered, pouring himself a whisky. He topped up Lucas's glass too, but Ally refused. Her head was already woolly.

'Darling, why don't you go to bed?' Ned said to his wife. 'Everything's absolutely fine.'

Mary put a hand to Ned's face. 'Are you sure?'

Ned kissed her palm and smiled. 'Of course, I'm sure. Stop being such a worry-head.'

Before she went, Mary emptied the jug of mead into Lucas and Ally's mugs. 'It's best drunk warm. Sweet dreams, my dear ones.'

On impulse, Ally leaned up and kissed Mary's cheek. 'You're so like my Mum,' she said, suddenly tearful.

Mary's chin trembled. 'I'm touched,' she whispered. 'I wish I'd had a daughter like you.'

No one spoke as she left. Ally blinked back tears, glad of the dim light. She was choked with sudden emotion. They sat on in silence, drinking. Ally felt strangely light-headed and yet hyper-sensitive to everything around: the gulping in Lucas's throat, the kitchen clock knocking like a heartbeat, candle wax running onto the table like hot tears. The shadows in the corners seemed to hold their breath.

In some deep part of her mind she could see as clear as a picture, John on a ferry, standing at the rail and staring at Battersay until it was just a speck on the horizon, and then gone.

Ned broke the spell of her dream-like state. 'It's not me who has trouble sleeping before a sailing trip,' he said quietly, 'it's Mary. She gets very wound up and anxious.'

'Jeez, I don't blame her,' Lucas said, 'you're brave to carry on sailing at all.'

'Or foolish,' Ned said. 'Is that what you're really thinking?'

'No, course not.'

'It's Mary who insists we go.' Ned sighed. 'Sometimes I wonder –'

'Wonder what mate?'

'If we should stop. Call it a day. Go and live in the Pennines or somewhere far from the sea.'

Ally was befuddled. She wanted to join in the conversation but her tongue weighed like a stone. Her words came out slow and slurred.

'Not mean zat.'

The men looked at her puzzled.

'Joo-nee ...' She wanted to ask what would happen to Juniper if they left but couldn't pronounce her name.

Ned and Lucas carried on speaking in low voices like conspirators. Their voices buzzed in her ears. What language were they speaking? Ally leaned forward; her balance went and she felt a rush of nausea like seasickness. She grabbed the chair arm to stop herself falling.

To her alarm, the fire began to hiss and flames of blue and green leapt up from its red-hot core. All at once, a giant black beetle scuttled out of the fire and raced towards her. Ally screamed and threw her mug. It landed on the massive creature with a sickening crack and squelch.

'Ally, what the hell –?' Lucas cried, as hot mead splashed his hand.

Ally sat rigid and sweating, unable to utter a word. All she could do was point at the crushed beetle. Its innards were oozing like ink out of its shattered shell yet it was reforming and growing in size.

Ned rushed forward and grabbed the mug. 'It's okay, it's not broken. Spills don't matter. You alright Lucas? Let me look at that hand.'

'I'm fine.'

'Run it under the cold tap, go on.'

Lucas staggered to his feet and lurched across to the sink. The whole room was rolling and dipping like a ship. Ally screwed her eyes shut but the sickening motion didn't stop. She heard water thunder from the tap, like the crashing of waves. Donny's body bobbed in front of her, black as a bloated beetle. With a gasp of horror she opened her eyes. Ned's face loomed towards her, his voice surging and receding.

'... too much to drink ... steady on ... nothing there ... Mary's mead ... lie down?'

He tried to pull her up but she resisted with all her might. He wouldn't make her stand on the carpet where Donny's body lay. She shook with terror, trying to find her voice. *Help me!* The words rang in her head but nothing came out.

CHAPTER 57

Glasgow

'Just drop me here,' John told the taxi driver. It was a street away from his destination, but he wanted time to get his hammering pulse under control. Turning into St Mungo's Place, it was as if he had never been away. Sycamores and beeches still hid the fronts of Edwardian villas and the pavements bucked and cracked over their giant roots.

He felt in his pocket for Flora's heavy cross and ran his thumb over it for courage. *Give me strength and wisdom to face her.* John did not know if he prayed to God or Flora or both, but he knew he needed all his self-control today. He had stayed too angry for too long with his unloving mother. She had reasons for being as she was, he realised that now, so he must not judge her. Marion should be pitied not hated. It was time they had a heart to heart – he would take anything she flung at him – as long as they cleared the air about the past and stopped blaming each other for things beyond their control. *I want to us to love each other, what is so difficult in that? We're mother and son. Surely the strongest of bonds?*

John braced himself to pass the stone pillars and walk down the short drive to his parents' house. His courage drained away. It was madness to think he could mend the rift with his mother after all this time. With any luck she would be out playing bridge and he wouldn't have to confront her. He just needed half an hour to go through his father's files and find what he was looking for. He'd discovered nothing on the Net but he was sure he'd remembered correctly: photos from a Highland Games when he'd been a young priest. As his boots crunched on the gravel, further doubts plagued him: his father might have cleared out the old newspaper cuttings – it was so long ago – or more likely his mother would have done it in one of her unsentimental spring-cleans and made a bonfire of them.

He stood on the shallow stone steps, gazing up at the solid house with its severe black door and plain sash windows, unadorned with any ivy like others in the street. The paintwork needed re-doing, he noticed with surprise. John hesitated. Should he ring the bell like a visitor or use his key and go straight in? It no longer felt like home and he didn't want to startle anyone.

Oh my God, John, just do it! It was Ally's voice in his head; she would have leapt forward and leant on the bell till someone answered.

He rang the bell twice. No one came. He was just putting his key in the lock, relieved the house was empty, when the door opened.

A small, stooped man in a baggy cardigan and brown twill trousers peered up at him. It took a couple of seconds for John to recognise the thin-faced, bespectacled man as his father. He'd shrunk and his grey hair had thinned to a few strands plastered across the top of his head.

'John?' he gasped.

'Yes Dad, hello,' he smiled, 'sorry to just turn up.' He moved to hug the old man, but Duncan Balmain stuck out a hand. They shook hands self-consciously, his father hanging onto John's with both of his.

'John, John, it's good to see you. Are you well? What brings you to Glasgow? Your mother's not here.'

Relief and regret battled inwardly. 'Dad, let's go inside.'

'Of course. Come away.' Duncan stood aside.

John was assailed by the familiar cloying smell of polish and carpet freshener. He sneezed.

'Coffee?' Duncan asked, leading the way to the kitchen. 'Your mother won't be long. What a surprise for her.'

John's heart twisted at the choice of words; there was no pretence she would be pleased to see him.

'I can't stay long. I'm heading down to Dumfries.' He came straight to the point. 'I wanted to take a quick look at your newspaper archive.'

His father turned and gave him a pained look. 'After six years I think you can spare the time to have a cup of coffee with your old dad,' he chided.

'Sorry, of course,' John said, 'I'd like that very much.'

At the side counter John straddled a high stool of chrome and mock red leather, remembering how his mother had stripped out the old 1960s kitchen and replaced it with a mock retro version. His father, twelve years her senior and decades behind her in taste, had stood by and watched in quiet bafflement.

'How is it going, John? Are you making any money as an artist?'

'Not much,' he admitted, 'but my needs are few.'

'Always the aesthete,' his father winked.

'I will pay you back one day.'

Duncan held up his hand. 'I won't hear of it. That money would be coming to you anyway. Just see it as a payment on deposit.'

'That's not the point Dad –'

'Come, let's sit in the study. These days I can't climb up those pylons your mother calls chairs.'

His father's den was still as scruffy and utilitarian as John remembered: a large desk and captain's chair in the window, three metal filing cabinets lined up against the opposite wall and two Parker Knoll chairs either side of a gas fire that was too small for the high-ceilinged room. There was a chill to the north-facing room despite the day being sunny and warm.

Duncan questioned him about life on Battersay, expressing sorrow for Donny's suicide. 'A terrible thing to happen.' He shook his head and sucked in his breath. 'But old Bethag, still as spry as ever?'

''Fraid not,' John sighed. 'Her dementia is getting worse and she's stopped going out. I still visit the care home and read to her. She really appreciated the book you sent her on folk tales, by the way.'

Duncan nodded. 'She was always spinning you yarns about the islands, so I thought it was just up her street.'

'It was a kind thing to do. Bet you did it without Mum knowing.'

'No point upsetting her,' his father said, 'their interests were always different. Your mother thought all those stories a bit – what shall we say? – pagan.'

'Ironic don't you think?' John grunted. 'Given the circumstances.'

'Circumstances?'

'Yes, the thing that brought them together in the first place, the fact that –' John stopped. His father was looking perplexed. Surely it wasn't possible that he didn't know? Or was he just surprised that his son did? While he grappled for the right words, his father changed tack.

'And tell me John,' Duncan smiled, 'have you been seeing any more of the young lassie you mentioned in your last letter? The one who was taking an interest in your sculpture. She sounded just right for you.'

John squirmed. Why on earth had he mentioned Ally to his father? He had been too easily flattered by her interest in his work. No one since Caroline had believed in him as an artist.

'We're not that friendly,' John said, 'and she's already in a relationship.'

'That's a pity,' Duncan said gently.

John gulped down his coffee. Their conversation about Battersay exhausted, his father began chatting about the daily routines of his life in retirement and his articles on early Scottish saints for various magazines.

'You'll have to wait for any news on the neighbours till your mother returns, I can never remember who is doing what.'

'Dad,' John said, growing anxious about his mother's impending appearance, 'do you still have those newspapers from when I was in Dumfries?'

Duncan frowned and hauled himself out of his chair.

'Don't get up,' John said, 'just tell me where.'

'No, no, I'm not that ancient. I'm pretty sure I can lay my hands on them. Your first parish?'

'Yes, in the early '90s.' John followed to the filing cabinets, watching impatiently as his father pulled out a drawer and slowly leafed through the dozens of buff files in each blue pocket.

'Maybe they're in the next one,' Duncan muttered, replacing the files and moving onto the drawer below.

Finally, at the bottom of the second cabinet, John's father cried, 'Ah-ha, here we are. I knew I hadn't thrown any of them out. We were awfully proud ...' His words trailed off. He looked warily over his spectacles. 'Not that I'm not still proud.'

'It's okay Dad,' John smiled, 'thanks for these. Can I spread them out on your desk?'

Duncan waved a hand. 'Go on, be my guest.'

Scouring the newspapers and parish magazines, John was transported back to his first enthusiastic days as a priest, full of energy and optimism. He stared at a black and white photo of himself, tall and fresh-faced in long black robe in front of a red-brick church, and another of him grinning in shorts and T-shirt among a clutch of children in football strips. He turned the musty pages of newsprint.

'Don't think that local paper exists anymore,' Duncan said, hovering at his elbow.

'You've probably got some antiques on your hands Dad,' John said dryly.

'What are you looking for son?'

'I'm not sure,' John said cautiously, 'it's just a hunch.'

He scanned each page, running his fingers over headlines and peering at photos for clues. But there was no sign. Perhaps he'd imagined it or remembered wrongly? John sat back in frustration. He was more disappointed than he'd thought possible. What a waste of time; he should have stayed on the island where he could have been of more use. The note he had left for Ally at the hall would make his behaviour seem even more bizarre and unstable than ever. God, what a mess.

John began to gather together the scattered newspapers.

'I'm wrong about it all,' he said, 'and I suppose that's a relief.'

'Are you going to tell me what this is all about?' Duncan asked.

John let out a long sigh. 'The woman you asked about – Ally Niven.'

'Aye, what about her?'

John's words died on his tongue. The front door opened and slammed shut, followed by a sharp tap of heels on the hall tiles. His insides knotted.

'Duncan! You left the inner hall door open again. Leaves all over the vestibule.'

Father and son exchanged looks. 'That's your mother home,' Duncan said.

John stood up, his hands clenching and heart racing. Just the sound of her footsteps plunged him back to boyhood and his anxiety to please, his steeling himself for a scolding.

'We're in here, Marion darling,' Duncan called out, crossing swiftly to the door.

It opened from the other side before he could get there. 'Goodness me, I wish you wouldn't bring guests into the study when we've got a perfectly good sitting-room, dear.' Marion's laugh was false. 'What will they think of us?'

'Darling, look who's here?'

John heard the tension in his father's voice.

He stepped towards her. 'Hello Mum.'

She visibly recoiled.

'Isn't this a lovely surprise,' Duncan said almost pleadingly. 'John says he hasn't got long. But I'm sure we can persuade him to stay.'

'So,' Marion found her voice, 'the prodigal returns, does he?'

'No,' John answered, 'he's just on a flying visit.'

The hard blue-eyed stare she gave him made his spirits shrivel.

'Well don't expect the fatted calf,' she said with that laugh that always set his teeth on edge.

154

CHAPTER 58

Kulah

Today I can hear the rain; it patters on the stone outside the door and spits down the chimney into the fire. My daughters are playing with The Baby, kissing her fingers and singing songs. Bethag is like a second mother; less babyish now. She has stopped calling me Mammy.

We don't hear the footsteps approaching – the breeze must be in the wrong direction – so we don't understand the sharp rapping on the door. We stare at each other. Bethag's mouth falls open.

'Keep still,' I hiss.

The holding of breath might keep them at bay. But the knocking comes again and the door begins to open at the same time, slowly as if the caller does not really want to come in. In that long small moment – as light is easing around the door and a man's foot appears – I act.

I leap from the cooking stool towards Seanaid and snatch The Baby from her arms like an eagle lifting a lamb. I am so quick that surprise does not have time to settle on my firstborn's face. Turning with Baby in my arms, I see Sam stepping into the room with rain dripping from his bonnet and his too-short jacket.

He stares at us, his face lifting in a puzzled smile. 'You've got a baby.'

'Hello Sam,' I say, 'what brings you here?'

'Where did the baby come from?'

'Sit down laddie. Will you take a cup of water? It's a long climb up from the village. Do you have some news for us?'

The Baby grizzles in protest at my too firm grip. My daughters are mute.

'Bethag, pour Sam a drink.'

Sam takes off his wet bonnet and moves to the fire, taking the cup of water and draining it off noisily. I jiggle my granddaughter as we all wait for Sam's answer. He gawks at us as if he might have stepped into the wrong house, still puzzled by what he sees.

Abruptly, the reason for his journey comes back to him.

'The ship,' he grins. 'They're coming.'

'The men?' Bethag gasps.

'Aye. Iain Mhor has seen it through the binoculars. They're gathering at the pier. Christina said I wasn't to bother coming up here 'cos they didn't want you standing with them. "Crocodile tears and smiles", that's what she said.'

'She's a poisonous bitch,' Seanaid said hotly.

'They can't stop us,' said Bethag, 'can they Mother?'

'Not if we want to go.'

I look into the faces of my daughters and see confusion. Our secret world with The Baby has just ended and a new uncertain one is about to begin. Once Sam steps outside this house and runs to the village carrying his news of a baby like a hot coal, everything will change. I see it

155

unravelling like a frayed rope: the hostile village, the salt-encrusted men, the beatings.

'I'm coming with you Sam,' I tell him. 'And I'm bringing my baby.'

'"Bringing my baby",' he repeats as if the words don't make sense.

'Yes. You can call her Marie.'

'No Mother,' Seanaid springs up, 'I won't let you –'

I face her. 'You will. The baby is mine. Your time on Kulah is coming to an end. When the ships begin to return you'll be free to go.'

I see the struggle on her face: the deep yearning to escape and the physical pull towards me and The Baby. I don't give her breathing space to think, picking up the patchwork blanket and wrapping it around her child.

'Come Sam.' I chivvy him towards the door.

'Shall I tell old Seamus about the ship and the men?' he asks.

'He already knows,' I answer.

Sam nods, not finding this strange. My daughters follow me wordlessly into the rain as if under a spell. Outside the breeze jostles us as we pick our way through boggy puddles to the path. The burn is rising and chuckling, sweeping towards the cliff. Out to sea, silver waves dance and rush for the shore.

I cannot see the ship, but I can feel it coming.

CHAPTER 59

Glasgow

It was Duncan who persuaded John to stay the night.

'You said yourself there was no reason now to rush off to Dumfries, so why not stay? You can't get back to Battersay until tomorrow.'

Conversation had been strained until his mother went out to a parish fundraiser, leaving them to fix supper for themselves. John made a risotto of ham, peppers and tinned asparagus.

'Let's take it in the study,' Duncan said. 'Have a look in the pantry for a bottle of wine while I get the fire on.'

They ate from trays on their knees and talked about St Ninian and early Celtic missionaries.

'There's a dig going on in Galloway that I'd love to go and see,' said Duncan. 'Discovering old hermits' cells by the sounds of it.'

'Why don't we go together?' John said on the spur of the moment. 'I've got nothing to rush back for.'

His father's face lit up. 'Would you really? That would be splendid.'

'As long as Mum will give you a pass out,' John said dryly.

'She'll be happy to have me out from under her feet.'

They fell into companionable silence. Then John asked, 'how did you and Mum meet? You've never told me the details.'

Duncan twisted his small crystal wine glass between thin fingers. 'At a whist drive in the church hall. She was so lively and pretty; I couldn't help but notice her.'

'And she you?' John smiled.

Duncan gave a short laugh. 'No, I wasn't really her type; too shy and bookish. It was a while before I figured on her radar.'

'So if you went to the same church you must've known her family well?'

His father frowned in thought. 'Not really. I think they moved into the parish when the new estate was built – we got a big influx then.'

John's interest quickened. 'What sort of people were they, Mum's people?'

Duncan shrugged. 'Fairly ordinary, decent sorts. Father was a low-grade civil servant and mother a housewife. Your mother didn't really get along with them. We didn't see much of them after we married and moved the other side of Glasgow.'

'Dad,' John hesitated, 'where does she keep her birth certificate?

Duncan gave him a startled look. 'Your mother?'

'Yes. Could I have a look at it while she's out?'

'Why would you want to do that?'

'I'm interested in my family history, that's all.'

His father looked nervous. 'Her personal things are in the bedroom. But I wouldn't like to open things without asking her first.'

157

'Come on,' John said, dumping his tray on the floor, 'we can do it before she gets back.'

As Duncan led a reluctant way upstairs, he turned to John. 'Is this something to do with – with – Caroline?'

John's heart thumped. 'No, why should it be?'

'I thought perhaps you're still angry with your mother for the way she behaved. It was unforgiveable of her making you break it off like that, threatening she'd harm herself.'

'Kill herself,' John corrected.

'Yes, well, your mother wasn't thinking rationally. She knows that now. The last thing she wanted was for Caroline to ...'

John ground his teeth. 'Please Dad; I don't want to talk about it.' He carried on mounting the stairs.

His parents' bedroom was unchanged; the built-in cream cupboards and matching dressing-table with brass handles and the same sheepskin mats hiding the worn purple carpet by the twin beds. Pink bedspreads matched the candy-striped wallpaper and velvet curtains. It reeked of his mother's flowery perfume. A cross between a little girl's bedroom and a bordello; John felt guilty at the unkind thought.

Duncan was already pulling out a cardboard box from the bottom of the wardrobe. 'It'll be in here somewhere.'

John went eagerly through the pile of papers his father passed to him: school certificates, shorthand and typing qualifications, mementos from her First Communion, birthday cards. There were childish drawings which John did not remember doing, but his heart leapt to think she might have kept some of his. Finally he found it: a thin official document in a faded brown envelope. The names were written in neat, looping black ink. His breath stopped in his throat.

Marie Susan McBride. Not Marion but Marie.

Abruptly, the light snapped on. 'What's going on in here?'

CHAPTER 60

Kulah

The weather gets worse by the minute. Halfway down to the village, the wind changes direction and strengthens. It swings around and slaps us full in the face, so that we must hunch over and push against it to make ourselves go forward. My arms ache with gripping The Baby. My daughters hold onto each other to stop themselves slipping on the loose wet stones. One of them holds the back of my blue plaid. Sam has rushed ahead, whooping into the gale.

By the time we come over the final ridge, the village is hard to see, the smoke from the houses melting into grey mist. Curtains of rain whip across one after the other to reveal the harbour and the Black Rock, and then close them off again.

'I can't see anything,' Bethag calls out. 'Is the boat in?'

Picking my way carefully, anxious not to drop The Baby, I press on. If it is in, then we shall not shy away from the greeting of the men.

We pass our home. It looks out to sea with dead eyes; no light burns in the window or fire warms its stone. The street is deserted, save for a goat huddling in a doorway. A line of gulls hang over the cliff like bunting, flapping hard to stay there.

'There they are, down on the quay,' Seanaid shouts. Her sharp eyes can see what mine cannot; the villagers herded onto the rocky shelf around the harbour.

'Is the boat in?' I echo Bethag.

'No. I can't see it. Someone's on the far side looking out. Maybe Iain Mhor with the binoculars.'

We reach the steep steps, soaked through. The Baby's crying is muffled by the thick blanket and I feel a stab of guilt for bringing her out in such weather. Yet I cannot let her go; I have started on a path that has no way back.

As I stumble towards the women, they press back, shawls pulled up and shrouding their disapproval.

Sam waves and calls out, 'She's got a baby. She's called Marie.'

I see the shock in their eyes, heads turning as the news ripples through the throng.

'The disgrace,' Christina cries, yanking Sam by the arm. 'Don't speak to her.'

He laughs. 'Poisonous bitch!'

Suddenly, Bethag notices Iain Mhor doing a wild dance on the opposite cliff. Christina's twins are there too.

'Look, he can see them!'

The old man is flapping his arms like a madman. He takes off his cap and flings it away, his white hair lifting like spume. He gesticulates at one of Christina's twins; points him back towards the pier.

'Happy as a lark,' someone laughs.

159

'No,' Seanaid says, 'something's wrong.'

CHAPTER 61

Glasgow

John's mother must have come in the back way or they would have heard the front door. She marched into the room, her bafflement turning to indignation.

'Are those my letters you've got there?'

His father struggled up from kneeling down. 'We're not reading your letters, dear.'

'How dare you? Put them back at once.'

'Yes, of course.' Duncan began a hasty gathering of scattered papers.

'Don't give him a hard time,' John said, 'it was all my idea.'

She gave him a furious look. 'Prying into my most personal things – what gives you the right?'

He steeled himself. 'I was looking for this. Your birth certificate.'

'What on earth for?'

'I think you know why.' John stood up. He towered over her. For a moment, a look of alarm flickered across her face, then was gone.

'I've absolutely no idea. You're both behaving bizarrely as usual.'

'The lies and cover up have gone on long enough, Mum. I want things out in the open once and for all.'

'Duncan,' Marion snapped, 'have you been telling tales? 'Cos if you have, I'll never forgive you.'

'Dearest, I –'

'Dad's said nothing; it's Bethag who's told me the truth.'

'Bethag? That daft old nurse?'

John pulled the silver and blue cross from his pocket and held it up. It glinted in the electric light. 'Recognise this?'

'Of course. It's the cross I gave you when you entered the priesthood. The one day I actually felt proud of you.'

John flinched but went on. 'I know where it came from. You had it from when you were a baby.'

'So what if I did?'

'Bethag recognised it – when you came to see me in the hospital after my accident, remember?'

'Of course I remember,' Marion said, 'that woman was fussing over you as if you were her own child.'

'Because she felt responsible for me. Once she saw Flora's cross on you she knew she was dealing with family.' John stepped forward eagerly. 'Her mother's cross *on you*. You were the baby she had been searching for – the baby she had promised to look after – *Marie*. But you know all that, don't you? That's why you were kind to Bethag all those years. You knew she was your aunt.'

His mother looked aghast. John pressed on, knowing he must speak now of what tormented him most, or the bitterness would never leave him.

161

'I know now why you were so hard on me growing up, but there was no need to feel such guilt.'

'No,' Marion clutched her throat, struggling to compose herself, 'please don't say it.'

'It needs saying, Mum. I know you were illegitimate. Bethag told me. And I know it was a big deal a generation ago, especially for us Catholics.' He looked at her with compassion. 'You never shook off that shame, did you? You took it out on me because you felt that any child of yours would be unworthy too. But it doesn't work like that.'

His father spoke up. 'Marion, I don't understand.'

In a strained voice she said. 'Let him finish.'

'That's what you told Caroline, wasn't it?' John challenged. 'That I wasn't good enough to be a husband and father. I'd be passing on bad seed. She told me you'd used that very expression. You did, didn't you?'

'Yes I did,' she whispered, her eyes glinting with emotion.

John felt his anger stir, despite his attempts to control it. He remembered the final bitter row with Caroline and her dismissive words: *Your family's really screwed up – I can't cope with it.*

'You turned her against me,' John accused. 'You didn't have to make threats about killing yourself to stop me running off with her. She'd already called it off. Caroline pretended not to care about the things you said, called it superstitious claptrap. But it changed things between us; the way she looked at me. She thought you were mad. Like mother like son. That's what we argued about.'

Suddenly Marion struck, slapping him hard on the jaw. John reeled back in shock, his hand going to his stinging cheek.

'Don't you blame me for her accident, you pathetic boy,' she blazed. 'You were the one who let her drive off in a temper.' Her look was hard and furious. 'The saints were looking out for her that day, taking her into their heavenly arms. They weren't going to let her make the mistake of marrying my *bad seed.*'

Duncan came between them. 'Please stop it. Don't say any more. You'll regret it.'

Marion shoved him away. 'Oh, no I won't. I've kept it bottled up for too long.' She rounded on John. 'You think I was mad with guilt at being illegitimate, do you? That I said to Caroline that you and I were both tainted goods? Well I did no such thing – I told her the God's honest truth.' She spat out her words. 'It's not me whose a bastard, it's you John, you!'

He stared at her, winded. She came at him, stabbing his chest with a blood-red fingernail. 'You ruined my life. I had everything in front of me – career, romance, travel. It made me sick when Caroline said you were going off to live in America. I was the one who should have gone to America – I had a job lined up as a secretary – but what happened? I got pregnant with you.'

John looked at his father pleadingly. 'Dad, is it true?'

'Oh, don't ask him,' Marion shouted, 'he wasn't the father – he just married me out of pity. Your real father was a no-good bastard at the factory.'

Duncan cried out, 'please don't say it, dearest.'

Her laugh was savage. 'Say what? Rape? Am I not allowed to speak the truth in my own house to my own dear son?' She swung back to John. 'You want the truth, don't you? Your evil father forced himself on me after a work's dance, in a back lane. I didn't scream so he told everyone I'd begged him for it. And do you know what? You look just like him. Even as a little boy I could see the man you were growing into; his height, his black hair and eyes, his huge hands.' She shuddered. 'Every time I looked at you I felt sick with disgust. That's why I wanted you to go into the church, so you wouldn't ruin some other woman's life,' she cried, 'like he did mine!'

John felt like vomiting; he broke out in a sweat. His mother's face was a livid red and her hate so palpable it seemed to suck air from the room. Duncan tried again to intervene but John warded him off. 'I need to know,' he rasped, 'is that what you told Caroline? That I was capable of being a rapist?'

'Yes,' Marion screamed, '*yes.*'

Stunned and beyond speech, John gaped. She was deranged. His mind reeled with what she had just told him. It was too awful to contemplate. All he could do was grasp onto the belief that she was still a Gillies, like a talisman that would protect him.

'But – but your name was Marie.'

'So are thousands of other girls. I hated it, changed it to Marion when I left home. Marie was the innocent girl that man destroyed.'

John realised he was still clutching Flora's cross.

'And this?' he forced himself to ask. 'Bethag knows this is Flora's cross and it was given to Seanaid's baby Marie. So how did you have it?'

'I'm nothing to do with that pagan nurse,' Marion was dismissive. 'That cross was given to me by my godmother. And no, she wasn't one of your precious Gillies women. She was Sarah Potts, a housekeeper in Edinburgh. I've no idea how she came by it – probably picked it up in a pawnshop. One of those Kulah heathens must've sold it. They're little better than tinkers.'

John balled his fists. 'They're as Catholic as you Mother,' he said through gritted teeth, 'and with ten times the compassion.'

'Then go back to your island tinkers,' Marion hissed, 'and get out of my bedroom.'

John pushed past her, flinging away the birth certificate. As he left the room he heard Duncan quietly sobbing.

CHAPTER 62

Battersay

Over here, help me!

Ally was being tossed on a rough sea. The ferry reared up, juddering on steep waves and then plunged down again. She could see a man on the far side of the deck, clinging onto the railing with bulky arms, his dark hair lifting in the gale. Not Lucas then. Nor Ned. Someone she knew. A well-worn coat. Familiar, yet not quite.

She reached out and pulled herself towards him, clinging to metal ladders and flapping tarpaulin. But every time she grew near him, the ship pitched and she slipped back to where she started.

I can't hold on any more.

Ally was crying in frustration. She was utterly exhausted. She knew if she lost sight of the man at the rail then she would give up and slide into the ferocious sea. But the man could not hear her cries and never looked round.

The roaring of the storm grew louder, drowning out her faint words. Ally looked behind and saw a huge throng of people huddled together, clinging onto each other to stop them sliding off the deck. Their moaning was like the battering wind. They held out their arms and told her to join them before it was too late.

'Okay, okay, I'm coming.'

Ally gave up the struggle and let herself drift towards them. It was such a relief not to have to battle against the storm and the rolling of the ferry. They opened up their arms – soaking, salty, woolly arms – and took her in.

Thank you, thank you.

They closed in around her and it was suddenly dark and the musty smell of sweaty, damp clothing was overpowering. In panic, Ally realised they had no faces and they were dragging her to the nearest railing.

'You have to go now,' said a woman. She sounded like Bethag.

But I don't want to. Please let me stay.

Strong arms lifted her up and tossed her over the side and as she flew through the air, the man at the far side turned to watch.

Ally sobbed. *John, why didn't you try to stop them?*

His mouth was opening and closing but she couldn't hear what he was shouting. Then she was lost in the darkness and the ship disappeared under a wave.

It's alright, I'm here.

A man's deep reassuring voice.

Ally was safe in bed. John's bed. She felt his arms go around her.

Oh, I've missed you. Ally wept, relief settling on her like warm blankets.

Me too. John was kissing her damp forehead.

They were wrapped in his animal skin cover and he was caressing her, kissing away her fear.

I knew you wouldn't let me drown.

I've always loved you; you know that, don't you?

Yes.

CHAPTER 63

Light spilled in from the uncurtained window. Ally winced as she tried to open her eyes. A sharp pain shot between her brows; she closed them again. She was still fully dressed. Her mind was a complete blank.

Slowly does it. Pieces of the previous evening began to collect in her sore head: the bar meal, a bottle of red wine to herself, Mary knitting, Ned – had he been there? – Lucas helping himself to whisky, and pouring one for her.

'Oh, God,' Ally groaned. How had she got so drunk? There had been something else too. She had a fragment of memory of her screaming, of fear pinning her to the chair.

'You awake, girl?'

Ally jolted, her eyes flying open. She didn't recognise the room. Turning in the bed, she gasped in shock.

'Lucas! What the hell are you doing here?'

Lucas in crumpled T-shirt and blond hair awry, squinted at her, his face creased from a hangover.

'I sleep here,' he said, 'it's my bed.'

'I don't get it,' Ally said, her head throbbing. 'How did I ...?'

'You were screaming like a banshee. Mary thought it best you didn't sleep alone in case you choked on your vomit or tried to fly from the window.'

'Oh, no,' Ally winced, 'how on earth did I get like that?'

Lucas propped himself up on an elbow and viewed her. 'Reckon it was Mary's mead – strong as stink – and you were knocking it back like it was alcopops. Ned says Mary adds in something narcotic to help sleep, but it gave you the horrors.'

'I had the weirdest dreams. They were really scary.'

'Yeah? Well you were shouting out for that mad priest.'

'Was I?'

Lucas ran a finger down her cheek and smirked. 'I know how to chase those nightmares away.'

Ally sat up, batting Lucas's exploring hand away. 'I'm never touching that mead stuff again; it's poisoned me.'

'Me neither,' Lucas said, sinking onto his back.

Ally swung her legs over the bed and shakily stood up. Crossing to the window, she lifted the lower sash to let fresh air into the stale room. Voices carried on the still morning air, muted but arguing. She crouched down to listen unobserved.

Lucas grunted, 'naughty, naughty.'

Ally shushed him and leaned closer to the open window.

' ... don't be silly, darling, you really haven't thought this through.'

'Oh, but I have Ned; I've been thinking of nothing else.'

'It might tip her over the edge – it could be dangerous.'

'I can't leave her.'

'But usually –'

'It's different this time.'

'I don't see why …'

Their voices trailed off as Ned and Mary moved away. Ally heard Myrtle bleat in the distance.

'So,' Lucas said, 'were they talking about us?'

'I think it was about Juniper,' Ally said, puzzled. 'Something about not leaving her. Mary sounded all stressed out.'

'Yeah, well I think Ned's mad taking Mary on this trip; it's clear as day she's agoraphobic – and probably scared of sailing. Perhaps she's backing out.'

Ally shook her head. 'No, I got the impression she meant taking Juniper with her.'

Lucas snorted in disbelief. 'That would be totally nuts.'

Ally reached down for her discarded shoes.

'What can I do to persuade you,' Lucas said, holding open the covers, 'to come back to bed?'

She regarded him; he was such an opportunist.

'Nothing. I need a bath and I've got to work this afternoon.'

Lucas sank back with a sigh. 'Pity.'

Ally thought how easy it would have been to slip back into their former relationship, but she didn't trust that he had turned over a new leaf. It struck her suddenly how she didn't want Lucas back.

'We'll talk about us later, okay?' Ally said. 'Straighten things out before the trip to Kulah.'

CHAPTER 64

Kulah

One of Christina's twins is running across the cliff top towards the steps. His screams are carried on the wind.

People surge back along the quay and scramble for the steps. The elderly are left sheltering in the derelict pier house, shouting in confusion for someone to tell them what is happening.

Up high, the gale has grown ferocious and the sea beyond the harbour is boiling with waves half as high as the Black Rock. The rain comes on harder, tumbling out of a sky turned purple with rage. The light has almost gone.

'Stick together!' I order, but no one is listening.

They battle along the ridge, some crawling on their hands and knees to avoid being whipped over the edge.

Then out of the half-dark, we see pale lights tossing back and forth in the spray out beyond the stacks.

'There it is,' Bethag screams.

The ship is pitching and rolling as the sea flings it between salty fingers. It rears up, and then disappears. Surely they won't try to enter the harbour? It would be suicide. The only thing they can do is to turn into the sea and ride out the storm.

All this is going through my mind, as I clutch The Baby and pray frantically.

'They're standing on the deck,' Seanaid cries. 'Oh Holy Mary, I can see them!'

We stand transfixed, helpless to do anything but watch.

All of a sudden, over the bellow of the sea there is a roar like a wounded beast, a noise of metal tearing on rock that screeches and judders through me. Briefly, the wind rips a hole in the rain and we see the ship, bows in the air, impaled on the Black Rock. Men are jumping or being hurled into the waves. They bob like ducks, thrashing in the spray and then sucked below.

Around me the women scream and wail and fling out their arms as if to catch their men. But the sea will not give them up. The mist drops again and we see nothing.

Pulled by invisible rope, we all huddle together, clutching on, forgetting the angry words and spiteful thoughts that have kept us divided. The horror of what we are seeing overshadows all our past troubles. We are anchored together, joined in a babble of prayers and frantic words of encouragement.

When the cloud breaks, we see in the dying light the sea sucking and howling against the stacks of rock as before. But the ship is gone. All sign of the men has vanished. Not one head remains above the waters.

A groan rises up above the din of the wind. Around me, the women clutch their stomachs and gasp for breath like fish being gutted. I bury my face in The Baby's blanket and weep.

Someone tears at my plaid, ripping it from my head. I can feel the anger in them before I see who it is.

'It's her fault!' she sobs. '*She* did this. I *heard* her.'

Distraught faces turn towards me.

'I heard you,' she accuses, 'praying for a storm. Cursing my father! You're a wicked, wicked witch!'

As she hurls her words like knives, Bethag's face is contorted in hate.

CHAPTER 65

Battersay

Ally struggled through the day at the hall. She had never felt so lethargic and detached, as if her limbs belonged to someone much slower and older.

'Boy, you look rough,' Calum said. He hovered in the kitchen doorway as if he wanted to tell her something.

'What is it?' Ally asked.

Calum hesitated, then said, 'It's nothing important. I'll catch you later.'

It left her feeling uneasy. Perhaps he was trying to tell her that there would be no work for her when she got back from sailing. Was she about to be sacked? Surely Ned, as Chair of the Hall Committee would have some say in it or told her if that was likely. But then it was Calum and Shona who dealt with the day to day running.

Ally felt nauseous as she cut up onions and opened tins of corned beef to make a tray of hash. All the time, anxiety fluttered inside that her days there were numbered. But would that be such a bad thing? *How long are you going to stick it out here?* Lucas had wanted to know. Perhaps it was time to call it a day and return to London, pick up the pieces of her old life?

At the end of work, she hung around making a list of the meals she had made and frozen in containers to help over the next few days. Ally waited for Calum to reappear and tell her what was on his mind. But the crofter did not come. Eventually she locked up.

'Oh well,' she sighed, 'goodbye hall, been nice knowing you.'

Ally set off for the coastguard's cottage to collect warm clothes for the trip. The front door was stiff from damp and not being in use. A sour smell like rotting seaweed met her as she stepped inside. She tensed. 'No more dead sea creatures please,' she muttered.

The house was deathly quiet with that musty, neglected feel of unlived-in places. The kitchen was just as she had left it over a week ago; an upturned mug on the draining board and two of Ned's books on the table. She scooped the books into her backpack and went upstairs. She hadn't slept there since the day Lucas had turned up out of the blue and given her a massive fright. Ally doubted she could sleep another night here; she was on edge just standing in the cramped attic. How had she lived here for weeks? It was claustrophobic. The low sloping ceiling seemed to press in on her more than ever and the tin roof creaked and rattled in the evening breeze.

As Ally quickly gathered up clothes she couldn't shake off the sensation that some presence was with her, standing behind, their breath on her neck. She kept looking round and reassuring herself in a loud voice.

'There's no one here. Stop being such a wuss. Nothing to worry about.' She rammed socks and sweatshirt into the bag. 'Lucas where are you when I need you? You'd make a joke of it all.'

She hurried back down the ladder, heart pounding in her eagerness to be gone. In the gloom of the corridor, she stopped to listen. There was a dripping noise coming from the bathroom. Ally was desperate to leave but knew she ought to make sure all the taps were turned off. She hurried through the open door. The hot tap over the bath dripped steadily in the silence. She leaned across to tighten it and flinched; the metal was still warm. Switching on the light for a better look, Ally saw there were splashes of water on the curling linoleum. Someone had been using the bath, and recently.

Puzzled, she reached for the towel hanging on the back of the door. It was wet. The bathroom was always a damp room but she hadn't used the towel in over a week.

'This is just weird.'

She fled the house without bothering to jam the front door closed behind her. What was the point? Someone was helping themselves to the place anyway. Ally had never been able to relax there; it had never been home. This was the final straw; some creep coming in and using her bath, drying off on her towel.

'You win,' she shouted at the forlorn looking house. 'I'm never coming back. I hope they knock you down!'

CHAPTER 66

Reaching the end of the track, Ally saw the local bus as it hove into view on its final run of the day back to Bay. On the spur of the moment she stuck out her thumb.

'Can you drop me at the turning to Bay House, Alec?'

'Okey-dokey. Jump on board.'

She had promised Ishbel that she would call in and see Bethag before she went and there would be no time in the morning; Ned had said he wanted to sail with the dawn.

Daylight was waning from the sky as she walked up the long grassy track to the home. The days were already shortening, though it was just into September. The windbreak of pine trees creaked and sighed; lights were on in the large bay windows.

'It's Ishbel's day off,' Morag told her brusquely, 'and it's after visiting hours.' She was Neil MacRailt's sister and hadn't spoken to Ally since the disturbance outside the coastguard's cottage over Juniper, where Neil had been frogmarched away.

'I promised to call in,' Ally stood her ground. 'I'm off sailing in the morning and won't be able to visit for a few days. Please Morag.'

The woman gave a disapproving tut but nodded at her to go in. 'She's in bed. If she's sleeping don't wake her up.'

Bethag's room was in darkness. Ally peered until her eyes could pick out the old woman lying in bed, her face shrunken and ghostly pale in the twilight.

'Bethag, it's Ally. Are you awake?'

'Ally?' she croaked. 'The lassie from the hall?'

'That's right,' Ally smiled and approached her. 'Sorry I haven't brought you any baking this time.'

'Och, don't you worry,' Bethag said, 'it's nice to get a visit. Can you help me sit up?'

Ally pulled her up and propped her on pillows; her arms felt thin and brittle in her hands.

'Scones next time I come,' Ally declared, 'you're wasting away.'

'I've no appetite, dearie.'

'Do you want the light on?'

'No, I prefer the dark. I can look out but she can't look in on me.'

Ally felt a stab of unease. 'Who's looking in on you?'

Bethag said nothing.

'Would you like me to read to you, like John does?'

'Where is John?' Bethag fretted. 'I miss my boy.'

Ally put a hand on hers. 'I know you do. I do too if I'm honest. He'll be back soon, I'm sure. He cares about you a lot, always protecting you from nosey people like me.'

'He's a good boy.' Bethag sighed, 'I've burdened him with too much. Perhaps that's why he's gone away.'

'What burdens, Bethag?'

A troubled look came over her wrinkled face. Bethag shook her head. 'I knew he wouldn't tell. But it's a terrible cross to carry, and him being a priest too.'

'Would you like to tell me? Is it about you and John being related?' Ally held her breath.

'Oh no, not that,' she sighed. Bethag stared out at the gathering night. The minutes ticked by on the brass clock on her bedside cabinet. Ally knew that this old islander held the key to what troubled John and perhaps to much more that was strange and unexplained about Battersay and Kulah.

'Aye, I'd like you to read to me, Ally,' she said at last. 'But draw the curtain first.'

Curbing her frustration, Ally did as she was asked. 'Is this the one John's being reading to you?' She picked up a book from the bedside: *Tales & Prophecies of the Outer Isles.* It was marked halfway through a chapter on North Uist.

'Aye, carry on where he left off, please.'

In the soft lamplight Ally read aloud, a bloodthirsty tale of rival clans fighting over a tidal island and an elite archer who could pierce both eyes of a seal with one single arrow. Ally felt queasy, remembering the dead seal left to scare her. She glanced at Bethag, but she was listening intently, her face calm.

'Go on lassie.'

On she read about the fate of the mighty MacGorries, their sea-bound strongholds, feuds, romances and untimely deaths. Towards the end of the chapter they had run into trouble with the law by plundering a Spanish merchant ship of its cargo of raisins and wine.

'The doomed ship broke up in a fierce storm,' Ally read, 'and the men of the clan went down to the shore and spirited away the booty, seeing nothing wrong with taking what the sea rendered up to them.'

'Stop,' Bethag suddenly said, 'I've heard enough.' Her hands moved across the bed covers in agitation.

Too late Ally realised the reference to the shipwreck must have upset her.

'Sorry. Would you like me to read something else?'

'Thank you, but no. I'm tired now.'

Ally put down the book and helped make Bethag comfortable.

'Will you turn off the light and open the curtain before you go?' the old woman asked.

As Ally did so, she said, 'I'll be away for a few days. I'm going to Kulah.'

Bethag gasped, 'Kulah? Don't go, please don't go. It isn't safe for a lassie like you.'

Ally smiled and took her hands in hers. 'It's okay, I'm going with experienced sailors – Ned Rushmore and a friend of mine.'

Bethag's frown lessened a fraction. 'As long as there are men with you.'

'Yes, big strong men, I promise.'

For a moment they both gazed out of the window. A band of golden light was sinking beyond the headland into the sea. Bethag's frail grip suddenly tightened.

'There she is,' she hissed, 'over there.'

'Who? Where?'

'Can't you see her? Coming over the hill. She's always coming over that hill.' The old woman trembled as she pointed. Anxiety gripped Ally. She peered hard. Perhaps there was something moving on the skyline – the head and shoulders of a walker – but it could just be a trick of the half-light.

'She'll never let me be, never. But what more could I do? It was all her fault,' Bethag whimpered, 'all her fault.'

Ally put her arms about her in comfort. Her heart hammered as she forced herself to ask, 'Bethag, is the woman you see wearing a tweed coat and a blue headscarf?'

Bethag nodded and whispered so faintly, Ally was unsure if she heard correctly. 'Aye, my mother's blue plaid.'

CHAPTER 67

Glasgow

Duncan found John in the dark of the bowling pavilion two streets away, the red glow of his cigarette giving him away.

'I guessed you'd be here. Always caught you smoking round the back as a boy.'

John felt numb. He liked it this way. He knew as soon as it wore off there would be pain like being gored. Like the pain of losing Caroline and blaming himself for her death. And the ache of seeing the empty space in his bed where Ally would never lie again, of hearing she was back with Lucas. He had thought himself cursed by the tragedy of Kulah, but Bethag had been wrong when she had confided in him as a trainee priest that they were related. They never had been. The curse he bore was far worse; a rapist for a father and a mother who was repelled by his very existence.

'Your mother's gone to stay the night with a friend,' his father said. 'She's done it before when she gets too fed up with me.'

'You knew about my real father?' John asked.

'Yes.'

'God, you must have regretted marrying her. She wasn't even grateful and then you had to pretend I was yours.'

Duncan gripped his shoulder with surprising strength. 'You were mine. I was the one brought you up, not him. I never regretted it, not for a minute.'

John didn't believe him. 'How could you bear to have me around when my own mother couldn't? You're just trying to be kind.'

'No,' Duncan said, shaking him gently, 'I loved you. You were such a loving, giving little boy, so curious about the world, a deep thinker, but able to see joy in the simplest of things. It broke my heart to see the way Marion rejected you – too frightened to let herself love you because of what that awful man had done. It blighted her life but I didn't see why it should blight yours too. I saw that I had to do the loving for both of us.' Duncan paused and then added, 'you are my greatest joy and I love you still, my dearest boy.'

John's eyes stung at his father's kindness; he knew how hard it was for him to talk of his deepest feelings. John had let himself believe that his life was forever blighted by the past, yet all the time he had ignored Duncan's love, like an overlooked gift.

'Thank you, Dad.' He reached for his father and hugged him tight.

CHAPTER 68

Battersay

Sollas lay shadowed in the gloaming as Ally came over the hill. She had run most of the way back from the care home to try and shake off the tension that had gripped her since Bethag's talk of hauntings. Lights blazed out of Shona and Calum's home and she could see Shona standing at the sink, washing-up. One of the twins was tearing around outside with the dog.

Ally longed for a brief moment of real, uncomplicated domestic life. She didn't care if Shona gave her an earful, it would be better than Bethag's frightened whisperings or her own edgy thoughts. Besides, she wanted to know what it was Calum had to tell her.

'Hi Tor!' she called out. 'Is your dad inside?'

The dark-haired boy flew at her like a bluebottle and grabbed her legs. 'Nee-oww, I'm a fighter jet. You're dead.'

Ally flopped to the ground and pulled him with her. He giggled. 'Stop tickling, that's not fair.'

Shona heard the commotion and came to the open door.

'Tor get yourself upstairs and in the bath now,' she ordered. 'Oh, it's you.' She stood, arms folded at sight of Ally.

'She wants Dad,' Tor said.

'Go on, scoot.' Shona steered him inside. 'Calum's up the top field. I suppose you've come about the phone calls. Well, I can tell you now it wasn't me.'

'What phone calls? I don't know what you're talking about.'

Shona looked wrong-footed. 'I thought Calum had said something.'

'I think he was trying to this morning, but didn't.' Ally said, 'Shona, can I just come in for a minute? You know I'm away tomorrow.'

Reluctantly Shona nodded and led the way to the kitchen. Ally felt a pang of nostalgia at the cosy chaos and couldn't help saying, 'I've missed coming over here.'

'Aye, well, it's not been easy.' Abruptly, Shona's frosty expression relaxed. 'Would you like a drink? I've some cider in the fridge.'

'I'd love that, thanks.'

They sat on kitchen chairs and shared a can, keeping to safe subjects: the twins being back at school and arrangements for the hall while Ally was away. Soon Shona was teasing her about men.

'That Lucas is a good-looking guy, right enough. And coming all this way to see you? Must really want you back, you lucky woman.'

Ally laughed. 'He's all talk – I don't think he means half of it.'

'That's not what it looks like to me,' Shona snorted. 'Larking about in the Co-op – the boy couldn't keep his hands off you, according to Sandra. And don't think I haven't seen you holding hands on romantic walks.'

'That doesn't mean anything,' Ally blushed.

'It's no wonder Balmain did a runner. He could see he's no competition for the hunky blond Australian.'

'That's got nothing to do with why he left.'

'Oh,' Shona scrutinised her, 'so what was it?'

Ally shrugged; she could never say anything about Donny's obscene drawings to the Gillies.

'Well, I take my hat off to you, Ally. Two men falling at your feet and you not bothered about the pair of them. And now you're sailing off into the sunset with Dr Ned.'

'Shona! There's absolutely nothing going on there, believe me,' Ally was indignant.

Shona laughed. 'I was just teasing. And Mary's much too possessive of her Ned to allow anything there.'

Calum tramped in. For a moment he looked between them as if trying to gauge what he saw.

'It's okay,' Shona said, 'we're having a truce. It's safe to come closer.'

Calum smiled in relief, shrugged off his jacket and poured himself a mug of stewed tea from the teapot. After a few minutes of chat about the croft, Ally said, 'so tell me about these phone calls.'

Shona and Calum exchanged glances, then he got up and left the room.

'We had no idea honestly,' Shona said.

Calum returned with a printout. 'Our phone bill,' he explained. 'There were entries that didn't make sense, all to this same number.' He pointed. 'Do you recognise it?'

Ally peered. A London number; it looked familiar.

'Calum rang it,' Shona said, ''cos we couldn't think what it was.'

'Aye, I did.' Calum looked embarrassed.

'So whose is it?' Ally asked in bemusement.

'It's for *Lara* magazine.'

'*Lara's*?' Ally exclaimed. 'How on earth –? But I only rang the once, that first time I came to your house. So what are you saying? That I sneaked in here to make calls to my boss?'

'No, we're not,' said Calum.

'I admit,' said Shona, 'that was my first thought. But we looked at the days and times of the calls and knew it was when you were at the hall – when we were all out at work.'

Ally was completely baffled. 'So you think someone else was coming in and using your phone?'

'Either that,' Calum hesitated, 'or my brother Rory made the calls.'

'Rory? But why would he?'

'I don't know, but I'm going to get it out of him when he gets back. He's working away at another fish farm in Harris till the end of the week.'

Ally looked between them and felt a stirring of unease. 'You have a hunch, don't you?'

Shona said, 'Rory's a sly one, always listening into other's folks' conversations and always on the lookout for ways to make easy money.'

'He's not a bad boy,' Calum defended, 'just a wee bit lazy.'

177

'I bet he listened into your phone call and made a note of the number after you'd gone,' Shona said, 'just in case it came in handy. It's the kind of thing he'd do.'

'But it still doesn't make any sense,' Ally puzzled. 'What good would *Lara* magazine be to Rory?'

'Tell her what you think,' Shona said. 'Go on.'

Calum looked uncomfortable. 'The calls were made in the few days before that article came out about you and Birdwoman – the one with the picture of you swimming. I think my brother might have taken the photo and sold the information – he has a digital camera.'

Ally's insides lurched. 'But it wasn't *Lara*'s who ran the story. Even if Rory was behind it, my boss Freya would never have touched it.'

Shona gave her a pitying look. 'Well you know her and we don't, but she's a journalist, isn't she? When it comes to the fuss over Birdwoman, common sense and decency seem to fly out the window. She could have sold it on, couldn't she?'

Ally shook her head. 'I just don't believe that.'

Calum touched her shoulder. 'You're probably right and we didn't mean to upset you. We'd decided not to say anything till after your trip and Rory comes home, but then you turned up.'

Ally was shaken. She stood up. 'Well it's too late to do anything about it now. I'll speak to Freya when I'm back on Friday.'

Calum said sheepishly, 'you can come and use our phone.'

At the door, Ally turned. 'So does that mean you no longer think I'm behind all the bad publicity?'

Shona was defensive. 'We never said you were. We just think you were wrong to try and make the bird-witch into your friend. It's just brought more trouble. And you weren't straight with us about you being a journalist, so is it any wonder we were suspicious?'

'Okay, I can see your point, Ally admitted. 'I'm sorry if I spoilt things between us, 'cos I really appreciated how kind you were when I came here.'

Unexpectedly, Shona grabbed her in a hug. 'Away you go before I start liking you again and want to swap you for the twins.'

Ally laughed and hugged her back. 'Well you won't have to bother about either of us pesky witches for the next few days. I think Mary's got it into her head to take Juniper with us; doesn't want to leave her alone with you lot.'

Shona cried, 'she's far too soft for her own good that woman.'

Calum looked worried. 'It's a crazy thing to do.'

'I agree, but Ally's got the gorgeous Lucas to keep her safe,' Shona teased.

Ally waved them goodbye. It was getting late and she still had to pack. She was keen to discuss the mystery of the phone calls with Lucas and see what he made of it all.

Calum called out, 'Oh, by the way, did Lucas pass on the note?'

'What note?'

'I picked it up in the hall yesterday and forgot to give it to you. Saw Lucas passing earlier and gave it to him.'

'Okay, thanks. Who was it from?'

'Didn't recognise the writing. But it had a drawing of a seagull on the envelope.'

CHAPTER 69

Kulah

No one sleeps; I cannot imagine ever sleeping again. I have retreated to our cold cottage with Seanaid and The Baby. I think Bethag is at the pier house keeping vigil; she has put herself out of my reach. The storm rages on without a care, through the night and the next day and the next.

When the gale sweeps on to somewhere else and the sea settles, we search the rocks. They are covered in dead birds, dashed against the cliffs. Sam risks all by scaling the rock face to reach caves that only the seals know. They are empty. There are no survivors.

The first body that bobs into the harbour is Neilac's. The next day, two more follow. But the swell is too great for the rowing boat and they cannot be landed. The MacRailt women are driven mad by the sight.

The keening of the women cuts through me. From dawn to dusk, the air is full of their wailing. If I flew on wings to the farthest corners of the sea, it would still find me.

Seanaid has been struck dumb by the horror of it all; only The Baby makes human sounds. I cannot bear to hear it.

I walk the cliff paths all day. At night I stand above the harbour waiting for Tormod and my punishment, but neither comes.

'When the next boat arrives,' Seanaid breaks the silence, 'I'm going with Rosamund Marie. I'm never coming back to Kulah ever again.'

CHAPTER 70

Battersay

'Where have you been?' Ned came hurrying up the dark track to meet Ally. He sounded angry.

'Sorry, I went for clothes then ended up visiting Bethag and the Gillies.'

'We've been worried sick.'

'I'm fine, what's the matter?'

'Come inside quickly. I'll explain all.'

Ally had never seen him so agitated. Walking through the hall and down the passageway to the kitchen, she was met by a pungent fishy smell. Mary sprang up from her chair by the fire.

'Oh thank goodness you're safe.'

In astonishment, Ally saw Juniper curled up on the hearth like a cat, her head burrowed under her arms. She was snoring loudly. Mary took Ally's hands.

'She'll be reassured to see you when she wakes. I'll make up a camp bed for you here. You don't mind that do you? She's had such a shock.'

'What's happened?' asked Ally in alarm.

'Somebody's had a go at her,' Ned said.

'I went up to the cottage this afternoon and found her in a terrified state,' said Mary, her voice shaking. 'She wouldn't come out, so I gave her a calming tea. Eventually she let me come close.'

Ned said, 'Mary coaxed her down here. She has a nasty cut and bruise on her face – been hit by something heavy. I've cleaned the cut.'

'That's terrible,' Ally gasped, 'poor Juniper. Have you reported it?'

'To that plod Melville?' Ned was scathing. 'You've seen how useless he is in protecting her. Anyhow, judging by the state of her fingernails, her attacker probably came off worse.'

'It's made up our minds though,' Mary said, sounding tearful. 'We can't leave Juniper behind. She's just not safe here. I'd never forgive myself if something happened to her while we were away.'

Mary steered Ally towards the table and a plate of cold food. Ally sank down shakily on a chair. She didn't feel like eating, but she downed a mug of water thirstily. Something about the way Ned and Mary hovered over her made her more nervous.

'What is it?' she asked.

They exchanged looks. 'Ally,' Ned said, 'have you seen Lucas?'

Ally put down the mug. 'Isn't he here packing?'

'No,' said Mary. 'We hoped he'd be with you.'

'I haven't seen him since this morning.'

'Oh dear,' Mary said, looking up at Ned, 'perhaps you were right.'

Ally's stomach clenched. 'Right about what?'

Ned went over to the dresser, opened the cupboard and pulled something out. He returned and put it on the table. Ally's mouth went dry. A camera.

'Mary found this in Juniper's house. Is it Lucas's?'

Ally touched it. 'Yes.' She looked at them in confusion. 'He'd never leave this ... What the hell's going on? Has something happened to Lucas?'

Ned said, 'You better come and see this.'

CHAPTER 71

Galloway

John pulled up his collar against the rain. The archaeologists continued working, their boots sunk in mud and cagoule hoods pulled up, looking like brightly-coloured monks. He watched his father pointing and talking animatedly to the dig leader.

'I'll meet you back at the pub,' John called over.

'Okay son!' Duncan waved back.

It was their second day in Galloway and the rain hadn't stopped.

'So fresh and invigorating, don't you think?' Duncan had said, not the least put off by the weather. He had insisted on taking John away for a couple of days and had booked a room at the Douglas Inn where the archaeologists were based. John's father was in his element quizzing them about the hermit's cell they had unearthed and testing out his theories on obscure Celtic saints.

John was content to sit in the background with a pint, reading. The wet, lush, tranquil surroundings of South West Scotland suited his bruised spirits. It was a world away from the fierce dramatic beauty of the Hebrides or the bleak unhappiness of his parents' home. Here was time to think. Somehow, in the next day or two he would have to decide what to do with his life.

John had been so sure that Battersay was his spiritual home, drawn to it by Bethag's possessive love and need for him. He had found contentment there in his solitary life as an artist – until Ally had come along and turned his world upside down. He felt a twisting in his guts just thinking about her. By the time he went back to the island – if that's what he chose to do – she would probably have gone back to London with the smooth-talking Lucas.

'I'm not sure there's anything to keep me on Battersay now,' he had said to his father their first night away. 'Now that I know I'm not related to Bethag, I don't have that feeling of belonging anymore. It's like losing a limb.'

Duncan had nodded. 'Don't be too hasty. You can be deeply connected to people without being their blood relation. It doesn't make Bethag any less important to you.'

On the way back to the pub, John stopped off at the newsagent's for a packet of cigarettes. It was a quaint shop with an old-fashioned bell, half the cramped room given over to photocopier, stationery and gifts. The walls were covered in framed photos for sale of bygone Galloway. John scanned them as he waited behind a man who was having a long mournful conversation about an ill neighbour with the assistant.

There were the usual sepia photos of farm workers and horses pulling antique ploughs and Edwardians in their finery on church outings and picnics. Then there were coloured photos of 1970s cars outside the Douglas Inn and girls in flared jeans and floppy hats at some local fair.

The most recent were of sword dancers walking down the main street and women dressed up in bonnets and crinolines in some re-enactment. One showed a line of orange-robed Buddhists splashing through puddles in sandals. He remembered hearing about the Buddhist retreat when he'd been a priest in Dumfries; there had been controversy at the time; some rivalry with an older commune that accused them of pinching members. John peered closer. In the background were a group of long-haired men and women, leading goats on ropes and carrying children.

He stood, trying to remember. Something nagged at the back of his mind. A memory began to resurface. He plucked the photo from the wall and stared harder. Turning it over, a label read, The Gathering 1990s. Anxiety twisted inside. What if he hadn't been wrong?

'Excuse me,' John interrupted the chat at the counter, 'do you know if the hippy commune is still going?'

They looked at him in surprise. 'Never knew there was one,' said the young assistant.

John pointed to the long-skirted women with the goats. 'There was a Buddhist retreat nearby.'

'Aye,' the man answered, 'there was – over at Kirk Newton. The Buddhists are still there but I think the hippies moved on years ago.'

'Is there anyone locally who would remember them? Perhaps one or two settled round here.'

The man shook his head. 'Not that I can think of. They were a strange bunch – kept to themselves.'

'Maybe the Buddhists would know,' the assistant smiled, trying to be helpful.

'They might,' the man grunted, 'but they wouldn't say. I've heard they're not allowed to speak.'

John felt disappointment. 'Okay thanks.' As he put back the picture, a thought occurred. 'Where did you get all these photos?'

'Think most of them were taken for the local paper,' said the young woman. 'Isn't that right Kenny?'

'Aye, but you'll find out nothing there,' he said, 'local rag went bust ten years ago.'

John bought his cigarettes. All he had to go on was a hunch and a half-memory. It was all too long ago; he would find nothing here.

As he turned to leave, the young woman suggested, 'Why don't you ask over in the library? They've probably got the archives for the newspaper – and they might know what happened to your hippies. Just a thought.'

John brightened. 'Thanks, it's a good one,' he smiled. 'Where will I find the library?'

She gave him directions. As he left, the man called Kenny said with gloomy relish, 'it closes at four – you'll be too late.'

CHAPTER 72

Battersay

Ally burst into Lucas's room. The bed they had both slept in just hours ago was still unmade; the pillows indented where their heads had lain. Ned followed her in, picking up a T-shirt and boxer shorts which had been discarded on the floor. She could imagine Lucas throwing them off as he walked to wash at the hand basin in the corner. She felt strange seeing Ned holding them.

'Looks like he left in a hurry,' said Ned.

Ally's heart drummed. She looked around desperately for any sign of his sports bag; in the wardrobe, under the bed, behind the chair. She had always admired his ability to travel light: two changes of clothes, swimming shorts, deodorant and a pair of deck shoes. Lucas never really unpacked, always ready to grab his bag and go at a moment's notice.

'Where is he?'

'Come downstairs,' Ned said, 'and we'll talk about it.'

'You think he's done a runner don't you?'

Ned didn't answer as he dropped Lucas's clothes onto the bed and ushered her out.

'Calum saw him earlier,' she said ,'cos he gave him a note for me. I think it might have been from John.'

Ned snorted. 'I bet the priest was maddened by Lucas turning up.'

Back in the kitchen, Mary asked, 'Did you two row about something?'

'No.' Ally felt confused. 'Well, not really. He didn't believe in all this business about Flora's ghost and the wailing voices. But he never said anything about leaving – he was looking forward to the trip. Lucas won't miss the chance to go to Kulah, so something must have happened.' She tried to quell the panic inside.

'Perhaps he got packed up and decided to go to the hotel for a last pie and pint?' Ned suggested. 'If he's on foot he might not be back till after midnight.'

'That's possible,' Ally said eagerly.

'Ned,' Mary said, 'why don't you ring the hotel to see if Lucas is there?'

He nodded and left the room.

'You mustn't worry,' Mary assured, putting a hand on her knee. 'He'll turn up.'

'I've got a bad feeling. Something's going on.' Ally told her about Calum's suspicions of Rory and how her boss at *Lara* might be involved in selling the salacious story of her and Juniper.

'Rory?' Mary was incredulous. 'I can't believe he'd do such a thing. He's such a nice boy. I used to babysit him when we first came here.'

'Well Calum and Shona seem pretty sure.'

'Don't jump to hasty conclusions.'

'They're going to wait and tackle him when he's back from Harris.'

185

'When is that?'

'End of the week.'

Mary nodded, her look strained. 'Do you think Lucas has something to do with it?'

Ally's chest tightened as doubts about Lucas gripped her once more. 'God, I hope not. That would be really paranoid to think he was involved, wouldn't it?'

Mary took a moment to answer. 'It would call into question why he came here in the first place. I assumed it was for love of you, Ally. He seemed so smitten. But he's hurt you in the past, hasn't he? Is it possible that he might be – well –? '

'Well what?'

'Doing it to please someone at *Lara*.'

Ally felt bile fill her throat. 'You mean Freya?'

'Lucas is ambitious. If somehow your magazine is involved in tittle-tattle about you and Juniper, perhaps he came here looking for more.'

'But Freya would have to sanction him coming all this way. Why would she do that? She's been a good friend to me. It was her idea that I took the summer off –' Abruptly Ally stopped.

'And that you came here?' Mary guessed.

Ally nodded.

'Then maybe she had her reasons,' Mary said.

'But she couldn't have planned that I'd make friends with Juniper and give her a scoop – that's ludicrous.'

'That might have been an unforeseen bonus for her and not her prime motivation. Perhaps she just wanted you out of the way and it was Lucas's idea to chase the story.'

Ally's head reeled. Surely neither Freya nor Lucas could be that coldly calculating? Unless.

'Is it possible,' Mary asked with a pitying look, 'that Lucas and your employer could be romantically involved?'

Ally tried to push away the same awful thought. 'No, she doesn't even like him. She warned me about him seeing another woman.'

Her heart missed a beat. It was Freya who had first sown the seeds of doubt into her relationship with Lucas, until Ally had no longer trusted him. Had Freya deliberately set about breaking them up so that she could have Lucas for herself? Her boss always got what she wanted – and Lucas was vain enough to be flattered into going to bed with her. Something else came back to her: the last phone call with Rachel. Her friend had been about to tell her that she'd seen Lucas with someone, when they'd been cut off. Perhaps she was going to warn her about Freya.

'I just can't believe they would both stab me in the back like that. I feel sick thinking about it.'

'I know it's a terrible feeling when people close to you let you down,' Mary said gently, 'but it appears that Lucas has been keeping things from you. Ask yourself how his camera ended up at Juniper's.'

186

Ally searched for an excuse. 'He could have dropped it by mistake and she picked it up – you know how she loves to collect stuff.'

'And is Lucas in the habit of losing his precious camera?'

'It's not impossible.' Even as she said it, Ally knew how unlikely it was; Lucas practically slept with his camera. 'Okay, so what are you saying?'

'That maybe,' said Mary, 'he went up there to take photos of Juniper because Freya or someone else from *Lara* asked him to.'

Ally shook her head in disbelief. 'Even if he was tempted, he wouldn't have left his camera behind.'

'Unless, he was too scared to retrieve it.'

Ally's insides turned to ice. 'You think it was Lucas who attacked Juniper, don't you?'

'In self-defence I don't doubt. If it was Lucas he must be covered in scratches – she clawed her attacker like a wildcat.'

Ally had a sudden image of the wounded Lucas fleeing Juniper and taking shelter at the coastguard's cottage – running himself a bath and bathing his wounds – weighing up whether he could get away with it or not. Being Lucas, he would want to brazen it out, sneak back and get his camera then deny being there. But that very morning, she had eavesdropped on the Rushmores and told Lucas they might be taking Juniper with them. He couldn't risk being anywhere near the woman, let alone confined on a boat with her. So Lucas must have legged it back to Sollas House, grabbed his bag and gone.

Ned returned. 'He's not been at the hotel, I'm afraid.'

'Mary's told me what you both think,' Ally said, jumping up. 'It's too horrible. I need to speak to Lucas. Can I use your phone?'

'Of course, but there's something you should –'

As Ally rushed past him, he put out a hand.

'Let her go,' Mary said.

With trembling fingers, Ally punched in the number to Lucas's mobile. She stood in the dark hallway, heart thudding as she waited. An automated voice said that the number could not be reached. Did that mean he was still on the island – somewhere without a signal – or was he deliberately not taking calls? She banged down the phone in frustration.

A moment later she picked it up and rang Freya's office number. Her boss's calm brisk voice said: *Freya Lomond. I'm away from my desk right now; leave a message, I'll be in touch soon, thanks.*

'It's Ally. We need to speak. I'm bloody furious about *Lara* being involved in stories about me and Juniper. I hope you've got nothing to do with this. If you put Lucas up to it, I'll tear your head off!'

Ally slammed down the phone, choking with anger. She turned to see the Rushmores staring at her.

CHAPTER 73

Kulah

The burial ground faces west, to Tir nan Og. The old chapel is buried into the rock and turf; it is a good place to sit and talk to the ancestors. I feel my mother's presence like a bright flame. It is a place of visions. When the men return, we must carry old Seamus here.

Someone leaves me oatcakes on a rock outside the chapel though I do not need food. I drink rainwater from the ancient stone font at the door which has never dried up even in the middle of summer when it doesn't rain.

I keep watch here and pray. Hunger does not touch me. I am waiting for the ship to come in or for deliverance, whichever comes first. Far away I hear the moaning of the wind like weeping. Day after day. No human can keep up a grieving for that long; so I know it is the elements.

Sometimes I catch sight of a boy running over the burial mound, gulls' feathers in his bonnet. I know his face but have forgotten his name.

CHAPTER 74

Galloway

John sat drumming his fingers at the end of the reading room which was emptying of people. The younger of the two librarians had taken pity on him when he'd pleaded for just a quick look in their newspaper archive, twenty minutes before closing.

'Did you belong to the commune yourself?' the chatty librarian with the long black plait and a badge naming her Lauren, asked.

'No,' John said, 'I'm just trying to get some info for a friend while I'm down here.'

She laid out heavy bound copies of the *Douglas Weekly* that she'd retrieved from the metal racks in the basement.

'I remember seeing their vans and trailers over at Kirk Newton when I was a kid. Some of them lived in tepees. I used to think how romantic,' she smiled. 'Now I think how did they manage without central heating and hot showers?'

'I heard they weren't that popular, is that true?' John began a quick scanning of the large news sheets.

Lauren shrugged. 'Didn't hear anything too bad. There was this really big guy in charge – we called him the Tartan Hulk – always wore a kilt and long hair. Some kids were scared of him but he was nice enough.'

'What about their children – did you ever play with them?'

'You're joking. Our mums said they were that dirty and scruffy we'd catch something off them. And they never came to our school – think they were home schooled. As far as I could see they had a ball living in the woods and making tree houses. Used to fire conkers and acorns at anyone walking over the hill – especially those long-suffering monks meditating outside.'

'Thanks for these,' John said.

'If you want to see the original photos, let me know. I'm afraid they're not digitised yet, so it's a matter of looking through the files. We might not have time now but you could come back in the morning.'

She left him to it. John worked quickly, flicking through to the issues that coincided with his time in Dumfries. The Tartan Hulk; yes he remembered a man fitting that description. It wasn't long before he found an article about him, next to his grinning bearded picture.

'First prize in the car lifting competition went to newcomer Olaf. This gentle giant is part of a colourful band of travellers who have put down roots in idyllic Galloway, setting up a community at Kirk Newton.

"Everything we grow is organic," said Olaf, "and this prize money will buy some more free range hens."

There were further benign references to the Kirk Newton Community over the following months: selling honey and eggs at the gates, holding a Halloween bonfire for the village, photographed at dawn on Newton Hill at the summer solstice, taking part in the local Gathering. But there were no other names given apart from Olaf; he appeared to be their spokesman and leader.

John skipped a couple of years. The memory he had was of being newly in Dumfriesshire when he'd helped set up a summer Highland Games to keep the local children occupied over the long holiday. A team of boys and girls had come over from Kirk Newton; everyone remembered them as they'd painted their faces blue and played in bare feet. There'd been a real holiday atmosphere with side stalls selling food, impromptu folk music, Sumo wrestling, races and team games.

'The library closes in ten minutes,' the older librarian called from the counter.

Hastily he scoured the pages for photographic evidence. Finally he found a picture of the massed teams in an August issue. He could just pick out himself with his team in the sea of grinning faces, but the image was taken from too far away to be distinct. It was impossible to identify the other adults involved.

'Have you got any more from this event?' John asked librarian Lauren.

She glanced at her colleague who nodded. 'Give me a minute then.'

While he waited, John flicked on. Abruptly the reports on the community had grown critical: the incomers were taking valuable seasonal jobs from locals; one of them had lost his licence for driving an untaxed unsafe vehicle, the fire brigade had been called to put out a fire which was blamed on 'wild commune kids' and a woman called Neave was being prosecuted for giving tattoos with unclean needles that had nearly killed a man with septicaemia. He turned back a few pages to before the tournament; he must have missed it.

The story he had been searching for leapt out at him. Next to it was a picture of Olaf with his arm around another man – younger and bearded – but recognisable. Bullseye: Ned Rushmore.

CHAPTER 75

Battersay

'I can't go on the trip until I've spoken to Lucas or Freya,' Ally protested as Mary steered her back into the kitchen and poured her a herbal tea.

Ned didn't try to hide his annoyance. 'Are you going to let these unworthy people spoil this special voyage?'

'I just need to know for certain. Can't you see that?'

'What difference will a few days make? If it turns out that they've both betrayed you then you're only going to feel worse. It'll ruin the sailing for you and we can't change our arrangements so late in the day.'

'Than you'll have to go without me.'

Mary looked pained. 'But think of Juniper. We need to keep her safe.'

'I'll look after her here then.'

'And what happens if you take off for London before we get back?' Mary chided. 'No, we simply can't leave Juniper like this. She's in a vulnerable state after the attack.'

'She can be unpredictable,' Ned added, 'you know that. We're the only people she can truly trust.'

'You're special to her,' Mary said.

'Don't you want to come?' Ned demanded.

'Yes, but – Oh God, I don't know what to do!'

Juniper stirred. Mary put a finger to her mouth.

'Sorry,' Ally whispered, feeling contrite.

Mary put a hand on her head and stroked back her hair. 'Please come, dear one.'

Ally wrestled with her feelings. 'I really want to but I need to know what Lucas is playing at. If he was the one who attacked Juniper, I'll never forgive him – or forgive myself for leading him to her.'

Mary stood up, looking agitated. 'I'm going to ring Peter-the-Pier in Bay. He'll know if Lucas left on the ferry or not.'

A tense few minutes followed while Ned paced the kitchen. They didn't speak. Ally knew she had angered him and felt bad; none of this was his fault. If it wasn't for her, there would be no spotlight on Juniper and Lucas would never have come to the island. She had endangered Juniper and was disrupting the Rushmores' cherished annual pilgrimage to the waters where they had lost Ossian.

Ally got up and went towards the doctor. 'Ned, I –'

Mary's return interrupted her apology. 'I've spoken to Peter.'

'What does he say?' Ally asked tensely.

'As you feared; Lucas left on the evening ferry. I'm so sorry my dear.'

Ally felt punched in the stomach. How had she allowed herself to be taken in by Lucas for a second time? She felt a wave of humiliation and guilt over Juniper. She crumpled to her knees next to the sleeping woman. 'Oh Juniper, forgive me,' she whispered and kissed her oily hair.

Mary said, 'we all need to get some sleep.'

191

Ned stood over Ally, staring down.   'So you'll come with us tomorrow?'

Ally nodded, her hand resting protectively on Juniper. 'Yes please.'

'That's my girl,' he said, and smiled for the first time that evening.

CHAPTER 76

Galloway

'Tragic couple take refuge in Crazy Celtic Commune'. John skimmed the article; it was largely quoting from a national tabloid that was wallowing in the tragedy of a son lost at sea, and yet blaming the over-liberal parenting of the Baby Boomer couple who had been so irresponsible as to take their child to sea in a storm.

' "Ned and Mary just want to be left alone," said Olaf, the self-styled chief Druid of the commune. "They've found peace and meaning with their fellow Celts. We are very close to the spirit world here."

When asked if the bereaved couple were in contact with their dead son, Olaf, a stocky six feet tall, turned aggressive and ordered the reporter off his land.'

John felt admiration for the no-nonsense druid. It was cheap of the local paper to pick up on the cruel tabloid article. Olaf had been kind to offer the Rushmores a safe haven in which to lick their wounds and no doubt the commune had given them purpose. He stared at the photo of Ned with Olaf; he had an inkling when he first saw Ned on Battersay that he knew him from somewhere but could never place him. The only time he had knowingly come across members of the commune was at the summer games.

The librarian Lauren returned with a file of photographs. 'Sorry, I'll have to rush you.'

'Thanks. Do you know what became of Olaf, your Tartan Hulk?' John asked, as he searched the file.

She shook her head. 'Betty might know – she lives out that way.' She beckoned to her colleague.

'Oh, him,' the grey-haired librarian said, drawn into the conversation. 'He was a strange fish. We always used to wonder how a man like him could afford to buy the land at Newton Hill.'

'There are plenty of rich eccentrics,' John said.

'Yes, you're right,' said Betty, 'and he was probably one of them. He certainly wasn't a real Celt – not even a Scot. He might have gone around like someone out of *Braveheart*, but local gossip said he was an Englishman from Essex.'

John snorted. 'So what happened to English Olaf and the rest of them?'

'I'm not exactly sure. One day they seemed to be there and the next they were gone and the estate was up for sale. I think a couple of the families stayed around trying to live in the old stables but they got evicted when the place was sold.'

'Who's there now?'

'The Buddhists took it over,' said Betty. 'The grounds and woods were much larger than their old place and they seem to like to wander about.'

'And Olaf definitely left the area?' John asked. 'So there's no chance of speaking to him?'

Betty shook her head.

Lauren suggested, 'maybe the Buddhists would know where he went.'

John nodded and flicked briefly through the file. There were plenty of shots of children's races and some of the musicians, but no close-ups of people from the commune.

'I'm going to have to close now,' Betty said brusquely.

'What is it that you're looking for?' Lauren asked.

John hesitated. 'This sounds strange, but I'll know it when I see it. I have a memory of a body painting competition – I think it was won by someone from the commune – someone with a bird of prey on his body.'

'That's no surprise,' said Betty, 'half of them were covered in tattoos and piercings.'

'I thought there was a photo in a local paper,' John said, 'but I must be wrong.'

He handed back the file.

Lauren said, 'I can have a better look through the archives tomorrow. Give me till the afternoon.'

As John made his way back to the pub he questioned his whole reason for trying to unearth Ned Rushmore's unhappy past. He had disliked the doctor from the moment he met him on Battersay, but that was more to do with Ned's pestering Bethag for ancient cures and fuelling stories about him being a de-frocked priest. He had resented Ned's interfering ways and superior attitude. Yet Donny had had his doubts too; he'd begun to tell him something about Ned once then had changed his mind. And why hadn't he followed up Donny's drunken ramblings about the swimmer with the eagle on his back? What was it the young fisherman had wanted to tell him the night he'd died?

Yet wasn't he being just as bad trying to find evidence that Ned was not to be trusted? And wasn't it more to do with jealousy over Ally? It infuriated him the way she looked up to Ned as some sort of Celtic guru. But that didn't mean he was a danger to her. So what was he doing here, wasting his time chasing half memories and rumours? And what, if anything, did the mysterious Olaf have to do with it all?

'Ah, there you are,' his father greeted him with a smile. 'You look like you could do with a pint.'

CHAPTER 77

Battersay

The island reflected a perfect image in the glassy water at dawn. They slipped out of Sollas Bay with the engine making a low puttering noise, the bows creating soft ripples. Pale gold light shimmered on the sea and shone on the white beach. To Ally's delight, a seal surfaced right behind and followed their progress. As the sun strengthened, she could see for miles; every crevice in the cliffs was crystal clear and the whitewashed houses looked close enough to touch.

'Isn't it looking beautiful this morning?' Mary murmured. 'You stay and enjoy the view; I'll sit with Juniper.'

Ally nodded and Mary went below. That morning, Juniper had been difficult to wake and heavy to manhandle into the Citroen 2CV. Now she lay below, sleeping once again. Ally suspected Ned had given her something strong to sedate her for the journey and keep her calm.

She gazed at the receding land, catching sight of the hall and a smattering of blue and orange tents. As they edged further out, Bay House came into view. Bethag would be waking and drinking her first cup of tea of the day. If they managed to land on Kulah, she would bring the old woman souvenir shells and pebbles to put on her window sill and remind her of home.

In the tranquil dawn it seemed impossible to believe in a troubled ghost walking the cliffs or that its people lay under a curse. It was one of the most stunning places she had ever visited and Ally felt a pang of regret to see it diminish before her eyes. Still smarting from Lucas's cowardly running away, and Freya's likely involvement with him, she looked on Battersay with renewed fondness. Despite the early pranks, she liked its people, her uncomplicated job and the outdoor life. And for a time she had found the most intense passion of her life in her relationship with John. Her heart twisted to think how she had misjudged him so badly too. Yet John was too embittered by his disastrous affair with Caroline and his loss of faith in women to forge a normal relationship. His interest in her had turned out to be unhealthy, but it didn't stop her aching with loss for him.

Ally reached into her bag and pulled out the book that she'd picked off the shelf on impulse an hour ago. *Tales & Prophecies of the Outer Isles.* It was just the book to get her in the mood for Kulah: a copy of the same book which she had read to Bethag.

'What's that?' Ned grinned, standing at the tiller. The strained tired look of the previous night had left him.

Ally held it up.

'Ah,' he said, 'that was written by an old tutor of Mary's.'

'Really?'

195

'Yes, delightful old boy. She took me to meet him once. Bit of a one for the female students; all the pretty ones got invited to tea. Very knowledgeable about Scottish folklore; that was his speciality.'

'Where did Mary study?'

'Edinburgh University.'

'So did I!' Ally exclaimed.

'Yes I know. It was on your CV. It's probably the reason I hired you. Always had a soft spot for Edinburgh graduates.'

Ally looked down at the book and noticed the author for the first time: Roland Mountjoy. 'I did a module in Scottish Studies but I don't remember this name.'

'He was more or less retired when Mary was there in the early '70s. I think there's still a Mountjoy lecture that celebrates his interests. Anyway, we've him to thank for setting us off on our lifelong love of all things Celtic.'

As they pulled further out to sea, a light breeze began to lift. Juniper's cottage could be clearly seen and the tumbled remains of the old settlement. Whoever had first lived there had wanted an uninterrupted view of marauders from the sea.

Abruptly, Ally caught sight of the religious statue rearing up like a stack of white rock: Our Lady of the Seas. The clarity of the light was so dazzling that she could make out the corroded faces of mother and child. The pitted hollows looked like shadowy tears.

Ally shivered. They repelled her and yet evoked a choking sadness. The breeze sighed and the boat began to rock.

Seeing it from this angle, it seemed less that the child clung to its mother than the mother was tugging her infant to her, roughly, protectively. Before, Ally had thought her a weak, helpless portrayal of womanhood; a victim. She was meant to embody all the pain and sorrow of women who lose their men at sea. But seeing her towering above now, Ally was struck by her muscular fierceness, her desire above all else to keep her child safe. This Madonna would put up a hard fight. In that moment of realisation, something about the robed woman spoke to her, as if she was attempting to reach out and tug Ally landward.

She stood up.

'What are you doing?' Ned was startled.

'Getting a better look. I thought I heard something.'

'I'd rather you sat down.'

For a moment Ally had an overwhelming desire to jump from the boat and swim back to shore. She gripped the side to stop herself.

'Are you all right?'

Ally battled with her sudden panic at leaving dry land. That's all it was; nerves at the thought of going far out to sea in a yacht without knowing the first thing about sailing. There were no whispering voices.

'I'm fine.' She sat down quickly with her back to the island.

'You can help me get the mainsail up in a minute.'

196

Ally nodded. She opened the book on myths to stop her staring back at the statue. The flyleaf was personally inscribed by the author.

'To Mary, with admiration, your friend and teacher, Rollo.'

CHAPTER 78

Galloway

'Why exactly are we here John?' Duncan asked, keeping pace with his son up the woodland path.

John didn't answer until they reached the summit of Newton Hill. He gazed down on the rooftops of the Buddhist retreat, barely visible through the canopy of beech, oak and birch.

'You know why. I want to see if this woman Neave remembers anything about Ned Rushmore.'

Returning to the library that morning, Betty had tracked down a former commune member still living in the lodge house at Kirk Newton, doing caretaking duties for the Retreat. She wasn't on the phone. Lauren had run off a copy of the photo with Olaf and Ned.

'But what is it you're expecting to find?' his father persisted. 'Aren't you being a little bit obsessive about this so-called quack doctor?'

John pulled out his cigarettes and took his time lighting one while he weighed up whether to unburden his suspicions to his father.

'I've been going over things in my mind for a long time,' John said, blowing out smoke, 'trying to make sense of things going on in Battersay. It's not just that Ned Rushmore and I have never seen eye to eye, it's that I've never trusted him. I think he's a fake. Not that I have any evidence – and anyway, what did it matter so long as he wasn't trying to practise medicine? His herbal mumbo-jumbo probably isn't harmful – it's largely old remedies he's pinched from women like Bethag.'

'So,' Duncan frowned, leaning on his walking stick, 'why the suspicion?'

'It's to do with Donny MacRailt, the boy who killed himself.' John drew hard on his cigarette and told his father about Donny's confession at seeing Birdwoman on Kulah years before she was discovered.

'But that's not all that haunted him. He was becoming more and more paranoid about the Devil – or someone he thought of as the Devil – a man with a bird tattoo. Donny said he'd seen him crouched on a rock at Kulah that first time he saw Juniper, but because of his father's angry reaction he didn't dare mention him and afterwards wondered if he'd just dreamt him. He said he'd only ever told two people – me and Ned Rushmore. I thought it was all the stress of the media attention over Juniper and falling out with his father. He'd also started self-medicating with booze and dope – I'm pretty sure Rushmore was supplying him – so I reckoned he was having psychotic episodes. He was really frightened.' John paused, drawing on his cigarette. 'Ally, the woman I was seeing, found these graphic drawings Donny had done of Juniper being attacked by a monster with an eagle on his back. They were pornographic – spooked her. There was one of her too. I began to wonder …'

'Go on,' Duncan encouraged.

'What if this monster wasn't just in Donny's mixed up head? What if the Devil was human and he felt under a real threat? Maybe Donny thought Juniper and Ally were at risk too and that's why he was putting his fears down on paper.'

'You think it might be this Dr Ned?'

'I never got the chance to speak to Donny about it before he ended it all, and I feel guilty as hell about that.'

'You're not saying that Rushmore is responsible for his death, are you?'

'Not directly, no,' John admitted. 'But maybe Rushmore was worried Donny knew something about him – had recognised him as the man with the bird tattoo – so was keeping him drugged up and feeding his paranoia until it tipped him over the edge.'

'Does he have a bird tattoo?'

'He's heavily tattooed – part of his Celtic image – but I've never seen his back.'

His father gave him a sceptical look. 'It all sounds a bit tenuous to me.'

John ground out his cigarette. 'I know how it sounds. But then it came back to me where I'd seen Rushmore before – down here. And I have this memory of this body painting competition which was won by one of the commune – a guy with a big bird on his back. I'm convinced it's Rushmore and I want to find out more about him from people who knew him in the '90s. Because if Donny was right, then Rushmore's got something to do with Kulah at a time when Juniper was living there undiscovered. He sails out that way every September. Don't you think it's odd that in all that time he never reported a sighting of Juniper?'

'What does your friend Ally think of all this?' Duncan asked.

John flushed. 'I haven't discussed any of this with her – she's a fan of Rushmore's – and we had a falling out. I downloaded Donny's pictures from her camera,' he said, his look sheepish, 'to have a better look. She got the wrong idea. I left her a note telling her not to go on this sailing trip he's organised – but knowing her she'll do just the opposite.'

His father put a hand on his shoulder. 'Then I hope you're wrong about this man and that it's only straightforward jealousy on your part.'

John felt a chill go through him. 'I hope so too, but I can't shake off the feeling that Rushmore is somehow mixed up in all this Kulah business. I think Donny was onto something that Ned doesn't want anyone to find out.'

CHAPTER 79

Kulah

I, Flora Gillies, am a priestess. I kneel on the damp earth of the burial chamber, next to the bones of the ancestors. They come to me in dreams and speak their wisdom. They tell me I must save my people and bring them safely home or the spirits of the men will wander forever.

I know what I must do now. I come out into waning daylight which stings my eyes but my spirit soars. No longer do I feel the wind through my clothes or the cuts on my bare feet. I go into every house and spread the news.

'I have seen the men. Come with me!'

They are worn out with crying, grief reducing them to rags that snap in the wind. My heart swells with compassion, even for the disbelieving.

'Have faith,' I tell them.

I see fear on the faces of some. They know I have the power of the saints on my breath; I can say; 'let it be done' and it is done.

'Do not be afraid.'

I take The Baby from her mother's breast and bid her follow. Seanaid flaps after me like an anxious hen. Soon all their fears will be gone and there will be laughter on Kulah once more. They trudge after me as if stones weighted their shawls.

CHAPTER 80

At sea, off Kulah

Outside it was dark. The boat rolled around in the swell. Ally lay below on a tiny shelf that passed for a bunk, feeling wretched. She had no idea what time it was, drifting in and out of fitful sleep. The last thing she remembered was throwing up her sardine sandwich over the side of the boat and Mary rubbing her back in comfort. Ned had given her something to help her sleep. Whatever had possessed her to come on this trip? It came back to her how easily she succumbed to seasickness.

'Mum-muh,' Juniper whimpered in her sleep, on the lower bunk. The air was rank with that oily fishy smell of hers.

Ally leaned over and put out a comforting hand. 'Know how you feel.'

Just the change of position made her nauseous. It was no good lying there; she would never get back to sleep feeling this bad. Gingerly, Ally swung herself out of the bunk and fumbled her way over the crates and boxes stacked in the hold. It seemed there was enough food and supplies to keep them at sea for weeks. Perish the thought.

There was something about food that nagged her aching head; some thought she'd had earlier which had seemed out of place. What was it? It had gone for now. Looking at the piled provisions, Ally wasn't sure she could ever eat again. She hoped Ned's sailing friends had good appetites.

She emerged into a cold salty bluster. Two shadowy figures sat close together, sharing a blanket. Behind them she could just make out a gigantic cliff face.

'Dear girl,' Mary said, 'how are you feeling?'

'Felt better,' Ally grimaced. 'Where are we?'

'Anchored off the Black Rock,' Ned said.

Ally's pulse quickened. 'You mean this is Kulah?'

'Just about. Exciting, isn't it? Come and sit with us,' Ned beckoned, 'and watch.'

'Watch for what?' Ally stumbled towards them, trying to keep her balance.

'The dawn,' said Mary.

Ned patted the bench beside him. Ally sat down and he pulled the rug over her knees too, putting an arm around her.

'Here I am with my two favourite women, in one of my favourite spots on earth. What a lucky chap, eh?'

Ally glanced at Mary, feeling uncomfortable, but she smiled back. 'Yes you are.'

'What are the chances of getting ashore?' Ally asked.

'Good,' Ned said. 'The wind's dropping. I reckon after sunrise we'll be able to enter the harbour.'

'Where's that?' All Ally could see was a wall of forbidding rock.

'Through there,' Ned pointed to a stack that jutted out from the black mass.

Straining her eyes, she could just make out an archway in the rock.

'And you're quite sure we're allowed to land? I thought it belonged to some trust that didn't want the bird life disturbed.'

'It does,' Ned said, 'but there's nobody here to stop us, is there? As long as we respect the island we aren't doing any harm. And we won't be staying long,' he added, 'just overnight if the weather holds.'

Ally was struck by his confidence. 'You've landed here before haven't you?'

Ned winked. 'Just don't go telling the authorities. This place was never meant for rules and red tape.'

Ally felt uneasy. 'How many times?'

'Hush,' Mary whispered, before Ned could answer, 'just listen to nature.'

As they sat waiting and her head began to clear of its grogginess, Ally became aware of sea birds stirring, their muted cries growing as they sensed the dawn.

Even before crimson light bled into the sky from the eastern horizon, the shriek of gulls announced the day, wheeling about the high cliffs. As the sun came up they clattered overhead, their huge white wings catching blood red in the early light, and dived into the inky water. The rocks were scarred with white droppings from thousands of birds; the cliffs seethed with screaming fulmars. She pulled up her hood, deafened by the din.

Ned rose and began giving orders, reeling in the anchor and steering the boat on course for the rocky entrance. She watched the couple work in tandem, wondering again how they could put themselves through the ordeal of sailing these waters where Ossian had drowned. Yet they appeared to gain comfort from being there.

Suddenly it struck Ally that they were at the very place where the ship full of returning Kulah men had been wrecked. This was the Black Rock and they were heading for the narrow passage where the ship had tried to enter on that stormy day in 1946. Her stomach lurched as they bobbed closer to the forbidding cliffs. Far below, must lie the wreck and the remains of the men: Bethag's father and his shipmates.

Ally clung on as they pitched back and forth, riding the swell, the sail glowing pink in the sunrise. Anxiety welled up inside. What if they went onto the rocks too? Or maybe they wouldn't be able to sail out again and got trapped on Kulah? She stared up at its fortress-like walls and the colonies of mighty birds; it didn't look habitable. There seemed to be no speck of green field or even rough grazing; all was bald, vertical granite. How could anyone live in such a place?

Poor Juniper. How on earth had she survived here for years? Worry for the strange girl made her even more anxious.

'Will Juniper be okay?' Ally called out.

'What?' Ned put a hand to his ear.

'Juniper,' Ally shouted over the cacophony, 'I hope she doesn't freak out when she sees where we are.'

'Why should she?' Ned bellowed. 'She's with her own kind here.'

Ally was taken aback. It seemed a rather callous joke. But Ned's expression was serious with concentration. Mary's back was to them as she worked a rope. She hadn't heard the exchange.

Minutes later they were sweeping in under the echoing archway, the air ringing with screeching and the clank of rigging. It was like being in a giant flooded cave and they swung violently from side to side as the current sucked them through. Ally's heart drummed. She half expected to hear the wailing grief of the Kulah women, the air felt so thick with fear and sorrow. *It's birds screaming not humans,* she had to remind herself.

'Watch out!' Ned bawled.

A dark shape came hurtling past, making Ally cry out in alarm. A huge black bird flew low, the flap of its powerful wings nearly knocking her off her feet. Its mournful call rang like a warning then it was gone.

'Cormorant,' Ned shouted.

Ally wished she was back at the hall serving up food to campers or drinking tea with Bethag in the care home conservatory. Or back in the kitchen at Sollas House among the strings of onions and dried herbs; anywhere safe and on firm ground.

A plate of cold food on the kitchen table. That was the thought that had troubled Ally earlier. The table set for one, for her. Not for two. Why had there been no food laid out for Lucas the night before last when they had expected him to be with her? That's what had puzzled her. Had Dr Ned and Mary already known that Lucas wasn't coming back? And if so, why hadn't they said anything?

The next moment, they were through the archway and into a sheltered bay like a watery amphitheatre, steep grassy terraces banking away into misty crags.

Ned climbed on the seat, rocking the boat.

'Careful!' Mary gasped.

He paid no attention, flinging out his arms. 'Kulaaaah!'

His shout bounced around the harbour like a ghostly echo: *Kulah, Kulah, Kulah.*

CHAPTER 81

Galloway

John expected a middle-aged hippy type to come to the door, not a plump woman in elasticated trousers and pink jumper with a neat bob of greying hair and no make-up.

'Neave Roberts?' he asked, doubtful this could be the woman who was once in trouble for using contaminated needles in tattooing.

'Yes. Have you come for the course? You need to go to the side gate and ring the bell.' She had a soft lilt to her voice with a trace of Welsh accent.

John explained his interest in the commune and produced the photo.

'I haven't got my glasses,' she said, waving it away. 'Were you a friend of Ned's?'

'We lost touch.' John didn't want to lie outright.

'I think they settled in the Hebrides. Read about him in some article on Celtic homeopathy. Not that I follow the news. Don't have TV, never listen to radio. They drown out thought, don't you think?'

'Yes,' John agreed. He waited for her to invite them in but she stood guarding her door.

Duncan stepped forward. 'I'm terribly sorry to ask this, but could I come in and use your bathroom? Embarrassing but old age ...' He smiled apologetically.

Neave hesitated then said, 'of course, come in.'

John glanced at his father; there was nothing wrong with the old man's bladder but it had done the trick. She directed Duncan upstairs and John into a tiny red sitting-room with a green sofa piled with mismatched cushions.

'I'll get us some lime cordial.'

She came back with tumblers full of the pale green liquid and put them on the wooden floor. John helped himself. He passed her the photo. She pulled out a pair of reading glasses from a desk drawer.

'Yes, Olaf and Ned.' She tapped the photo. 'What do you want to know?'

'Tell me about Olaf,' John said, 'what sort of guy was he?'

'We all loved him. He was full of energy and ideas. Built the Community from scratch – very in tune with the earth, people, animals, kids – everything.'

'Did he have his own family?'

Neave gave him a surprised look. 'We were all his family. We weren't bound by conventional laws. We had our own way of ordering society – the old Pictish matriarchal way.'

'Sounds interesting,' Duncan said, appearing in the room. 'Can you explain that?'

Neave squatted on the floor, giving John's father the other half of the sofa, despite his protests.

'We were all equal,' she said, sitting very erect with short fat fingers clasping her glass, 'but the most spiritual among us ruled on any disputes and guided the others. And the women druids were the most powerful because we kept control of the lineage – the children – and descent passes down through us, you see.'

'I see,' Duncan said, looking bemused.

'So,' John said, 'it's not important to know who the father is as long as you know the mother?'

'Exactly,' Neave answered, flashing a smile. 'We got to choose the father for each child. Obviously the more virile men were popular – the ones with the true Celtic characteristics of strength and good looks and wisdom.'

'Like Olaf?' said John, avoiding his father's astonished look.

'Like Olaf,' Neave agreed.

'And Ned?'

Neave's smile disappeared. 'Things were more complicated with Ned.'

John waited for her to elaborate, hoping his father wouldn't feel the need to fill the awkward silence.

'He would probably have embraced the Celtic way,' she continued, 'but Mary was a bit of a problem – she was more conventional – still in the grip of the old patriarchal ways of monogamy. She wanted Ned to herself.'

'Not surprising after what they'd been through together,' John pointed out, 'losing their only son Ossian. I can imagine how it would make her anxious about losing Ned too.'

Neave gave a derisive laugh. 'She had no need.'

John wondered what she meant, but she didn't elaborate.

'Did you keep any photos?'

'No, all the images I want are in my head – or in my dreams.' She took a long slug of her drink.

At the risk of annoying her, John asked. 'You were a tattooist for the Community?'

She gave him a sharp look. 'Body artist.'

'Did you – paint many bodies?'

'Yes. There was always some event to celebrate. I did temporary paintings too – the children liked to put on woad for games and competitions.'

'Yes, I remember that – quite terrifying for the other kids,' John laughed. 'So your designs were in great demand?'

'They were until some local drunk made trouble.'

'The accusation of dirty needles?'

Neave bristled. 'I was a scapegoat. Olaf paid my fine but said I had better stop. The locals were out to get us by then, they hated how successful we'd become. And the bad publicity around Ned and Mary didn't help – no one had bothered us till they came.'

'That must have been very difficult for you,' John sympathised.

'I took up painting pots and tiles instead. Inanimate objects can't sue you.' She drained off her cordial.

'Did you do Ned's body paint before you gave up?'

'Yes, he was very keen.'

'So you did the eagle on his back?'

She frowned. 'No, Ned didn't have one.'

'Are you sure?'

'Quite sure.'

John hid his frustration. 'Oh, I must've been mistaken then.'

Neave hauled herself up. 'Olaf did though.'

'I'm sorry?' John was startled. 'Say that again.'

'Olaf's the one who had an eagle across his back,' Neave said. 'It's a symbol of wisdom and knowledge.' She took their empty glasses. 'And virility of course.'

CHAPTER 82

Kulah

'What about Juniper?' Ally asked, stepping into the small dinghy.

Mary looked undecided, fiddling with a leather pouch around her neck. 'Best let her wake naturally. When she does, we can come back for her.'

Ned loaded up a camping stove and a couple of boxes; Mary clutched a pile of bedding while Ally carried their small tent and a backpack of warm dry clothes. In a matter of minutes they were climbing out onto the tiny strip of shingle beach between sheer cliffs, the water blue and calm.

Ally's heart lurched with excitement; finally she was going to explore this mysterious island that had held her imagination all summer. They even planned to stay a night here. Tonight she would read Roland Mountjoy's book by torchlight and listen out for the ghosts of Bethag's family. Its remoteness scared and thrilled her; only a handful of people in the world had stood where she was now.

She helped Ned pitch the tent on the narrow grassy bank above, next to a large ring of stones.

'From photos I've seen, this is where they used to have communal feasts – the equivalent of barbecues,' he told Ally. 'And do you see up there?' Ned pointed to a line of ruined stone houses on the skyline. 'That's what remains of the village.'

'I haven't seen photos of the island, only the ones Bethag has of her family.'

'You must get Mary to show you when we get home. She's got quite a collection. Roland gave them to her. He was an excellent amateur photographer and spent a summer here collecting folklore.'

'Then he must be the man who took pictures of Flora Gillies and her daughters,' Ally exclaimed. 'The photographer signed them with an R.'

Mary cooked a breakfast of eggs and bacon on the portable stove. Ally was still feeling queasy from the voyage but the salty bacon and steaming tea revived her. As the mist lifted off the high peaks, Ned led them up the hillside to the ruined village. Bracken and brambles grew out of the deserted houses, their roofs fallen in and windows gaping.

Ally peered inside one darkened cottage; it smelt of damp earth and animals. All of a sudden, something darted out of the shadows. She gasped as a wild goat jumped past with a bleat and raced up the stony track, disappearing over the ridge.

'He probably got more of a fright than you did,' Ned teased. 'Come on, let's see where it went.'

The path petered out and the climb became a scramble over boulders and up loose scree. Ally ended up on hands and knees. She felt dizzy looking down, the hillside dropping away on all sides to the sea. The wind was stronger up there; it whistled and moaned, buffeting her towards the edge. Ally froze. Panic pounded in her chest.

'Wait! I don't think I can go higher,' she called out. Mary and Ned turned around.

'I think there's a plateau ahead,' Ned coaxed, coming back for her. He held out a hand. 'Just take your time and don't look back.'

'I'm sorry I can't. I get vertigo.' She was shaking so badly that Ned beckoned Mary down.

'She can't do it, my love.' He crouched down beside Ally. 'Come on, turn around and just sit. I've got hold of you.'

Ally inched round, digging her fingers and heels into the gravelly mountainside. Her head spun and vomit rose in her throat. She closed her eyes. Mary sat down on her other side and slipped an arm through hers.

'I'm sorry,' Ally whispered, 'I'm ruining your walk.'

'Don't worry; the view is just as stunning from here.'

Ally opened her eyes and allowed herself a cautious look around. The old village lay below, clinging forlornly to the grassy slope. Goat tracks trailed away on all sides along the cliff tops and dark-haired goats peppered the crags. She had no idea how they kept upright on the vertical rock face. Gulls kept up an incessant noisy calling. And far, far below, the sea sucked and sighed, and stretched away over the horizon.

'We'll go down there,' Mary pointed out a grassy mound set well apart from the village on its own promontory, surrounded by a ring of stunted trees. 'It'll be more sheltered.'

'Looks a bit too near the edge for me,' Ally fretted.

'We'll take it slowly,' Ned promised.

With Ned and Mary taking an arm each, they coaxed Ally back down. Quickly, her panic subsided. In the grassy dip by the mound she couldn't see the sickening drops.

'I don't know what scared me so much,' she said, feeling foolish, 'I've climbed higher mountains in Europe. I just felt so sick.'

Mary put a cool hand on her brow. 'You need to take it easy. It'll pass. Sit for a minute.'

'What is this place?' Ally asked. Only up close was it apparent that the large green mound was man-made, with steps down and a doorway; a sunken building with a turf roof.

'It must be the chapel,' Ned said, circling it, 'the one Rollo talked about.'

Mary nodded. 'He reckoned it was built on the site of a much older burial ground – probably Iron Age.'

'Come and have a look round here. There are lots of old graves.'

Ally followed. Weathered headstones, their names and dates almost smoothed away, dotted the ground in the shade of gnarled hazel and rowans. There were other mounds with no markings.

'Not much room in a place like this for burials,' Ned mused. 'They must've reused old graves, I imagine.'

Ally touched the prickly dried lichen that clung to a Celtic cross and felt a rush of emotion. The place was full of souls: generations of Kulah men and women. As a stiff breeze rustled the gnarled branches, she felt a strong presence of these long dead islanders. But it didn't feel peaceful like other ancient graveyards. Maybe it was the restless pounding of the sea below, out of view but a constant noisy threat.

'I wonder why these ones have no headstones,' she puzzled.

'Perhaps they were the most recent,' said Ned, 'and they never had time to erect them – or didn't have the manpower.'

Ally's heart stopped. Under one of these undulating ridges must be where Flora and Seanaid lay. She could almost see Bethag kneeling distraught over the newly dug graves and hear her keening.

'You look in need of a sit down, poor girl.' Ned steered her back to the sheltered side.

Ally flopped down beside Mary who was sitting with her face raised to the sun like a contented cat.

'Tell me more about Roland Mountjoy.' Ally wanted to chase away bleak thoughts of the doomed Kulah women.

'A very charismatic man – even in his '70s – and still handsome,' Mary said, smiling at Ally. 'I think he caused quite a stir here. Came at the end of the war when the women had been left to cope alone and hadn't seen such a manly creature in years.'

Ally thought of Bethag and her sister Seanaid – mere teenagers at the time – and Bethag's searching for a baby that had something to do with John.

Ally was weighing up whether to mention this when Ned said, 'Yes, the old goat got a Kulah girl pregnant, didn't he?'

'Not an old goat,' Mary reproved, 'but yes, it was Seanaid Gillies, Bethag's older sister. She gave birth to a baby girl.'

'Really?' Ally exclaimed.

Mary nodded. 'But you know about Seanaid, don't you?'

The intense look she gave Ally made her uncomfortable. 'What do you mean?'

'Calum says that when Bethag gets confused she mistakes you for her sister.'

'Yes, she does. It's such a sad story. Bethag says Seanaid died in the flu epidemic at the end of the war.'

Ally glanced across at the silent empty village and tried to imagine it busy with the women. 'But the baby must have survived, mustn't she? Because Bethag went looking for her. Do you think …?' she hesitated. Mary nodded in encouragement. 'That she found her niece in Glasgow and that John is her grand-nephew? That would explain why she's so fond of him and he's so protective of her.'

Ned said, 'Well that's fascinating. I've always wondered why Bethag doted on that talentless man.'

'He's not talentless,' Ally defended.

'No he's not,' Mary agreed, 'but I don't believe he's related to Bethag.'

'Why not?' Ally asked.

'Rollo talked to me about his illegitimate child – his *daughter* – but by the time he found out about her, she'd been adopted.'

'How very sad for him.'

'Yes, he would have loved a child. His wife couldn't have any.'

'Was he able to find her?' Ally asked.

'Not exactly,' Mary said, 'adoption agencies didn't give out information in those days. All he knew was that his daughter had gone to a professional couple who moved to Yorkshire.'

'So she couldn't have been John's mother then?'

'No, she couldn't.'

'But Flora's cross – John has it.'

Mary shrugged. 'Perhaps the adoptive parents gave it away to stop their baby being traced.'

'Or one of the islanders took it and sold it,' Ned suggested.

'So Bethag's been wrong all these years about finding Seanaid's child? She'll be really upset – I don't think we should tell her.'

'Maybe not so wrong,' Mary said quietly. Ally felt uncomfortable under her steady gaze.

'What do you mean?'

'I think you were sent to Battersay for a reason Ally. I think Bethag found Seanaid's grandchild instead.'

Ally's insides somersaulted. 'You can't mean me?'

'Yes, why not?' Mary said, taking her hand and squeezing it. 'Your mother grew up in Yorkshire, didn't she? I think the ancestors have led you home for a purpose. Think of the disturbance in the spirit world since you came, dear child. You've heard the women crying and you've seen Flora's ghost – more than that – you've seen Juniper possessed.'

'Fits of rage you mean,' said Ally, trying to rationalise Juniper's bizarre outbursts, 'the tantrums of a woman who can't make herself understood.'

'You understand her. I believe it is Flora speaking to you through her.' Mary's expression remained calm but her eyes shone with excitement. 'Whatever terrible things have gone on, whatever spirits are wandering restlessly, only you have the power to exorcise them. It's your duty to help them find peace.'

Ally was dumbfounded. 'That's ridiculous,' she laughed, snatching her hand back, 'I don't have any powers and I can't possibly be related to Seanaid.' She looked at Ned. 'You don't believe this surely?'

His look was hard to fathom. 'I trust Mary's judgement. She's a wise woman. She was adamant you should come on this trip. If she thinks you have powers then you will have. Dear girl, you must overcome your modern cynicism and allow your ancient spirit to guide you.'

Ally's insides turned cold. For the first time, she felt really nervous in their company. Their Celtic beliefs had been quaintly eccentric – up till now. She did not like the idea that they had deliberately planned to bring her out to Kulah. She felt suddenly very alone and vulnerable.

Her throat tightened. 'I don't understand. What could you possibly want me to do?'

210

'Rest,' Mary smiled, 'don't look so worried. You'll come to no harm here. This evening we'll have a ceremony to placate the ancestors. And then it will all be over.'

CHAPTER 83

Galloway

'Why did the commune get closed down?' John asked Neave.

'For someone who pretends to know Ned and the Community, you ask a lot of questions,' she answered, growing suspicious. 'Who exactly are you?'

'John, tell her the truth,' his father urged.

John came clean. 'I used to be a priest in Dumfries. I remember Ned from those days and I'm worried that he might be mixed up in something bad in the Outer Isles – some sort of cover-up. But the man my friend described had a bird tattoo on his back.'

'I can't help you,' Neave said abruptly, 'I think you should leave.'

Duncan intervened. 'We don't want you to say anything against your old friends, but this is important. A dear friend of John's may be at risk – she could be sailing with the Rushmores right now. We just want to know if we should be concerned about Ned or whether my son's worrying about nothing. Please, is there anything else you can tell us about either of them?'

Neave slowly put down the empty tumblers and stared out of the window. For a long time she was silent. Finally she said, 'Olaf and Ned are brothers.'

'Brothers?'

'Yes. Olaf is the older.'

'Tell us more, please,' John urged.

'Olaf – I don't suppose that is his real name – made a lot of money in the '80s in overseas property; that's how he could afford to buy the land here. He gave Ned a refuge after they lost their boy but I don't think Ned and Mary ever got over it.' She continued to look at the trees. 'After a year or so of not getting pregnant with Ned, Mary wanted Olaf to give her a son – she was desperate – and thought it would be the next best thing to Ossian, seeing as Olaf shared Ned's DNA.'

'And did she get pregnant?' John asked.

Neave shook her head. 'Olaf wouldn't sleep with his brother's wife.'

'So what happened?'

Neave sighed. 'Mary tried to take her own life. She was admitted to a psychiatric hospital. After a few months she came home but didn't settle and took off without telling anyone where she'd gone. Ned was beside himself with worry but Olaf said they should just let her come back in her own time. Olaf was becoming more and more of a recluse; you could tell he was getting sick of communal life. It was a bad time.'

'But Mary came back?'

Neave turned to face John. Her look was sombre. 'Yes, she came back – with a baby.'

CHAPTER 84

Kulah

'What does placating the ancestors involve?' Ally asked with a nervous laugh.

Back by the shore, she felt safer and Mary had made a delicious lunch of fresh bread and goat's cheese and peppery salad. The strange atmosphere at the ruined chapel was dispelled, yet Mary seemed more edgy and preoccupied.

'Praying and singing mostly,' Mary answered, 'and offerings of food and drink.'

'And me?'

'You'll repeat the names of the dead.'

'That's all?'

Mary didn't answer; she was staring distractedly at the yacht waiting for Ned to reappear.

Ned returned in the dinghy with a groggy Juniper who squatted down close to Ally. Ally looked at her anxiously, wondering if she realised where she was. At that moment she looked small and vulnerable, hunched in a rug.

'You okay?' Ally worried. 'You look terrible.'

'She's fine,' Ned said. 'I think those sleeping pills have reacted with the travel sickness ones. They're still wearing off.'

'She can sleep a little longer,' Mary said as she handed round cups of water. Her hands were shaking. 'From the spring in the village; it's the freshest you'll taste anywhere.'

'How did you know where to look for it?' Ally asked.

Mary glanced away, flustered. 'Rollo told me.' She got up and shook crumbs from her clothes. Picking up a backpack and thermos, she said, 'I'm going up there to meditate for a bit – mentally prepare.'

Ally nodded, but Ned jumped up. 'I'll come with you, darling.'

'No,' she was firm. 'I want to do this on my own.'

They watched her go. She cut a lonely figure, picking her way back up the hillside, long plait of hair bouncing off her shoulder like a young girl.

'You do realise why she's chosen today to speak to the dead, don't you?' Ned said.

'Is it to do with Ossian?'

He nodded. His look was so sorrowful that Ally felt a rush of pity. Ned said, 'It's twenty three years to the day he died.'

CHAPTER 85

Galloway

John stared at Neave non-plussed. 'Mary had another baby? Whose was it?'

'Mary claimed it was Olaf's. He denied it but it was curtains for the Community. Olaf put the place up for sale immediately, said it was getting too commercialised and it was time we all moved on. He wanted somewhere more remote.'

John's heart went cold. 'Like an island out in the Atlantic?'

Neave nodded. 'More than likely.'

'Did Ned and Mary go with him?'

She shrugged. 'I don't know; it was all pretty chaotic. They disappeared off about the same time.'

Duncan asked, 'would either of them be a danger to women?'

Neave's eyes widened. 'No, I couldn't imagine that.'

John and his father exchanged looks.

'Well that's a relief,' said Duncan.

Neave looked uncomfortable. 'But Mary might be.'

'Mary?' John was astonished.

'She's the jealous type and very unstable. Ned thought he could look after her, but she needed proper psychiatric care in my opinion.'

John felt an icy chill go through him.

'I need to get back to Battersay.'

Duncan thanked Neave for her help. As they swiftly left, John asked, 'what was Mary's baby like?'

'She was a little girl – a dark-haired baby girl.'

John's heart thumped. 'Called?'

'I forget.' Neave shrugged. 'She cried at lot, that's all I remember.'

CHAPTER 86

Kulah, 1946

On the strip of turf between the chapel and the cliff, I, Flora Gillies, cradle The Baby and nod out to sea, ignoring the plaintive cries of the women. The sun is blazing like a forge iron as it drops below the horizon.

'The prophecy of the ancestors has come about.' I raise my voice. 'I was wrong to question it. There was nothing we could have done to stop the disaster, do you understand that? Last spring I heard the cuckoo.'

A groan goes around.

'But, women of Kulah, there is hope in the prophecy too.'

'What do you mean?' Margaret calls out. 'How can that be?'

'I have dreamed dreams and seen visions here, in this very place. The red boat: I have seen it in the sunset. And the woman of the red hair has given birth to the baby: this baby.' I hold her aloft.

Seanaid steps towards me, holding out her arms. 'Please Mother –'

I cling on tight. 'This baby was meant to be. The Seer saw it ten generations ago. Do not be ashamed. We are not being punished because of her – none of us. Would Flora Gillies lie to you? Am I not the one who has led you through the valley of the shadow of death? It is the power of the ancestors that has kept me strong; I feel them all about me.'

'Where are the men?' Christina cries. Others take up her call.

'They are here,' I shout, 'get down on your knees and thank the saints. Your prayers are about to be answered.'

CHAPTER 87

Kulah, the present

The wind strengthened during the afternoon. Ally awoke stiff and cold, her discarded book open and pages crackling in the breeze. She'd fallen asleep in the sun; now it had slipped behind bulky clouds. The boat lolled in the bay. Juniper lay curled in her blanket snoring. Ally looked around. No sign of Ned or Mary.

She checked her watch; it was after seven and she felt empty as if she hadn't eaten all day. Rummaging around in a crate, she found a container of homemade shortbread and demolished three biscuits at once.

Ally stood up and shivered. It was too cold to stand around waiting; she would go up to the chapel and see if she could help with anything. The sooner they got this weird ceremony over the better. Best if Juniper slept through the whole thing rather than see Mary getting upset over Ossian. She wondered if she could persuade the Rushmores to set sail again that evening? She really didn't want to stay on Kulah after all. Mary's belief in her being Seanaid's granddaughter was creeping her out, as was this place.

What did you expect? She could hear John's wry voice. Naively, she'd imagined some quaintly atmospheric place that time had forgotten but had preserved like some Hollywood Highland set of picturesque cottages and secret coves. Instead, Kulah was grimly rugged and utterly abandoned, wrapped in an air of desolation so profound that the very rocks seemed locked together in grief.

'John, I wish you were here now,' Ally said, gripped by a deep pang of longing for the man. 'I don't care about the stupid drawings.' What would he make of Mary's attempts to placate the spirits of Kulah? Would he feel sorry for a mother still in mourning, or exasperated by her pseudo paganism? Knowing John, probably both.

Ally pulled up her hood, tucked the book into the crate and set off up the track. Looking back, she made a mental promise to Juniper that she would take her back to Battersay and look after her there – in the coastguard's house if necessary. Hurrying through the deserted village, she kept her eyes on the distant promontory so as not to dwell on the tumbledown homes and their sad ghosts.

Arriving at the burial mound she saw the remains of a picnic laid out on the grass. A wooden bowl with gnawed chicken bones and bread crusts, untouched apples and two horn beakers tipped on their sides. She picked one up and sniffed. They had been drinking Mary's potent honey mead. Ally searched around the graveyard but there was no sign of them.

'Ned, Mary!' she called out.

The wind sighed back, rattling the trees. The twilight was fast approaching as mist descended. There was going to be no spectacular sunset tonight to please the ancestors. Cautiously, Ally stepped beyond the trees and peered along the cliff edge. It was deserted. Alarm began to

216

spread from the pit of her stomach. She called out again. Where else could they have got to?

She arrived back at the turfed chapel. Had they gone inside? Ally stared down the narrow steps cut into the slope that ended in a small dark entrance. It hardly looked big enough for an adult to squeeze through. Gingerly, she descended. She could smell a pungent dankness; the opening gaped black as a tomb.

As she inched forward, she could hear a soft moaning. Ally stopped. From a half-stooped position she could see a candle flickering on the floor. It cast a weak light over a barrel-roofed chamber. At the far end were stacked old crates, creels and empty tins. The floor was littered with small bones – rodents or birds? It looked and smelt more like a rubbish dump than a chapel. Her stomach flipped over as it suddenly struck her; this must be where Juniper had sheltered and led her grim existence. But tins? Had she salvaged food washed ashore from shipwrecks?

There was a sudden sob from close by. Startled, Ally glanced to her left. It took a moment to work out what she was seeing. Mary, long grey hair flowing about her shoulders was kneeling on a bed of bracken, eyes closed, rocking back and forth. Beside her, Ned was trying to comfort her. 'I'm sorry, so sorry.'

Ally turned and crept back up the steps.

CHAPTER 88

Galloway

John rang Calum and Shona. There was no reply, so he left a message. Had Ally gone sailing with the Rushmores? And if so, was Lucas with her? He had some stuff to tell them about Ned and Mary that could be linked with Juniper and Kulah and maybe Donny. Please could they ring back a.s.a.p.

He and Duncan went back to the library.

'How can I find out more about the wildlife trust that owns Kulah?' he asked Betty the librarian.

Half an hour later they had the name of the man who had set up the trust: Oliver Rushmore, millionaire and ornithologist.

'This must be your man Olaf,' Duncan said. 'Looks like he was the owner all the time that Juniper was stuck there. The question is, did he know about her?'

Anxiety had gripped John ever since hearing about Mary's dark-haired baby girl. He steered his father outside.

'Is it possible that Mary could have abandoned her daughter on Kulah?' he asked. 'She just doesn't seem the type. She's nutty about kids.'

'Well Neave said she was in a bad way mentally when they left the commune.'

'But why would she do that? And what about Ned – did he know? Surely they couldn't have been so callous?'

As they walked to the car, John tried to picture what had happened after the haven of the commune had collapsed.

'Do you think the two brothers and Mary retreated to Kulah and started their own community?'

His father looked sceptical. 'Like hermits, you mean?'

'Yeah, Neave said Olaf was becoming a recluse. Perhaps Ned and Mary found they couldn't hack it and ended up abandoning the little girl.' John guessed. 'Left her to fend for herself.'

'But why? And what became of Olaf?'

John stopped in his tracks. *Olaf and Juniper*. 'What if he stayed on Kulah bringing up Juniper? She might be his daughter after all. Ned and Mary might have kept them supplied. That would explain how Donny saw a man with an eagle tattoo; Olaf not Ned.'

'But that was years ago. Why did this Olaf not come forward when Juniper was rescued?'

'Something must have happened to him,' John said.

'But it still boils down to Mary abandoning her child,' Duncan pointed out. 'It's not natural.'

John gave him a grim look. 'Not all mothers feel a bond with their children.'

Duncan put a hand on his shoulder. 'I know; I'm sorry son.'

They were pulling out of the library car park when John's mobile rang.

'Calum? Thanks for ringing back. I may be overreacting but I'm worried about Ally. Is she –?'

Duncan glanced at his son as he fell silent listening to Calum. John frowned in concentration.

'*What*?' he suddenly barked. 'Good God!'

Duncan pulled the car into a bus stop and cut the engine.

'No, this isn't Juniper's doing,' John said in agitation. 'Listen, I've been finding out a lot about the Rushmores and a brother of Ned's called Olaf. I think Olaf was keeping Juniper on Kulah. Donny saw them both years ago on the island and I think the Rushmores found out.'

John's anger grew at something Calum said. 'For God's sake man, Juniper's the victim in all this – she's Mary's daughter. Yes! Because I've just discovered the link. If the Rushmores have taken her as well as Ally, then that's very sinister. They're dangerous people – possibly murderers from what you've just told me. We have to get to Ally and Juniper. Okay, tell Melville I'm on my way back. I'll try and get on the Barra flight today.'

When John finished the call, he looked ashen.

'What's happened?' Duncan asked.

'It started with calls from Ally's boss, Freya. She set the alarm bells ringing about Lucas. Couldn't track him down. He was expected back in London two days ago.'

'And?'

John swallowed. 'They've found a body up at Juniper's cottage.'

'It's Lucas?' Duncan gasped.

John nodded grimly. 'Yes it's Lucas.'

CHAPTER 89

Kulah

Ally watched a puffy-eyed Mary emerge from the underground chapel. She could not rid her mind of the image of Mary and Ned's distress, just feet away from the detritus of someone's hideout. Didn't it strike them that this must have been Juniper's dismal refuge? But they made no mention of it and only the thought of the anniversary of Ossian's death kept her from challenging them.

'You're nervous, but there's no need,' Mary said, wrapping herself in a plaid. She looked suddenly old.

Ned followed, swaying in the wind. He was glassy-eyed and drunk.

Ally glanced around. She didn't like the way the mist was rolling down from the crags behind, closing in on them. 'Maybe we should have the ceremony back at the harbour. The weather's on the turn.'

'No,' Mary snapped, 'it has to be done on the cliff facing west.'

'Why?'

'Looking across to Tir nan Og, of course; where our loved ones are.'

'Let's get this over with then,' Ally said, 'before Juniper wakes up.'

'Yes, it's time,' said Mary. Ned began to gather up the flask and horned mugs, but Mary was impatient. 'Leave all that.'

Ned dropped the horns but held onto the flask. As soon as they stepped around the mound towards the cliffs, a stiff wind carrying a spatter of rain buffeted them sideways. Mary led them forward.

'It's too windy,' Ally called out, anxiety crawling in her stomach. 'Don't go so near the edge please.'

Steel grey light glinted through the low cloud and merged with the choppy sea. What if they could not sail tomorrow? She looked round at Ned. He was strangely silent and subdued. Mary turned and gave a tearful smile.

'It's fine. Take my hand. Don't be afraid.'

When Ally hesitated, Mary linked an arm through hers. 'Come on, we'll hold onto each other; that way, no harm can come.'

Once through the ring of trees, the roar of sea and wind hit them. Overhead, birds gathered, flapping madly to stay near the ledges on the rock-face. Mary led her to a promontory where heather gave way to a strip of crumbly path and tufts of spiky grass. From here the world was a vast open expanse of endless sea and scudding clouds. Ally snatched her arm free and held back.

'That's far enough,' she said, heart hammering. The view was making her light-headed. 'Please don't go so near.'

'There must be a sunset,' Mary frowned, scanning the horizon.

Ned unscrewed the flask and took another swig of mead. 'Here, Ally, this will do you good.'

Ally took it and drank. The liquid burned down her throat. She had an instant memory of being drunk on it with Lucas; the smell made her suddenly nauseous and she handed it back. Ned snatched it and drained it off. His moodiness didn't unnerve her as much as Mary's growing agitation.

'How long do we have to wait?' Ally demanded, shivering in the wind. The spatters of rain were strengthening.

'Till they come,' Mary said in irritation.

'Who?'

'The women – the ancestors – my Ossian.' Mary cocked her ear. 'Listen, can't you hear them? I can hear them.' Her look was feverish. Ally stared at her. *She's unhinged.*

Ned flung out his arms and bellowed, '*Ossian!* Ossian, come to us!'

In an instant, Mary was in front of him. She raised her hand and slapped him hard in the face. Ned reeled back, stunned.

'It's not time, you stupid man,' Mary shouted tearfully. 'How dare you call up my boy's spirit like that? I shall decide, not you.'

Ally watched, appalled, wondering if she should intervene.

'Mary, my darling,' Ned staggered to stay upright. 'Let's just do this.'

'Not yet. We wait for the sunset.'

Now Ally was really scared. 'Look Mary, it's almost dark. There isn't going to be a sunset. Do your thing and then get off the cliff edge. This is really dangerous.'

Mary swung round, fury in her face. Ally flinched.

'Of course there will be one. It's written in the prophecy.'

'What's the prophecy got to do with anything?'

'*Everything.* It's why we're here – why you're here.'

Ally's heart drummed. 'Me? I've got nothing to do with all this. I'm not Seanaid's granddaughter for goodness sake.'

Mary grabbed her wrist, her voice pleading. 'You are the red-haired woman who is going to give me the child.'

Ally struggled in panic. 'What child?'

'The child that will reunite us with the ancestors – with Ossian. It's the second half of the prophecy – when everything will be alright again.'

'I don't have a child.' Ally threw off her hold.

'You're pregnant,' Mary said, her look desperate, 'I know you are. I can tell when a woman is carrying a babe in her womb. It's probably Balmain's but I put you with Lucas just to make sure.'

'You did *what*?' Ally was stunned.

'Got you drunk so he could have you – he wanted it – and I had to make sure.'

'Mary you're sick in the head,' Ally gasped, 'and I'm not pregnant.' She looked at Ned beseechingly. 'This has to stop now.'

Ned looked stupefied.

Mary wailed, 'he doesn't understand. No man understands what it is to carry and nurture a baby, only to have him snatched away.'

'I lost Ossian too,' Ned cried.

'You let my boy drown!'

'No Mary,' Ned groaned, 'don't say that.'

221

'Your brother was twice the man that you are, I see that now. I should have stayed here with him when I had the chance.'

'You don't believe that, my darling.'

Ally was aghast. 'What do you mean stayed here?'

Mary cried, 'this is my true home. Ossian is here – I feel him with me. And Olaf. Tell her about Olaf, Ned,' she challenged.

'No.'

'Tell her!'

Ned looked stricken. 'My brother. He owned Kulah. He brought Mary here with the baby.'

Ally felt winded. 'What baby?'

'Juniper,' Ned said, his eyes welling with tears.

Ally stared at Mary. 'Juniper is your baby?'

'Mine and Olaf's.'

'You left your own daughter to die on Kulah?' Ally accused.

'To *live* here,' Mary said, 'with her father – brought up as a true Celt – living off the sea and her wits – unsullied by modern life.'

Ally was horrified. 'Juniper was the victim of some sick experiment of yours?'

'Tell the truth, Mary, for pity's sake,' Ned pleaded. 'Juniper was never your baby – nor Olaf's.'

'Yes she was.'

Ned looked desolate. 'No my darling, she wasn't yours. You took her, didn't you? From some poor family of asylum-seekers in Glasgow. You saw her lying in a blue blanket and thought it was a boy, so you stole her.'

'That's not true!' Mary covered her face.

'Olaf told me,' Ned said. 'That's why he shut down the commune and got you far away. To save you from prison.'

Mary screamed, 'I had to have a child. At least Olaf understood that!'

'What you both did was wrong,' said Ned. 'And I'm just as much to blame. I've stood by and done nothing – covered up for you. But how else could I make it up to you for losing Ossian? I'll never forgive myself. But now Mary please,' he begged, 'it all has to stop.'

'It can't stop,' Mary sobbed. 'We all have to go together – just like the women of Kulah.'

'What do you mean, go together?' Ally's throat was so tight she could hardly breathe.

Mary scrabbled at the pouch around her neck and pulled something out, holding it aloft.

Ally was terrified. Mary was out of control. How could they get her away from the cliff edge without endangering them all?

Suddenly she saw what Mary was dangling from her hand; a Maori charm made of bone.

'Where did you get that?' Ally gasped.

'From Lucas of course!'

Ally felt dread claw her insides. 'What have you done to him?'

CHAPTER 90

Kulah, 1946

Frightened and confused faces stare back at me, Flora the priestess, but one or two show a glimmer of belief. How feeble they are. They are weak so I must be strong. I throw back my head and begin a psalm. The sound stirs them. Quickly the chanting spreads. We stand, buffeted by the wind, stoking up courage like fire.

I take off my mother's silver and turquoise cross and, holding it up in one hand while cradling The Baby in the other, lead them in prayer. I beseech Our Lady and the Saints to save us.

'Oh, Sea Mother, come to us. Take your weary children into your arms and rock us to sleep. Come now and take us. Bring us to our men folk. We have such longing in our hearts. Keep us apart no longer.'

'No longer,' Margaret cries, her arms lifting in supplication. Others follow, until there is a swaying, sobbing band of the faithful.

'How can we bear it without them?'

'Take away our pain.'

'I want my Daddy.'

'Help us Holy Mother.'

Our wailing rises like a vortex, sucking in all our grief. We are one strong woman; one voice. Birds screech overhead on mighty wings turned golden in the sunset. It is a sign. They will lift us up and carry us over.

'The men are calling us,' I encourage, 'the ancestors are calling us. Soon our troubles and labours will be over. Listen, the very stones of Kulah are calling us. Can you not hear them in the noise of the birds?'

'Yes, yes,' they weep, 'we do, we do.'

'There is no point in being here now. Why should we suffer any more? Kulah belongs to the ancestors.'

'Yes, we have suffered enough.'

'Come then, my people,' I urge, 'it is time.'

I am full of the power; I am a chariot of fire. Slipping the cross around The Baby's neck, I step towards the dying sun.

'We must go before the sun sinks. It is lighting our way home.'

I feel them about me, moving together in the twilight, chanting and screaming our desire. People are fainting and being held up by loving arms. Soon all the pain will be in the past. I smile at my daughters and hold out a hand. I have promised to take care of them. Now there is no need for Seanaid to leave because we are all going to be together forever.

'Go, my friends. Tonight we will be in paradise with the others.'

Margaret links arms with Morag and they step off first, calling out for Neilac and their husbands. Others surge forward, stumbling and grasping for hands. The air rings with the cawing of birds and the names of the dead. *Donald, Alastair, Tormod, Iain, Murdoch* – the names of the men of Kulah – echo off the rock.

Seanaid grabs my arm. 'Mother, no, no.' Her face is swollen with crying.

'Don't be frightened my lamb.'

'My baby,' she gasps. 'Please don't. My baby – '

I put one strong arm about her trembling shoulders; The Baby in the crook of my other. Bethag moves towards us too, her face in shadow. She knows that life without us will not be worth living. United again; the Gillies women.

My youngest lurches to my other side, not wanting to be left behind. Then I'm stepping off the cliff.

CHAPTER 91

Kulah, the present

'My God, Mary,' Ned gasped in horror, 'tell me you haven't harmed Lucas?'

Mary gripped on tight to the charm. 'He was dangerous; I had to stop him,' she whimpered in the wind. 'I told him to go and leave us alone, but he just laughed at me.'

'Tell us what you've done!' Ned shouted.

'His essence is here with us – he will help us travel to the other side – guiding his unborn child.'

Ally was shaking uncontrollably. 'Is he dead?'

Mary sobbed, 'He tried to grab the camera from me – I shoved him – his head hit a stone – I didn't mean …'

Ally clamped a hand over her mouth to stop herself vomiting.

'Please Mary, don't do this,' Ned pleaded, 'come away from the edge.' He stumbled forward.

'Stay back,' Mary hissed, holding the charm aloft. Gulls swooped and screeched overhead. Sudden icy rain arrived like needles.

Ned began to babble. 'I knew nothing of this Ally, please believe me. I thought Lucas had left the island. You do believe me, don't you?' He reached out in supplication.

Ally turned to face him. The next moment she was being grabbed by the hair from behind. Ally's scream froze in her chest at the feel of a cold blade pressed to her throat.

'Mary no!' Ned gasped.

'Keep away from her,' Mary shrieked. 'There's no other way out. She has to come with me, don't you see that?'

Ally tried to blot out the thought that the knife nicking her skin was the one she had seen Mary use routinely in her kitchen – sharp and long. Shockwaves of fear turned her bowels to water. She was seconds away from death. Mary was going to slit her throat or take her over the precipice. *Keep her talking.* Ally latched onto the still small voice in her terrified mind.

'Tell me about Lucas, Mary?' she gasped. 'I want to understand.'

'He hurt Juniper – prying with his camera,' she hissed. 'That's all he wanted – photos to impress your boss. So I did it for you too, didn't I? That's when I realised what the ancestors were telling me – Lucas was meant to come with us.'

Ally's ears buzzed; she thought she would black out. Ned stood paralysed with shock. *Humour her.*

'You're not to blame,' Ally said faintly, 'but why are we here, Mary?'

'To follow the women. They knew how to end their torment; they showed me the way.'

'Women?'

'The women of Kulah – you've heard them too – heard their crying.'

225

'But they died of the flu. They're buried in the graveyard.'

'No, there was no flu. That was the story they told afterwards to cover up the scandal.'

Ally swallowed. 'What scandal?'

'Mass suicide,' Mary cried. 'They threw themselves off the cliffs. Flora led them so they could be reunited with their loved ones.'

'I can't believe that.'

'It's true. Bethag told me. It troubled her Catholic mind.' Mary was panting now, her grip on Ally's hair agonising. 'The survivors had a terrible time trying to retrieve the bodies. She wanted them buried in hallowed ground so there would be no purgatory for Flora and the others. You remember don't you, Ned?' There was desperation in her voice as she appealed to her husband. 'How I had to provide her with remedies to help her sleep? A very guilty conscience.'

'Oh, dear God,' Ned was suddenly galvanised. 'You mustn't do this, Mary. Let Ally go!'

He lunged towards them. The next moment Mary was screaming and thrusting the knife at Ned. He yelled as the blade slashed his wrist. He fell back in shock as blood streamed down his arm.

'I'm so sorry,' Mary sobbed. With a sharp jerk, she pulled Ally backwards towards the edge. Ally fought to free herself, but Mary had her by the throat and she gagged for air.

'No,' she spluttered, 'please!'

'Mary,' Ned gasped, clutching at his wound, 'my darling, don't.'

'Come with me,' Mary pleaded, 'Ossian is calling us to him.'

Ally hooked a foot around Mary's and brought them both down. They slid towards the precipice, wind and rain whipping hair into their eyes. Ally tried to scramble back, but Mary tore at her arm, dragging her with surprising strength.

'You can't deny the ancestors,' she shrieked.

'Ned,' Ally screamed, 'help me!'

She dug in her heels but could find no purchase in the thin soil and loose wet stones. Ally tried to turn, flailing and scratching at Mary's face. Mary bit her hand and then sunk her teeth into Ally's cheek. She roared with the pain. Nearby, she could hear Ned's weeping entreaties. She felt him scrabbling at her leg, trying to help. Ally jabbed a finger into Mary's eye. Mary unclenched her teeth. Ally tried to roll away. Mary yanked her by the hair. It felt like her scalp was lifting.

Mary's strength seemed superhuman as she pulled Ally with her. Ally felt the cold rock of the cliff face against her thigh and then her leg was kicking against thin air. She was going over. She tore at the ground, ripping her nails. Mary was wrapped around her in a tangle of plaid, hanging onto her, forcing her to look down. Black rock dropped away to crashing foaming waves in the gloom. Even the birds that wheeled from hidden clefts far below looked like miniatures.

This is it. A sudden calm came with the realisation that there was nothing left she could do. Flora Gillies was claiming them. Mary was ending her nightmare – and taking Ally with her. There was a deafening shriek of fulmars and then she was clinging to Mary's plaid as they slipped over the edge.

CHAPTER 92

Kulah, 1946

'Mother!' The name is being screamed as I go. 'Mother, help me.'

Moments before, I felt the nothingness beneath my right foot, the lurch in my gut as I step into thin air.

I know I must carry my burdens with me to the other side. But suddenly my arms aren't heavy enough. I spin around as I tip away from wet earth. My arm is tugged sharply backwards. I feel The Baby slip from my grasp.

The dusk is full of screaming – women and birds – and my arms reach out for what I am about to lose. A hand grabs at mine.

'*Seanaid.*' My daughter's name tears from my gaping mouth.

Then we are falling together; my Seanaid and I. Icy air whistles past, black rocks turn before my eyes. I am a sinking stone. Panic, cold fear and hot anger tumble with me.

Mother, help me!

These are the last words I hear. But they are not Seanaid's words; they are mine. My last conscious thought is this: it is I, Flora Gillies, who is crying for my mother.

CHAPTER 93

Battersay

'We have to go tonight,' John insisted to DI Stewart who was investigating Lucas's murder. High winds had nearly grounded the small plane to Barra, and the ferry trip to Battersay had been hazardous as the storm grew. Now it was dark.

'It's not safe,' the police officer cautioned. 'We'll try at first light. We're as anxious as you to bring in the yachting party, but I'm not going to endanger life needlessly, Mr Balmain.'

'But lives are already in danger,' John fumed. 'Ally and Juniper are alone with a couple of crazies.'

'The Rushmores are under suspicion yes, but –'

'No buts about it. They cold-bloodedly murdered Lucas. They obviously have no intention of returning. They've cut their ties – no coming back.' John banged his fist on the inspector's desk. 'I know how these people are thinking – they're living the pagan dream – they'll have no compunction about sacrificing Ally and Juniper with them. That's why they've taken them along.'

'That's pretty wild speculation. It could've been Juniper who attacked the victim – apart from the blow to the head, he was also covered in scratch marks. And we need to speak to Alison Niven. Perhaps she and Lucas had an argument before she left –'

'You can't suspect Ally?' John shouted in disbelief.

'We have to keep an open mind.'

'For God's sake!'

'I'm sorry,' Stewart was firm, 'I'm not sending out a boat or helicopter in this weather.'

'What about the coastguard?' John demanded.

'The nearest is two islands away and can't take off in these conditions either.'

Calum took John firmly by the elbow; his high-handed angry manner was only making the detective more stubborn in his refusal.

'Come on John; Shona's got a pot of chilli for us.'

They drove in the rain-lashed dark, Calum hunched over the steering wheel, the windscreen wipers working at maximum. Visibility was down to a few yards as the car was buffeted from side to side. John's stomach knotted as they passed the road end to Sollas House. No lights gleamed through the storm.

'I still can't get over Juniper being Mary's child,' Shona said, doling up steamy bowls of chilli and rice at the messy kitchen table. 'Fancy treating her like that; it's bloody unbelievable. If only we'd known.'

John said, 'She was always going to be someone's daughter.'

'Aye,' Shona said, 'you're right. You've always been right about the bird girl, haven't you?'

'Tell us more about this Olaf guy,' Calum asked.

229

As they ate in the fuggy kitchen, John told them what he knew of Ned's brother, his retreat to Kulah and Donny's confession about seeing Juniper and the eagle swimmer.

'So you reckon poor Donny was being hounded by the Rushmores for knowing too much?' Shona asked.

'Who knows,' John sighed, 'but someone was supplying him with drugs and he was increasingly paranoid. I think they were deliberately trying to tip him over the edge. Maybe they were worried that Donny might have seen Mary there too.'

He pushed away his half-eaten food. 'Think I'll risk the storm for a smoke.'

Shona stopped him with a hand on his arm. 'Don't be daft – you'll get blown away. Smoke in here.'

She poured them both more red wine. Calum refused.

'I used to enjoy a glass or two with Ally,' she told John.

'Or three or four,' Calum grunted.

John's heart squeezed at the thought of Ally sitting where he was, laughing with Shona.

'We used to gossip about you,' she smiled.

John fumbled with his cigarette and lighter.

'She's going to be alright,' Shona encouraged. 'They may have no intention of harming her, you know.'

'I won't forgive myself if anything's happened,' John admitted, his expression pained. 'I pushed her away. We had this great thing going and like an idiot I had to go and spoil it. It was a kind of self-protection, I suppose. I was so afraid of losing her, just like –'

There was silence as he smoked, avoiding their embarrassed looks. He'd drunk and said too much.

Gently, Shona said, 'you really love her don't you?'

John's dark eyes were full of sorrow. 'Yes,' he whispered, 'more than anything.'

***

Sometime in the early hours, the wind dropped. The sudden silence woke John from an edgy sleep on the Gillies' sofa. He got up and made tea, taking it outside. It was still dark. He smoked. A bird gave a weak chirrup. The air was fresh and full of oxygen.

John was gripped with foreboding. What if the storm had scuppered any chance of saving Ally? Gradually, light leaked into the inky sky. He ground out the cigarette and went to wake Calum.

CHAPTER 94

Kulah

The helicopter swayed in the stiff wind out over the Atlantic, the clattering blades making conversation a shouting match. DI Stewart and another armed policeman sat in front. The police boat would take another four hours to arrive. Calum pointed. John scanned the blurred view. Suddenly in front of them, a jagged fringe of rock loomed out of the cloud.

The helicopter veered south, dipping sideways to avoid the crags. Kulah.

'Where on earth can we land?' John bellowed.

Calum shrugged. He had never been out to the island before.

Minutes later they were dropping below the mist and sweeping in over a tight circular bay, ringed by massive cliffs. John's heart thumped. Pieces of yacht lay bobbing in the swell like a smashed toy. Plastic crates and debris dotted the shingle. Had they even made it ashore?

'Looking for somewhere better to land,' the message was relayed from the pilot, as they swept upwards once more.

John bit his knuckle in frustration. They circled the island searching for signs of life but, with low cloud, visibility was poor.

'We might have to return later,' Stewart shouted in warning.

Just as they were giving up hope, weak sunshine began to penetrate the cloud. They circled once more as the mist lifted. Stone settlements clung on to the drenched hillside, the tracks between glinting like running streams.

They returned to the bay and dropped onto the uneven grassy area for the police to disembark. John insisted on climbing down. 'I know the Rushmores – I can negotiate.'

'Me too,' Calum said.

The helicopter took off again to search from above, hanging in the pearly sky like a fractious bird, then moving off. The place was eerily empty and quiet, save for the muted call of gulls. They soon found a couple of soggy boxes, their contents scattered and picked over by seabirds.

'They got ashore at least,' said Calum.

Further up the slope, the police found a small ripped tent impaled on a rock, pegs still attached.

'Gale must have carried it up here,' Stewart said. 'No one could have slept in that.'

Nothing stirred as they picked their way uphill, cautiously searching each ruined cottage. The old settlement was deserted.

'Where the heck could they have taken shelter?' Calum asked.

'There are isolated bothies on the map,' said DI Stewart. 'We can search those.'

'Doesn't seem likely,' his sergeant pulled a face, 'and the tracks look washed away.'

John said with impatience, 'Mary knows this island – she probably lived here for a while with Olaf and Juniper. She will know where to hide.'

'If hiding was her intention,' Stewart said ominously.

John was chilled by his words. What had the Rushmores really planned to do on Kulah? Desperation seized him; he must find Ally. John hurtled up the sodden mountainside.

The helicopter clattered into view once more.

'Hang on,' Stewart called out, 'they've seen something. They think it's a body.'

John's heart raced with dread. They scrambled after the helicopter over a westerly ridge, plunging through ankle deep bog. It hovered over a circle of battered trees. Beyond, John could make out a strange shaped mound. He saw something move and dashed forward. Stewart blocked his way.

'It's not safe, stay back.'

But John took no heed, barging past and racing through the trees. Standing at the mound, gazing up at the helicopter, was a woman with wild matted hair and filthy clothes: Juniper. Beside her lay the lifeless form of Ned Rushmore.

CHAPTER 95

Juniper heard the voice again; the one in her head.

How long have we waited for revenge, Juniper? Look at the men coming over the brow of the hill. There, the dark one with the fierce eyes and the old soul leading them – showing no fear – don't trust him. The others carry terror like weights tied to their boots; they are no match for us.

Or was the voice separate, outside of her?

They have a right to be afraid. You are the Bird-witch and I am Flora Gillies your spirit – your guide. Don't forget how I kept you company all those years: I was your mother, your protector, your guardian. You were nothing but a trembling, puking child without me.

It frightened Juniper to hear it; it tempted her to lose control.

There is anger in your belly like a raging fire; can't you feel it? How many years of purgatory have we suffered, we women of Kulah? From the beginning of time, men have been the cause of our suffering. We bear the scars of their cruelty: burns on our skin, bad seed in our wombs, abandoned, imprisoned, maddened by grief.

Look how he stands before us now – the tall dark one – just like Rollo once stood with smiles and gestures and sweet words of comfort.

'Juniper, where is Ally? You're safe now; there's nothing to be afraid of. I won't let anyone harm you.'

Don't listen to him; don't let your heart flutter like a wounded bird. You must not give in to the honey in his voice; it is the sound of sweet treachery. Feel the knife under the plaid; run your thumb over the cold sharp blade to give us courage. Don't fail me now Juniper. I must have vengeance!

***

John stepped closer. Ned's dead face was gaping up at him.

'Stay back!' the detective bellowed behind.

Juniper looked at John with wild eyes full of terror or anger. Glancing at the mound behind, he could see it was some sort of sunken burial mound or grave-house. Where were Ally and Mary?

'Ally? Ally!' he shouted.

Juniper raised an arm as if to ward him off and opened her mouth wide, letting fly a harsh noise like a furious bird.

He tried to reassure her.

'I know what Mary did to you. She will never be allowed to hurt you again – no one will. Just show me where Ally is.'

'Balmain, stop! She's got something under her cloak.'

In an instant, Juniper was hurling herself at John, wielding a long kitchen knife. He dodged sideways. The armed policeman drew his gun.

'No,' John barked, 'don't shoot.' He lunged at her legs, bringing her down in a tackle.

The policemen were on her at once, seizing her arms and wrenching the knife from her grasp. Juniper kicked and writhed with superhuman strength, punching Stewart in the face and biting the sergeant.

'Bitch!'

Calum waded in and caught a kick in the groin. He doubled over in agony. She bared her teeth and screamed so loud, John's ears pulsed in pain. Her eyes rolled with fear. Suddenly he knew what he had to do.

Scrabbling to his feet, he bellowed, 'hold onto her.'

Standing tall, John flung his arms in the air and to the astonishment of the other men began to shout.

'Saints of Kulah help us! Mary Mother come and rescue your daughter Juniper. She is burdened with unhappy spirits. Come to her now and release her.'

Juniper continued to scream and pant with fury. John leaned towards her and held her look.

'Whoever you are, leave Juniper now. In the name of the Holy Mother and the Holy Child, I call on you to go!'

He stared at her unblinking. Her dark eyes defied him; her face contorted with hate. John felt dread tighten around his heart. Whatever possessed the maddened woman was too strong for him to combat. Stewart was right; Juniper could have murdered Lucas. If she had killed Ned she could have harmed Ally too.

Ally. A sharp pain of fear gave him the spur. He stepped over Juniper, ignoring the brutal kicks to his shins, his look unflinching. John placed his hands on her head.

'I know who you are,' he said with deathly calm, 'Flora of Kulah. You have been wronged. Your spirit has wandered for too long. It is time for you to join the ancestors. Go; leave this young woman and be at peace!'

Something in Juniper's look changed. She writhed against the constraints of the policemen's hold but they hung on grimly. Then she started to shudder, convulsions contorting her body. Her head was red-hot to the touch. John flinched but kept his hands there.

Abruptly the fight went out of her. Juniper went limp. Her eyelids fluttered and closed. John stood back, panting hard as if he had just run a race. He felt an icy coldness like a shadow falling over him. For a moment he couldn't breathe. Then it passed by. Stewart looked at him in bewilderment.

'She's gone,' John said, completely drained. 'Flora Gillies is finally at rest.'

Juniper opened her eyes. The sergeant tightened his grip again but she didn't try to resist. She looked around as if unsure of where she was or who they were.

Suddenly her chin trembled. She gulped, her eyes watering, and then she leaned over and was sick.

John crouched down beside her, pulling her tangled hair from her face.

'It's okay,' he murmured, 'don't be frightened.' He rubbed her back.

Juniper started to cry. It was the first time he had heard her sound human.

'Come quickly!' It was Calum who shouted from the steps of the subterranean chamber. John hadn't noticed that he'd gone. 'Leave her,' Calum said sharply, 'I've found Ally.'

CHAPTER 96

Ally knew that she had died. She had gone over that slimy, jagged cliff in a bundle of plaid and flying limbs into stormy nothingness. That was why she was lying buried in a dark womb of a place. This was the afterlife. Yet her mind was still plagued by the terribleness of those moments before death: Mary's screaming, the madness of her words, and the horror of knowing Lucas had been killed.

How could she still feel sick when she was dead? And she ached all over, her cheek throbbing and skin stinging as if she'd been lashed. She wanted to open her eyes but she knew that was nonsensical: there was nothing to see.

Someone was shouting. *Calum's voice*? Her mind playing tricks. Perhaps the echo of familiar voices stayed like a fading memory after you died?

'In here, look!'

A bright beam of light suddenly hurt her eyes.

'Ally?' *That voice*. Warm hands touched her face, her neck. 'She's still alive. Oh Ally, thank God.' Strong arms went around her.

'Careful, you shouldn't move her. We don't know how injured she is.' Calum's voice again.

Ally felt warm breath on her face; she forced her eyes open. Dark eyes studied her and the familiar handsome face – the last person she'd thought of as Mary dragged her over the edge – was leaning over her.

'John?' she whispered.

'It's me,' he smiled, 'you're going to be okay.'

'I don't understand,' Ally said faintly, 'where am I?'

'On Kulah – in some sort of chapel.'

Ally started to tremble violently. 'It was terrible – Mary tried to kill me – she went into the sea – oh God – and Lucas – she killed him too –' Fear throttled her.

John pulled her close. 'It's over.' He kissed her hair, 'I promise you it's over. The police are here. The Rushmores can never harm you again – nor Juniper – she's under arrest.'

Ally's heart jolted. *Juniper*. That was how she was here, alive in John's arms. The memory rushed back with the force of the tide: Juniper looming like a furious eagle, arms outstretched, screaming on the precipice, and her strong claw-like hands tearing at Ally's legs and dragging her back.

Ally's eyes flooded with tears. 'She saved me,' Ally gasped. 'Juniper saved my life.'

CHAPTER 97

Battersay

Shona fussed around Ally like a mother hen while she recovered her strength at the croft house in Sollas. Bad bruising and cuts – Mary's teeth marks showing purple on her cheek – were the worst of her physical injuries, but she was emotionally traumatised. Ally was content to sit in the garden wrapped in a rug out of the wind or take short walks to the beach. Her life was in limbo.

'Don't rush into any decisions,' Shona advised, 'you know you can stay here as long as you like.'

The kindness of the Gillies left her tearful, yet the experiences of the past weeks made her question everyone's motives, especially those closest to her. Lucas, Freya, Ned, Mary – they had all used or betrayed her in some way. How could she be so wrong about people? Mary in particular – the woman she had loved because she had reminded Ally of her own mother – had left her with a feeling of vulnerability that made her question everyone; even her friends. Given her flawed judgement, could she allow herself to love John? Often Ally found herself weeping for no reason. The future yawned in front of her like a chasm. She knew she would have to fully understand what had happened on Battersay and Kulah before she could take the next step.

Gradually she gathered the facts like random pebbles and tried to arrange them into a pattern that made sense. The truth about Calum's brother Rory had come as a further shock. He had been kicked out of the family home for his part in 'that Rushmore business', as it was coming to be called by the islanders. Mary had paid him to scare Ally off; it was he who had harassed her at the coastguard's house. When Ally had questioned why, Shona had been scathing, 'cos he's a waster – he'd do anything for easy money, that one. That's why he sold that picture to your boss – got too greedy.'

'But why should Mary want rid of me when she didn't even know me?'

'Rory said it was jealousy,' Shona said. 'Saw your picture on your application and worried that Ned would fancy you. I think her biggest fear was that he would find a younger woman and go off and have a baby with them. No one lasted two minutes at the hall if they were young and female. It was all in her head, 'cos he'd have walked over hot coals for her.'

'Poor Ned,' Ally said, 'what an unhappy life he must have had.'

'Don't waste your tears on that man,' Shona was brusque. 'He left Juniper on that island like a prisoner. He could have saved her years ago but didn't. Think of the poor family in Glasgow; those asylum-seekers. You're the one who heard him tell how Mary stole their baby. They're the ones you should feel sorry for, not Ned Rushmore.'

But Ally couldn't help dwelling on Ned's pathetic end. Juniper had dragged him to the burial mound perhaps in an attempt to save him, but he had died of hypothermia and loss of blood as the storm raged around him. Ally acknowledged that Ned had tried to save her and belatedly bring a stop to Mary's murderous plans. Yet he had been weak and gone along with Mary and Olaf's bizarre experiment with Juniper; someone else's child. He had failed the girl time and time again. And what then had become of Ned's brother Olaf? The question continued to nag. No one seemed to know.

Ally had spoken to Freya and handed in her notice.

'I'm so sorry about everything,' Freya had pleaded down the phone, her usually composed and efficient manner quite gone. 'It was Lucas's idea to go to Battersay not mine, you must believe me. There was absolutely nothing going on between us. Please come –'

'I don't believe you,' Ally cut her off. 'I've spoken to Rachel; she saw the two of you together. I just want to know one thing: was the plan to get rid of me for the summer just so that you could have Lucas for yourself?'

There was a long pause. Freya sniffed into a tissue. 'No, of course not, it just happened.'

Ally closed her eyes. She would never really know why Lucas had turned up on Battersay but she suspected he had been trying to have his cake and eat it; to string her along while pleasing Freya with a scoop. And now he was dead.

'You'll never know the damage you've done,' Ally said quietly.

'If there's anything I can do,' Freya said, 'the job is always there –'

Ally had put the phone down on her.

In the past couple of days, she had begun to get restless and talk about returning to the hall. Routine, purposeful work; chopping carrots, rubbing butter into flour, pulling trays of syrupy flapjack from a hot oven was what she craved. Ally pottered around the Gillies' kitchen making soup, bread and gingerbread figures for when the twins came in from school.

The afternoon was blustery – she was pegging out washing – when Ally heard the throaty rattle of John's blue van. She sensed his arrival before he appeared on the single track road. He had visited twice before, but it had been awkward between them. Shona had been there, too eager for things to go well, allowing no space for talk of difficult subjects: the deaths on Kulah and Juniper's breakdown and removal to hospital.

'Don't go bothering the lassie about all that,' Shona had said with a nervous laugh. 'It's all over. She needs cheering up. Talk about something happy for goodness sake.'

But they couldn't. John had sat politely with a mug of tea, looking like he'd rather be anywhere but there, his handsome face pinched with tiredness. Ally felt he was just coming out of a sense of duty.

'Give me a ring if you want to come over,' he had said as he left the second time. Ally hadn't rung. She wasn't sure why. Perhaps it was to do with not wanting to revisit John's home since she and Lucas had trespassed and gone through his things. They had spoilt previous happy memories.

Ally went to the end of the path and waited, arms crossed and heart hammering. She watched John climb out of the van, his dark hair tangling in the wind.

'Feel strong enough for a walk?' he asked straight away.

Ally said, 'I'd like that. Just give me a minute to put something on my feet.'

***

John led her away from Sollas and Juniper's peninsula, to the bay beyond the coastguard's house. Shona had been and cleared out Ally's things and brought them over to the croft. The cottage looked forlorn as they skirted past and kept going.

They hardly spoke, scrambling over heather and rocks and down a large dune to a crescent of white beach. It was a stretch of the shore on the way to Bay that Ally had hardly explored. Immediately she took off her trainers and plunged her feet into cold sand.

'Can I talk to you while we walk?' John asked. His expression was unsure, boyish. 'You don't have to say anything. Just listen. Then afterwards you can ask what you like.'

Ally's heart sank. What fresh revelation was she going to have to confront? Her look must have shown her reluctance. John gave a tight half-smile.

'You need to know who I am, Ally. And I need to speak these things aloud to make them real.'

'Okay,' she agreed. 'Walk and talk.'

As they wandered up the beach, side by side but not touching, John unburdened his past. He told her everything about his damaged relationship with his mother, his burden of guilt over Caroline's death and the terrible confrontation in Glasgow over Bethag and the old woman's mistaken belief that Marion Balmain was her long lost niece.

'My adult life has been constructed on a lie,' John said, 'a tragic mistake. I believed Bethag was my great-aunt – wanted her to be because she was so kind and loving. I thought my mother rejected me because of her shame at being illegitimate and adopted, but it was because of who I am – *me* – the replica of the man who raped her. She physically loathes me because I'm half made up of that man.'

'But you're not,' Ally protested, 'you are your own –'

'Wait,' John held up a hand, 'let me finish.'

He stopped and turned to look out across the sea. It glinted in mellow September light.

'My mother believes, given the wrong circumstances, that I am capable of doing what that man did to her. It's what she told Caroline and the knowledge poisoned my fiancée's love for me – once it was in her mind she couldn't be free of it.'

Ally swallowed down words of protest. He looked haggard from the effort of his confession; she was suddenly afraid of where it might lead.

239

'I'm still trying to get my head round what my mother told me,' John said, 'trying to work out who I really am.' He rubbed a hand over his face.

Ally touched his arm but he flinched from her contact.

'I'm not after your pity, Ally,' he said harshly, 'I just want you to know what sort of man I am. There must be no more secrets and misunderstandings – you deserve the truth – and I'm in no doubt that you deserve better than this.'

Ally stood staring at him for a long moment.

'Can I speak now?' she demanded.

John shot her a look, his face tensing as he nodded.

'I see what you're doing. You're throwing all this at me in an attempt to push me away again.'

His eyes widened. 'No, I'm not –'

'My turn to speak John,' Ally was abrupt. 'You have such a low opinion of yourself that you can't imagine anyone else loving you, so it's easier for you to end things with me before I have a chance to end it with you. That's right, isn't it?'

John pulled a hand through his hair in agitation. 'No, that's not true.'

Ally grabbed his arm and shook him. 'Just because your mother rejects you – and Caroline was too cowardly to stick by you – you think every other woman you get close to will end up feeling the same. But love doesn't work like that!'

He frowned down at her, his eyes searching. 'Love?'

'Yes, you idiot,' Ally cried, 'I don't believe in all this sins of the father stuff that your mother has filled your head with. Anyway by the sounds of it you're much more like Duncan, that lovely man who brought you up and who you obviously think the world of. He's been the one who has moulded you into the passionate, tender man I fell in love with.'

John grasped her hands. 'And now you know everything, do you still love me?'

Ally pulled his hands up to cradle her face, delighting in the touch of his warm roughened fingers.

'Yes, John, I love you.'

At last he smiled, letting go a cry of relief. 'Oh God, Ally, I thought I'd lost you.'

He pulled her close and kissed her. For a long moment they held each other tight. Ally was engulfed in feelings of deep tenderness and yearning. She knew then that John was the only person in the world whom she could really trust to make sense of what had happened. Whatever they decided in the long term, she knew that at this moment, all she wanted was to be with him. And the way that he held her and stroked her hair, Ally knew that John's love for her was just as fierce.

As they walked on hand in hand, Ally spoke of the things that still troubled her. She knew that she could say anything and John would understand. They talked of the mass suicide of the Kulah women and what could have driven them to such desperation: grief, hunger, mass hysteria or something more atavistic, a longing for the spirit world? Their leader, Flora Gillies, must have been a woman at the end of her tether.

'After I came to Battersay,' John said, 'Bethag confided in me that her mother had committed suicide and not died of the flu, but she didn't want anyone to know. That's why I was protective of her.'

'And I kept nosing into her life,' Ally said ruefully. 'Poor Bethag, she must have been so traumatised seeing her mother and sister die like that. Why didn't she jump too?' Ally puzzled. 'Was it to save the baby?'

'Yes, I believe so. It helped her hold onto her sanity.'

'So why was she then separated from her niece?'

'When Kulah was evacuated, Bethag was only fifteen or sixteen – and the baby was illegitimate – so she would never have been allowed to bring her up.'

'How very sad,' Ally sighed. 'Apparently Rollo told Mary that the baby was adopted by Yorkshire people. That's why Mary wanted me on Kulah – she was desperate for me to be Seanaid's grandchild. But my mum wasn't adopted. Isn't it strange to think that maybe somewhere in the world Seanaid's daughter still lives – perhaps grandchildren too?'

John slid an arm around her shoulder and pulled her to him protectively. 'I can't bear to think about what Mary tried to do to you,' he shuddered. 'If it hadn't been for Juniper being there …'

'Don't John,' Ally whispered, pushing away the traumatic memory.

'Sorry,' he said, quickly kissing her head.

They stood watching the sea, then Ally forced herself to ask, 'Is it really possible that Juniper was possessed by Flora Gillies?'

'By something,' John was cautious.

'But you used to rubbish that idea when I first knew you – superstitious nonsense you called it.'

John's smile was rueful. 'I said a lot of high-handed things when I first met you. You've challenged my thinking on many things.'

'Have I?'

He kissed her on the lips in answer.

'Then it's also possible,' Ally said, 'that the woman in tweed and the blue head shawl I saw could have been a manifestation of Flora too? Some sort of paranormal disturbance?'

'Yes, I think so. Just in the way that people really did hear the wailing of the women.'

'So it took another tragedy like Juniper's abandonment – or maybe Donny's death – to stir things up again.' Ally tried to grapple with the idea but gave up with a shake of the head. She wasn't sure she really believed it.

'What will become of Juniper?' she asked.

John sighed. 'Who knows? One thing is certain; the authorities won't let her live wild in an insanitary hovel again. There's talk of trying to trace her birth family, though that's a long shot. It's two decades ago and if they were asylum seekers like you said Ned claimed, anything could have happened to them.'

'It's heart-breaking,' Ally said, 'she must be so traumatised by it all. I wish I could do more for her.'

'Well, perhaps you can, given time. We'll make an effort to keep in touch. You were about the only person who got through to her.'

They put their shoes back on and scrambled back up to the road.

'This Olaf guy,' Ally puzzled, 'did he really exist?'

'According to Neave from the commune he was very much alive.'

'So where is he now? Did Mary kill him too?'

John shrugged. 'Seems to have disappeared without trace. The police think he probably had an accident years ago and was washed out to sea – that's why Juniper was left for so long on her own.'

'But he ran the trust that owned Kulah, didn't he?'

'It appears Ned was running that; forging his brother's signature and submitting accounts each year from an address in Oban so as not to draw attention to the island, I suppose.'

'I hate the thought that he might be out there somewhere experimenting on some other vulnerable kid.' Ally shivered. 'I guess we'll never really know what went on with the Rushmores or why they tried to invent this warped pseudo Celtic world around poor Juniper.'

John said, 'I think it's probably quite simple. Grief for their lost son; that's what it's all been about.'

His words broke through her jumbled thoughts like a shaft of light. Her heart squeezed with pity. It felt better than the hurt and anger that had plagued her over the past two weeks.

'Oh, John. You're so right.'

He took her hand. 'I think it's time we visited Bethag.'

Ally's stomach knotted. 'I'm not sure I'm ready. I can't talk about Kulah to her – and I don't think I could bear her calling me Seanaid and getting distressed.'

John put his arms around her and squeezed. 'If she does, we'll leave. She may not be my great aunt, but she's a dear friend and she loves to be visited. Come on.'

***

'She's in her room,' Ishbel told them, coming forward and hugging Ally. 'It's good to see you lassie. No more sailing trips, do you hear? Leave Kulah to the birds. It's never been fit for humans.'

'Don't worry, I will.' Ally hugged her back.

Bethag was sitting up in bed listening to Gaelic radio. The room was over-warm and the window closed.

'John!' she said, raising a shaky hand in delight. 'Come and sit next to me. And who is this with you?'

'It's my friend Ally,' John said swiftly, 'she works at the hall remember?'

Bethag looked puzzled, her mouth opening. Ally tensed.

242

'Aye, Ally,' the old woman nodded. 'The scone-maker. You've not been to see me in ages.'

Ally relaxed, sharing a look of relief with John. She came forward and kissed Bethag on her downy crinkled cheek.

'Sorry I've been a bit under the weather. But tomorrow I'm going back to the hall to make scones especially for you.'

Bethag gave a small chuckle. John sat down in the chair and pulled Ally onto his knee. The old woman laughed again.

'More than a friend I see.'

As Ally glanced round at John, she caught her breath. 'Bethag, you've framed it.' She picked up the photograph on the bedside table. 'The picture of your family.'

Her heart squeezed to see the straight-backed handsome Flora sitting between her two teenage daughters and gazing at the camera; gazing at Rollo, the man who had got Seanaid pregnant. She could imagine only too vividly the cramped, peat blackened cottage on the steep hillside, and the excitement that Rollo and his camera must have caused to the isolated women.

Her hands shook as she placed the frame back on the cabinet. Did that photo capture the moment when fate took a disastrous turn for the Gillies? The point at which Rollo was accepted into their home, when Seanaid fell in love with him? Did the proud Flora sense danger; is that why she sat with a protective hand on each girl's arm?

Bethag's look wandered from the picture to the view outside the window: a heathery tract of moor dipping away to the cliffs.

'She's gone,' she murmured.

Ally and John exchanged glances.

'Who's gone, Bethag?' he asked.

'She doesn't bother me anymore.' The old woman pointed at the photograph, her faded blue eyes glinting with tears.

Ally leaned forward and touched her trembling hand. 'The woman in the tweed coat and the blue scarf? You saw her too, didn't you?'

Bethag gazed at Ally for a long moment and then nodded.

'So she's at peace now?' Ally said, heart thumping. 'Your mother's at peace?'

Bethag gave a look of confusion. Then she raised her finger again and prodded the glass.

'No, it was Seanaid I saw. She's been so very sad.' Bethag sucked in her breath, suddenly agitated. 'Aye, she's given me no peace. But I did the best I could. We would have buried her if we'd ever found her.'

'Of course you would,' John reassured. 'You have nothing to blame yourself for. The sea can be a place of burial too.'

Bethag nodded, finding comfort in the idea. Her face relaxed as she looked lovingly at John. 'And I saved her bairn, didn't I? What more could I have done?'

'Nothing more,' Ally said swiftly. There was no need for John's old nurse to ever know the mistake she had made. 'You've helped put Seanaid to rest, and that's all that matters.'

Bethag smiled, her face girlish as the crease of worry left her brow. 'Thank you lassie.'

Ally and John walked down the drive, arm in arm, pondering what had just happened. Ally looked over to the Standing Stone, almost camouflaged against the hazy moorland, and wondered how it had once had such a powerful tug on her imagination. What did it matter if the ghostly presence had been Flora or Seanaid? Both had died in traumatic circumstances. But now it was all over. Kulah had reclaimed its own and Battersay looked serene and untroubled under a pearly sky.

'This place is truly beautiful,' Ally whispered.

John stopped abruptly. 'Come home with me Ally.'

She hesitated. 'What are you offering?'

His look made her insides flip. 'Definitely drink, food, hot bath, bed,' he said, his dark eyes challenging. 'Possibly marriage or just growing old disgracefully – but either way both of us together.'

Ally's heart leapt in her chest. She kissed him on the lips. 'Okay – all of those – though not necessarily in that order.'

'Really?'

'Yes, really,' she smiled.

'Excellent,' he grinned, throwing an arm around her shoulder.

They hurried down the road laughing and holding each other tight. From a bird's eye view, Ally thought, they were two people bound so closely that it must be hard to imagine them apart.

***

INTERVIEW WITH THE AUTHOR

What gave you the idea for the novel?

One summer my youngest brother had this mad-cap idea for some of the family to go wild camping on the Outer Hebrides off Scotland. We were used to holidays on Skye, where my father's family came from, but knew far less about the remoter Outer Isles. They are very wild and romantic islands, steeped in history. You really feel as if you're at the edge of the world and daily life is ruled by the weather – at least it is if you are camping! Battersay was inspired by Barra in particular. I thought it the perfect place for the heroine of the modern story, Ally, to retreat to with her bruised heart.

What about Kulah and the flashbacks to the 1940s?

Kulah is based on the even remoter MacLeod island of St Kilda. I have never been out there but have had a fascination for the place for years. Unlike my fictional Kulah where the populace hung on until after the Second World War, St Kilda was evacuated in 1930 – the last remaining 36 people unable to make ends meet. What must life have been like for those hardy folk? We often think nostalgically back to a simpler, more natural way of life where everyone was bound by strong communal ties, but I didn't want to romanticise the past. The dark side to my supportive tight-knit fictional community was the condoning of domestic abuse and social bigotry.

Flora Gillies, your Kulah heroine, is a very strong character. Is she based on anyone in particular?

No, Flora is the archetypal Highland woman; strong, resourceful and fatalistic. She will do anything for her people and her family, but ultimately trusts in a higher power. And all the Floras I can think of (from Jacobite heroine Flora MacDonald to our former clan chief Dame Flora MacLeod) have all been feisty!

Was the tragic shipwreck a real event?

There was no such incident off St Kilda, but there was a tragedy off the island of Lewis at the end of the First World War when a ship called the HMS *Iolaire* sank within sight of home in 1919. 205 returning soldiers were drowned. This took a terrible toll on the bereaved women and families and I wanted to explore the effect of such a trauma on a small close-knit community over time.

Where did the idea for the Birdwoman Juniper come from?

She leapt straight into my head from a YouTube clip I was watching of St Kilda with a cacophony of seabirds! What would it be like to live on such a rocky island once it was abandoned with only seabirds for company? This striking image came into my mind of a 'birdwoman' living wild – a sort of Northern Mowgli of the seabirds – only able to speak their language. Who was she and how did she get there?

There is a supernatural element to the story that you haven't used in your other novels. Why is this?

Having grown up with the clan legends and folklore of my MacLeod past, I'm open to the idea of ghosts! Gaelic culture is full of prophecies – predictions made by Seers – and incidents of 'second-sight', even in quite modern times. I've always been intrigued by such beliefs and wanted to leave room for a paranormal explanation (haunting and possession) as well as a rational one (mental stress).

If you have enjoyed THE HAUNTING OF KULAH, you might like to read another mystery by Janet: THE VANISHING OF RUTH.

1976: friends, Marcus and Ruth, go missing in Afghanistan during an overland bus trip to Kathmandu. A generation later, Ruth's niece Amber, haunted by the disintegration of her family, determines to get at the truth of their disappearance. Was it murder, as her father suspected, or a suicide pact as the police believed?

Tracking down the trip's bus driver, Cassidy, Amber starts to piece together a lost world – the mystical vibrant hippy trail to India – and colourful characters like Juliet, who imagined herself the reincarnation of an Edwardian traveller. As the mystery surrounding her aunt and the charismatic Marcus unfolds, Amber begins a journey of discovery of her own, that will lead her not only into the dark secrets of the past and lost love, but face to face with a tragedy much closer to home.

Bonus content:

*Interview with the author about her own overland adventure as an 18 year old that inspired the story
*Discussion notes for reading groups

WHAT READING GROUPS HAVE SAID ABOUT THE NOVEL

'Loved the book – couldn't put it down!'

'I would strongly recommend this book as a good read.'

'Wonderful. Kept me guessing all the way through. A pleasure to read.'

'It would make a fabulous screenplay – the split stories, great characters, wonderful locations and a well-resolved murder mystery at its heart – and there was a lot of enthusiasm in the room for the idea!'

'I thoroughly enjoyed this journey through time and distant lands without leaving the comfort of my armchair. The contrast between the Victorians, the hippies and the modern day was fascinating.'

'I really enjoyed reading this. It held my attention with a great plot. It was enthralling and I wanted to keep reading to find out what happens. Good characters which I believed in.'

***

Janet welcomes feedback on her novels. If you wish to do so, or to find out more about her other novels take a look at her website: www.janetmacleodtrotter.com

Lightning Source UK Ltd.
Milton Keynes UK
UKOW041514250812

198070UK00002BA/2/P